THE COP AND THE COWBOY

Taylor let the detainee out of her police car and he straightened to his full height. He looked, Taylor noticed, as if he were already in costume for the Old West shoot-out the town staged every night for the tourists. . . .

He scanned the street, studied storefronts with interest, watched people walking and jumped when a car passed. His eyes sparkled and his lips twitched: If it weren't for his stature, *he could have been a little boy in a toy store.* . . .

AN ECHO IN TIME

Praise for the novels of

SHERRY LEWIS

WHISPERS THROUGH TIME

"A tension-filled story [with] great characters . . . it's catchy, it's witty, and it's a fast ride down a steep hill."
—*Rendezvous*

"Terrific . . . A pleasant surprise."
—*The Romance Reader*

A TIME TO DREAM

"*A Time to Dream* captivated me from the beginning. . . . By slowly unraveling the mystery surrounding the protagonists, Ms. Lewis creates a romantic aura amidst a sea of conflict."
—*Rendezvous*

An Echo in Time

Sherry Lewis

JOVE BOOKS, NEW YORK

This is a work of fiction. Names, characters, places, and incidents are
either the product of the author's imagination or are used fictitiously,
and any resemblance to actual persons, living or dead, business
establishments, events, or locales is entirely coincidental.

TIME PASSAGES is a registered trademark of Penguin Putnam Inc.

AN ECHO IN TIME

A Jove Book / published by arrangement with
the author

PRINTING HISTORY
Jove edition / September 2001

Visit our website at www.penguinputnam.com.

ISBN: 0-515-13156-3

A JOVE BOOK®
Jove Books are published by The Berkley Publishing Group,
a division of Penguin Putnam Inc.,
375 Hudson Street, New York, New York 10014.
JOVE and the "J" design
are trademarks belonging to Penguin Putnam Inc.

PRINTED IN THE UNITED STATES OF AMERICA

10 9 8 7 6 5 4 3 2 1

For JoAnn,
who got me through this book
in ways only she will ever know

Prologue

THE ATTACK CAME out of nowhere—three gunmen, maybe four. Sam Evans threw himself to the ground and took cover behind a stand of trees. Sweat broke out on his brow and ran into his eyes. He dashed it away and tried to get a bead on one of the gunmen, but shadows blanketed the mesa. He couldn't see a thing.

Wind howled. Dust and grit flew. Noise, confusion, and dirt seemed to be everywhere.

Sam's ranch, the Cinnabar, lay in the center of the Montezuma Valley, far below the mesa. Closer—at the base of the mountain—was the Lazy H Ranch, property of the woman he'd once loved. Sam had put Olivia Hamilton behind him, but he was here tonight for her. He couldn't leave the valley without making sure her property didn't fall into Sloan Durrant's clutches. He couldn't leave Kurt Richards to fight the battle alone, even if Kurt had stolen Olivia from under Sam's nose.

The gunfire stilled and Sam took a heartbeat to look for Kurt. He'd been at Sam's side only a minute before, and

Sam could only hope that he'd found his way to safety somewhere.

He forced himself to breathe slowly and struggled to find the control that had served him so well all his life. He wasn't about to waste ammunition until he could see someone or something moving.

Kurt must have decided the same thing, because the sudden silence was almost eerie. Sam just hoped that didn't mean Kurt was injured—or worse.

Painfully aware of the sound of his own heartbeat, Sam cursed the wind for masking the noises their attackers must surely be making. He swallowed, felt grit between his teeth, and wondered how long he and Kurt could hold off their attackers.

Without warning, a shadow broke free from the trees and started running toward the edge of the cliff. Sam kept his rifle trained on the moving shape, squinting to see if it was friend or foe.

It ran. Stopped. Ducked. Spun around and waved both arms as if trying to get Sam's attention. A shot rang out, barely audible over the wailing wind. A volley of shots joined it, and the shadowy figure began to run again. It had to be Kurt, but what was he doing?

Whenever Sam began to doubt Kurt's story about coming from the future, the damn fool did something to wipe away Sam's suspicions. Dancing about like that in the middle of a gunfight was about the stupidest thing Sam had ever seen. Kurt was going to get himself killed.

A sound to Sam's left pulled him around just in time to see one of Sloan's men creeping out of the bushes. The man's rifle was trained on Kurt. Sam took aim and fired. The man dropped, but his buddies answered with half a dozen shots in Sam's direction.

Sam crawled on his elbows through the trees to take up a new position. He struggled to keep Kurt in his sights through the swirling dust. Why didn't he turn around and come back? Was he running away?

No, Kurt wasn't the type to turn tail. Nor did he look like a man on the run. If he wasn't running *from* something, what was he running *to*? There could be only one answer . . .

Olivia.

Sam scanned the landscape for several agonizing moments before he saw her standing on the edge of the cliff, bathed in moonlight like an invitation for their attackers. He sucked in a breath and everything inside him grew cold.

What in the hell was she doing here? Where were the men Sam had left behind to watch her?

Sam spat out an oath along with a mouthful of grit. Kurt had seen her first, thank God. He had only a few feet to go. But what Sam saw next made his blood freeze.

Directly in front of Kurt, the wind picked up speed. The dust created a thick, dark cloud, and Sam knew Kurt couldn't see the strange hole that yawned in front of him. If Sam hadn't known better, he'd have sworn something had happened to his eyes. The hole looked for all the world like a wrinkle in the landscape, shifting shape, waiting for Kurt to draw closer. Another few yards and he'd be there.

With a certainty he couldn't have explained, Sam knew it was the doorway through time that had brought Kurt here. And with an equal certainty, he knew it would take Kurt back again if he got too close. Away from Cortez. Away from the Lazy H. Away from Olivia.

Much as Sam hated losing, even *he* knew Kurt and Olivia belonged together. She'd already lost a husband. Sam couldn't bear the thought of her heart breaking over a second loss.

Sam had already made up his mind to leave Cortez. Olivia had Kurt. Jesse, Sam's kid brother, had a lovely bride-to-be, and once Sam left, he'd soon have the Cinnabar, as well.

Sam had nothing but dreams of a fresh start and a vague idea of traveling to Montana to find it. There was nothing to keep him here.

Swearing under his breath, he darted out of his hiding place and ran, absolutely certain that he'd be shot before he reached his target. He let out a bellow for courage and plowed into the storm. His shout must have carried through the din, because Kurt stopped, crouched, and spun back toward him.

Sam kept roaring to bolster his courage and hoped it would distract Kurt long enough to let him accomplish his own mission. If not, it would make him a damn pretty target.

The wind picked up speed, swirling, blinding him, sucking him closer and closer. He caught a glimpse of Olivia and experienced one brief pang of regret. He heard his name, more a whisper than a shout, but he didn't let it stop him.

Gunshots echoed all around him, but miraculously, none of the bullets found their mark. Still roaring, he passed Kurt and purposely headed into the crease in time. A second later the hole seemed to grab him, and he knew he couldn't turn back.

The force of the wind sucked his breath away. A strange roaring echoed in his ears. Dust and lights nearly blinded him. One second his chest felt as if it might explode, the next as if a terrible weight might crush it.

And then, suddenly, everything grew almost supernaturally quiet, the lights in front of his eyes disappeared, and Sam's entire body went limp. The only thing he was aware of was the helpless feeling of falling into utter blackness.

Chapter 1

Sam AWOKE WITH a start to the strangest sound he'd ever heard. A roar, almost like the sound of a locomotive, followed by a *whoosh* and a gust of hot air blowing across his face. He sat up quickly, but the pain in his head forced him back to the ground with an *oomph*.

Pain in every inch of his body made him long to sink back into oblivion. When it didn't come, he inched one eye open and tried to focus. Colors swam in front of him. Dirt and rocks spun around him. The tangy scent of weeds, sage, and pine tickled his nose.

Where was he? The last thing he remembered . . .

His eye opened a bit wider. No, that had to be a dream. He must have fallen asleep in one of the pastures. If he opened his eye a little further, he'd find himself in his wide bed at the Cinnabar.

The sound of another approaching locomotive forced him to acknowledge that he wasn't dreaming. He dragged to his knees and focused on a strange ribbon of black with two yellow lines in the center. It stretched away in both directions as far as he could see and disappeared over the low rise of a nearby hill.

Definitely a road. Couldn't be anything else.

Sam crawled closer and touched it. Rock. Sleek. Gray.

Altogether, the strangest thing he'd ever seen.

His head pounded, his arms and legs ached, but the sound grew closer. He sat heavily and rubbed his temples, but the effort was almost too much. All at once a . . . a . . . what *was* that? shot past too quickly for him to get a good look at it, but it hadn't been much bigger than a buggy.

Saints alive, could it move!

He sank bank onto his heels and rubbed his face, and images from last night's ambush flashed in front of his eyes. He'd jumped into that hole, only half-believing that he'd actually make it to the future. Now he thought maybe he'd actually done it.

Well . . . Never let anyone say Sam Evans didn't do things up in a big way.

When the pain in his head began to subside, he looked around slowly at the jagged snow-covered mountains cutting into the sky and forming a bowl around the valley. Black-green trees scrabbled up the mountainsides and crept into the valley at their feet. In the valley's center, a series of rolling hills covered in tall grass and willows stretched away in either direction.

Where was he? This sure didn't look like the Montezuma Valley.

He searched until he found his rifle in the dirt, half-hidden beneath a bush. Forcing himself to concentrate, he dusted the rifle off and made sure it would still work. He had only a few rounds of ammunition left, and the good Lord only knew whether he'd find game in these hills or how long he'd have to wander before he found civilization.

Struggling to his feet, he rested the rifle on his shoulder, chose a direction, and set off. Unless things had changed in the past hundred years or so, roads led to towns, and towns meant food and shelter.

He could hear another of those strange locomotive-wagons approaching, so he stepped off the road and waited. It took only a second for him to catch his first glimpse of reflected sunlight. It disappeared behind a hill and emerged again a second later. Another dip, another hill and the dog-gone thing was on a level with him.

It streaked toward him and he steeled himself, expecting the sound and the rush of hot air that would nearly knock him off balance. But this wagon didn't rush past. It slowed, passed in a blur of white, and came to a stop just a few feet from him.

It was the strangest thing Sam had ever seen—low and sleek and topped by a collection of red, blue, and white bubbles. The bubbles began to turn, throwing beams of colored light across the landscape, and a door on the wagon opened.

A man wearing a shirt and trousers the color of tanned deer hide stepped out onto the road. He wore a holster on his hip that held not only a revolver but a whole slew of other contraptions Sam didn't recognize.

He was little more than a boy with a smooth face and a youth's air of self-importance, but he looked Sam up and down slowly. "Good morning, sir. Are you lost?"

More lost that you can imagine, son.

"Not exactly."

"Where are you headed?"

"Town."

The kid took a quick look around. "Where's your car? Did you break down somewhere?"

"Car?"

"What are you driving?"

"I'm on foot."

"Hitchhiking?" The boy gave him another appraising glance. "Would you mind letting me see your firearm for a minute?"

Sam tightened his grip on the rifle. There were two things a fella never messed with—a man's horse and his gun. "Is there some reason why I should?"

The little guy held out an impatient hand. "The rifle, please."

Sam started to refuse, then caught the glint of sunlight off a metal badge on the kid's chest. "You a lawman?"

The boy squared his shoulders and lifted his chin. "That's right. Sheriff's Deputy Donald Dumont."

Sam still wasn't thrilled to hand over his rifle, but he

couldn't think of a good reason to refuse and he didn't want to start off his new life in trouble with the law.

The deputy spent a minute looking the rifle over, then glanced back at Sam. "What is this, an antique?"

"I suppose it might be."

"Is it loaded?"

"You bet it is. What kind of fool would wander through the wilderness with an unloaded rifle?"

The boy tucked Sam's rifle under his arm as if he had no intention of returning it. "You want to tell me what your plans are when you get to town?"

"Don't have any. Just looking for a place to stay."

"Looking for a place to stay with a loaded rifle?" The deputy narrowed his eyes and motioned Sam toward his wagon. "I'm going to have to ask you to step over to the car, sir. Put your hands on the trunk and spread your legs."

Sam had never taken kindly to being pushed around, and he never did anything without a good reason. He squared up himself, which put him a full head above the deputy. "You mind telling me why I should?"

"Because I told you to." Unbelievably, the little pip-squeak drew his revolver and leveled it at Sam. "Now, move."

That revolver made a difference in Sam's thinking. Fig-uring the "car" must be the wagon with the lights on top, he started toward it and looked around for a steamer trunk so he could calm the little guy. "Put my hands where?"

The deputy gave Sam a shove toward the car's tail end, kicked his foot gently to spread Sam's feet apart, and started patting Sam's leg. Now, that might not have been too bad, but he made a big mistake when he started moving his hands up Sam's leg.

Jerking upright, Sam spun around and put an arm in the deputy's throat. He gave him a shove backward, and the deputy sprawled in the dirt, losing his grip on his revolver. Sam kicked it out of the way and stood over him. "Oh, no, you don't, little fella. You just keep them hands to your-self."

Before Sam could catch his breath, the deputy's foot shot

straight up and caught him in the very area he'd been trying to protect. Searing pain sliced through him. Tears filled his eyes. He fell, unable to breathe or see or think, and a cloud of choking dust billowed up around him.

In a flash the deputy scrambled after his gun and aimed it straight at Sam's head. "Get up."

Sam couldn't even speak, much less move.

"I said, *get up*. Assaulting an officer is going to earn you a nice long stay in jail."

"Assaulting an officer?" Sam croaked. "Seems to me, *you're* the one who was trying to get fresh."

"Don't get smart." The little guy's hand trembled so badly, the revolver bounced around in front of Sam's face.

Damn and blast, the little fool would probably shake the gun into firing. Sam took a deep breath and managed to struggle to his feet. He put up both hands to show he wasn't going to fight.

But that wasn't enough for the little guy. "On your head," he ordered. "Put your *hands* on your *head* and keep 'em there."

Sam did his best, but the pain kept him hunched over and protective instinct made him want to keep certain areas covered.

Red-faced with fury, the deputy shoved him toward the car. "You, mister, are about to become a guest of Heartbreak Hill, Montana."

Sam stumbled, caught himself, and drew a little straighter. "Did you say Montana?"

"That's right."

"I *made* it?"

"If this is where you were aiming for."

A slow smile spread across Sam's face. He took another look at the mountains, wondering if there were silver mines in this neck of the woods or they'd been played out a long time ago. He'd find out soon enough, he supposed. Meanwhile, he had the chance he'd been wanting. A chance to test himself in a place where nobody knew who he was. A chance to prove himself—if only *to* himself.

And, as Kurt had told him when their situations were

reversed, there were worse things than a few days of free room and board. Especially when a man was out of touch, so to speak, with his surroundings.

As for landing in a town called Heartbreak Hill . . . Well, if that didn't sound like the perfect place for Sam, he didn't know what did.

His smile spread to a grin, and he sketched a bow at the deputy. "Well, now, I'd be pleased to come with you, son. Why didn't you just say that in the first place?"

"I'm telling you, Taylor, you oughta let me handle your campaign. I've got a million ideas, every one of 'em good."

Taylor O'Brien looked up from the filing cabinet she'd been rifling and smiled at her father. He sat easily in the huge rolling chair he favored when he visited her office and ran a hand across his shock of once-red hair. "I'm sure you do, Pop. But I know how busy you are. I think Ruby and I can handle it."

Charlie O'Brien snorted a laugh. "Busy? With what? I haven't had a blasted thing to do since they made me retire. And I can't think of anything I'd *rather* do than help my little girl be reelected county sheriff."

Taylor found the file she wanted and nudged the drawer shut with one hip. "Ruby has some really good ideas, Pop."

"Better than mine? I doubt that."

Taylor believed that her father had a million ideas, but there was a huge gap between her definition of a good idea and his. In the two years since he'd retired, he'd been in nearly as many troublesome scrapes as her ten-year-old son, Cody. In the past couple of weeks she'd had to pick him up from a poker game after he'd lost every cent in his pocket, extricate him from an argument with a neighbor over borrowed tools, and smooth ruffled feathers at the Moosehead Lodge when he'd refused to pay for an under-cooked steak.

She sat behind her desk and flipped open the file. "I appreciate the offer, Pop, but you could *really* help by just staying out of trouble."

Charlie snorted again. "I don't go looking for trouble. You know that. It just finds me."

"I'm sure it does. But that brings up another thing. I'd like you to stop saying that in front of Cody. He's starting to get ideas."

"Well, then? You see? That's all the more reason you should let me be in charge of your campaign. It'll keep me busy, and I won't have so much time to spend with Cody while you're working."

"It's tempting." Not *entirely* true, but she didn't want to hurt him.

"It's smart." Charlie relaxed in his chair and grinned at her. "Who's prouder of you than your old dad is?"

She pushed the file to one side and gave him her full attention. "Nobody."

"And who wants you reelected more than I do?"

"Nobody." Taylor studied his eager face and felt herself caving. She'd always hated disappointing her father. "What do you have in mind?"

Charlie popped upright. "For one thing, I think we need to gussy you up some. Get you looking like a female again."

Taylor shook her head wearily. "I should've known you'd throw that old argument at me, but it won't work. I'll win the election—*if* I win—on my abilities and the issues, not on the way I look."

"Looks can't hurt."

"*Looks* aren't important to the job."

"But they're important to *folks*, and folks is who's going to be voting." Charlie leaned forward and wagged one finger at her. "I'm not the only one who remembers the way you used to dress, and I'm not the only one who thinks you should start caring about yourself again."

Taylor closed the file with a snap. "How I *look* isn't anyone else's business. It's been ten years since I *gussied up*. This is who I am."

"No, it's not."

"Yes, it is." She stood abruptly. "Have you been asking people what they think of the way I look?"

"Asking? No. I haven't been *asking*." Charlie shrugged casually. "But if someone wants to express their opinion, I'm not rude enough to shut 'em up."

"And you expect me to believe they're just stopping you on the street to tell you what they think of my hair or makeup?"

"What makeup?"

Taylor let out a frustrated sigh. "Look, Pop, no matter what you think, I happen to like the way I look." Okay, so that wasn't entirely true, either, but the things she didn't like would have taken money and surgery to fix. Taylor just wasn't that vain.

"I didn't say you aren't pretty. You're damn pretty, just like your mother was. It's just that maybe you don't do all you could to accentuate your features."

In spite of herself, Taylor laughed. "Where on earth did you hear that?"

"*The Sally Show*. I like watching when they do what they call makeovers."

Taylor blinked a couple of times, trying to adjust to the mental image of her father, who'd held the county title of arm-wrestling champ for nearly fifteen years, who'd come home bruised from a night out with the boys more than once, who'd ridden rodeo and roped bulls and gentled wild horses, watching makeovers on daytime television. Maybe she *did* need to find something for him to do.

But did it have to be on her campaign?

Ruby Phillips had been Taylor's best friend since before either of them could remember. She'd known Charlie nearly as long as Taylor had, and though her loyalty ran deep, she wouldn't be thrilled by the thought of having him underfoot. She'd already suffered more than her share of embarrassment at Charlie's hands.

Not that he *meant* to embarrass anyone. It's just that Charlie was . . . well, *Charlie*. God love him, but he was one of a kind.

On the other hand, he *did* know how other people his age felt. And Heartbreak Hill's senior population was large enough to make his input valuable. Taylor's opponent, Hutton Stone, had a leg up with folks over fifty, just by being one of them. Involving Pop in the campaign might just help her win.

Surely, Ruby would understand.

Taylor reached for the can of Diet Pepsi she'd opened a few minutes earlier and took a long drink. "All right, Pop. I'll talk to Ruby and see if there isn't something you can help with. But Ruby's still in charge."

Charlie shot to his feet, grinning as if he'd just been handed a winning lottery ticket. "Hot dog! You won't be sorry, Sweet Pea. I can promise you that." He picked up the worn John Deere cap he'd left on the edge of her desk and settled it over his graying hair. "I'd better get myself home and start thinking of a few ideas."

Taylor eyed him over the rim of the can. "I thought you said you already had ideas. A million of 'em."

Charlie smiled, not at all embarrassed at having been caught. "Well, I *did* have the one."

"You'd better make the others better than that one, or I'll change my mind." Taylor flipped open the file on her desk again, glanced at her watch, and argued with herself for a moment before asking, "Would you mind looking in on Cody after school? I don't want him conning Anna into believing he doesn't have to do his chores—again."

Charlie nodded as he pulled open the door. "That little girl is no match for him, you know. You ought to let him stay with me."

"Anna's not a little girl. She's eighteen."

"She's still no match for that boy. He's an O'Brien. Besides, I'm right next door. Cody could run over in the mornings when you leave, and stop by after school. You wouldn't have to be late when Anna doesn't get there on time."

"Tempting . . . but, no. You and Cody together all day?" Taylor shuddered. "I love you, Pop, but the way trouble finds the two of you when you're separate, I don't think that's a very good idea."

Charlie scowled. "We're not *that* bad."

"I'm glad neither of you gets into *real* trouble, but you're both . . . exuberant. Besides, you've already raised your family. I promised myself when I took this job that I wouldn't impose on you."

"Taking care of Cody isn't an imposition. He's my grandson."

"Yes, and I love that you feel that way. I just want to make sure you *keep* feeling that way. Asking you to baby-sit while I work would be the quickest way I know of to ruin it." She left her desk and crossed the room to stand beside him. Sliding one arm around his shoulders, she stood on tiptoe and brushed a kiss to his whiskered cheek. "I think we should save the days you and Cody spend together for special occasions."

Charlie's scowl deepened, but the glimmer in his eyes softened his expression. "All right. If you say so. Can't say I agree with you, but I won't argue." The sound of an approaching car drew his attention to the window, and the glimmer changed to the familiar glitter of curiosity. "Speaking of trouble," he said under his breath, "here comes that useless deputy of yours."

"Donald isn't useless." Taylor craned to see over his shoulder. "He's just young. Honestly, Pop, how's he supposed to get any experience if nobody ever lets him do anything?" She broke off when she realized that the patrol car was creeping toward the office at a snail's pace and caught the I-told-you-so look on Charlie's face. "What is he doing?"

"Beats me. He's *your* deputy." Charlie leaned a little closer to the window. "Looks like he's bringing someone in with him."

Taylor groaned silently. Heartbreak Hill didn't have any real crime. Nothing that called for an arrest, anyway. But every once in a while Donald arrested someone just to make himself feel important. With the campaign heading into the final months, the *last* thing she needed was trouble.

Sighing, she stepped out onto the old-fashioned board-walk behind her father and waited while Donald parked the patrol car. A stranger sat in the backseat, craning to see out the windows. She couldn't see much, just a dusty black cowboy hat and a drooping mustache that bracketed the man's mouth, but it was enough to tell her that Donald had arrested someone she didn't know.

Trust Donald to end the summer with a bang.

She strode toward the car while Donald climbed out and resituated his hat. "What's going on?"

Donald jerked his head toward the backseat. "I found this guy wandering along the edge of the highway out near Solomon's Bend."

"So you arrested him? On what charge?"

Charlie couldn't seem to resist the urge to put in his two cents' worth. "Loitering, probably. Or dressing funny. Or maybe he's got too big a mustache. Is there a law about that?"

"Very funny, Pop." Taylor waved him away from the car. "What's the charge, Donald?"

Her deputy unlocked the back door and assisted his prisoner onto the street. The man straightened until he stood well over six feet tall—a good foot taller than Donald—and glanced around with undisguised interest. He looked as if he were already in costume for the Old West shootout the town staged in the square during the summer months.

Donald slammed the door and took his prisoner by the elbow. "How does carrying an unlicensed weapon grab you? A *loaded* weapon? Or resisting arrest?" He looked straight at Charlie, challenging him. "Or assaulting an officer?"

Taylor darted another glance at the prisoner. Taking those arms, legs, and chest into consideration, the man looked twice Donald's size. If he'd tried to hurt Donald, her deputy wouldn't be here now. And the man didn't look even slightly concerned, nervous, angry, or sorry. In fact, she couldn't tell if he was even paying attention.

He scanned the street, studied storefronts with interest, watched people walking, jumped when a car passed, and turned a quizzical expression toward a ringing telephone. His eyes sparkled and his lips twitched. For all his size, he looked like a small boy in a toy store.

Donald jerked his head toward the back of the car. "Get his weapon from the trunk, okay? I'm putting him in a cell before he loses his head again."

The request snapped Taylor out of her momentary stupor. "Is something wrong with the car? You drove up so slowly—"

"The car's fine. It's just that anytime I went faster than five miles an hour, Wyatt Earp here went crazy, acting like I was trying to kill him or something. It took me more than forty-five minutes to drive ten miles."

Taylor bit back a smile and opened the trunk. "Well, then, why don't you let me book him? You look like you could use a break."

Charlie came up behind her and nudged the trunk open. His gaze shot to her face, then flashed back to the trunk. "Do you know what that *is*?"

"Not exactly." Taylor lifted the rifle gingerly and checked for the safety. "It looks old. Is it an antique?"

"I'll say. It's probably well over a hundred years old." Charlie hopped back onto the boardwalk with more agility than he'd shown since he retired. "Where did you find that?"

The cowboy blinked several times and focused on Charlie's face. "The rifle? I bought it in Cortez."

Great voice, Taylor thought before she could stop herself. Deep, clear, and bass. Perfect for an actor. He must be here for the shoot-out.

Charlie pushed back his cap so he could see better. "Interested in selling?"

"No."

"Then how about the name of the dealer you went through? I know a couple of people who'd give their eye-teeth for something that nice."

And Charlie'd probably like to collect a hefty finder's fee. Taylor stepped in front of him. "Not now, Pop. We have work to do."

"Exactly." Donald gave a put-upon sniff and tried to tug his prisoner toward the office. "I'm telling you, we need to get him booked before he goes crazy again."

"Take a break," she said again. "I'll handle it from here. You can file your report later."

Donald quirked an eyebrow at her. "You sure you can handle him? He's strong as an ox."

"If I can't, I have no business being sheriff."

The cowboy looked startled, then turned to Donald with a deep scowl. "I've never hit a lady in my life, you little pip-squeak. The only reason I belted *you* is because you tried—" Two crimson splotches flared in his cheeks, and he flicked a glance at Taylor. "Well, *you* know what you tried. No need to spell it out in front of the lady."

Donald's mouth opened and shut a couple of times, and he looked as if he either wanted to disappear or hit something. "I didn't *try* anything. I was frisking you. It's standard police procedure."

Obviously, Donald and the stranger had gotten off on the wrong foot, and if the look on Donald's face was anything to go by, things were about to get worse. "Take a break," Taylor said for the third time. "That's an order. Don't come back for at least an hour."

Donald's mouth flapped for a few seconds, but in the end he let go of the prisoner and stormed off down the boardwalk, muttering under his breath.

"You, too, Pop. The show's over. There's no need for you to stick around."

"I don't mind staying. You might need me."

"I'll be fine. This is my job. And you promised to look in on Cody for me, remember?" Without giving Charlie a chance to argue, she led the cowboy into her office, shut the door, and settled her prisoner in one of the chairs in front of her desk.

He didn't put up any resistance, even when she released one wrist from the handcuffs and clipped the free end to the arm of the chair. While she checked the other wrist to make sure the cuff hadn't cut off his circulation, he studied her office as if he'd never been inside one before.

"Well, I'll be," he mumbled as he looked from one thing to another. "I'll be." When the fax machine rang, he jumped halfway out of his chair and pulled back as if he'd just seen a rattlesnake. "What's that?"

For a big guy, he wasn't so tough. "It's a fax machine. Haven't you ever seen one before?"

He shook his head and leaned a little closer as the wheels began to squeak. When paper started rolling out of the machine, he jerked backward again. "What's it doing?"

"Printing a transmission." Taylor found the form she needed and perched on the edge of her desk. "Let's start at the beginning," she prompted. "What's your name?"

"Evans."

"Is that your first name or your last?"

"Last." He turned his warm gray eyes directly on her and smiled for the first time. "The whole thing is Samuel J. Evans, but you can call me Sam."

"All right . . . Sam." The name fit him somehow, like a comfortable old pair of jeans. "Where are you from?"

"Most recently, Colorado."

"You mentioned Cortez outside. Is that where you live?"

"Near there." He made himself more comfortable—or as comfortable as he could be handcuffed to the chair.

"Do you have an address?"

He ran his free hand over his chin. "I guess that would be the Cinnabar Ranch—at least it used to be."

"Used to be?" Taylor shifted her weight to make herself more comfortable. "How long ago did you leave?"

"That all depends." He craned forward to glance at the newspaper on her desk. "That the right date?" At her brief nod he tilted his head to calculate. "Last thing I remember, it was the end of August . . ." He half-stood to watch a car go by, but the handcuffs pulled him back into his seat. He shook his head in wonder and grinned at her. "Amazing."

"What is?"

"This whole thing." He waved his free hand vaguely. "Never would've imagined."

"What did you mean when you said, 'the last thing you remembered' . . . ? Have you had a memory loss?"

"Not exactly. You asked how long ago I left. Well, it was the end of August when everything went blank."

She checked his eyes for signs of drug use, but they looked clear and bright. She couldn't smell alcohol on his breath, either. Maybe he suffered from some chemical imbalance. "Do you have blackouts often?"

"No. Just the one." He cocked an ankle across his knee and tried to rest his arm on the chair but the handcuffs pulled his hand to his lap again.

"Are you on any sort of medication we should know about?"

He shook his head slowly. "I'm not sick, ma'am."

"Okay. I'll take your word for it." She looked back at the report. "What's your Social Security number?"

"My what number?"

"Social Security."

He shook his head as if she'd confused him. "I don't know what that is."

"It's a number assigned to you by the government. You know, to keep track of the taxes they deduct from your wages. Haven't you ever had a job?"

"Just on the ranch. Never have worked for anybody else."

"But surely you filed a federal tax return."

"Not that I recall."

Oh, great. A tax protestor. Taylor set her clipboard to one side. "Do you have any identification, Mr. Evans? Maybe a driver's license or state ID card?"

" 'Fraid not."

Taylor held back a frustrated sigh. He wasn't making this easy. "Maybe I should contact your family. Is there anyone in Cortez I could call for you?"

"I don't think so."

"Friends?"

"Not anymore."

"Is there *anyone* I can contact? The charges against you are fairly serious."

He leaned forward and met her gaze steadily. "What charges? Carrying a gun? I didn't shoot anybody. Putting that young whippersnapper in his place? He deserved it. 'Sides, I didn't hurt him—other than his pride."

"But you did assault him—"

"What he did to me was a sight worse. Any judge in his right mind would agree."

"What he did to *you* was well within his rights as an officer of the law."

Sam looked deep into her eyes—deep enough to leave her flustered. "Now, how would you know that? You weren't there."

"Well, no. I wasn't, but—"

"And I'll wager that if he'd tried something like that on *you*, you'd be a might upset."

"He's an officer of the law," she said again. "He had every reason to check for concealed weapons. If he'd taken you into custody without frisking you, it would have been with reckless disregard for his own safety—and mine. And *yours*, too, for that matter."

"If that's all he wanted to know, he could have asked."

Taylor stood and tried again to gain the upper hand. "You may very well be an honest, upstanding citizen who would have confessed to having a dozen knives hidden in your waistband and boots, but Deputy Dumont couldn't take the chance. If he hadn't taken adequate precautions when he arrested you, I would have fired him."

"Poor fella." Sam turned those gray eyes on her again and frowned so deeply the tips of his moustache almost touched beneath his chin. "Tell me, Sheriff, are you always this bristly?"

He looked so amused, so damn superior, Taylor's fraying patience snapped. She fished the handcuff keys from her pocket and unlocked the cuff attached to the chair. "Okay, Mr. Evans. That's enough of that. We'll finish this later, when you're ready to cooperate."

"I *am* cooperating."

"You've been completely *un*cooperative. But don't think you've won. Patience and time are two commodities I have in abundance." She led him through the door to the temporary holding cells and locked him inside one. "I'll contact the court to find out when your arraignment will be. Meanwhile, I suggest you spend some time trying to remember something about yourself. And while you're at it, try to drum up some friends and family. I have a feeling you're going to need them."

Chapter 2

SAM LAY ON the narrow bunk of his cell, hands linked beneath his head, and stared at the ceiling while he listened to the sounds all around him. This was a strange, strange world he'd leaped into. Everything moved at lightning speed and noise assaulted him from every angle. Things roared, banged, whirred, rang, and buzzed constantly. Music floated in through the door that led into the sheriff's office and he had no idea where it was coming from. Her office wasn't large enough to hold an orchestra, but he'd swear he could hear one in there.

He looked forward to exploring this new world and discovering everything in it . . . once he got out of jail and stopped hurting so much. Time would probably ease the pain, but getting out of jail might be a bit of a problem.

He unclasped his hands and stood, a little worried in spite of himself. He'd never seen a woman like the sheriff. Taylor, the old man had called her. *Taylor*. Kind of an odd name for a woman, if you asked Sam.

Maybe it fit. Her dark red hair was cut short as a boy's, and she dressed like a man in trousers and a shirt, but the curves those clothes revealed left no doubt in Sam's mind that she was a woman.

Other than Olivia, he'd never seen a woman with quite

so much hellfire and damnation in her eyes. And intriguing eyes they were. Not quite green. Not exactly brown, either. He'd definitely seen flecks of gray and even some blue when the light hit them just right. A man could spend a lifetime just trying to figure out what color they were.

Not *this* man, of course. Sam wasn't about to blow his chance by getting involved with any woman—especially one like the sheriff. The top of her head might only reach his shoulders, but that look in her eye convinced Sam that only a fool would mess with her.

As if she'd felt him thinking about her, the sheriff opened the connecting door and looked him over slowly. "I'm going to run over to the diner for lunch. I'll bring something back for you when I'm finished. Any preferences?"

She seemed a whole lot calmer, so Sam crossed to the door of his cell and gripped the bars. He didn't care what he ate, as long as it was free. "Anything's fine. You choose." When she started to close the door again, he called out, "Ma'am? Could I ask you a couple of questions?"

Taylor hesitated, then gave a quick nod. "What is it?"

"You said I'd need friends and family. Mind tellin' me why?"

"If you don't want to stay in jail until your trial, you'll need someone to post bail for you."

"What will happen if I don't have any friends or family?"

She took a couple of steps closer. "None?"

"I'm not from around here."

"We can call someone in Colorado—or wherever. Maybe someone would be willing to wire you the money."

"Not likely. What other options do I have?"

She lifted one shoulder. "The judge might release you on your own recognizance, but if you're as tight-lipped with him as you've been with me, that's doubtful."

"I'm not being tight-lipped. I just don't have the answers you want."

Taylor's eyes roamed his face skeptically. "Well, then, do you own anything a bail bondsman might be willing to take as collateral? A house somewhere? A car?"

Sam leaned his arms on the crossbar in front of him,

realizing for the first time just how much he'd left behind and how precarious his position was. "The only things I own are the clothes on my back, that rifle on your desk, and the things you had me take out of my pockets."

"Nothing else?"

"Not a thing." He'd never been destitute before, and he wasn't sure he liked the feeling. "I'm in bad shape, aren't I?"

"Maybe." She took another step closer to his cell. "Why don't you tell me your side of the story about what happened between you and Deputy Dumont?"

"Will it make a difference?"

"It might. You never know."

Sam ran a hand along the back of his neck. "I didn't assault him so I could get away, if that's what you're wondering. And I didn't resist arrest. Matter of fact, I told him to go ahead and bring me in. The *only* thing I did was to teach him a lesson about putting his hands where they didn't belong. If I'd wanted to hurt the little runt, he wouldn't be here now."

To his surprise, Taylor smiled, and the smile transformed her face. "That's what I thought." The smile faded again quickly. "But that doesn't change the facts, Mr. Evans. The fact is, you *did* assault him. He has a legitimate complaint. And you *were* carrying a loaded weapon along a public road."

"I wasn't planning to use it."

"Then why did you have it?"

Sam shrugged. "I just had it. I brought it with me."

Taylor's eyes narrowed and her mouth curved into a scowl. "You came all the way from Colorado—on foot—and nobody stopped you for carrying a loaded weapon before you got here?"

Maybe he should be a little more honest with the lady sheriff. Surely, she'd understand about time travel. It had been a hard concept for Sam to grasp when he first heard about it, but here in the twenty-first century, people probably did it all the time.

"I didn't come on foot," he told her. "I came through time."

"You . . ." Taylor gave him an odd look. "You did *what*?"

"I came through time. Sort of traded places with a friend of mine so he could stay in the past and get married."

"You're talking about time travel?"

"That's the deal. Left right in the middle of a gunfight and landed here on the side of the road."

"You don't really believe that, do you?"

"Why not? It's true."

"I don't appreciate being jerked around, Mr. Evans."

"The name's Sam, and I haven't touched you, lady. You know I haven't."

"That's not what I meant." She snapped a glance at the door and took several deep breaths. "Tell me, do you travel through time often?"

Sam laughed. "No. I didn't even know it was possible until just a few days before I did it." He rubbed the back of his neck and stretched to get some of the knots out. "And now that I know how much it hurts, I'll think twice before doing it again. Have you ever done it?"

"No. No, I haven't."

"Well, take my advice. Don't. I feel like a herd of cattle stampeded across my chest and half of 'em slept on my legs."

"I'll take your word on that." Her lips curved, but the smile looked forced and brittle. "Just exactly *how* did you come through time?"

"Some strange sort of hole in the middle of a storm. I don't know what you'd call it."

"Uh-huh."

"The durned thing sucked me up and nearly turned me inside out."

"I see. And what time did you come *from*?"

"Last thing I remember, it was the end of August, eighteen and eighty-nine."

"So, you jumped through a hole in a storm and came

forward . . ." She broke off to calculate. "You traveled a hundred and twelve years?"

"Exactly."

"Why a hundred and twelve? Why not a hundred? Or *two* hundred? Wouldn't it be easier to leap a nice, round figure?"

"Well, now, how would I know that?" Sam was starting to think he'd misjudged. "You don't believe me, do you?"

"I didn't say that."

"You didn't have to. It's written all over your face. You think I'm crazy."

"I don't think you're crazy. Why would I think that? But it's getting late, and I really should get lunch."

"Right." Sam leaned one shoulder against the bars of his cell and stuffed his hands into his pockets. "Good idea."

She took advantage of the moment to slip through the door and, with one last insincere smile in his direction, closed it with a bang.

Well, now. He'd really done things up pretty, hadn't he? Apparently, time travel *wasn't* common here after all. The only thing he'd done was to convince the sheriff that he was touched in the head.

Not exactly the result he'd been going for.

Sam paced from one end of his tiny cell to the other, trying to come up with a new plan. Telling the truth about the time travel wasn't the best idea he'd ever had. But what could he say now? The sheriff had given him a perfect solution earlier. If he hadn't already thumbed his nose at it, he could have claimed that he'd lost his memory. He'd just have to think of something else.

He didn't know how long he paced before the door creaked open. He whirled toward it, expecting to see the sheriff again. Instead, he found himself looking at a gangly young boy with a shock of blond hair hanging in his eyes and a sprinkling of freckles across his nose. He wore a pair of short pants that hung off his narrow hips and a shirt that dwarfed him. They fit so badly, Sam figured they must have been hand-me-downs from an older relative . . . *much* older.

The kid's eyes flew open when he saw Sam inside the cell, but curiosity pulled him through the door. "Who are you?"

"Sam Evans. And you?"

"Cody O'Brien." The kid tilted his head, and his sudden resemblance to the sheriff was startling. "Have you seen my mom?"

"Your ma's the sheriff?"

Cody nodded.

"She went to get lunch. Said she'd be back soon."

"What are you in jail for? What did you do?"

"Had a string of bad luck." Sam didn't want to go into the particulars. "Look, kid, why don't you go watch for your ma in the other room? I have some serious thinking to do."

"What about?"

"Life."

Cody nodded as if he intended to leave, but his feet must have been be connected to some other part of his brain. They carried him another couple of steps closer. "Did my mom arrest you?"

"Her deputy did."

"Donald?" The kid made a face and moved to the cell next to Sam's. He stepped onto the lowest crossbar, gripped the bars high above his head, and leaned back as far as his arms would stretch. "I'll bet Mom hates that."

"Why?"

"Because it means Donald'll be bragging about this for weeks, and Mom hates it when he starts acting all weird like that."

"Is that right?"

Cody pulled himself close to the bars, then fell back again, scooped the lock of hair off his forehead, and shook it back into his eyes immediately. "What did Donald arrest you for?"

"I don't really think that's important."

"Are you a real criminal?"

"No."

"Then why are you in here?"

Sam crossed to the far corner of his cell and sat on the edge of his cot. "I thought you were looking for your mother."

The kid set up a rhythm, pulling himself close to the bars, laying back again as far as his arms could reach. Up, back. Up, back. "I was. But if she's just gone to get lunch, I'll wait until she comes back."

"She might be a while."

Cody gave his head a shake. "Naw. She always gets something and brings it back here—even when she doesn't have somebody locked up. Grandpa says she's a workaholic."

Sam lay back on the bed and stared at the ceiling. "What does that mean?"

Cody stopped rocking. "You've never heard of a workaholic before?"

"If I had, I wouldn't have asked."

"It means she's, like, addicted to working or something. Grandpa thinks she needs to get married, but every time he says so, Mom goes ballistic."

Sam didn't need help interpreting that word. He might not recognize it, but what little he'd seen of Sheriff Taylor left no doubt in his mind how she'd react to that suggestion. "So that means your ma's not married? What happened to your pa?"

A strange expression crossed Cody's face. He fell back again as far as his arms would allow. "My *pa*?"

"Is he . . . on the other side?"

"Side of what?"

Sam tried again. "Is your ma a widow?"

Cody nodded uncertainly. "Yeah. Yeah, she is."

"I'm sorry to hear that."

Cody hopped to the floor and shoved his hands into his pockets. "It's okay. I'm used to it."

Sam raised one eyebrow at the boy's reaction. Maybe things were different in this time, but Cody's reaction still seemed a little coldhearted. Sam hadn't always gotten along with his own father, but he'd still grieved when the old man passed on. "How long has your pa been gone?"

"Just about my whole life." Cody darted a glance toward the door to his mother's office before adding, "I don't really remember him."

"And your mother has to work here to support you?" Judging from the kid's clothes, she wasn't having an easy time of it.

Cody scowled as if he'd never given his mother's predicament much thought. "Yeah, I guess she does."

Sam mulled that over while the boy walked up and back in front of his cell. After a minute or two Cody stopped in front of his cell. "Grandpa says you have a really cool rifle. Can I see it?"

"Do you know how to use one?"

"Sure. Grandpa taught me."

The boy sounded confident, but the way his eyes darted around the room made Sam doubt he was telling the truth. And he was pretty sure that letting the sheriff's son blow off a foot wouldn't earn him any favorable marks. "I don't think so."

"Why not?"

"Because you're too young. And because it's mine. I don't want anyone messing with it."

"I won't mess with it. I just want to look at it."

"No."

"Just for a minute?"

Sam moved closer and put on his deepest scowl. "I said 'no,' boy. And that *means* no."

"I won't break it."

Sam fixed Cody with a look he knew could intimidate. "Hasn't anybody ever told you no before?"

Cody shrugged, completely unaffected by Sam's disapproval. "Sure they have. But my mom's so busy, I can usually get her to change her mind if I bug her long enough."

"Well, that won't work on me. I don't have a thing to do."

"Yeah, but you can't get out to stop me, either."

"Maybe not." Sam purposely kept his voice low. Ominous. He knew how intimidating he could be when he tried.

"But I can raise one helluva ruckus if you try to get to that rifle. Loud enough for your ma to hear even if she's ten miles off." He gripped the bars in front of him and scowled a little harder. "I'll get out of here *some* time. Keep that in mind before you do something stupid."

He held the boy's gaze without blinking. There was something about Cody that brought Jesse to mind. The same stubborn tilt to his chin. The same expression of belligerence mixed with uncertainty. Apparently, going from boy to man hadn't changed a whole lot over the years.

After what felt like forever, the boy took a deep breath and turned partially away. "Yeah? Well, I didn't want to see your dumb old rifle, anyway. It's probably not even real."

Sam didn't bother setting him straight. He wanted to leave the kid *some* dignity. "How old are you, anyway?"

"Almost eleven."

Tough age. "So you're the man of the house? Or do you have an older brother?"

Cody's shoulders straightened almost imperceptibly. "It's just me and Mom, so yeah, I guess I am the man of the house."

"Your ma's probably glad she's got you, then, isn't she?"

"I guess so."

A sound from the outer office caught Sam's ear a second before Taylor burst in. Her gaze shot straight to Sam's cell. "Why is this door open?"

Sam nodded toward Cody, who'd slipped into a corner. "I have a visitor."

"Cody? What are you doing here in the middle of a school day? And why are you back here? You know better than this."

"I was looking for you," the boy mumbled. "I thought you might be back here."

"You didn't answer my first question. Why aren't you in school?"

"They sent me home—for fighting."

"They *sent* you home? Why didn't they call me?"

"I dunno." Cody kicked at something with the toe of his

shoe. "I wasn't doing anything wrong. I was just talking to Sam."

"To *Sam*?" Taylor glared at Sam as if he'd dragged the kid back here against his will. "You're already on a first-name basis?"

Sam opened his mouth to defend himself. The boy rolled his eyes impatiently.

Taylor didn't give either of them a chance to get a word out. "Wait for me in the other room, Cody. I'll be there in a minute. And we'll be talking about school, so don't think I've forgotten." Dejected, Cody slipped out behind her and Taylor turned on Sam with a vengeance. "How did he get back here?"

"Opened the door and walked through, I suppose. But he wasn't bothering me." *Much.*

"Bothering *you*? You think *that's* what I'm worried about?" She raked her hair again. "He's a child. He has no business being back here."

"It wasn't as if I invited him, ma'am. And I couldn't exactly make him leave."

That seemed to douse some of the fire in her eyes. "No, I suppose you couldn't." She sighed heavily. "I'll talk to Cody—*again*—about staying away from the holding cells. But if he does come back here, I don't want you talking to him."

Sam had too much respect for a mother protecting her young to risk getting between them. Even though he didn't completely understand her anger, he inclined his head. "If that's how you want it."

"It's how I want it." She let out a deep breath. It seemed to come from the bottoms of her feet and took the rest of the starch out of her with it.

"I don't want to upset you again, but you ought to know that he asked to see my rifle."

Taylor glared at him. "How did he find out about that? No . . . No, let me guess. My father, right?"

"I believe the boy mentioned his grandpa."

An angry red flushed her cheeks. "What did you tell him?"

"I said no."

She let out a little laugh. "And he listened to you?"

"He knew I meant it."

"I see." Her shoulders turned to stone again. "Well, thank you. I'll make sure the rifle's locked up, then I'll bring your lunch." She disappeared into the other room and returned a few minutes later carrying a small white box and a red cup with white letters on it. "Hot turkey with fries," she said, sliding the food through a small opening in the door. "I didn't know what you wanted to drink, so I brought you a Coke."

"A Coke?" Sam picked up the cup but its sides were so soft he nearly crushed it. A *paper* cup? Who'd ever have thought it? And a lid made of glass that let him see the drink inside. Fancy.

She might call it Coke, but it looked like coffee to Sam. Only cold. Cold coffee had never appealed to him, but he was thirsty enough to try anything. He tried to figure out how to drink from it, but the only access he could find was a small X-cut in the lid. Holding it to his mouth, he tilted back his head, but only a few drops came through. More dribbled down his chin and onto his shirt from the edges of the lid.

He lowered the cup to have a second look and caught Taylor watching him with a quizzical expression. "I *did* bring you a straw."

"Oh. Right." Whatever that was. He looked again at the things she'd brought and noticed a long round tube of paper that looked just about the right size to fit through the hole in the lid. Feeling proud of himself, he started to push it through.

"You might want to take the paper off first."

He glanced at her. "Right."

"You act as if you haven't ever seen a straw before."

"I haven't." He juggled the cup and the straw and tried to figure out how to take off the paper. "Isn't there some way to drink without this?"

"You could take off the lid."

He laughed and tossed the straw onto his bed. "That's a

relief." He removed the lid, surprised at how easily it bent in his hand. "What is this?" he asked, holding it so she could see what he meant. "It can't be glass."

"No, not glass. It's plastic."

"Plastic." He turned it over in his hand and studied it for a moment. "Well, now, isn't that handy?"

"You've never seen plastic before, either?"

"Not that I can recall."

She nodded toward another bundle on top of the white box. "Your silverware is made of plastic, too."

He flicked the plastic lid with his thumb. Seemed a bit flimsy to eat with, but he supposed he'd get used to it in time. Suddenly cotton-mouthed from thirst, he took a huge gulp. Something fuzzy crawled up his nose, a chunk of ice fell into his throat, and the drink exploded as he swallowed. Vile stuff tasted like cold sugar water, only worse. A fit of coughing shook him, but he managed—barely—to hold on to the cup.

"What the hell *is* that?" he demanded when he could breathe again.

"You've never had a Coke before, either?"

"No." He looked around for some place to leave the vile stuff and finally settled for a corner of the floor. "And I hope I never do again."

"I'm sorry. I thought you might like it." She didn't *look* particularly sorry. Her lips twitched as if she was struggling not to smile, and he could distinctly hear laughter in her voice. "I'll get you something else. What would you like?"

With that twinkle in her eye, she was downright pretty. Too bad she was forced to dress and act like a man to put a roof over her boy's head. Sam forced his gaze away from her face. "Do you have water?"

"Yes, of course. With or without ice?"

"How is it you have ice?" Sam asked with a glance at the single, high window in his cell and another at his cup. "It's not even winter."

"Freezers. They make ice whenever we want it."

"Then I'll have some."

"Anything else?"

"I don't know." He slid a hesitant look toward the white box still waiting for him. "Any surprises in there?"

She laughed softly, caught the look he sent her, and clamped her lips together. "I don't think so, but why don't you look before I leave?"

He picked up the box and took a moment figuring out how to open it. Whatever it held *smelled* good enough to eat. "The sandwich looks edible," he said when he had the box open, "but I have no idea what these stringy brown things are."

"They're French fries. Potatoes cooked in hot oil. Try one. If you don't like it, I'll get you something else."

Sam had always been partial to potatoes, so he took an experimental nibble, chewed thoughtfully, and nodded. "Not bad. I'll keep 'em."

"Good. I'll be back in a minute with your water." She left him alone, and Sam settled in to eat. He might not be any closer to getting out of jail, but at least he wouldn't starve to death.

He ate slowly, pondering his future, and listening to the whirring, banging, buzzing, ringing, and roaring going on all around him. In time, he supposed he'd get the hang of living in the twenty-first century.

He'd better. He had a pretty good idea he was here to stay.

Chapter 3

TAYLOR GRIPPED THE steering wheel as she pulled out of her parking spot and maneuvered through a knot of tourist traffic. She couldn't wait for Labor Day when the worst of the summer rush would be over until next spring. She could make it that long. Then she could concentrate on the election.

She took her eyes from the road just long enough to glance at Cody, who sat on the other side of the car, arms folded across his narrow chest, mouth drawn in a thin line. When he realized she was watching him, he turned away so she couldn't see his face.

"All right, buster," she said now that they were alone. "Spill it. What were you fighting about?"

"Nothing."

"Mmm-hmm. Mrs. Wilson is always expelling people for doing nothing—especially on the third day of the school year." She braked to avoid a slow-moving car. "You might as well tell me. I'll be talking to her about sending you home instead of calling me."

"It was nothing." Cody hunched a bit further into the seat. "And she didn't send me home. She called Grandpa."

"Which is how you found out about Mr. Evans's rifle." It all made sense now. "You know what you did at the jail was dangerous. Mr. Evans is a prisoner—one we know absolutely nothing about." Except that he might be sick, delusional, injured, or a visitor from the past. "What if something happened to you, and I wasn't there to protect you?"

That earned a quick glance. "I'm not a baby. And anyway, nothing happened."

"It might have."

"But it *didn't*."

"I realize that," Taylor said through gritted teeth, "but the point is, it *could* have. Especially if you'd gotten your hands on Mr. Evans's rifle." She chanced another glance at him. "Do you have any idea how dangerous that could have been?"

"I'm not stupid, Mom. I wouldn't have shot myself."

"Accidents with guns happen all the time, Cody. Nobody *thinks* they're going to happen, and they don't plan them. That's why they're called accidents." She took a deep breath and tried to keep her voice level. "You're too young to be playing with guns."

"I wasn't going to *play* with it."

Bad choice of words. Of course, he wouldn't think of it as play. "You're too young to be *handling* guns, then. I want you to promise that you won't even think about doing something like that again."

Cody turned away and mumbled under his breath. "I don't know why you're making such a big deal out of it."

"Because it *is* a big deal. We were lucky." Realizing that she'd strayed from her other big concern, she tried to go back. "I'm not happy, Cody. I think we may have to keep you home from the scout camp out this weekend to give you some time to think about all this."

Cody scooted a little closer to the door. "I don't care. I don't want to go, anyway."

"Okay." Taylor didn't believe him, but she wasn't going to argue that point.

"I already told Grandpa I didn't want to go."

"I thought you liked camping out with your friends."

"Well, I don't." Cody folded his arms and shifted even

closer to the door. Any further, and Taylor worried that he'd fall out.

"You've always liked going before. Do you mind telling me why you've changed your mind?"

"Because."

"Because why?"

Cody shot her a look that would have made the flowers in her front garden wither. "Why should I go when everybody else is taking their dad along. I don't *have* a dad."

Taylor's stomach buckled as if he'd hit her there instead of landing a blow to her heart. "You have Grandpa."

"Yeah. A *grandpa*." Cody hunched his shoulders as if he thought she might try to touch him. "But nobody else is taking a grandpa, are they?"

The pain on his small face shocked her. Where had this unhappiness come from? "Lots of boys don't have fathers," she reminded him gently. "Like Matt Price, for instance. And Sean Covert."

"Their dads don't live with them," Cody argued, "but they *have* one. It's not the same thing."

This was her fault. One thoughtless, careless decision as a teenager had put the anguish on Cody's face today. One stupid decision that she'd foolishly thought would affect only her.

If she could go back and do it over again . . .

She stopped herself sharply. If she could do it over again, would she change anything? Would she make a decision that might mean Cody would never have been born? True, the circumstances of his birth hadn't been ideal, but how could she regret the choice that had brought Cody into her life?

She slowed at the four-way stop near the FoodWorld and checked for traffic before driving on. "You have a dad, too," she said at last. "You wouldn't be here if you didn't."

Cody's scowl deepened. "Yeah? Then who is he?"

That was the question she'd dreaded for ten long years. If she answered it, Cody would know where he came from, but she'd be opening a door that was better left shut.

"He doesn't live in Heartbreak Hill anymore," she said,

praying that would be enough to satisfy her young son.

Cody shifted back toward her, his face suddenly eager. "So?"

"I don't know where he is."

"*So?* At least tell me his name."

She stole a quick peek at him. "That would be enough for you?"

"Yeah. Sure."

For now, Taylor added silently. One of these days Cody would want to search for his father, and what would happen then? Nate had left town so fast when he learned she was pregnant, all that was left of him were the skid marks on the highway.

His desertion had finally shown her what Charlie and her friends had been telling her all along—that Nate Albright was selfish and self-absorbed. She'd been nothing more than a diversion—an easy, eager, willing diversion too young to see the truth, too naive to understand that his whispered vows of love were what he'd used to get the only thing he'd wanted from her.

"So—?" Cody prodded. "Who is he?"

She couldn't bear to hurt Cody further, but she couldn't lie to him, either. "I met your dad the summer before my senior year in high school," she said slowly. "He was here working on one of the guest ranches near town."

"Is he a cowboy?"

"Not exactly. He'd spent his whole life in the city and wanted to try his hand at life out here." She sent Cody a thin smile. "He wasn't really cut out for it. He thought Heartbreak Hill was boring."

"Sometimes it is."

"I guess it can be," she said. "But most of the time it's just right. Not so large that you become invisible to your neighbors, not so small that everyone has their nose in your business."

"Yes, they do."

Taylor pulled into her driveway and shifted into park. "Maybe a little," she admitted. "But the folks around here generally mind their own business."

"Since when?"

The question set off warning bells. She shifted in her seat to face him. "What's going on, Cody? Has somebody been bothering you?"

"No more than usual. Why did he leave?"

"I don't think he was interested in being grown-up and taking responsibility for someone beside himself. Is this why you were fighting?"

"Responsibility for me?"

"And me. Tell me, Cody. Is this what you were fighting about?"

"So? What was his name?"

Taylor resisted the urge to grab his shoulders and make him answer. "His name was Nate."

"Nate *what*? I know it wasn't O'Brien 'cuz that's Grandpa's name."

"Albright." She managed to get the name out around the growing lump in her throat. *Please, God, don't let Cody want to find him.* She didn't think she could bear to lose even part of her son to a man who had never shown the slightest interest in his existence.

"So my name should be Cody Albright?"

"Your name should be what it is—Cody O'Brien."

"But it *should* be Albright." Cody unbuckled his seatbelt and flung open his door. "You know what? This really sucks . . . big time. I *hate* not having a dad, and I hate the things kids say about you because of it."

Before she could react, Cody slammed the door and raced up the sidewalk toward the house. Taylor slowly released her death grip on the steering wheel and leaned her forehead against it instead.

She had the uneasy feeling that Cody had answered her question.

The next morning Taylor stood at the counter of Deke's Family Restaurant and waited for her breakfast order. Her eyes burned from fatigue and her head pounded with worry. Cody had been quiet and withdrawn all evening—not at all his usual chatty, energetic self. She hadn't known what to say to him, and the silence between them had grown thick and heavy.

Since he'd been expelled for the rest of the week, she'd left him sleeping. She'd asked Anna to have him call as soon as he woke up. Until then, she'd be on pins and needles, hoping he'd call and wondering whether a good night's sleep had made a difference in his attitude.

She leaned an elbow on the shiny chrome-lined counter and forced a smile so nobody would ask what was wrong. She hadn't had enough sleep to work up a believable lie.

"You and I need to talk," a voice said sharply in her ear as a soft cloud of Eternity filled the air around her.

Smiling with relief, Taylor turned toward her dearest friend. "Oh, Ruby. You don't know how glad I am to see you."

Ruby's perfectly plucked eyebrows arched. "You might change your mind when I'm through with you."

She was, quite simply, the most beautiful woman Taylor had ever seen up close and personal. Her perfect brown hair swung just past her shoulders in layers. Her makeup was always done to perfection, and even in jeans and a T-shirt she looked as if she'd stepped out of a fashion magazine. Luckily, her easy, down-to-earth personality made it possible for Taylor to like her anyway.

"You'll never guess who just left my office," Ruby said with a saccharine smile.

"Who? Do I care?"

"Oh, come on, Taylor . . . guess." The sweetness vanished and anger sizzled in Ruby's eyes. "His name starts with a *C*."

Taylor thought for a second, remembered her conversation with Charlie the day before, and groaned aloud. "My dad."

"Bingo." Ruby pulled a piece of gum from the ever-present pack in her purse and wedged it into her mouth. "He brought a list of things he wants me to do."

"What kinds of things?"

"Let's see if I can remember. He expects us to stand on a street corner and wave to people as they commute to work. He wants me to tie balloons and pictures of you on telephone poles. And this is my personal favorite—he thinks we should set up a booth at the county fair and give away homemade preserves to gain votes. Preserves you and I make in our spare time, of course. No sense wasting a perfectly good opportunity to get you married off and find me a second husband."

"I am *so* sorry." Taylor took her friend's arm and led her away from curious ears. "I was going to call you last night, but Cody threw me a curve and I forgot all about it."

"Then it's true? You *agreed* to this?"

"In a way. Yes. But it won't be so bad. It's just something to keep him busy. He knows you're in charge."

"Does he? I guess he forgot." Ruby smoothed back a lock of hair and adjusted an earring. "Look, Taylor, your dad's a sweetheart. He really is. And you know I love him almost as much as my own dad."

"But?"

"But I wouldn't want *my* dad working on the campaign, either. Charlie's absolutely convinced that every one of my ideas stinks to high heaven, and he's not shy about saying so."

"I realize it's not going to be easy," Taylor said under her breath, "and you have every right to be angry with me. But I just didn't have the heart to tell him no. He's at loose ends. Bored. He's been watching daytime talk shows on television, for heaven's sake. I'm just hoping this will keep him out of trouble."

Ruby's expression didn't soften a bit. "If that's what you're worried about, why didn't you hire him to work at the sheriff's office with you? That would have kept him busy."

"He wants to work on the campaign." Taylor smiled weakly. "He wanted to run the campaign, but I told him he'd have to work under you. And I'm sorry I forgot to tell you. I don't know what else to say."

"You *could* say that you've changed your mind." Ruby leaned against the counter and closed her eyes. "Oh, hell, Taylor. Just promise that you'll have a long talk with him and make absolutely sure he knows who's in charge."

"I can definitely do that."

"I should box your ears for this. The only reason I don't is because I wouldn't be able to say no to my dad, either."

Taylor hugged her quickly. "Thank you. I owe you one."

"At *least* one," Ruby grumbled. "So, tell me. What did Cody do last night that threw you such a curve?"

Taylor glanced over her shoulder to make sure no one could hear and lowered her voice for good measure. "Three days into school, and he's been expelled for fighting. But that's not the worst part. He asked about his dad."

"You're kidding."

"I wish. Out of nowhere, it suddenly bothers him that he doesn't know who his dad is. He didn't tell me until I tried grounding him from the scout camp out this weekend. Then he said he'd already decided not to go, even if Pop takes him."

"Did you tell him about What's-his-name?"

Taylor tried in vain to massage some of the tension from her neck. "I told him Nate's name. That's what he really wanted."

Ruby started toward one of the booths in back of the large room. "What'll you do if Cody tries to find him?"

"I don't know." Taylor followed her and slid onto the bench. "I used to be so afraid of this happening. But after a while, when Cody never showed any interest in Nate, I let myself believe he never would." She toyed absently with the napkin holder in the center of the table. "You know, I never even think of Nate anymore. I rarely even remember that Cody *has* another parent."

"Who wants to remember Whosit?" Ruby twisted a ring on one of her fingers. "I prefer to think that Cody is the result of immaculate conception."

In spite of the gnawing worry, Taylor laughed. "It isn't the fear of Cody searching for Nate that worries me, as long as Nate's the same selfish scumball he used to be. But what if he isn't? What if he wants to be part of Cody's life?"

Ruby shook her head firmly. "He won't. If he did, he'd have come looking already. It's not as if he doesn't know where to find you."

"Maybe he wants to know Cody but he's afraid to make contact first. Maybe he's one of those parents who decides to let the child make the first move."

Ruby's mouth thinned. "I doubt it," she insisted, but Taylor could see the the idea disturbed her. "Even if Nate *has* suddenly grown a heart—which I doubt—you're *not* going to lose Cody."

"I'm not sure I can prevent it. He's not acting like himself at all." Tension made Taylor's neck ache. She rolled her head from side to side, but it didn't help. "When I got pregnant, I didn't have any idea how deeply this would affect Cody. I'm pretty sure that's what he was fighting about at school. I think some kids have been saying things about me."

"What kinds of things?"

"Cody didn't say, but I can guess."

"When you decided to run for office, we talked about this. We knew the past might come up again."

"I know. It seemed manageable as an abstract possibility. Today it just seems overwhelming." She caught sight of the waitress carrying her order to the cash register and stood. "I wish I had time to deal with this, but I have to go. We have a prisoner, and he needs breakfast. And I have an appointment with Cody's teacher at ten."

Ruby stood with her. "What prisoner? When did that happen?"

"Yesterday. Donald found this guy wandering the side of the road carrying a loaded rifle. I can't decide if he's sick or crazy."

"Donald? He's both."

"No, the prisoner. He claims he traveled through time from the past. I think he actually believes it."

Ruby tugged the strap of her purse to her shoulder. "Great. A crazy man. Just what we don't need. How soon can you get rid of him?"

"His arraignment is tomorrow." Taylor moved slowly toward the cashier. "He'll be transferred to the jail in Helena unless he makes bail."

"Perfect. We don't need any kind of trouble this close to the election." Ruby swung toward the door and tossed a grin over her shoulder. "We're going to be too busy making those homemade preserves."

Five minutes later Taylor tried not to drop one of the Mountain Man Breakfast Specials as she crossed the street. It was a beautiful morning. A few soft clouds butted up against the mountains—pearl drops in a sea of blue sky. The sun warmed her shoulders, but she could feel its summer strength ebbing a little more every day. She should be in a wonderful mood.

She checked for traffic and stepped off the curb. The scent of bacon, eggs, and toast made her stomach bunch and knot. She didn't often indulge her craving for a big breakfast, but she had the feeling she'd need all the energy she could get today. Protein power. Eating something might even help her headache.

The clock on the corner chimed eight o'clock, and she groaned. She'd been hoping to get to the office before Donald, but she'd spent too long crying on Ruby's shoulder. She'd be lucky to squeak in ahead of him now.

It wasn't that she didn't trust Donald. But he was young, and sometimes an inflated sense of his own importance got the best of him. Getting taken down by a prisoner—even a bruiser like Sam—had punctured a hole in his fragile ego. He'd be looking to pump it back up today.

When the lid on one of the breakfasts shifted, she stopped beside a parked car, rested the boxes on its hood, and worked the flimsy tabs into their holes. As she picked up the boxes again, two men on the next block caught her eye. She gave them a quick once-over, but it still took a full three seconds to realize she was looking at Charlie talking with Hutton Stone.

What was that about?

It wasn't that she didn't trust Charlie. She just wanted to make sure trouble wasn't stalking him again. She shifted direction and headed toward them. Hutton wore his usual dark suit and tie. His graying hair was still slightly damp from his morning shower. But the cloud of aftershave around him made Taylor feel as if she'd been tossed into the bottle.

Hutton had long ago lost the slim face of youth; now he sported a bulldog's jowls that wobbled when he talked and the buttons of his shirt had to work to meet the buttonholes.

Taylor's headache kicked up another notch, along with a flicker of paranoia. Charlie noticed her, and a wide grin split his face. "*Here* she is," he said to Hutton. "We can get the whole thing set up right now."

That laid to rest any hope they'd been discussing the weather. Taylor turned a benign smile on Charlie. "Set what up, Pop?"

He slid an arm around her shoulders and gave her a gentle squeeze. "Hutton and I have been talking about scheduling a debate between the two of you."

Hutton smiled as if he'd never heard a better idea. "I'm certainly game."

Taylor tightened her grip on the boxes, half wishing she could throttle Charlie instead. Her thumb punched a hole in the top box and landed in something gooey and still slightly warm.

Pop knew she had a mortal fear of public speaking. He was the one who'd signed the permission slip to let her transfer from speech class in high school, for hell's sake. She'd never been any good at thinking on her feet and getting those thoughts out of her mouth. "I don't know, Pop. That's something we're going to have to discuss with Ruby."

Hutton's slightly protruding eyes took a long look down his hooked nose. "You don't sound very enthusiastic."

His tone jangled her nerves. "That's because I haven't even had a second to think about the idea. In the future, I'd appreciate it if you'd contact Ruby about campaign-related things instead of buttonholing my father on a street corner."

Hutton's thick lips curved into a satisfied smile. "Oh, but this isn't *my* idea. Charlie's the one who suggested it."

Taylor's thumb jammed farther into the box. Ruby would kill Charlie when she heard about this—if Taylor didn't beat her to it. She pulled her thumb out of the egg goo and sent her father a look that she hoped left no doubt about how she felt. "Then I apologize," she said to Hutton. "Let me run the idea past Ruby and we'll get back to you." And Ruby'd better think of some graceful way to get her out of it.

Hutton shrugged as if he didn't care one way or the other. "Fine with me." He palmed his slicked-back hair and turned his gaze up the street. "I wouldn't want to push you into anything that makes you uncomfortable."

Taylor forced a smile. "I never said a debate would make me uncomfortable."

"No, I guess you didn't." Hutton's smile turned downright sleazy. "Are you sure you're up to this?"

"Up to what?"

"Campaigning. I mean, you've never actually been through a *real* election before."

It was true that she'd more or less fallen into office after a stroke had forced the former sheriff to retire. Also true that the special election held then had been little more than a token one and that Taylor had sailed through it unopposed. But she refused to let Hutton think he could intimidate her. "I think I'm up to the challenge."

"I hope so. Elections have a way of bringing out the worst in people—or maybe I should say the worst *about* people." He held up both hands quickly. "Not that anyone in *my* camp would sling mud. I'd fire anyone who dared to do something underhanded. But people around here do have long memories, and a person's morals are mighty important when it comes to a job like sheriff."

His meaning couldn't have been more clear if he'd painted it on a wall. He planned to make sure no one forgot that she'd been pregnant and unmarried at seventeen.

Ignoring Charlie's huff of outrage and disbelief, Taylor forced her voice to stay level. "Then I guess I'm lucky that

I've never tried to keep secrets. Everyone in town already knows my past."

"Ah, yes." Hutton shook his head sadly. "But there's a big difference between ignoring something and forgiving it."

"What is there to forgive?" Charlie demanded. "My daughter's never hurt anyone in her life."

"That's not how some people see it." Hutton let his gaze drift down the street again. "It's one thing to turn a blind eye when someone's living quietly in your community. It's quite another to elect someone like that to a public position—a position many consider a role model for our children. Parents might not want their children to be told they should look up to someone in Taylor's . . . circumstances."

Taylor thought about her miserable young son. She knew in that moment that Hutton Stone was somehow responsible for Cody's fight, his questions, and his current unhappiness. One of the breakfasts slid from her hand and landed at her feet. Egg slimed out of the box onto her boot and across the sidewalk. Hash browns tumbled out into the dirt. Strips of bacon curled out from the box lid and the scent suddenly made her nauseated.

Red-faced, Charlie took advantage of her distraction to plant himself directly in front of Hutton. "Is that how you're going to approach this election?"

"Cool it, Pop." Taylor didn't blame Charlie for wanting to pop Hutton in the nose, but Hutton would return the favor with an assault charge, which wouldn't do either of them any good.

Hutton tried to look innocently surprised. "Surely you know *I* have no problem with Taylor. We all made mistakes when we were kids."

"My son is *not* a mistake," Taylor cut in. "I won't let you or anyone else make him an issue in this campaign. Maybe I didn't marry Cody's father, but that has absolutely nothing to do with my ability to do my job."

"Once again, I must point out that I never said it did." Hutton's gaze flickered here and there, and Taylor realized that a few people were beginning to take an interest in them. Hutton cleared his throat and raised his voice to make sure nobody missed what he said. "Really, Sheriff, there's no reason to get upset with me. As always, I'm concerned about my friends and neighbors."

"So am I."

"Then we have no disagreement, do we?"

"Of course not." Acutely aware of the people shuffling closer, Taylor forced her stiff smile to stay in place, but she was so furious she could hardly see. She'd have to come back to clean up the mess she'd made. Right now, she had to put some distance between herself and Hutton Stone before she did or said something that would make everything worse.

When she realized Charlie hadn't moved, she called to him over her shoulder. "Are you coming, Pop?"

Charlie muttered something to Hutton, then caught up with her at the corner. He locked his hands behind his back and matched her stride as she crossed the street. "I'm sorry, Sweet Pea. I didn't mean to stir up something like that."

"Sorry doesn't help, Pop. From now on, I don't want you doing *anything* or talking to *anybody* without Ruby's okay or mine. If you can't promise that, I don't want you to help on the campaign at all." Her father's face fell, but she was too angry to back down. "That's if there even *is* a campaign after today."

Charlie grabbed her arm and stopped her in her tracks. "What do you mean by that?"

"I mean, if my past is going to get stirred up, maybe I'll just drop out."

"Now don't go rushing into anything," Charlie cautioned.

"Why not? How much thought did you give to what you started back there?"

Charlie's gaze faltered. "I admit it wasn't one of my brighter moves, but don't let that stop you."

"There are worse things than losing, Pop. If Hutton Stone stirs up the past, Cody will go through hell, and I won't let that happen no matter what it costs me." Jerking her arm away, she left Charlie staring after her. A tiny piece of guilt twinged her, but she ignored it.

She meant what she'd said.

Chapter 4

SOMETHING WAS BOTHERING the lady sheriff this morning. Even Sam could see that. Her eyes were hard and worried, the skin above her nose puckered as she went about her business. She slammed in and out of the front office a few times, snapped at her pip-squeak deputy—not that Sam minded *that*—and finally marched into the back room to slide another of those white boxes of food into his cell. She tossed a glance at him and one knife-sharp word after it: "Breakfast."

Sam pushed to his feet, battling the dull ache that had worked into his back and neck from sleeping on the tiny cot. Stepping over the boots he'd tugged off during the night, he picked up the box.

She was already halfway out the door, but Sam ignored the scent of breakfast—which smelled as good as anything he'd ever come across—and called after her. "Ma'am? Do you have a minute?"

Hours of uninterrupted thinking had Sam worried that he'd have trouble convincing a judge to set him free. He had to try to get out of jail before his case went to the judge. And that meant convincing Taylor O'Brien that he was neither dangerous nor crazy.

She stopped with one hand on the door. "What is it?"

"Mind if I ask you about my chances of getting out of here?"

The crease between her eyes deepened. "The judge will have to tell you that after your arraignment."

"And when will that be?"

"We're scheduled for tomorrow at ten."

Close as Sam could figure from the morning shadows that stretched across the ground behind the jail, that left him a little more than twenty-four hours. "And what'll happen at this arraignment?"

Taylor's hand loosened on the doorknob and slid down the side of the door as she turned to face him. "The judge will decide whether to release you on bail or keep you in jail until your trial."

"What will happen if the judge doesn't let me out?"

"You'll be transferred to the jail in Helena to wait for trial." She wiped her hand across the back of her trousers, drawing Sam's unwitting attention to the soft swell there. "My deputy tells me you refused representation by an attorney. Are you sure you want to go into court without one?"

Sam pulled his gaze away from the back of her trousers. "Not entirely. But I don't know any attorneys, and I seem to be a little short of money. Last I knew, lawyers weren't all that happy about taking on clients without it."

"If you can't afford one, the court will provide an attorney for you."

"Free? They'll do that?"

"Well, yes. It's the law." Her scowl settled in even deeper. "Don't tell me you haven't heard of that, either."

"Sorry."

"I don't believe you." She inched closer to his cell. "If you've watched even one cop or lawyer show on TV in the past twenty years or so, you know about court-appointed attorneys."

Sam shook his head slowly. "If you'll remember, ma'am, I haven't been around over the past twenty years or so. I don't even know what a T-V is."

"You're still claiming that you come from the nineteenth century?"

"Just telling you the truth."

"All right." She came a little closer. "For the sake of argument, let's pretend that I believe you." Obviously, she didn't, but Sam wasn't going to argue. "When my deputy read your rights to you yesterday—"

"My rights?" Sam moved the food to the other side of the cot where it wouldn't tempt him. "What would those be?"

Taylor's eyes turned the same dark green as the junipers back home. "Your rights. My deputy read them to you before he arrested you."

"Sorry, ma'am, but the little fella didn't read anything to me. Of course, I was a little indisposed at the time. It was all I could do to get back on my feet after your deputy . . . knocked me flat."

She gave a little half-smile full of skepticism. "I still don't believe that my deputy is capable of knocking you flat."

"Guess he wanted to show me who was in charge."

"Donald's half your size. How did he take you down?"

The memory made Sam's face burn. "I'd rather not say."

"I'd rather you did."

"Would it make a difference?"

"It might."

"Let's just say he . . . well, he . . ." Sam turned sideways so he wouldn't have to look at her. Much as he wanted out of this cell, he still couldn't get the words out. "I'd rather not say in front of a lady."

She made a noise somewhere between a laugh and a huff. "I'm the sheriff, Mr. Evans. If my deputy used unnecessary force when he arrested you, you'd damn well better tell me."

He couldn't resist taking a peek at her face. Poor thing, having to pretend to be so tough all the time. That look in her eye reminded him of Olivia, so bristly and determined to make her way in the world. "I'm pretty sure *he* doesn't think it was undue."

"Right now I'm not concerned with what he thinks." Taylor came right up to the cell. "I'm concerned with what *you* think. If you're going to plead police brutality when we get in front of the judge tomorrow, I want to know."

"I wasn't planning to *plead* anything. I figured I'd just tell my story. Figured the judge might be interested in what happened."

"Why don't you tell *me* what happened?"

"No offense, ma'am, but as I said, there are some things I don't discuss with ladies—this being one of them."

She huffed again and her eyes hardened. "Would you just forget that I'm a lady for a few minutes?"

He took in the nip of waist between the soft swell of breasts and hips, the shapely legs outlined by slim-cut trousers and the gentle curve of her cheek. "I don't think I can do that, ma'am."

"Try."

"I know you're trying to be tough and all, but I don't think there's anything you can do to make me forget that you're female." He treated himself to another long look at her. "It's just not possible."

Her cheeks flushed bright red, and she took a couple of backward steps. "Mr. Evans—"

"No insult intended, ma'am."

Her mouth snapped shut again, as if he'd confused her. "None taken, I suppose." She regarded him intently for a few seconds. "Tell me, Mr. Evans, do you really believe that you came here from the past?"

"I'm not in the habit of lying. Where I come from, a man's word is his bond. Lying is for cowards and cheats. I'm neither."

"No," she said slowly as her eyes roamed his face. "I don't suppose you are. I just wish I could believe you."

"If I could prove it to you, I would."

"You could try. Maybe it would help if you told me something about where you came from."

"About Cortez?"

"If that's really where you came from."

"And how will that help you know whether I'm lying or

not? It's not as easy to prove that you're from the past as it is to prove you're from the future. Anything I tell you about that time is probably in a book somewhere. If I'd known I'd find myself in this position, I might've brought a few things along."

"Yes, well, I'm sure it was a surprise." She leaned one slim shoulder against the wall. "Why don't you tell me *how* you got here?"

He checked her eyes to make sure she wasn't trying to pull a fast one on him. Get him to say something crazy and then use it against him. But she looked genuinely interested, and this just might be a way to get her on his side.

"Like I told you before, what I did was take someone else's place," he said. "Fella who came from your time and fell in love with . . . with the widow who lived on the neighboring ranch." It felt strange to refer to Olivia that way, but he saw no need to give the sheriff information she didn't need. "When it looked like he was going to be pulled back here, I took his place."

Taylor shook her head slowly. "You took his place."

"On the spur of the moment."

"I see." She ran her fingers through her hair and left it mussed. "Didn't it occur to you that it might not be so easy to get along in a strange time?"

Sam had the strangest urge to reach through the bars and smooth her hair, but he resisted. "I didn't exactly have time to think about it."

"You didn't think about money? About food and shelter? About anything?"

"Like I said, I didn't have time to think. We were in the middle of an ambush when this hole opened up in the sky behind Kurt. I didn't want him leaving Olivia alone, so I ran into it. Didn't have time to start thinking until I woke up here, and by then the deed was done. Next thing I knew, your deputy was taking my rifle away and shoving me up against the trunk." He was proud of himself for remembering the term.

Taylor didn't seem to notice how brilliant he was. "If

you hadn't run into my deputy, what would you have done?"

"My first thought was to find a town." He smiled wryly. "Guess I've done that, haven't I? Next thing I had in mind was finding work or maybe hunting food for a few days. Wasn't sure what I'd find in town. I know my way around a ranch, but I had it in mind to try something new. Any chance there's a silver mine nearby?"

"Sorry. No. Heartbreak Hill was never much of a mining town. In fact, that's how it got its name. Miners came here hoping to strike it rich, but every last one of them left heartbroken." She folded her arms and turned so that her back pressed against the wall. "The town probably would have disappeared like so many others, except that it was in a central location between other mining areas and a few shopkeepers got the idea to settle here and provide services the miners couldn't get anywhere else."

"Well, I'm disappointed to hear that. When I first started thinking about leaving the Cinnabar, I gave some thought to trying my hand at mining."

"What made you decide to leave Cortez in the first place?"

"I had a brother who wanted to run the ranch more than I did, but the old man left the whole thing to me when he died. Jesse—that's my brother—was planning to get married. He and his wife-to-be wanted a place of their own. The Cinnabar should've been his, anyway. He liked all the book work that went along with running it." Just thinking about Jesse brought a lump to his throat. He cleared it and kept talking. "Leaving seemed like the best way to let him have the place, and my other obligations were taken care of, so there wasn't much point in staying."

"This brother of yours . . . Can I contact him about posting bail for you?"

"Not unless you can get a message back through more than a century."

"Right." The skepticism flooded her eyes again. "Let me try to reach him. You say his name is Jesse? Same last name as yours?"

"Yes. But it won't do you any good to go looking for him."

"What about this neighbor of yours . . . Kurt Richards? And Olivia. What is her last name?"

"It was Hamilton when I left, but if they made it through that night, I'm sure she married Kurt shortly afterward." He thought about the ambush and asked impulsively, "Do you suppose you could find out what happened to them after I left? I'd like to know whether they bested Sloan Durrant and his men."

Taylor pulled a small ledger and pen from her pocket and jotted down a few notes. "Sloan Durrant? Who's he?"

"He was the banker in Cortez at the time. Greedy son of a . . . gun. Planned to take Olivia's land away from her—especially that stretch up on Black Mesa."

Taylor's gaze shot to his again. "*The* Black Mesa?"

"You've heard of it?"

"Of course I have. It's one of the most famous historical sites in the nation."

"Well, I'll be." Sam grinned slowly. "Then Kurt and Olivia saved it."

"Someone did." Taylor's expression changed subtly. Not that she looked convinced, but at least she seemed a little less doubtful. "And you're saying that your friends are the ones who are responsible for preserving it?"

"I don't like to brag, but I like to think I had a *little* something to do with it, myself." His smile faded. " 'Course, the history books probably wouldn't mention me, would they?"

Taylor shook her head. Hard. As if she was trying to shake off something that had landed on her. "It's a nice story, Mr. Evans—"

"Sam. Please. Nobody ever calls me Mr. Evans. Makes me feel like I'm putting on airs."

She shook her head again. "Well, I'm sorry to hear that, but you are a prisoner in my jail, and I think it would be best to keep things formal. As I was saying, it's a nice story. But you're right. Everything you've told me could have come straight out of a history book, or off the Internet."

"The what?"

"Never mind. The point is, you still can't prove who you are or how you got here, and you still don't have anyone to post bail for you."

And she still wasn't going to let him out of jail.

Sam sank back onto his cot without looking and landed right on top of the box holding his breakfast. He jumped up again, but not before egg soaked clean through the back of his pants. He stood there dripping, looking like a damn fool in front of the lady sheriff, who bit her lip to keep from laughing.

Sam couldn't see how things could get much worse. But a second later the door banged open in the outer office and a woman's voice cut through the background noise that never stopped.

"Taylor? Where are you?" A clatter of footsteps, and a dark-haired woman loomed into the doorway, eyes wide, mouth set in a thin line. She wore the brightest colors Sam had ever seen in his life, and carried a pouch that looked like a saddlebag over one shoulder. Earrings dangled from her ears, a gem sparkled at her throat, rings flashed from several of her fingers, and the scent of strong, sweet toilet water wafted in with her.

She was pretty enough, for all that she'd covered every inch of her face with paint and her fancy water stung his eyes. When it came to women, Sam preferred the natural kind—like Taylor, there. Pretty as they came, and all natural. Why, putting fancy paint on that face would be almost sacrilegious.

Taylor stepped away from the cell as if she'd been caught filching apples from the neighbor's tree. "Ruby? What are you doing here? What's wrong?"

"Your dad just told me that you're thinking of quitting the campaign. Tell me it isn't true."

"I haven't decided anything yet."

"Then you *are* thinking about it?" Ruby looked as flattened as if someone had run over her with a horse cart. *"Why?"*

"In a word, Cody."

"Explain."

Taylor glanced at Sam and gave her head a crisp shake. "Later."

"But this is ridiculous. You *can't* back down now."

"I can, and if it's best for Cody, I will." Taylor stepped around her friend and looked back as if she expected the woman to follow her.

The woman's bag let out a high-pitched chirp like a cricket. A silly little noise, but it stopped both women in their tracks. While Ruby fished around inside the bag, it chirped again. After the third time, she pulled out a small black box and held it to her ear. "Hello?"

Intrigued, Sam moved a step closer. That earned him a quick, dark glare, so he retreated again and watched as she carried on a conversation with the little black box. ". . . I don't know. I thought I left it on my desk. . . . No, no, next to the flyers . . . It's not? Where in the world could it have gotten to?" She turned her back and cupped her hand around the box. "Did *Charlie* go anywhere near my desk after I left? I see. Well, that explains that."

Taylor listened as carefully as Sam did, and the mention of her father's name made her sag against the door frame. "What's he done now?"

Ruby waved a hand at her. "Well, he can do his best, but that still isn't good enough. You saved the text on the computer, didn't you? And Taylor's picture is still there? Good. Good. Then reprint it. And this time, don't leave it where Charlie can see it." She pulled the box away from her ear, jabbed a finger at it, and stuffed it back into her bag. "It seems that Charlie doesn't like the picture of you we put on the brochure, and by the strangest coincidence, the master copy has disappeared."

Taylor groaned. "He *took* it?"

"No one actually saw him do it, but it wasn't there when Gordy came from the print shop to pick it up. I'm sure Charlie will say it's only a coincidence that he was making phone calls from my desk just before it disappeared."

Taylor looked so distraught, Sam felt kind of sorry for her. "I'll talk to him. I promise. I'll make *sure* he understands he can't do things like that."

Ruby rolled her eyes, but there was fondness behind the exasperation. "I'll talk to Charlie myself. You don't need to worry about it. Besides, if you decide to drop out of the campaign, we won't have a problem, will we?"

"I suppose not."

Ruby put an arm around Taylor's shoulder and gave her a quick squeeze. "I don't want you to quit. You know that. But you also know how much I love Cody and I wouldn't do anything I thought was bad for him. I just don't understand how watching you try for something you want, and get it, could possibly be bad for him."

"If you'd heard Hutton Stone this morning, you wouldn't say that."

Ruby's red lips puckered. "*Now* we're getting somewhere. What did Hutton say?"

Again, Taylor looked at Sam and again she shook her head. "Let's go into my office."

Ruby took a long look at Sam, as if she'd noticed him for the first time. "So, this is the prisoner who claims he's a time traveler?"

Taylor's gaze faltered and her cheeks burned, a little embarrassed, maybe, at having Sam find out she'd been talking about him. She reached for Ruby's arm and tugged her toward the door. "Let's not talk about this now."

Ruby slipped out of her grasp and raked her eyes across Sam again. She wasn't the friendliest woman Sam had ever met. "I know what's going on here. It's so obvious, I can't believe I didn't snap when you told me about him." She came right up to the cell and glared at him. "You're working for Hutton Stone, aren't you?"

"No, ma'am. I don't even know who that is."

"Oh, come on. You don't really expect me to believe that."

"Don't know why not. It's the God's honest truth."

"Uh-huh." She folded her arms and paced in front of his

cell. "And you think the sheriff and I are stupid enough to believe that wild story about traveling through time? What did Hutton do, pay you to make Sheriff O'Brien look foolish?"

"No, ma'am." From the corner of his eye, he saw Taylor watching him. "I wouldn't take money for something like that."

"Is that right?"

"Yes, ma'am."

"I don't believe you."

Taylor raked her hair again—one quick, jerky movement so full of agitation it worried Sam a little. "Hutton Stone *did* send you, didn't he?"

"No, ma'am. Like I said, I don't even know who the man is."

"Well, you can tell Hutton Stone that he'll have to do better than this to bump Taylor out of office." Ruby grabbed her little black box again. "Come November, she'll still be sheriff, and he'll still be selling real estate." She turned to Taylor and lowered her voice, but not by much. "I knew Hutton was underhanded, but this is beneath even him."

"I don't work for Hutton Stone," Sam said again. No sense letting somebody be accused of something he didn't do. And besides, Sam wasn't anxious to be tarred by a dirty brush. "I'm not working for anybody at the moment."

"Right." Ruby punched the box several times and shooed Taylor toward the door. "You can't keep him here. You're just playing into Hutton's hands."

"But—" Taylor looked as confused as Sam felt. "What about the charges against him? He did assault Donald."

"That's nonsense. This whole thing's a setup. Nobody in his right mind would believe that this guy assaulted Donald and left him in one piece." She put a hand on Taylor's shoulder and guided her into the outer office. "Do whatever you have to do, but get him out of this jail before—"

The door clicked shut on the rest, and Sam stood there for a few minutes, dripping egg on the floor and feeling as if one of those fast-moving cars had run him over. He wasn't used to having his integrity questioned, and he didn't like it. But he had the sinking feeling that the worst was yet to come.

Taylor was back before the sun had a chance to move in the sky. Sam guessed it had been less than half an hour. "Deputy Dumont has decided to drop the charges against you," she said as she worked the key in the lock. "You're free to go."

"You believe your friend, then?"

"I don't know what I believe." The lock gave way, and she swung the door open. "I only know I want you out of here."

"What I told you is true. I'm not working for anyone."

"I don't know what your game is, Mr. Evans, but I don't want any part of it."

"I don't have a game, Sheriff. I'm just looking for a place to land on my feet."

"Well, let me give you a piece of advice." Her eyes flashed through colors and finally settled on dark, brown, and stormy. *"Don't* land in Heartbreak Hill."

"You're running me out of town?"

She rested one slim hand on her hip. *"I'm* strongly suggesting that you move on."

Sam gathered his boots and glanced at the egg-crusted back of his pants. He didn't look fit to start a new life. Still, there must be some reason fate had dropped him just outside Heartbreak Hill. He'd like to stick around and find out what it was. "Will I be breaking some law if I don't leave?"

She lifted her chin and glared at him. "I wish I could say yes, but I'm not going to lie. I can't force you to leave town, but you'd be doing us both a favor if you did. If you stay and I find out you're connected to Hutton Stone in *any* way, you'll wish you'd taken my advice."

Sam tried to take her seriously, but she was such an itty-bitty thing, he could have picked her up and slung her over his shoulder if he'd wanted to. Her gun was almost as big as she was.

He followed her into the outer office and accepted his

hat when she thrust it at him. "You know, ma'am, this isn't any of my business, but working to support that boy of yours can't be easy on you. Can't you find something easier? Something more . . ." He searched for just the right word. "More ladylike?"

Her face flamed, her eyes burned, and her nostrils flared slightly. "More *ladylike*? Is that what you said?"

"I didn't mean offense, ma'am. It's just that you're a lady. You have a boy depending on you. I understand that. But aren't there things you could do that aren't so rough? Dressmaking, maybe."

She looked for a second as if she might slap him. "Thank you for your concern," she said as if she had to grind each word out between her teeth, "but my son is no concern of yours, and neither am I."

"I didn't mean—"

"You can tell Hutton Stone he just made a *big* mistake. I was thinking of dropping the campaign, but you've just convinced me otherwise. Now, get out."

"Can I get my rifle back?"

She growled—literally *growled*—at him, stormed across the small office, and unlocked a cabinet against the far wall. She jerked his rifle from inside and shoved it into his hands.

He checked the chamber and discovered it had been emptied. "Ammunition?"

"You don't need ammunition. Not in my town. And if I catch you with any, I'll have your butt back in that cell so fast it'll make your head spin. Is that understood?"

"Understood."

She gripped her desk hard, as if she thought it might get away if she loosened her grasp even slightly. "And if you want to keep your freedom, don't you ever, *ever* patronize me again."

"I wasn't intending any offense."

"Well, you sure delivered."

Women, Sam thought as he let himself out into the bright summer sunlight. They made absolutely no sense. No sense at all.

His mother had fretted herself to death, hating the harsh

life on the Cinnabar Ranch, wishing for parlors and teas and ladies to visit with, dreaming about lace and satin and silk and servants, and resenting his father for taking her away from all the softness she thought she deserved. Taylor had practically bitten his head off, and all he'd done was express a little honest concern that life could go easier on her.

If women couldn't be consistent, how was a fella supposed to know how to act or what to say to them? Good thing Sam had no plans to get involved with one any time soon.

He stood for a moment and let his eyes adjust after being locked up inside for so long. He relished the warmth of the sun on his face and shoulders, scanned the horizon, and followed a thick line of pine along a gully on one of the nearby mountains.

He was free. Not only from jail, but from everything that had held him back in the past. He was free to make a new life. Free to fail miserably. Either way, it would be his doing. There'd be no more relying on his father's reputation, living up to someone else's expectations, or worrying about disappointing someone.

A man couldn't ask for more than that.

Chapter 5

EVERY TIME TAYLOR stepped into Heartbreak Hill Elementary School, she felt as if she'd been transported back in time. Instead of twenty-eight, she felt ten or eleven—uncertain, ungainly, and unattractive. The scent of school lunch, sweaty young bodies, industrial-strength cleanser, and varnish did it to her without fail, and she always needed a few seconds to remember that she wasn't that little girl anymore.

She didn't have to keep her chin up. She didn't have to ignore Kip Mikesell and DeWayne Beers who were close friends now, but who'd been merciless teases when they were kids. She didn't have to dread the annual mother-daughter tea or envy friends who had mothers and could actually attend.

She took three deep breaths while she oriented herself and tried to forget everything that had happened that morning. She didn't want Hutton Stone or Sam Evans to distract her while she talked with Cody's teacher. Checking her watch, she set off toward the fifth-grade hall.

Curious kids glanced up as she passed classrooms; a few who knew her waved. Others looked away. She held on to her nightstick and keys as she walked, trying to minimize the jingling that accompanied her whenever she was in uniform. With her handgun locked in the trunk, her empty holster swung against her leg with every step.

She wasn't the same person who'd gone to school in this building, but that unhappy little girl still existed inside her. The girl who'd lost her mother when she was a little younger than Cody; who'd spent hours trying to get her too-thick, too-curly hair to conform to the popular hairstyles; who'd suffered through braces on her teeth and clothes picked out by a father who was well-meaning but totally out of touch.

Taylor hated remembering. If she hadn't needed to help Cody, she wouldn't have let the memories play, even for a second. Over the years she'd grown adept at shutting down any emotions that made her uncomfortable.

She paused at the drinking fountain and gulped a mouthful of tepid water, swiped at her lips and chin with the back of her hand, and steeled herself to meet with Mrs. Wilson, who'd always left Taylor feeling intimidated.

Her classroom had changed little over the years. When Taylor was a student here, the walls had been covered by artifacts Mrs. Wilson had picked up on her travels around the world. If anything, the walls were more cluttered now, but Taylor couldn't tell which treasures were new and which had been here before.

Shelves of award-winning books—Mrs. Wilson didn't let her students read anything else—still lined the wall behind the teacher's desk and the desk occupied the same corner it always had. A list of assignments written in Mrs. Wilson's perfect cursive took up one side of the chalkboard. Only the reading posters of sports figures and celebrities gave any sign that time had passed. The faces were all ones today's kids would recognize.

Mrs. Wilson looked up from her desk as Taylor entered. She didn't look as if she'd aged a day. Her short-cropped hair was still the same honey-blonde, and Taylor could have sworn she'd owned those same sensible shoes and skirt back in 1984.

Her glasses hung on a gold chain around her neck and swung slightly as she stood. "Ah, good. You're right on time. We'll be able to talk before the kids come back from recess."

Taylor smiled as if she'd just received an A on a spelling test and crossed the room—which had once seemed a whole lot bigger. "Thanks for meeting with me. I'm very concerned about what happened yesterday."

"So am I." Mrs. Wilson motioned for her to sit in a kid-sized plastic chair in front of her desk and resumed her own seat. "At the time I wasn't sure I agreed with the principal's decision to suspend Cody, but after a little more thought I think giving him a few days to think about what happened is the wisest thing to do."

Taylor didn't agree, but she'd promised herself she wouldn't jump to conclusions. "Why don't you tell me exactly what happened? Cody was a little vague."

Mrs. Wilson sat back in her chair and glanced toward Cody's empty desk. "That doesn't surprise me in the least. To tell you the truth, Taylor, I think Cody is a very unhappy little boy. His unhappiness is coming out in a variety of unacceptable ways."

"Cody's not usually a fighter," Taylor assured her. "It's just that things are a little tough for him right now. I know part of the reason, but I'm hoping you can help me understand the rest. What happened yesterday? Why did he get into the fight?"

"Cody didn't tell you?"

"Not specifically. He said something about not liking what kids were saying about me, but after that he clammed up. I'd like to know who said what."

"It may not be easy for you to hear."

"I'm pretty sure it won't be, but I don't care about that. I *do* care about my son and what he's going through."

Mrs. Wilson smiled softly. "I'm glad to hear that, but not a bit surprised." She stood and took a moment to get her thoughts together, pacing the tiny square behind her desk as she always had when faced with a problem. "Keep in mind that I don't think the kids are responsible for this," she said after what felt like forever. "We all know that kids often echo what they hear at home."

Unfortunately.

Mrs. Wilson flicked a brief smile at Taylor before she went on. "Some of the other students have been taunting Cody about not having a father. They've only been in school three days, and already the teasing is almost out of control. Believe me, I've done my best to stop them, and after we've been in school for a few hours they calm down. But the next morning they're at it again."

She stopped pacing and rested her hands on the back of her chair. "Cody endured the teasing as long as it was directed at him. Yesterday morning, one of the boys said something about you, and the others took up the chant. Cody flew off the handle—not that I blame him. The boy used a particularly harsh word."

"What word?"

"He called you a whore."

Taylor appreciated the way Mrs. Wilson looked her straight in the eye, just as she had when Taylor was eleven and convinced she was stupid because she didn't understand math. Mrs. Wilson had never tolerated self-doubt, and that direct eye contact didn't leave room for any.

Taylor expelled a shaky breath. "That's pretty much what I expected you to say." She straightened her shoulders under the teacher's gaze. "Did anything happen to the other boy?"

"He received a suspension, as well. His parents were here within an hour, arguing with the principal to have him reinstated."

"Did Mrs. Coats rescind her decision?"

"I sat in on the meeting." A touch of warmth and a flicker of humor danced in Mrs. Wilson's eyes. "She knew I'd have something to say if she backed down."

Taylor managed a weak smile. "Thank you."

"I hate injustice. You know that. But I'm afraid that yesterday's fight is a symptom of a deeper problem with Cody. He's obviously feeling the lack of a father in his life."

Taylor didn't want that to be true. "It hasn't been a problem before."

"I'm afraid it has. I understand that Cody has been making up stories for a couple of years."

Taylor's heart sank and her palms grew damp. "About his father?"

"I'm afraid so." Mrs. Wilson drew a thin notebook across her desk and consulted it. "His father has been everything from a government spy, to an undercover police officer, to Brad Pitt."

A horrified laugh squeaked out of Taylor's throat. "Well, at least he gives me credit for good taste," she said when Mrs. Wilson looked at her strangely. She sank back against her chair and clutched the seat so she wouldn't lose her balance. "I had no idea this was going on. Why didn't his other teachers say something?"

"I can't answer for them."

"What do you suggest I do?"

"You might consider getting Cody some counseling. The right therapist might be able to help him work through these issues."

And give Hutton Stone a great big rock to throw at her in the campaign.

Taylor shook the thought away the instant it formed. How could she think about the campaign at a time like this—even for a moment? What kind of mother did that make her?

She stood and held out a hand. "Thank you, Mrs. Wilson. I'll do that."

Mrs. Wilson didn't take her hand. "I said, consider it. There may be other ways—better ways—to handle the situation. Cody might balk at the suggestion that he needs therapy. And I think we both know what Hutton Stone would do with the information that Cody was getting psychiatric help."

"He'd have a field day. But the campaign doesn't mean anything compared to my son's well-being. If Cody needs help—"

"The campaign may very well contribute to Cody's well-being. His one claim to fame, so to speak, is having a mother who's successful and—in his words—'afraid of nuttin'.' "

"He said that?"

"He's proud of you, Taylor. That counts for a lot."

Before Taylor could process that, the bell signaling the end of recess blared. Mrs. Wilson stood and came out from behind her desk. "I wouldn't rush into anything if I were you. Keep an eye on Cody for a few days and see what happens. He'll be back in school on Monday, and if I have anything to say about it, this will be the last incident of its kind."

Doors banged open in the corridors and a multitude of shouting voices disturbed the relative silence. Surprising herself, Taylor gave in to the impulse to hug the teacher. "Thank you, Mrs. Wilson. That's exactly what I'll do."

Running feet echoed in the hallways, and two red-faced girls burst into the room, skidding to a stop when they saw Taylor. She had no desire to face a roomful of students wearing the same look of horrified fascination as those two little girls she'd just seen.

Muttering a good-bye, Taylor hurried from the room and ducked out the nearest door. Mrs. Wilson would have to work a miracle to wipe that look off their faces, but even her best efforts wouldn't touch the parents who'd put it there in the first place.

By the end of the day Taylor was so exhausted she could hardly see. She drove home, but she'd only gone two blocks before she decided it might have been safer to walk. It would have taken toothpicks to keep her eyes open more than a slit, and her reflexes were sluggish at best.

The more she thought about her conversation with Mrs. Wilson, the more confused she became. The more she thought about Ruby's assertion that Hutton Stone was responsible for Sam Evans being here, the angrier she became. But even anger couldn't keep her going.

The minute she got home, she'd call for a pizza. Then she'd take a hot bath and veg on the sofa while Cody watched TV. She didn't think she could handle anything more demanding.

The only thing that had gone right all day was that she hadn't seen Sam since she released him. She'd kept her eyes open, even phoned the local motels during the afternoon, but nobody had rented a room to him. She hoped that meant he'd taken her advice.

What would Hutton Stone do next? She didn't want to spend the rest of the campaign looking over her shoulder, doubting everything, distrusting everyone. It wasn't like her to be suspicious, and she didn't like the way it made her feel.

Damn Hutton Stone, anyway. And damn Sam Evans, too. If she never saw him again, she'd be happy.

She pulled into the driveway and shut off the car with a sigh of relief. She'd made it home without killing anybody. If she *ever* got this tired again, she'd walk or catch a nap at the office before she got into the car. Even her bones ached.

Gathering her things from the seat beside her, she dragged up the back steps and into the kitchen. The blessed sound of silence—unusual whenever Cody was around—caught her the second she entered the house.

She tossed her purse onto the kitchen table and headed toward her bedroom to change. "Anna? Cody?" She unbuckled her service belt and pulled off her shoes halfway down the hall. "Where is everybody?"

She picked up her shoes and flexed her feet in the soft carpeting of the hallway. It was one of her little-known secrets that she hated shoes. They were the first things off at night and the last things on in the morning, and it felt like pure heaven to get out of them today. Everything bothered her from the way her blouse fit to the cuff of her socks. She was *so* ready for the day to be over.

Inside her bedroom, she tossed her shoes in the general direction of her closet and unbuttoned her uniform shirt. Before she could get out of it, a piece of paper stuck to her mirror caught her attention.

Mom. Me and Grandpa are at his house. Come over okay?

Ignoring his grammar, she tugged a T-shirt from her drawer and over her head. Trust Charlie to ignore her wishes and send Anna home early. After the stunt he'd pulled at the campaign office that afternoon, she was ready to have a serious talk with him—tomorrow.

She tossed her uniform pants after her blouse and found a pair of cutoff jeans in the bottom of the clean laundry basket—a mound of clothes waiting for her to fold whenever life slowed down long enough. She strode down the hall and out the back door, minced across the hot driveway in her bare feet, and threw open Charlie's door a minute later.

Charlie's coffee cup, two plates covered with chocolate cake crumbs, and Cody's Seahawks cap sat on the table. Laughter burst through the door from the living room. She recognized Charlie's laugh and Cody's, but she couldn't place the deep, booming bass laugh that mixed with theirs.

She bit her tongue. Even upset, she wouldn't light into Charlie when he had company. She even kept that promise for a good thirty seconds—right up to the instant she stepped into the living room and saw Sam Evans sitting on the low-slung plaid couch between her father and her son.

His legs were so long, his knees poked up nearly as far as his nose and he looked slightly ridiculous and out of place sitting there. But the blood rushing to Taylor's face wiped out every bit of humor she might otherwise have found in his appearance.

At least now she knew where he'd disappeared to.

None of them had noticed her yet, but she soon put an end to that. "What are *you* doing here?" she demanded.

Three sets of eyes snapped to her face, but none of them looked even slightly sheepish. Cody's feet were on the couch beneath him, and he bounced up and down like a small child. Charlie waved her into the room as if they'd just been killing time until she got there.

Sam managed to unfold his knees and shoot to his feet as she entered the room. He dipped his head and reached up as if he intended to tip the hat he'd left lying on the coffee table. "Ma'am." He looked to Cody with a scowl. "On your feet, young man. A gentleman always stands when a lady comes into a room."

To Taylor's surprise, Cody scrambled off the couch and stood at strict attention. "Mom." They made quite a pair standing there, Sam in full western regalia, Cody in hip-hop *chic*.

She rounded on Charlie. "What is he doing here?"

"Sam?" Charlie ran a slow hand along his chin. "I invited him."

"I could have guessed that," Taylor snapped. "The question is, why?"

"Because I wanted to. Poor fella was wandering around town with nowhere to go."

"The *poor fella* should have left town like I told him to."

"I don't think I can do that, ma'am. Not until I find out why I was brought here."

"Oh, will you *stop* calling me *ma'am*? It's driving me crazy. I know why you're here as well as you do. This shy cowboy act isn't fooling anyone." Except maybe her dad and her son.

Charlie pushed to his feet and scowled at her. "I'll thank you to remember your manners, young lady. Sam's my guest. There's no call to speak to him that way."

"Do you know who he *is*?" She wagged one finger in Sam's direction as if Charlie needed a reminder. "He's working for Hutton Stone. He's here to make me look stupid before the election."

Charlie shook his head and pushed her hand down to her side. "He told me that's what you and Ruby think, but it isn't true."

"How do you know that?"

"Because he told me."

"And you *believe* him?"

"I don't have any reason not to." Charlie patted his stomach absently, the way he always did when he began to get hungry. "I thought a man was supposed to be innocent until proven guilty. Or have things changed without me knowing?"

Under other circumstances, Taylor would have offered to start supper. But she wasn't about to cook for Sam Evans. Instead, she plowed her fingers through her hair in frustration. "No, things haven't changed. But has he told you where he comes from? Has he *told* you?"

"Oh, Mom, it's so cool." Cody bounced in front of her, his little face alight with more enthusiasm than she'd seen in a long time. "Can you imagine? It's just like Michael J. Fox in that movie, you know?"

"No, Cody, I can't imagine. Traveling through time is impossible. You know that."

"If it were impossible," Sam said, "I wouldn't be here."

Taylor took Cody by the shoulders and pulled his face around to look at her. "Cody, listen to me. He's lying. It's not possible to travel through time. When you see it in the movies or on TV, it's make-believe."

Cody jerked away. "I know that, Mom. Jeez. I'm not stupid."

"Then how can you believe *this*?"

"Because this is different." Cody threw himself back onto the couch and pulled away when she reached for him. "This is *real*."

Instinctively Taylor looked to Charlie for backup, but she should have known better. He shook his head as if she'd brought home a lousy report card. "You might be the sheriff when you're downtown, but you're still my daughter in this house. I won't have you accusing my guests of lying."

"Oh, come on, Pop. You can't expect me to act as if *I* believe this. You're playing right into Hutton Stone's hands."

"Nonsense." Charlie dropped heavily into his chair and fumbled on the end table for one of the cigars he was trying to give up. Scowling at her as if it were her fault he couldn't find one, he waved her toward a chair. "Sit down and quit hovering. Cody's staying for supper. You might as well, too."

"With Mr. Evans? No, thank you." She jerked her thumb toward the door and fixed Cody with her most motherly look. "It's time for you to say good-bye. We'll eat at home."

"I don't wannu."

"I realize that, but I want you to, and the last time I checked, I was still your mother." While Cody got slowly to his feet, she turned the look on Sam. "I don't know how you got to my father, but *I* call the shots where it comes to Cody. I told you once already, and I'm telling you again to stay away from him."

"Aw-w-w, Mom."

She motioned Cody quiet and kept her gaze locked on Sam's disconcerting gray eyes. Not for the world would she let him see that he bothered her in the least—even though his gaze kept dropping to the hem of her cutoffs as if he'd never seen legs before. "Do I make myself clear, Mr. Evans?"

He dipped his head. "Perfectly, ma'am."

"Good." She ushered Cody out the front door and paused before she shut it. "And *stop* calling me, *ma'am*."

Hours later Taylor leaned back in the chair in front of her laptop computer and rubbed her burning eyes. She'd been searching since after dinner, but she couldn't find any information on Sam Evans. At least, no information that helped.

There were about a million Sam Evanses listed on the directories she accessed on the Internet, but narrowing the list down to the one sitting in her father's house was nearly impossible. She *had* found several listings under Evans in the Cortez vicinity, and tomorrow she'd start making phone calls. If Sam was part of that family, she'd know soon.

If not . . .

Well, if not, she could always send his prints off to the FBI lab for identification. For all she knew, his name wasn't Sam Evans at all.

She took a long drink from the Diet Pepsi at her side and stood, stretching her arms high above her head, bending at the waist to work some of the kinks from her back. Pacing to the kitchen window, she pulled back the blind and looked at her father's house across the narrow driveway.

The house was dark. Everything looked peaceful. But how could she go to sleep knowing that Pop was alone with a stranger? A stranger with tall tales and eyes that looked as if they could bore through a person if he turned them on you at just the right angle?

She shivered in spite of the warm night and lowered the blind, wrapping her arms around herself as she walked into the hallway to check on Cody.

He'd finally, reluctantly fallen asleep—but only after pouting at her for hours while he sat in front of the TV. Somehow, taking him away from the excitement had gotten all tangled up in his mind with not having a father. And the blame for both landed squarely on Taylor's shoulders.

Just a few days ago Cody had been the one thing in her life she was absolutely sure of. Now she felt as if she'd lost even that.

After making sure Cody was sleeping soundly, she let herself outside and sat on the back porch where she could keep an eye on Charlie's house. She didn't know what she expected. Maybe nothing.

The warm night breeze wrapped around her shoulders and set the wind chimes Cody had made for her in school in motion. She tilted back her head and listened to the soft sound of the hard-baked clay disks mingled with the strident chirping of crickets. It should have been a soothing sound, but she couldn't shake the nervousness that began deep inside and worked its way in slow coils outward.

Someone drove past with a radio turned up too loud— one of the Beesley boys from down the street she guessed—and the deep, pounding bass sent shock waves through the quiet night. After a few minutes she became aware of another sound. Something she couldn't identify at first, but definitely out of place. A soft scuff of shoe against the ground. A click as a door closed.

She was on her feet as soon as the sounds registered, wishing she'd thought to at least put on shoes. If Sam was

up to something, she'd be hard-pressed to outrun him in
her bare feet. She might have stepped inside and grabbed
a pair of sandals, but the footsteps moved stealthily away
from the house, and she didn't want to take any chances.

It couldn't be Pop. He'd never moved that quietly in his
life. It had to be Sam.

Scarcely daring to breathe, she slipped into the shadows
where he couldn't see her. A second later he stepped into
the moonlight, tall, dark, and ominous-looking.

He lifted his face to the sky and stood there, unmoving.
From where Taylor hid, it looked as if his eyes were closed,
as if he were simply breathing deeply of the clear night air.
If she hadn't known better, she might even think he looked
young and innocent. Almost boyish. As young and guileless
as Cody.

But she *did* know better. He was up to something. She
could feel it in every cell of her body. She held her breath,
waiting for him to make his move.

He let out a sigh so heavy, so wistful, so . . . *heartfelt*,
Taylor almost felt sorry for him. "It's a beautiful night, isn't
it, Sheriff?"

Taylor froze. Blushed from the tips of her toes to the
roots of her hair. She must look ridiculous cowering here
in the shadows of her porch. For a split second she considered pretending she wasn't there, but that would only make
her look more foolish. Besides, what did she care if he
knew she was on guard?

Gathering her dignity, she moved back into the moonlight.
"Yes. Lovely. But that's not why you're out here, is it?"

He turned to look at her, the chiseled line of his jaw
clearly visible in the light, the long, lean line of him sil-
houetted sharply. His shoulders looked about five miles
wide when he stood that way, and she recognized the tone
of muscles that could only come from physical labor, not
a workout at the gym. "What do you think I'm doing?"

It occurred to her for the first time that if he could break
Donald in half without even trying, he could do a sight
worse to her. But she refused to let him think she was
nervous. "I don't know. Maybe meeting Hutton Stone so

you can give him a report. Who knows? Why don't *you* tell *me* what you're doing?"

"Getting some fresh air. Warming up a little. It's too cold in Charlie's house for me. Why in the hell does he have cold air blowing in through the ceiling?"

"Clever try." She moved a little closer so she could keep her voice low. She didn't want to wake Charlie or Cody. "It's a swamp cooler, and you know it. Charlie and Cody might believe your story, but you're going to have to do better than that to convince me."

He moved closer. Too close. His gaze slid to her bare legs, than jerked back up to her eyes. "I'll keep that in mind." That incredible deep bass belonged on the radio or television. It cut through the remaining distance between them and zinged straight through her defenses. "Any suggestions on how I'd win you over?"

"Like I'm stupid enough to tell you."

He shrugged, a lazy lift of both shoulders, and his mustache shifted around a lopsided grin. "Just thought I'd ask. No harm in that, is there?"

Taylor took a deep breath and let it out again slowly. Okay, so he was a good-looking guy. A *great*-looking guy, in fact. A great physical specimen. She could practically hear Hutton Stone plotting. Poor Taylor, all alone, without a man for so long nobody could remember the last time she'd been with somebody. Hutton was probably counting on Sam's looks—his *presence*—to affect her.

Well, it didn't.

"No harm in that," she said airily, and turned back toward the safety of her house. "It'll take more than good looks and cowboy charm to make me weak in the knees."

She slipped inside and closed the door behind her, but not before she heard Sam's soft, deep voice in reply. "Yes, ma'am."

She leaned against the door for a second or two, surprised to find that she needed to catch her breath, irritated by the finger-light shivers that traced up her spine, and annoyed beyond words by the fact that her knees were, in fact, just the tiniest bit wobbly.

Chapter 6

CODY WAS GONE when she woke the next morning, his bed abandoned with the covers dragged onto the floor, his pajamas in a heap by the window. She knew immediately where he'd gone. If not for Sam, she'd have tossed on her robe and run across the lawn to Charlie's. Then again, if it weren't for Sam, Cody wouldn't be gone in the first place.

What *was* it about the guy? she wondered as she tugged on a pair of jeans—long ones this time. Why did Cody find him so fascinating? Why did Pop believe his cockamamy story? Why had she woken several times in the night to find his voice haunting her dreams?

She had half a mind to confront Hutton Stone and demand that he get rid of Sam *now*. The other half warned her that she'd look even more foolish if she did. She had no proof that Hutton was behind this. She couldn't start flinging accusations in public. She'd made a mistake by letting Sam know her suspicions.

From now on, she'd have to keep her wits about her. She wouldn't say another word to Sam about Hutton until she had proof. Cool, calm, and collected—that's how she'd play it.

She found a T-shirt and pulled it on, moistened her fingers under the bathroom faucet and ran them through her hair, and took just a moment to check her reflection—which she'd have done even if Sam weren't there.

At least, that's what she told herself.

Outside, she sprinted across the dew-damp lawn and let herself in through Pop's back door. Cody was there, all right, sitting across the table from Sam, who somehow managed to look incredible with the shadow of a beard darkening his cheeks. One of Charlie's sleeveless white undershirts stretched across his chest and exposed his arms and shoulders.

He stood when she burst through the door, snagged a shirt from the back of a chair, and held it in front of him. Cody's smile evaporated, and Charlie paused in the act of stirring scrambled eggs on the stove to watch her, narrow-eyed, as if he didn't trust her.

Wasn't that rich? He was feeding Sam, giving him clothes and a place to stay. Acting as if *Sam* was family and *she* was the intruder. It almost made her forget her vow to remain calm.

"Well," Charlie said when she closed the door behind her. "Morning, Sweet Pea."

She smiled broadly and crossed the room to kiss him, purposely keeping her step light. "Morning, Pop." She turned to Cody then, still smiling, still acting as if this whole setup was natural. "Morning, kiddo. I figured this is where you were when I found your room empty."

Cody squared his shoulders, flicked a quick glance at Sam for approval, and lifted his chin. "Are you mad?"

"Of course not." She flashed her best smile at Sam, even though her cheeks were starting to ache from the effort, and sat in the empty seat beside Cody. "Are you planning to eat over here, or should I fix something at home?"

"Here." Cody's shoulders lost some of their starch, but his eyes still looked skeptical. "I want to hear Sam's stories."

"Oh?" She could feel an eyebrow arch, and she tried desperately to pull it back into line. "Sam's telling stories?

I'd love to hear a few, myself. Mind if I join you, Pop? Do you have enough?"

"Plenty." Charlie pulled two more eggs from the refrigerator, but he didn't take his eyes off her for more than a second. "You want bacon and sausage, too? Or should I see if I have a can of peaches or something?"

"I'll have whatever you're all having." She rested her chin in her hand and watched Sam try to fit his shoulders and arms into Charlie's shirt. "Did I interrupt a story?"

"Not a story, exactly." Sam gave up on the shirt and glanced around for something else to cover himself with. "I was just telling Charlie and Cody about how we did things on the Cinnabar."

"Really?" Did she sound interested enough? Or did her skepticism come out in her voice? "What kinds of things?"

"Breakfast for one." Unable to find anything, Sam hunched his shoulders and folded himself back into the chair. "We didn't have a fancy cooling machine like that to keep food in," he said with a nod toward the refrigerator. "Cody'd probably be the one to gather eggs before we could cook. And the cows would have to be milked, of course. I'm not used to waking up and having food sitting there waiting to be eaten." He looked her over slowly, his eyes as full of doubt as the other two. "And I can't get over the fancy cookstove. No fire to build? No wood to bring in? It's amazing."

"I'm sure it is." She battled the temptation to bat her eyelashes and pretend utter, feminine fascination. "And who did the cooking on this farm of yours?"

"Ranch. The Cinnabar is a ranch. My brother and I split the duties."

"No maid? No housekeeper? How perfectly dreadful."

Cody shot her a disgusted look that warned her she'd gone too far. Charlie slammed the lid down on the pan. "You're welcome to join us, but not if you're going to behave that way. Nothing's changed since you stomped out of here last night. Sam is still my guest, and I still expect you to behave."

She burned under the reprimand. She hated being treated

like a two-year-old—especially in front of Sam. She had half a mind to storm out again, but that wouldn't get her anywhere. "I apologize," she muttered with a quick look at Sam.

He didn't show any expression at all, just sat there, hard as stone, while his eyes moved across hers. "In all this suspicioning you've been doing," he said after what felt like forever, "has it ever once occurred to you that you might be wrong about me?"

They were all watching her, Charlie and Cody and Sam, waiting. The room fell so silent, she could have been the only one breathing. She could lie and say yes, but she'd spent Cody's entire life drilling the importance of truth into him and to lie now would undo everything she'd taught him. But if she said no, she'd seem hardheaded, stubborn, and unmoveable—not to mention slightly irrational.

"I don't know what to think about you, Mr. Evans," she said at last. "All I do know is that there's nothing in the world more important to me than my family, and if you aren't who you say you are, then I have every right to be concerned and want you gone."

"And what if I *am* who I claim to be?"

"Then I owe you an apology."

He smiled, and the skin around his eyes crinkled, almost as if smiling came naturally to him. "Sounds reasonable. I'll hold you to that."

She tried not to notice the way his eyes softened, the way his face seemed less rigid when he smiled. "And if I can prove you're *not* Sam Evans from eighteen-whatever?"

"If you can prove that, Sheriff, I'll leave. You have my word on it."

Sam watched in fascination as water swirled in the white porcelain bowl and then disappeared. Imagine. It was a helluva lot nicer than using the old outhouse, especially in the middle of the night. He'd flushed a dozen times already, and he probably shouldn't waste Charlie's water this way, but the whole process fascinated him and he hadn't been in the mood to experiment with the toilet in his jail cell.

All he had to do was push that little handle and it started all over again.

And then there was the way water just came out of the faucet whenever he turned the little silver handles. Hot water whenever he wanted it. A whole separate place for taking a bath. Soap that didn't feel as if it was going to burn your skin off. And even—if you could imagine this—a little box where he could stand and let hot water spray over him.

What a world.

He reached for the little handle just once more, but the sound of Taylor's voice in the hall stopped him. "What is he doing in there?"

"Flushing the toilet," Charlie whispered back. "He's fascinated by it."

"By the *toilet*?"

"Well, if you'd never seen one before—"

Sam pulled his hand back and wiped it on his pant leg, as if he could hide the evidence that he'd been about to push the handle again. Taylor's doubts about him hadn't abated one bit over breakfast. Only Charlie's repeated warnings kept her civil. If they'd been alone, she'd probably have him back in jail just for looking at her.

Unfortunately, there was plenty to look at. Her eyes, the shape of her mouth, the curve of her cheek, the tight fit of her shirt, the slim hug of her dungarees. Too bad she was so damned prickly. Sharp as a porcupine.

Oh, sure, he understood—in theory. After all, he really could be up to no good. He'd been a little less than friendly to Kurt when he'd first showed up at Olivia's farm, so he knew all about the doubts running through her mind. But he had to survive, and he wouldn't feel safe until he could convince her that he was on the up-and-up.

He just didn't know how a fella was supposed to prove himself if she wouldn't give him a chance.

The first step, he figured, was to convince her that he wasn't going to hurt the people she loved. Then, maybe, he could show her that he was a friendly sort. And then, if he was lucky, she might even start to believe him. It would just take patience.

With one last glance at the bowl, he let himself out into the hallway. Taylor, Cody, and Charlie were waiting there for him.

Charlie grinned. "Everything okay?"

"Fine. Thanks." He jerked his head back toward the door. "Just getting acquainted with all the new-fangled things you have in there." He ran a hand across the stubble on his chin and grimaced at its roughness. If he was going to win Taylor's confidence, he couldn't run around looking like a bandit. "Any chance you have an extra razor? I haven't shaved in two days."

"Not an extra, but you can use my electric." Charlie motioned him back into the bathroom. To his dismay, Cody and Taylor crowded at the doorway to watch. Charlie pulled a strange-looking metal thing with a long tail from a cupboard. He reached across the sink in front of Sam, stuck one end of the tail into a hole in the wall, and handed the contraption to Sam. "Just push that button to turn it on."

Sam nodded as if the instructions made sense and he could figure out how three small circles could get rid of two days' growth. He'd have preferred to do this without an audience, but it didn't look as if he'd get that chance. Taking a deep breath, he pushed where Charlie'd showed him to.

The damn thing came to life in his hand, buzzing as if a whole hive of bees had been trapped inside, wiggling as if it planned to jump on him while he wasn't looking. Instinctively he jerked backward and the contraption flew out of his hand.

Startled, he backed into the toilet, lost his balance, and crashed to the floor against the wall. The razor bounced off the edge of the counter and landed on the floor beside him, still buzzing and wriggling and writhing.

He scrambled to his feet and backed into the wall. But when he caught a glimpse of Taylor's face, he froze.

It wasn't that she was laughing at him. He might have

expected that. It was what the laughter did to her face that stopped him cold. He'd realized before that she could be pretty beneath that tough front she wore, but with amusement dancing in her eyes and the severeness tempered by laughter, with the morning sunlight bringing her hair to life, she was downright beautiful.

A little *too* beautiful.

Too beautiful to be living just a few feet away. Too beautiful to be watching him shave. Certainly too beautiful to be standing there in trousers and bare feet, as if they'd known each other forever.

He looked away while Charlie roped in the razor. But it was too late. Sam had learned the hard way that once a man realized a woman was beautiful, he couldn't *un*realize it. He couldn't ever look at her the same way again. It had happened just that way with Olivia. Sam had fallen in love with her when she was his best friend's wife, stayed with her after Harvey's death, and even made an offer for her hand. But Olivia never had seen *him* that way, and when all was said and done, she hadn't wanted him.

Sam never wanted to go through that kind of agony again.

Yet here he was, noticing all of Taylor's charms, forgetting that she wore her hair like a boy and dressed in men's clothing. Even glossing right over the fact that she hated him.

She took the razor from Charlie and held it out to Sam. "Very well done. You almost had me believing you."

He took it reluctantly, making sure not to touch her as they made the exchange. Ignoring the jibe, he looked to Charlie. "Don't you have another kind of razor? Something that's not alive?"

"My mom's got the one she uses on her legs," Cody offered.

Oh, no. No. Not if his life depended on it. *No way in hell* would Sam use the razor Taylor used on her . . .

No!

"That wouldn't work," Taylor said quickly. "It's too dull. He'd cut himself."

"You have new blades, don't you, Mom?"

"No. I used the last one." She backed out of the bathroom and glanced up and down the hall as if she couldn't figure out how to get away. "Why don't I just run down to the Stop-N-Shop and get a pack of disposables? I think that would be best." She nodded quickly and forced a smile. "Yes. That's what I'll do."

She disappeared before anybody could respond, but Sam stared after her, stunned.

Well, now, imagine that. Who'd ever have thought that a real live woman lay under all that stone? And who'd have thought that she'd be flustered by the likes of him?

That called for some thinking. Alone. Sam had never done well thinking deep while other people watched. He didn't like having someone wait for his decision, or keeping an eye on his face to see which direction he was leaning, maybe even put in an argument or two to sway him.

The question right now was what to do about Sheriff Taylor O'Brien.

Even if he'd been willing to ponder this around the others, he didn't want Charlie or Cody guessing what was on his mind. *He* wasn't even sure what was on it, and he didn't want anyone else getting ideas.

The door slammed behind Taylor, and Sam worked up his most casual smile. "Guess I've got a few minutes before she comes back."

"A few." Charlie turned back into the hallway. "You want some coffee while you're waiting?"

Sam followed him toward the kitchen. "Actually, I was thinking maybe I'd take a walk and get my bearings. I haven't seen much of the town yet."

"Think you can find your way back?"

Sam chuckled. "I've ridden miles of uncharted land back home and never had a problem. I think I'll be fine in town."

"Maybe I should give you some change for a pay phone and write down my number, just in case." Charlie started scribbling something on a scrap of paper, then stopped himself. "You know how to use a pay phone?"

Sam shook his head. "No, but don't worry about it. I'll be fine."

"I could go with him, Grandpa."

"Well, now, that's a mighty fine idea." Charlie jerked his head toward Cody. "Take the boy with you. He's lived in Heartbreak Hill all his life. He'll get you back safe and sound."

"That's not necessary," Sam said quickly.

Charlie poured a cup of coffee and sipped noisily. "Heartbreak Hill isn't like your big cities, but it's still probably more than you're used to. You're not used to traffic, for one thing."

"I'm sure I—"

Charlie shook his head as if he'd heard the last on the subject. "We don't need you getting hit by a car while you're out walking. One of us'll go with you the first few times you venture out. After you're more acclimated, you can wander about on your own."

"I'm not sure the sheriff will approve."

"You leave Taylor to me," Charlie said around another slurp. "I can handle her."

"Well, then, you're a better man than I am."

Cody bounced up onto his toes, eager to be off. Sam wished he could think of a convincing argument for leaving the boy behind. But until he could get some money in his pocket, he was at Charlie's mercy.

He nodded and motioned the kid toward the door. Maybe it wouldn't be so bad. Nothing said they had to chitchat the whole time. He'd just make it clear that he didn't want a lot of conversation, that's all. Cody would have to be satisfied with that.

He stepped out onto the porch and took a deep breath. In the past three days he'd already spent more time indoors than he usually spent in a month. He glanced up the street, amazed at how many houses folks squeezed into such a little space. Down the street was just as bad. Houses of all kinds, from single-story clapboard houses that would've looked right at home in Cortez, to log cabins, to fancy two- and three-story digs that must have cost a fortune to build.

Every house had a long stretch of lawn in front that made them look cool and inviting, even in the middle of the summer heat.

Cody stood beside him, bouncing onto his toes, falling back onto his heels, tugging at the waistband of his too-big trousers. "Which way do you want to go?"

"Which way is the best?"

Cody pointed up the street. "If we go that way, I can show you my school and my friend Justin Mooney's house." He shifted direction. "If we go *that* way, we'll end up back in town."

"I'm going to have to make myself a living. I can't impose on your grandpa forever. Maybe we should head for town."

"Grandpa doesn't mind. He likes having you around, I can tell. Are you sure you don't want to see my school?"

"I like your grandpa, too, but I'll still feel better when I find work."

"*If* you can find work. Justin's dad says there aren't many jobs around now that summer's over. He lost his job a while ago." Cody stepped off the grass onto the edge of the road.

"I'm sure I can find something." Sam fell into step beside the boy and let his gaze trail across the rooftops toward the mountains. He wondered what Jesse would think if he could see this. Would he count himself lucky to be running the Cinnabar, or would he figure Sam had gotten the best end of the deal?

Cody bounced up onto his toes in front of Sam's face. "So, do you want to see my school? It won't take very long. And see, the thing is, I told Justin about you and he wants to meet you. I kinda promised that I'd introduce you."

Sam felt a pinprick of concern. "Just what did you tell him?"

"Just that you're a friend of Grandpa's and you're really cool."

"That's good. The rest is our secret, okay?"

Cody nodded, but he looked disappointed.

"Maybe you should have asked me before you started making promises."

"I would have. I will next time." Cody shoved a lock of wheat-colored hair out of his eyes and walked backward so he could keep talking. "But the thing is? Justin? Well, he's always kinda rubbing his dad in my face. I mean, he's my friend and everything, but he's always showing off that he's got a dad living with him and I don't."

"That's hardly your fault."

"I know. But Justin sometimes acts like it is. Lots of people act like it is."

Sam slowed his pace. "They act as if it's *your* fault? How could that be?"

"Mom says that he didn't want the responsibility and that's why he left, so it kinda *is* my fault."

Sam stopped walking entirely. "Your mother told you that?" What kind of woman would say something like that to a kid? *Sorry, son, but your father died because he didn't want to take care of you.*

"You must have misunderstood her," Sam said decisively. "Your mother wouldn't have said that."

"How do you know? You don't even know her."

"It's just not the kind of thing a mother would say."

"Why not? It's the truth . . . probably."

"Even if it was, a mother wouldn't say a thing like that to her son." A seed of doubt floated through his mind as he remembered some of the things his own mother had said before she died. But that had been different. Sam had been an adult—or nearly so. Mean as some of her barbs were, they hadn't been completely heartless. Sam's mother had been a miserable woman, mean-spirited and miserly with her affection. Everything he'd seen of Taylor convinced him that she doted on this shaggy-haired son of hers.

"There's no telling why people . . . leave," he said, carefully avoiding any reference to death since Cody apparently didn't like to talk about it. "But I don't think that's why your father moved on."

"You don't?"

"No, I don't. I'm sure he loved you very much."

"You think?"

"I'm sure of it." Even if it wasn't true, what could it hurt to let the boy believe it? The man was gone. The boy needed something to believe in.

Certain that Taylor would be glad he'd cleared up the misunderstanding, he gave his hat brim a twitch and pivoted on the balls of his feet. "Now that I think about it, I'm not sure I feel like heading in to town after all." He scratched his chin and pretended to consider. "Why don't you show me that school of yours? And maybe I can meet your friend—if you think he'll like me. It's my considered opinion that a fella can't have too many friends."

Charlie met Taylor in the driveway when she pulled in more than an hour later. His hair stuck out at all angles, his eyes looked wild. If that wasn't bad enough, he was wringing his hands the way he did whenever something upset him.

"Don't shut off the car!" he shouted. "We have to go find them."

"Find who?" She was already running late for work and she still hadn't had breakfast. This was not a good morning.

"Cody and Sam." Charlie jerked open the passenger's door and slid inside before she could react. "Come on, come on. Put it in reverse and let's go."

"Wait a minute. You let Cody go off somewhere with Sam?"

"A walk. Just for a walk. Holy smokes, I'll bet something's happened to him."

"If something's happened to him," Taylor warned, yanking the gearshift into reverse and pulling out of the driveway to the squeal of tires., "I'll never forgive you."

Charlie tore his gaze away from the road and stared at her. "Sam?"

"Cody".

Charlie pushed at the air between them. "Cody's all right. I'm not worried about him. It's Sam. I shouldn't have let him walk around town on his own. He's not used to modern times. Anything could have happened to him."

Taylor stomped on the brake and squealed to a stop at the corner. "You sent my son off with a complete stranger—who's either working against me or *completely crazy*—and you're worried about *him*?" She was shouting by the time she got to the end of her question, but she couldn't help it. "Are you insane?"

Charlie stuck his nose into the air and looked down its bridge at her. "That's no way to talk to your father, missy. I'll thank you to show a little respect."

"Oh, no, you don't. Don't you dare play the injured party with me. My son is missing. Off in the company of some lunatic, thanks to you." She tried to swallow the huge ball of panic in her throat and got the car rolling again. "What is going on in your head, Pop?"

"What's going on in yours?" Charlie huffed out a breath and turned away. "Sam's a perfectly decent guy, not that I'd expect *you* to realize that."

"Oh? And why not?" She kept her eyes trained on the sidewalk, the trees, the yards they passed, praying for some sign of Cody. When Charlie didn't answer, she looked over at him and caught the smug smile on his face. "I don't believe this. You're bringing Nate Albright up at a time like this?"

"I didn't say a word about Nate Albright."

"No, but you were thinking about him, weren't you?" She slowed and searched the undergrowth as they passed the gully, but all she could see were deep patches of green shadow.

"Well, let's face it," Charlie mumbled, "you haven't been famous for picking out the best guys in the world. First, there was Whoosit, then Tony the Phony—"

"I had two dates with Tony Placencio," she protested. "*Two*. He doesn't even count."

"He was another loser, and you were pretty hot over him for a few weeks." Charlie folded his gnarled hands in his lap and put on an expression so self-righteous she'd have been tempted to slap it off if he wasn't her father.

"I was nineteen," she reminded him stiffly. "That was a long time ago."

"It still proves my point."

She hesitated at the intersection of Motherlode and Timberline, trying to decide which direction to take. "And what point *is* that?"

"The point that Sam's a nice guy who's telling the truth. The point that you give a loser like Nate Albright or Tony Placenta all these chances and you won't even look twice at a man like Sam. It's a sad thing for a father to admit, but you're going to end up an old maid if you're not careful."

Taylor gripped the steering wheel as if it held the last remaining drop of reason in the world. "You're not saying what I *think* you're saying—are you? You couldn't possibly be suggesting that I should date Sam Evans? Because if you are—if you're even *thinking* it—I'm going to start looking for a good psychiatrist."

Charlie sniffed. "I didn't say a word about dating. All I'm saying is that maybe you should get off your high horse and admit that you're not always the best judge of character."

Taylor didn't dignify that with an answer. She finished a sweep of Loden Way and turned onto Paintbrush. Ahead on the sidewalk near the school, she saw a crowd of people. Accelerating slightly, she drew close enough to identify about eight children surrounding one adult, who just happened to be wearing a dirty black hat and old-fashioned duster, whose scowling mouth was hidden beneath the twin swags of a mustache.

Considering how upset she'd been a second ago, the inadvertent smile that tugged at her lips seemed highly inappropriate. But the picture of Sam being followed by Cody and his friends, all with their tiny little-boy chests puffed out, all doing their best to match his cowboy swagger, was just too much.

"You see?" Charlie demanded. "Cody's fine. I told you he would be."

She wiped the smile away and pulled up behind Sam and his gaggle of admirers. "Yes, you did. And you were right, thank God. But, really, Pop—"

"The boy's fine," Charlie said again. "When are you going to admit that your old man just might know a thing or two?" He climbed out, shut the door, and hustled onto the sidewalk to join his new buddy.

Taylor clenched her teeth and followed. He was so convinced that Sam was on the level. Cody clearly adored Sam. Could they possibly be right?

No. Sam was up to something, she just knew it. As soon as she got to the office, she'd put out some feelers on the computer and make a phone call to the Cortez Police Department. If he'd run out on his family, they'd probably have a missing persons report. If not, she'd just broaden her circle and keep checking.

There had to be a record of him somewhere. And Taylor wouldn't give up until she found it.

Chapter 7

TAYLOR CARRIED A bowl of popcorn and two sodas into the living room and situated them on the coffee table in front of Cody. For days one thing or another had prevented her from talking to him about her chat with Mrs. Wilson, but she couldn't put it off any longer. She couldn't close her eyes and pretend that nothing was wrong.

Cody glanced with interest at the treats and scooted over on the couch to make room for her. "Do I have to stay home tonight? Can't I watch movies with Sam and Grandpa?"

"Another time, maybe. I haven't had much time alone with you lately."

"But they're watching old war movies."

"And you want to do that?"

"Sure." Cody scooped up a handful of popcorn and dropped once piece at a time into his mouth. "Grandpa says old movies will help Sam figure out what's happened since he left Colorado."

Taylor made herself comfortable beside her son and tucked her feet beneath her. "How clever of Grandpa." She reached for her can of soda. "But I'd still like you to stay home with me. I want to talk to you about my visit with Mrs. Wilson."

Cody's smile faded and his eyes narrowed. "Yeah?"

"She told me something that concerns me a little."

Cody reached for another handful of popcorn. "What? That I'm a troublemaker?"

"No. Mrs. Wilson likes you very much. She had nothing bad to say."

Cody slid to the floor to be closer to the bowl. "Then why are you upset?"

"Not upset. Concerned. She says that you're making up stories about your dad. Is that true?"

"I guess."

"Do you want to tell me why?"

Cody's hair fell into his eyes. He made no effort to move it out of the way. "I don't know why. I just do."

He looked so small in his oversized shorts and T-shirt, so young and defenseless and sweet. Taylor wanted to pull him into her arms and hug him the way she had when he was younger. She wanted him to climb on her lap and wind his fingers through her hair. But those days were gone.

"Are you trying to fit in? Trying to impress your friends?"

His face twisted, a mixture of embarrassment and irritation. "I don't know. Can't I make up stories?"

"Of course you can—if that's all they are and if you tell people they're stories. It's not okay to lie about who your dad is to deceive your friends."

"I don't tell stories to my friends."

"It's not okay to lie to anyone else, either."

Cody slid to the corner of the coffee table, apparently anxious to put some space between them. "I'm not a liar, Mom. I just make stuff up, that's all."

Taylor forced herself to stay in the same casual position so Cody wouldn't think she was getting angry. "I'm all for imagination," she said with a smile. "As long as it's used constructively. But honestly, Cody. Did you really tell people that your dad is Brad Pitt?"

His gaze dropped to the floor. "Once. A long time ago."

"Why?"

"Because Shelby Miner was bragging about how her dad

was doing some stupid commercial for a car place in Billings, and she was acting like everybody should kiss her feet or something." Cody shoved the lock of hair out of his eyes. "It was just a joke. Everybody knew it but her."

"Was the government spy a joke, too?"

"I guess so."

"And the undercover cop?"

"I don't know." Cody shifted onto one side and looked at his fingertips. "I didn't lie, Mom. It *can't* be a lie if you don't know the truth. When I told those stories, I didn't even know my dad's name."

Taylor straightened her legs and tried to keep her face neutral. "I'm not angry, Cody. I'm just concerned. I had no idea you'd been feeling bad about not knowing who your dad is." She moved closer and touched his shoulder. "I wish you'd told me before now."

"Why?"

"Because." Taylor stopped herself and thought carefully before she responded. "Because I'm your mom and I love you. If you're upset about something—about *anything*—I want to know about it."

"You wouldn't have told me."

"Why do you think that? You asked me your dad's name the other day, and I told you—didn't I?"

He nodded slowly. "Yeah. I guess."

Taylor smoothed her hand across his hair. "Is there anything else you want to know?"

"Where is he?"

"I don't know."

"Why doesn't he ever come to see me?"

"When I knew him, he wasn't interested in having a family. Maybe he still feels the same way. But it's his loss. He doesn't get to know what a great kid you are."

Cody kicked his legs out in front of him and thought about that for a few seconds. "Do you know where he works?"

"No, honey. We were kids. I wasn't even out of high school yet. I don't know what he did after he left here."

"Did you tell him when I was born?"

Taylor shook her head. "No. I was still hurt and angry, and I didn't think he deserved to know." She patted the cushion beside her and put her arm around Cody when he reluctantly joined her. "Maybe I didn't make the best choices at the time, but I can't change that now. I know you'd like to know your dad. I used to fantasize about knowing my mother after she died. But we can't make life be something it's not. We can only make the best of things the way they are."

Cody leaned against her shoulder, and for that moment he was the little boy who'd liked to snuggle with her when he was young. "But this is different," he said after a while. "Grandma was dead. You couldn't know her. My dad's still around."

Taylor tilted his chin so she could look into his eyes. "But he's made his choice, Cody. He doesn't want to be part of our family. Can you understand that?"

"I guess."

"And do you understand why it's not a good thing to make up stories about who he is?"

"I guess."

Taylor wasn't sure she'd gotten through to him yet, but she could tell from the look in his eyes that she'd reached the point of no return. He was shutting down, ready to stop listening. This wasn't going to be an easy issue to deal with. She'd have to take it one piece at a time and choose her moments wisely.

Standing under the hot sun, Taylor wrote a parking ticket, climbed onto the bumper of an RV that had been left poking out into the street, and wedged the ticket beneath the windshield wiper. Tourists swarmed in and out of the T-shirt and gift shops on Motherlode, stood in line for tables at Heartbreak Hill's four restaurants, and parked in places no one in their right mind would try to park.

Good for the economy. Not so good for her peace of mind. She hadn't had a quiet moment for days, or much chance to find out the truth about Sam.

Every evening she bit her tongue while Cody and Charlie

listened to every word that came out of his mouth as if he could predict the future. She had to sit across from him at meals because she couldn't pry Cody away, listen to his ridiculous stories because Charlie practically took her head off if she showed even the slightest disbelief.

She'd tried to make Cody understand why he needed to be careful, but Cody was as besotted as Charlie. He wouldn't listen to anything negative about Sam. After just four days Sam had zipped straight past stranger and become a close family friend in Charlie's and Cody's minds.

Jumping down from the RV's bumper, she scanned Motherlode to make sure everything else looked peaceful. As she started up the street, she saw the furtive figure of a woman slip out the back door of Hutton Stone's office. The woman wore a scarf over her head and kept her shoulders hunched, as if she didn't want to be seen.

Strange. Maybe someone working on Hutton's campaign. But in that case, why sneak out the back way? Ah, well, unless a crime was involved, it wasn't any of her business, and she didn't have time to waste speculating. She had a rare break in the action, and she knew just what to do with it.

Lowering her gaze to avoid being stopped, she hurried to her office. Once there, she found the number for the Cortez Police Department and dialed. Within minutes she'd been transferred to a man who announced himself as Detective Sweeney and sounded perturbed by the interruption. Her introduction brought no more than a mumbled, "Right. Okay. Whad'ya want?"

"I'd like to ask you a few questions about someone who claims he recently came from the Cortez area."

"He got a record?"

"I don't know. I'm not even sure I have his real name. I'm wondering whether you have any missing persons reports that might match his description."

"Okay. Let's start with the basics." The telephone amplified the smacking of lips, which made her wonder if she'd caught him having lunch. "What name did he give you?"

"Samuel J. Evans. Does that ring any bells?"

"Around here?" He smacked loudly and shuffled papers close to the telephone. "Are you kidding? We got about a billion Evanses."

"This one claims he lives on a ranch outside of town. The Cinnabar."

"The Cinnabar?" The detective snorted a laugh. "You *are* joking, right?"

"Not at all. That's what he told me when he showed up here four days ago."

"Uh-huh." He slurped a drink in her ear. "Funny fella, is he? Big joker?"

"Not especially. Why do you ask that?"

"Because, Sheriff, the Cinnabar Ranch is well-known in these parts. The Evans family owns it, but I can tell you right off, there aren't any Sam Evanses there. That's for damn sure."

"How do you know?"

"Because the name's been retired, so to speak. You know, like they do with athlete's jerseys? The one and only Samuel J. Evans disappeared from Black Mesa over a hundred years ago."

Taylor's throat dried and she had trouble swallowing. "What do you mean, disappeared?"

"Disappeared. Vanished. Some said he was killed in the famous ambush up there, but they never did find his body."

Taylor's stomach knotted and her shoulders tensed. She told herself the coincidence meant nothing. This Sam could easily have heard the legend of the real Sam Evans and incorporated it into his story.

"Hey," Detective Sweeney said suddenly, "you know what's funny? That ambush happened this month. Four days ago. Same time this guy showed up in your town. That's kind of odd, dontcha think?"

Taylor's arms began to tingle and she couldn't feel her legs. A sense of the surreal surrounded her. Her desk seemed far away, as if someone had put a fun-house mirror in front of it. The detective's voice suddenly sounded distorted and muffled.

She shook her head and tried to pull herself together. "You don't happen to have a picture of the missing Sam Evans, do you? Something from your local history books?"

"Well, now, I'm not sure. I could check with the Heritage Center if it's important. They'd be most likely to have something like that."

"Please do. It's terribly important."

"Mind me asking why you want *his* photograph? You aren't thinking you have him up there, are you?" He snorted laughter and hummed a few bars of *Twilight Zone* music.

Taylor tried to laugh with him, but it sounded more like she'd choked on something. "Of course not. I'm just curious to know why this guy would take the name of someone who's been dead for over a century."

"Mmmm. Okay, well, sure. I'll see if I can track down a photograph. If I can, you want me to fax it or mail it?"

"How about both? Fax first and follow up with a copy in the mail."

"Sure thing. And if you find out that it has anything to do with our Sam Evans, let me know, wouldja? Things've been a little dull around here lately."

She promised, of course, though she had a rough time getting the words out. It wasn't possible for their Sam to be from Cortez unless . . .

Unless his story was true.

Sam decided to watch his step around Taylor that evening. She was leaning against the far end of the table on the patio, her face set and drawn, her eyes narrowed as if she was just waiting for him to do something she could find fault with. In the late-afternoon shadows her hair had turned a deep mahogany and her eyes nutmeg brown.

Sam wished he knew how to defuse her anger and suspicion. He didn't expect them to become friends, but it would be nice if she'd stop hating him. At least she'd had the decency to wear long trousers again this evening. Sam considered himself a decent guy, but he wasn't made of stone. Even a saint would have a hard time not looking at a set of legs that shapely.

He pulled his gaze away and tried to stop remembering how she'd looked in those short pants just as Charlie slid a platter onto the table.

"Steaks all around. Hope you like yours cooked."

From across the lawn Cody let out a whoop and tossed his ball to the edge of the lawn.

Sam took a deep, mouth-watering sniff. "I prefer it that way. We never went much for raw meat back on the Cinnabar."

Charlie roared with laughter.

Taylor curled her lip in a semblance of a smile. "He means 'well done.' Pop doesn't consider anything cooked unless it's been turned to shoe leather. If you like yours rare or medium, you're out of luck."

Charlie crossed to his little barbecue pit and slid his hand into a mitten to pull four ears of corn wrapped in silver paper from the heat. "I don't like meat to talk to me when I cut into it, if that's what you mean."

"I don't think there's much danger of that," Sam mused. "I'll wager there's not much life left after you freeze it the way you did."

That half-smile tweaked Taylor's lips again. "Pop still won't take chances."

"Well, anything's fine with me," Sam told her. "I don't complain when folks offer me their hospitality."

She worked a spoon into a large bowl of raw vegetables. "I'm impressed. I wouldn't have expected a cowboy from the Wild West to have such excellent manners."

Charlie shot her a look. Cody froze halfway into his seat. They seemed as nervous about her mood as Sam was.

He smiled as if she didn't have an ax to grind—and wasn't grinding it on him. "My mother would be heartened by your compliment, Sheriff. She was determined that her sons wouldn't grow up coarse and unrefined."

Taylor slid onto the wooden bench across from him, linked her hands together, and rested her chin on the bridge they made. "Tell me about this brother of yours."

"Jesse?" Sam pulled back slightly. Not because he didn't want to talk about Jesse, but because just saying his name aloud made him nostalgic. "He's just a kid, really—at least that's how I always thought of him until just a month or so ago. He's getting married in a few months—or he would be if I were still back home. I guess he and Elizabeth married, had their family, and passed on by now."

His voice grew thick and his throat swelled. He cleared it roughly. No sense getting all teary-eyed. He wouldn't see Jesse again, and that was that. There was nothing he could do about it. "He's smart as a whip," he said when the lump wouldn't shrink. "And better suited to working with ledgers and such than I ever was. Sitting in one place too long always makes my legs twitch."

Cody reached across the table for the steaks. "Do you miss him?"

"Sure I do." Sam cleared his throat again. Took a hidden swipe at his eyes with his shirtsleeve. Caught Taylor watching him with an odd expression and tried to pull himself together. "Jesse's a great kid."

"Wouldn't you like to know what really happened to him?"

"Well, now, that'd be nice." Sam wiped his eyes once more and tried to smile. "But I don't suppose that'd be possible."

"It might be. I mean, maybe you could find out something on the Internet or something. You can find almost *anything* on the Internet. We can hook up with my mom's computer if she'll let us."

Not much chance of that happening, but Sam didn't want to add fuel to her fire. "Well, then, one of these days you can show me where this inter-net is and I'll see what I can find."

"Can we, Mom? Can we get on the computer after dinner?"

"I don't know, Cody. I'm supposed to meet Ruby after dinner so we can fold mailers."

"You can go. I know how to use the computer by myself, you know."

Taylor tilted her head and hesitation clouded her eyes. "Let me think about it, okay?"

Sam cut a bite from his steak and cleared the lump from his throat. "Wait a minute, son. I don't know anything about computers or inter-nets. I'm not sure I want to get on one until I'm sure it's not going to throw me."

Taylor's gaze slid to his, and for a split second she looked at him as if he were human. "It won't throw you."

"Still—"

"It's perfectly safe. If you'd like to look for information about your family, Cody can show you how."

Her eyes softened almost imperceptibly—just enough to make it tough for Sam to look away. Everyone and everything else faded into the background, and all he could see was her eyes, her hair, her lips. Time seemed to stand still as he watched the subtle rise and fall of her breasts.

She didn't seem any more able to look away then he could. Her breath came faster and her tongue darted nervously across her lips. The neck of Sam's shirt suddenly felt too tight, the sun too hot on his shoulders. He had the strangest urge to kiss her, to just pull her into his arms and cover her mouth with his. Simple. Just like that. No excuses, no explanations, no apologies. And he might have if Cody hadn't nudged his arm and reminded him that they weren't alone.

Sam had never believed in witches, but as he blinked out of the trance, he'd have sworn Taylor had put him under a spell.

"Okay, Sam? You wanna get on the computer after dinner?"

Sam wiped his suddenly damp hands on his pant legs. "You show me where this computer is and how to get on it. I'll do my best to stay on."

Taylor turned away, but not before Sam saw her actually *smile*. He had no idea what he'd said to bring it on, but he was almost sure he was responsible. He felt his own lips twitch in response, then caught Charlie looking at him and caught a whiff of trouble brewing.

Sam pushed to his feet and put some distance between himself and the table—himself and Taylor, anyway. He couldn't deny that he was attracted to her. What man

wouldn't be? He couldn't deny that inexplicable urge he'd
had to kiss her. But, then, any man with blood in his veins
would want that. Just *look* at her.

But no matter *how* Sam felt, he wasn't about to get
caught in another situation where he did all the feeling.
He'd lived through that once, with Olivia, and he'd lost in
the end.

He wasn't in the mood to lose again.

"You should have seen him," Taylor whispered into the
phone a few hours later. She paced the floor of her bedroom, far too aware of Sam hunched over the computer
with Cody across the hall. "They were genuine tears, Ruby.
You can't fake emotion like that."

"Nonsense. Actors do it all the time."

"But that's the point. I don't think Sam's acting." She
inched open her bedroom door and looked at Sam and Cody
in front of the computer on Cody's desk. Cody pointed and
clicked; Sam jerked backward, laughed at himself, and
inched forward to watch the images loading.

"You should see the way he acts with the computer," she
said when she'd closed the door again. "With the electric
razor, the radio, the microwave—with *everything*. Even the
best actor in the world would eventually let his guard down.
Sam never does. He's always in character, and I'm beginning to believe the character is genuine."

Ruby laughed harshly. "You *believe* that he's from the
nineteenth century?"

Taylor stopped pacing and dropped onto the foot of her
bed. How *could* she believe that? "I'm starting to believe
that he really doesn't know who Hutton Stone is. And if
he's *not* from the nineteenth century, at least he *thinks* he
is."

"So, he's crazy."

"I don't think so."

"Okay, then. Fine. We trust him, right? Is that what you
want me to say? My hell, Taylor. You've already canceled
our plans for tonight so he can play with your computer.
What's next?"

Taylor tugged her fingers through her hair. "I don't know. Maybe it would help if you spent some time around him. You could get a feel for what he's like and then tell me what you think."

"I can already tell you what I think," Ruby said archly. "I don't need to spend time around him. Why is this suddenly so important to you?"

Taylor closed her eyes and tried not to think about that moment before dinner when his eyes had touched a match to the kindling that lay inside her. She blamed Charlie for that. He's the one who'd put ideas in her head.

"Because of Cody," she said. "And because of Charlie. They're just so head over heels about him—"

"And that's the only reason?"

"Of course it is."

"You're sure this isn't about *you*?"

"Absolutely not."

"You don't have even *one* heel over your head?"

Taylor stood again and paced briskly across the room. She glanced out the window at the moonlight streaking across the driveway and tried to make sense of her emotions.

"Answer me, Taylor. What do you feel about this guy? If you're starting to care about him, I think you should tell me. Don't get me wrong. I've always thought you should have someone in your life, but not *this* guy. He's wacko."

"I don't know," Taylor hedged. "I'm starting to wonder if Cody and Charlie are completely off-base. I don't want to like Sam, but there's something about him that makes it hard not to. When he was talking about his brother, I cared that he was upset, but I *don't* care about him in the way you mean."

Ruby remained silent for several long seconds. Long, slow, agonizing seconds while she waited for Taylor to say something more. "I'd never bring this up under other circumstances. But in light of the talk Hutton's been stirring, people might be a little . . . judgmental about you getting involved with someone who's at all questionable."

"I'm not involved."

"He's living with your father, Taylor. Like it or not, you *are* involved. You know how politics are. People in public office have to be beyond reproach. The fact that he's living with Charlie and you're right next door could stir up a lot of gossip. It would also help if he wasn't crazy."

"What if he's not crazy? What if he's telling the truth?"

"Are *you* crazy?" Ruby took a deep breath for control. "You have to get rid of him before he becomes an issue. You don't have the luxury of waiting."

Taylor sank back onto her bed. "I know. But it's not as easy as it sounds. I can't force Pop to kick Sam out, and the more I fight, the more protective Pop and Cody become."

"Then don't fight him. Keep pretending to believe him. He'll eventually drop his guard."

"But that's so deceptive. I hate it."

"And claiming to be here from eighteen-whatever isn't deceptive?"

Taylor flopped backward and stared at her ceiling. She could always count on Ruby to inject a note of reason into any situation. "Okay. I'll see what I can do."

"Good. You had me worried."

"Don't be," Taylor said with more conviction than she felt. "He'll be out of our lives soon. I'll make sure of it."

But as she replaced the receiver, Cody's laugh twined with Sam's floated in from the next room. For the briefest of moments a coziness thick as warm honey floated through her, and she had the strangest feeling that she was experiencing a moment from her own future. A future in which Sam figured prominently and Cody forgot Nate Albright even existed.

She plugged her ears to block the sound. When that didn't work, she covered her head with a pillow. But she had a strong feeling that keeping her promise to Ruby wouldn't be easy.

Chapter 8

"YOU KNOW WHAT I've been thinking?" Charlie said as soon as she set foot in his kitchen the next morning. Cody had come in a few seconds before her, and had already headed off to look for Sam. "I've been thinking that maybe we ought to take Sam out to see something of the town tonight. *All* of us. The whole family."

Taylor reached for the coffeepot and poured a cup. "I'm not sure that's such a good idea, Pop. I don't want to give people the wrong impression."

Charlie scowled so hard, his forehead folded into accordion pleats. "*What* wrong impression? What are you talking about?"

Taylor carried her cup to the table and shoved the morning paper aside to make a place for it. "Ruby's worried that people will think Sam and I are involved. That could wreak havoc on the campaign."

"Ruby worries too much."

"Maybe. And maybe you don't worry enough." Taylor sipped and set her cup aside. "It's not that I don't like Sam, but I don't want people thinking that he's something he's not."

"Who's going to think a thing like that? He's staying in my house, not yours."

"Lots of people," Taylor said, growing impatient with his naivete. "Anyone who remembers that I wasn't married to Cody's father will speculate. Anyone who listens to Hutton Stone. Anyone who doesn't like me for some other reason."

Charlie cracked an egg into the frying pan. "Who cares about them?"

"I should if I want to win this election."

"So, you're going to let people dictate to you? You're going to let them tell you who your friends should be? You're going to let *Hutton Stone* tell you how to act and what to do?"

"No. Of course not." The very idea was ridiculous—if disconcertingly true. "It's just that—"

"It's just that you're not brave enough to be your own self?"

"No!" She hated that he could make her doubt herself, when just minutes earlier she'd been so convinced she knew what to do. "It's just that people expect public officials to be completely above reproach."

"You are."

"Yes, but they don't *know* that, do they?"

"If they doubt you, they need to clean their minds up. That's what I say."

"It would be a lovely world if the truth was enough, but it's not that way. These days people automatically assume the worst, and you have to prove yourself innocent."

"Well, that's just wrong."

"Yes, I know." She strode to the window and looked outside. "I know it's wrong, but that's how things work, like it or not."

She could see Charlie's reflection in the window. It lifted one shoulder and cracked another egg. "Well, sure, it'll work that way as long as you let it. Seems to me maybe you'd want to teach Cody something about standing up to the truth rather than folding to peer pressure. But maybe that's not what you have in mind for him."

She whipped around to glare at him face-to-face. "That's not fair, and you know it."

"And I always thought you wanted Cody to know you were proud of him, no matter what. But if you're going to act like you're ashamed of him—" He broke off and let another shrug and another pointed crack of an egg finish the thought for him.

"I'm *not* ashamed of him." Taylor forced her voice lower. "But even you have to admit that there are more desirable ways to bring a child into the world than the way I did it."

"I guess some folks would see it that way. Me, I figure the good Lord's got reasons for the way he lets things happen. I don't figure it's my job to second-guess him." He worked the salt shaker and pepper mill over the eggs. "That's kind of how I look at Sam being here, too. There's a reason for it, you can bet that. I don't believe in coincidences."

"Don't try to manipulate me with religion," Taylor snapped. "You haven't been to church in years."

"Neither have you."

"No, but I'm not the one who brought it up, am I?" She dragged her fingers through her hair, completely undoing all her hard work in front of the mirror that morning. She hated losing her temper, especially with Charlie—though he could be so exasperating it was hard not to get irritated. She leaned against the counter and took several calming breaths. "What am I supposed to do, Pop? I'm trying to get elected. Hutton Stone is going to do everything he can to make people question me, my beliefs, my ethics. This situation with Sam doesn't make things any better."

Charlie looked up from the stove. "Well, Sweet Pea, I guess that's up to you. You can bow down to other folks' opinions and live your life that way, or you can stand up for yourself and what you believe. I can't tell you which one to choose."

"You make it sound so simple. It's not."

Charlie smiled and flipped an egg. "The choice *is* simple. It's just the carry-through that's tough."

Taylor reached for the loaf of bread he'd left sitting on

the counter and popped four pieces into the toaster. "I hate when you do this to me, you know."

"Do what?"

"Tell me the truth when it's not what I want to hear." She sent him a weak smile. "I hate it when you make me see where I'm wrong."

"So, does that mean we're taking Sam out and about tonight?"

"You know that's what it means."

"Well, now, I think that's a fine decision. Just fine." He turned another egg and gave her a quick once-over. "Don't suppose you'd be willing to have that makeover before we go?"

Taylor laughed harshly. "Oh, so I'm supposed to ignore what people think on one hand, but when it comes to how I look, I'm supposed to care?"

"It's not for folks," Charlie said rigidly. "It's for yourself. You'd feel better about yourself if you accentuated your eyes and such."

"I feel just fine about myself."

"Well, it's up to you." Charlie's gaze drifted toward the top of her head. "But your hair looks real pretty this morning—at least, it did when you first came in. You've done something different *there*."

She slipped back into the chair she'd vacated a few minutes earlier and sipped her rapidly cooling coffee. "Hair's different."

"Well, of course it is."

"It's not because of Sam."

Charlie slanted a glance over his shoulder. "Well, now, I never said it was, did I? I don't believe I even mentioned Sam when I was talking about the makeover."

"No, but I know what you were thinking."

"Was I?" Charlie shook his head in wonder. "Well, imagine that."

"Look, Pop, I'm willing to be friendly to Sam, but that's as far as it's going."

"I never suggested anything else, did I?"

Not in so many words, but that sweetly innocent look on

Charlie's face made her worry. She just wondered if Sam had any idea what her father had up his sleeve.

Sam took in the town hungrily as he followed Charlie and Taylor along the boardwalk. The last time he was in town, he'd been not quite himself—locked up in the backseat of Deputy Donald's patrol car and still in pain. Now he wanted to see everything.

The weathered boards used along the main street made the buildings appear old at first glance. A hitching post ran the length of two full blocks, but Sam hadn't seen a single horse, so he figured they were just for show.

Folks also used perfectly good equipment as decoration— a harness here, an oil lamp there, horseshoes and whips and saddles and blankets. But inside, the stores were completely modern, filled with garish electric light and music and the incessant beeping Sam now associated with computers.

While Sam was lost in thought, Charlie stopped walking and Sam almost plowed into his back. Charlie pointed to a window full of images of people. "This is the photo shop. You take film in here to be developed. Have you ever seen a camera?"

"A couple of times." Sam took a closer look. "I had a picture made with my brother once when a fella with the equipment traveled through Cortez."

That got Taylor's attention. "Who has the picture now?"

"Now?" Sam hooked his thumbs in his pockets. "I wouldn't know. It was in the top drawer of my desk when I left the Cinnabar."

"When was the picture taken?"

"Not many years before I left. Maybe eighteen eighty-six or so. Why do you ask?"

"Just curious." She lifted her shoulders and the material of her blouse stretched tight across her breasts.

Sam tried not to look—at least he tried not to get *caught* looking. He'd seen more bare skin tonight among the folks in town than he'd seen in his entire life. But all the bare-legged and scantily clothed women couldn't hold a candle to Taylor.

There was something about the way she moved that intrigued him—something smooth and graceful but barely contained. It gave a man the impression that there was far more to her than she let on, and made a fella think that it might be worthwhile to find out what she had hidden beneath that veneer of control.

"Curious," he said, considering the possibilities. "You want to see what I looked like back then?"

She turned sharply to face him. "No. I want to see if you really existed back then."

"And a picture would prove it to you?"

"It might help." She averted her gaze quickly, and Sam had the distinct impression there was something she wasn't telling him.

He pushed his hat back on his forehead and studied the window once more. "Well, then, I wish I could produce it for you. It'd be nice to have you stop looking at me as if you think I'm going to murder you all in your sleep."

Her eyes darted to his again. "I don't think that. If I did, you wouldn't be staying with Charlie, no matter what he said. And you wouldn't spend one minute around Cody."

"Then, what *do* you think?"

"The jury's still out on that question." She started walking again, heading toward the center of town by Sam's calculations.

He fell into step beside her. "I don't suppose you'd give me a hint about what I could do to convince you I'm just a normal fella?"

Her lips curved slightly. She glanced behind her to check on Cody and paused at the corner to let a line of cars whiz past. "You could admit that you didn't come here from the past. That might make you seem a little more normal."

"You'd like me to start lying?"

"No. I'd like you to start telling me the truth."

"I've done that. You just want me to say what you want to hear."

Her cheeks flushed and she stepped off the boardwalk a little too soon. One of those cars came barreling along the road toward her. Without thinking, Sam grabbed her around the waist and lifted her out of the way.

She arched against him, twisting to get away. "What are you *doing*?"

"You were about to get yourself killed." He started to lower her to the ground as she twisted in his arms, and they were face-to-face, nose-to-nose, her mouth right there in front of his, inches away. If he'd leaned forward even slightly, he could have kissed her. Her breasts smashed against his chest, soft, full, and inviting. His reaction was immediate and would have been obvious to everyone around if he'd put her down, so he tightened his grip and held on. "You were about to get yourself killed," he said again. "Didn't you see that thing coming toward you?"

Her breath came faster than normal, her cheeks glowed, and her eyes seemed like pools of liquid amber. "It wasn't coming toward me. I was perfectly safe. And if you don't put me down this instant, you'll get a repeat of what my deputy did to you the day he arrested you."

That promise had just the effect Sam needed. He didn't even count to three before he put her down without giving away the overpowering reaction he'd had to her. "No offense intended, Sheriff." He gave his hat a twitch, lowered it over his eyes so she couldn't see them quite so easily, and hooked his thumbs in his pockets so he could give the impression that he held women that way every day of his life and it had meant nothing to him. "Just trying to do a good deed. Guess you'd prefer it if the next time you're about to get killed, I just let it happen."

"No. That's not what I'd prefer." She brushed something from the front of her blouse and tugged at the hem of it. "I don't mean to seem ungrateful, Sam. It's just that—well, it's just that you can't go around manhandling women without their permission."

Behind them, Charlie chuckled softly. Sam could almost feel Cody watching every move they made with those little eagle eyes of his. He had the feeling neither of them would've objected one bit if he'd kissed Taylor full on the lips while he held her there. But Taylor would've hated it, and Sam didn't make a practice of kissing women who didn't want to be kissed—no matter how tempting it might be.

He dipped his head in agreement. "I'll keep that in mind. For the next time."

She stepped off the boardwalk again, and Sam followed her this time. "I don't want to seem ungrateful," she said again when they reached the other side of the street. "If you really thought I was about to be hit—"

"I wouldn't have done it otherwise."

"Well, then . . ." She moistened her lips slowly, but she kept her gaze straight ahead. "Well, then, thank you."

A thank-you? Sam felt so damn triumphant, he had to fight to keep from grinning. "No problem at all." He glanced back to see if Charlie and Cody had heard that—kind of wanting to share the moment with someone who'd appreciate the progress he'd made—and found them lagging far behind. They had identical looks on their faces, secretive, pleased with themselves, and obviously delighted with the goings-on ahead of them.

Charlie leaned down to say something to Cody. Cody nodded, looked at Taylor, and grinned. Before Sam knew what was happening, Charlie lurched to one side of the boardwalk and gripped one of the posts to steady himself. "Blast! Blast it all! This damn knee again."

Taylor wheeled around to see what was wrong. Cody busied himself fussing around Charlie. Sam could only stand there and watch.

Taylor hurried back toward her father, her face tight with concern. "Pop? What's wrong? What happened?"

"Twisted this damn knee," Charlie growled. "I must have stepped on a rock or something." He nudged Cody. "You see any little rocks around, boy? Anything I might've stepped on?"

Cody glanced around quickly and lunged toward a pebble a few feet away. "This one, Grandpa. This is probably it."

"I suspect you're right, son." Charlie gave the stone a look and made a face. "Damn sharp little thing." He grimaced as if his leg was about to fall off. "I think maybe I ought to stay here and rest for a few minutes, Sweet Pea. Cody can stay with me. If I feel up to it, we'll meet you down at the square. If not, the boy'll help me get home—won't you, son?"

Cody nodded solemnly.

"If it's hurt that badly," Taylor argued, "I don't want you walking on it at all. I'll run home and get the car."

Charlie's pained expression slipped for half a second. "I don't want you and Sam to miss out on all the fun just because of me. It's not *that* bad. I'm sure I'll be able to get myself home. I just don't think I should stand on it for a long time. Besides, don't you need to be at the square—Minding the tourists?"

"I'll call Donald and ask him to cover for me."

Sam could imagine what a mess Donald would make of things on his own, but he didn't think Taylor would welcome his opinion.

Charlie scowled at her. "Nonsense. I wouldn't want you to get a reputation for shirking responsibility. You can't take time off just because your old man is careless enough to wrench his knee."

"Grandpa can lean on me to get home," Cody said. "And if his leg gets really bad, we'll just sit down and wait until you get back."

Charlie nodded up at her, and Cody did a remarkable job of looking utterly serious. Taylor shifted her gaze to Sam.

He did his best not to give the two conspirators away. "I don't suppose it'll hurt Charlie to sit here and wait. I'll be glad to walk on with you, Sheriff."

A quick smile of pleasure almost wiped out the calculated agony on Charlie's face. "I do think that would be best, Sweet Pea. The two of you go on, now. We'll catch up if we can."

Taylor nodded reluctantly, kissed Cody's cheek soundly, and brushed a quick peck to Charlie's weathered cheek before turning back to Sam. "You don't have to come with me if you don't want to."

Sam didn't want to look too eager, so he merely

shrugged and set off beside her. "I might as well. I don't have anything better to do."

To his surprise, she let out a short laugh. "You're quite the sweet-talker, aren't you?"

"Never saw much call for sweet talk," he said. "I always thought women could see through it too easily."

She pulled back slightly, as if he'd surprised her. "Well, of course we can. But we don't like being told that we're nothing more than relief from boredom, either."

It would have been so easy to point out that men didn't like to be accused of all manner of nefarious plotting, but he didn't. Better to keep things light. "Oh, you're much more than that, Sheriff. You're one of the most intriguing women I've ever met. It keeps me on my toes just trying to figure out how not to set you off."

She laughed again. "Have I really been so horrible?"

"I don't know if *horrible* is the right word. *Challenging* might fit better."

"You have to admit that your story isn't exactly easy to believe."

Sam stuffed his hands into his pockets and kept his elbows flat against his sides so he wouldn't accidentally brush against her and set off the reaction he'd worked to hide earlier. He slowed to study a poster urging folks to vote for Taylor's opponent. Didn't care much for the weasly looks of the guy. "Who is this Hutton Stone, anyway?"

"He sells real estate in town and wants desperately to put me out of office. He's old-fashioned and convinced that a woman can't be sheriff. He's been pretty vocal about it."

"I'll admit that I've never heard of a lady sheriff before," Sam said, "but I know a few who'd probably do a fine job. And I'm sure not going to tell you that you can't do the job. My mother didn't raise a stupid son."

Taylor laughed again and the look in her eyes was the closest thing to friendly Sam had seen since he'd first set eyes on her. He had the urge to gather her close again and take that kiss he'd been wanting, but he shoved that idea right out of his mind.

He liked this new side to Taylor, and he wanted to enjoy it for a little while longer. So he kept his gaze straight ahead on the plump backside and hairy back of a man wearing nothing but short pants, black socks, and dirty white shoes.

If that didn't keep Sam's thoughts in line, nothing would.

They walked in silence for a few minutes while the crowd thickened around them. Sunset was just around the corner, and the black-green shade on the mountains made Sam long to be in the thick of them. Elongated shadows from people, trees, and buildings stretched well into the street, and everything seemed to slow down, as if reaching a certain time of day set people moving at a different speed.

Even Taylor slowed down, strolling now instead of plowing along, nodding and smiling to people as they walked. Sam was a little disappointed that she hadn't introduced him to anyone, but he supposed she had her reasons. And he wasn't ready to wipe that soft smile off her face with questions.

She stopped in front of a shop with a window looking out over the boardwalk. A short line of people waited in front of it, each scanning a list printed on a board on the wall. "Are you up to an ice-cream cone? My treat."

A woman turned away from the window holding a brown cone-shaped cookie filled with mounds of something colorful. Before Sam could ask what it was, she licked the top color, crossing her eyes to keep watch as she put it to her mouth.

"More strange food?"

"Dessert, actually. Frozen flavored cream." Taylor motioned him into line. "You'll love it—if you don't already." Another person turned away from the window and the line inched forward. Taylor leaned against a post and looked him over carefully. "So, tell me, Sam. Have you ever been married?"

"Not yet. Don't plan to, either—at least not for a while."

"Have you ever come close?"

He wasn't quite ready to talk about Olivia yet, but Taylor seemed interested, not suspicious for once, so he offered a brief answer. "Once."

"Ah, so you've been in love."

"I have. And so have you."

Her cheeks flamed, but she looked so beautiful Sam didn't regret the observation that brought it about. "Yes, I have. Once. A long time ago."

"Only once?"

Her eyes narrowed to tiny slits. "What kind of question is that?"

"An honest one. It's hard to believe a woman as pretty as you has only been in love once."

She made a face at him. "I know I teased you about sweet talk, but you don't have to go overboard."

"That's not why I said it." He gave in to temptation and leaned close to her ear, taking a deep breath of the sweet and spicy scent that drifted up from her neck. "I said it because it's true. You're a mighty beautiful woman, Sheriff. And don't get all bristly on me for saying so. I told you I'm not in the habit of lying."

She pulled back ever so slightly. Sam might not even have noticed, except that her hair brushed against his cheek and he could hear the soft sound of her breathing. "I wish you wouldn't do that," she whispered. "With the election coming up, I can't afford to start gossip."

He righted himself slowly and glanced around. Some people didn't seem to notice them, but others seemed intensely interested in what they were doing. "This election of yours must be important."

"Very important." She ran her fingers through her hair and managed to put a few more inches between them. "I love my job—and I need it. I don't want to hand it over to someone else."

"Understood. I'll keep my distance."

Two more people stepped out of line, and Sam found himself at the window. He had no idea what to order, so he deferred to Taylor's judgment and came away carrying a cone filled with something pink, something white with nuts, and a third flavor that looked honest-to-god purple. He took an experimental lick and the burst of fruit flavor surprised him. Smiling, he tried another.

"Well?" Taylor joined him holding a smaller cone. "What do you think?"

"Incredible. I'm going to have to find work so I can come back for more."

Taylor led him off the boardwalk, checked carefully for cars, and started across the street. "You're going to find a job here in Heartbreak Hill?"

"I can't go on taking your father's charity forever."

"What will you do?"

"That, Sheriff O'Brien, is the question of the day. Of course, I haven't had a chance to do any looking yet, but I'm not sure what I'd be qualified to do in this world of yours."

She licked her ice cream thoughtfully. "I'm sure there's something. I suppose I could keep my eyes and ears open and let you know if I hear anything."

He smiled and filled his mouth with purple ice cream. "That's mighty nice of you, Sheriff. I'd appreciate that."

She slowed and tilted her head to look at him. "Look, I'm still not convinced about you, but you are staying with my dad. And he and Cody think so much of you . . ." She smiled softly. "I'm pretty sure you're not on Hutton Stone's payroll, so you can drop the 'Sheriff' bit and call me Taylor if you'd like to."

Sam wasn't sure why that pleased him so much, but he liked knowing that he'd slipped past some of her defenses. "I'd be honored."

They walked for a few minutes in companionable silence, the kind neither of them felt compelled to fill with idle chatter. Occasionally she'd point out something she thought might interest him.

Sam enjoyed just being out and about, seeing people, getting a feel for his new world and the folks in it. He enjoyed walking through the crowds and studying the clothing, catching snippets of conversation.

He caught Taylor watching him, her expression clear and only slightly curious. "Are things so very much different than what you're used to?"

"Not so very much. It seems that folks are just folks, no

matter when or where they live. But there are some differ-
ences. Kids don't seem to be quite as respectful toward
their elders as they should be, and men aren't nearly as
gentlemanly. I've only seen a handful of men actually
opening doors for ladies." He nodded toward a lanky guy
with bowed legs a few feet ahead of them. "That fella there
just gave the door an extra push for the lady behind him.
Didn't even stick around to see that she made it through."

Taylor laughed softly. "I guess that would be different.
Just so you're aware, some women find it offensive to have
doors held for them."

"Offensive?" Sam made it through his first flavor of ice
cream and moved on to the next. "How could manners be
offensive?"

"It has to do with wanting men to realize that women
are capable rather than needy, strong rather than weak."

"And what is it about a fella showing simple courtesy
that makes a woman feel weak?"

"It's not that the woman feels weak. It's that the man's
implying that she is weak by opening the door in the first
place."

"What if he's not implying anything? What if he's just
being respectful?"

Taylor tossed half of her ice-cream cone away. "I don't
have time to explain all the subtle nuances of sexual equal-
ity right now. Just don't be surprised if your sign of respect
isn't always appreciated."

Sam wasn't anywhere near ready to toss away his cone.
"Do all women feel this way?"

"Not all."

"How about you?"

Taylor shrugged. "If a man holds a door for me, I'll walk
through it. If not, I'll open it myself. It doesn't matter one
way or the other."

"Anything else I should know?"

"I'm sure there's plenty."

"I meant about you."

She froze. Shook her head quickly and looked away.
"I'm not that complicated."

Sam would have argued that, but he didn't want to ruin the mood. He followed her around a corner and stopped cold at the sight of a crowd gathered around a tree-lined square in the center of town. Hordes of men, women, and children clustered together, talking, laughing, shouting. Parents warned children to behave, then promptly let themselves become absorbed by something else so they didn't notice the little tykes' next escapade.

"What's this? Everyone in town must be here."

"Not many people from town, mostly tourists come to see the show." Taylor looked around quickly and motioned for him to follow—as if he hadn't been trailing behind her all evening. "Come with me. We'll get you a place where you can see the whole thing."

She led him through the thickening crowd and found a spot at the edge beneath a towering pine tree. "This looks like a good spot. I'll make a quick pass through the crowd and meet you back here in a few minutes."

Sam checked to make sure he wasn't blocking someone else's view, then leaned against the tree's trunk to finish his ice cream. "Whatever you say."

"Don't leave."

"I won't move a muscle." He held up the cone and added, "Except to eat."

She turned away to hide her grin, and Sam chuckled. As she walked away, he watched the enticing movement of her hips, the nip of waist, the crown of fiery hair, and he couldn't make himself look away until she'd disappeared. But when she did, common sense hit him like a board upside the head.

He stopped licking his ice cream and stared at the corner she'd just rounded. For all his big talk the other day, he sure wasn't acting much like a man who didn't want to get involved with a woman.

Chapter 9

TAYLOR WASN'T SURE how Sam did it. She didn't want to like him. She *certainly* didn't want to believe him. Yet here she was, grinning like a schoolgirl after less than an hour alone with him and wondering if maybe—just maybe—there was a reasonable explanation for how he got here.

What was *wrong* with her?

She waited while a man and woman hustled several small children out of Heartfelt Gifts, smiled at one tiny girl with curly hair who was howling as if her heart would break over a frog puppet in the window, and silently blessed the frazzled mother who went back into the store after it.

"So—who's the guy?"

The unexpected voice startled her. She turned and found Irene Beers grinning at her from just inside the doorway. Taylor didn't know Irene as well as she knew Irene's brother, DeWayne. They'd never run in the same circles or shared many interests, but DeWayne thought the sun rose and set on his little sister, and Taylor was always friendly when they met.

She glanced over her shoulder to see if she'd missed something. "What guy?"

"*What guy?*" Irene tapped one finger against her cheek

and jiggled her hips. "Let me think. Of the twenty strangers I saw you walking with tonight, which one could I *possibly* mean?"

The music on Irene's CD player changed to something soft and Native American. The scents of vanilla and cinnamon floated out of the open doorway. A short gust of wind from the mountains caught T-shirts hanging on hooks and tossed them gently.

"Sam's a friend," Taylor said. "He's staying with Pop for a while."

"A friend?" One strap of Irene's tank top slid down her arm. "That's all?"

Taylor should have expected Irene to show an interest in Sam. With her soft brown hair, big dark eyes, and full pouty lips, she was one of those women who were sensuous without even trying. She went through men the way some women went through chocolate. "There's nothing romantic between us, if that's what you're asking."

Irene's speculative gaze floated toward the square. Her lashes were so long and full, they formed actual shadows on her cheeks. "He's *very* good looking."

"I suppose he is." Taylor picked up a sweatshirt from a display table and looked it over. Next to Irene, she always felt plain as a brown paper wrapper. "I hadn't really noticed."

"You hadn't—?" Irene tugged her strap back into place and watched the stagecoach roll through the crowd toward the square. "You're kidding, right? How could you *not* notice?"

Taylor put the sweatshirt back on the table. "Well, maybe I noticed, but not in the way you think."

"That's sad. So, tell me what's he like? Is he nice?"

"I don't know him that well," Taylor said, trying to decide why Irene's questions bothered her so much. "He seems nice, I suppose." She didn't know why that felt like such an understatement, either.

"And you're *really* not interested in him? I mean, is it okay if I see what happens?"

Objections tumbled to Taylor's lips, but she wasn't certain exactly what they were. She didn't want Sam for herself, but she didn't like the idea of Irene adding him to her list of conquests. "It's just that Sam's . . . different," she said as Kip and DeWayne moved into position to make their entrance as the bandits. "He's not like other men."

"There's nothing wrong with that."

"No. I mean he's *different*."

"You mean he's gay?"

"No. No, not that. He's just . . . Well, he's old-fashioned. I guess that's the best way to describe him."

Irene's eyes glittered with anticipation. "That sounds wonderful, if you want to know the truth."

"The thing is, he's recently ended a relationship. I don't think he's ready to get involved with someone new."

"If you ask me, that's the best time to meet a man."

Maybe. If you're a bloodsucker.

Taylor frowned thoughtfully. "It was a tough breakup. Sudden and unexpected."

Irene put one hand on her hip and scowled. "Look, if you want him for yourself, just say so. Otherwise, let *him* decide whether or not he's interested. He's a big boy."

He certainly was. Taylor might have tried one more argument, but a shout from the square cut her off. People craned to see better, angry voices carried over the noise of the crowd. Taylor had seen the shoot-out so many times, she rarely watched it anymore. But she knew how it sounded—and it didn't sound like this.

She left Irene without a word and hurried into the crowd. People were packed together so tightly, she had trouble getting through and had to change directions several times. The sounds coming from inside the square grew louder. When only a few rows separated her from the action, she heard the unmistakable crack of flesh meeting flesh and tried to move faster.

When she finally pushed to the front of the crowd, she took in the scene with one glance. The stagecoach was in position, but the driver and shotgun rider were missing. The horses Kip and DeWayne rode in on pranced uneasily at the edge of the square, and she realized with horror that

Sam and DeWayne were squaring off against each other. Kip lay in the dust and was shaking his head to clear it.

Before she could move, Sam took a swing at DeWayne and connected. DeWayne staggered backward and landed a few feet from Kip. In a flash, Sam scooped up the prop rifle and aimed at a spot between them. "You two are going to stay right there and wait for the sheriff. Don't even think about trying to get away."

Taylor glanced around quickly to see what else Sam had done while she wasn't looking, and caught a glimpse of Hutton Stone pushing through the crowd on the opposite side of the square.

Damn!

She didn't even have time to ponder what this meant. She just strode into the square and said a prayer of gratitude that so far most people watching thought the fight was part of the entertainment.

Sam looked so pleased with himself, she almost hated to burst his bubble. But she couldn't pretend that everything was all right.

"Sam?" She kept her voice low, so it wouldn't carry into the crowd. "Do you want to tell me what's going on?"

"Sonofabitch came out of nowhere," Kip ground out before Sam could answer.

Sam gave him a warning nudge with the rifle barrel. "These two were trying to rob the stage. I couldn't see you anywhere, so I figured I'd help out until you could get back."

She touched his arm gently. "I appreciate your help. I really do. But they're not bandits. They're friends of mine, and they're putting on a show for tourists."

The triumph in Sam's eyes faded. "Friends?"

"Good friends." She nudged the rifle barrel toward the ground. "But there's no reason to let the crowd think there's a problem. Let's just act as if this is all part of the show."

Kip muttered under his breath. DeWayne nodded slowly and got to his feet, rubbing his jaw and sending dagger looks at Sam. "That's probably best. What do you suggest?"

"Somebody needs to get you two vicious criminals locked up in jail, so let's let Sam do that, and I'll try to get the microphone from Bailey so I can make the introductions." She glanced at Sam. "Do you remember where the jail is from here?"

He nodded miserably. "I see it."

"Fine. Then march these two over there. You two, ham it up." She touched Sam's hand and tried not to notice that she felt the contact all the way to her shoulder. "Just don't shoot them if they turn around and shake a fist at you or something. Wait inside until you hear your name, then come back and take a bow."

The tips of his mustache drew together beneath his chin. "Didn't mean to botch things for you."

"You haven't botched anything we can't fix," she assured him. "Just play it to the end and we'll be okay." She looked to Kip and DeWayne. "Are you two ready?"

"I suppose." Kip touched a quickly discoloring eye and drew his hand away. "But I want an explanation when this is over. The two of us owe this sumbitch."

"I'll explain everything later." Taylor had no idea what she'd say, but she would have agreed to almost anything to get the show back on the road. "But please forget about it for tonight."

"I'm not likely to forget it," DeWayne muttered. He brushed dust from his pants and raised his hands over his head. "Come on, Wyatt Earp. Let's get this over with."

Taylor turned away and, with a wave to the crowd, started toward the lean-to that housed the public address system. She hadn't even gone halfway when Hutton burst into the square.

"What in the *hell* is going on here?"

"Nothing, Hutton. Everything's under control."

"Under control?" Hutton started after Sam. "This man should be under arrest."

"Everything's fine," Taylor insisted. "It's all part of the show—which you're ruining, by the way."

Hutton swung to face her, his expression full of fire and fury. "He attacked Kip and DeWayne. *That's* not part of

the show, and you know it. I hold you personally responsible for this fiasco."

Taylor forced herself to turn away. "There *is* no fiasco.
Everything is fine."

"You call this *fine*?" Hutton swept his gaze across the
crowd, looking for support. "Those two men are hurt. *I* call
it criminal assault."

"Oh, for Pete's sake, Hutton—"

"We've seen how well you protect some of us. I'm curious to know if this is how you plan to protect the rest of
Heartbreak Hill's citizens."

Taylor clenched her fists to keep from smacking him.
"You're blowing this out of proportion. And I'm sure these
people don't want their summer evening ruined by local
politics."

Hutton glared at her. "The shoot-out has *already* been
ruined."

"You know, Hutton," she said as if he hadn't spoken,
"part of this job is adjusting to the unexpected. If you win
in November, I hope you'll do better at rolling with the
punches than you have tonight."

She turned away before he could argue, gratified by a
low rumble of laughter that worked its way through the
crowd. But her relief didn't last long. They might have
saved the moment, but she had the feeling that tonight
would come back to haunt her.

Hours later Taylor walked with Sam along the darkened
sidewalk toward home. Stars sparkled in the clear sky and
a warm breeze caressed her shoulders. Charlie and Cody
were nowhere to be found, of course. The longer she
thought about Charlie's injury, the more certain she was
that she'd been set up.

She could have throttled Charlie for pulling such a stunt.
Yes, she'd enjoyed getting to know Sam, but if Charlie
hadn't gotten cute, Sam wouldn't have been alone, and tonight's disaster would never have happened.

Poor Sam. He'd been subdued since the shoot-out.
They'd salvaged the performance, but he was still embar-

rassed by his part in it. A soft breeze tossed his hair and rippled the fabric of his shirt against his chest. And a very fine chest it was. Strong, broad, solid. She had the strangest urge to run her fingers across his shoulders, and it took all the self-control she had to keep her hands to herself.

He caught her watching him and pushed his hat back so she could see his eyes. "Did I do something else wrong?"

"Not at all. I was just . . . thinking."

"About anything special?"

"Not really." She kept her voice light and her hands in her pockets so they wouldn't dart across the distance between them. "Wondering whether you enjoyed yourself, I guess. What you think of our little town and the people in it. Just . . . thinking."

"Other than nearly ruining everything, I enjoyed myself just fine. The people are friendly and curious, just like folks in any other town."

Taylor drew to a stop in the night-shadow of an oak tree and watched a dark Chevy Cavalier pull into the driveway behind Hutton Stone's office. "That's strange. Why is Joe Mooney at Hutton Stone's office?"

"Maybe they're friends."

"I didn't think so." In fact, she'd been counting on the parents of Cody's best friend to vote for her. If she couldn't rely on them, who could she count on?

"Maybe it's not Joe Mooney," Sam suggested.

"It has to be. That's his car."

Sam touched the back of her arm and drew her away. Fire shot up to her shoulder and down to her fingertips. "You know there'll be talk tomorrow. Are you ready for that?"

She looked into his eyes and tried to swallow. "About the shoot-out?"

"About us."

Taylor blessed the night for hiding her quick blush. "What can they possibly say? It's not as if we were on a date or anything."

"They can say plenty." Sam slowed his step and raked his gaze across her face. "And they probably will."

"If it weren't for the election, I wouldn't even care." He was so close, she shivered in spite of the evening's warmth. "Or maybe I should say that I wouldn't care if it weren't for Cody. I'm used to being talked about. He's still young and easily hurt."

"And you think it'll hurt him if folks speculate about you and me?"

"Yes, if people start raking up my past, or if they start remembering too much about Cody's father."

Sam gave her an odd look. "It's not your fault Cody's father passed on. Why would anyone blame you—or him—for that?"

Taylor did a double take. "Passed on?"

"Even if your husband was the worst kind of scoundrel, that wouldn't be the boy's fault."

"Nate Albright was a scoundrel, all right. But that's not how most people would see it—especially if Hutton Stone has his way. He'd like them to start questioning *my* ethics." She tugged a leaf from the tree and rubbed it between her fingers. "But why are you under the impression that he's dead?"

"The boy told me."

"Cody did?" Taylor's heart squeezed painfully. "Apparently, Cody says a lot of things that aren't true. I'm not a widow. I've never been married."

Even in the soft moonlight she could see confusion gathering in Sam's eyes.

She hesitated to tell him more, but she couldn't bring herself to lie to him. "Nate wasn't my husband. That's the whole point. He was a young, handsome, exciting boy from the city who took my country bumpkin breath away and left me pregnant when he went back home."

She held her breath as she watched Sam's reaction, surprised by how much she needed him not to look at her differently or pull back in disgust. By how much she wanted that spark of interest to remain in his eyes.

Sam's mustache drooped and his eyes narrowed. "And you're worried that Hutton Stone is going to remind people about that and convince them that a woman who's been taken advantage of in the worst way is somehow to blame for her misfortune?"

"It would be easy to lay all the blame at Nate's feet." She wrapped her arms around herself and leaned against the fence. "But I wasn't taken advantage of. It wasn't as if he forced me to do something I didn't want to do."

"But he didn't stay around to suffer the consequences with you, either."

"He was young."

"So were you." Sam lifted his hand hesitantly, his eyes locked on hers as he reached toward her cheek and trailed one finger to her chin. When she didn't pull away, he smiled softly. "You must have been. You're hardly more than a girl now."

"I'm much more than a girl," she whispered hoarsely, not entirely certain whether it was a protest or a promise.

"I guess you are, at that." His gaze lit on her lips and settled there, and she knew he was thinking about kissing her.

Her heart jumped and every inch of her skin began to tingle. Whether it was logical or not, she wanted to feel his arms around her, to taste, to touch.

He waited, as if he could see the questions and answers on her face, then lowered his lips to hers, slowly, giving her ample time to change her mind and pull away. She couldn't have done that if her life depended on it.

His mouth touched hers gently. So gently. The bones in her legs liquified and her knees buckled so that he had to slip his arms around her to hold her up. She melted against him, savoring the feel of his granite chest and legs. His arms were as sturdy as the trunk of the oak tree that shielded them with its branches. She wrapped her arms around his waist, marveling at how solid he was.

Long before she was ready, his mouth left hers and he smiled down at her. "Does this mean we're finally friends?"

She laughed and loosened her arms. "I think it's safe to say that."

"And does this mean you finally believe the rest? Who I am? Where I came from?"

"I think we could say that, too." She ran her hands along his sides and grinned up at him. "It still sounds crazy to me, but I have to admit that you're pretty convincing."

"I'm not trying to be convincing," he said with a scowl. "I'm just telling you who I am."

"I didn't mean that to sound rude. It's just that . . . Well, try to put yourself in my place. What if someone came to you with a wild tale like this one. What would *you* think?"

"Someone did. I believed him. If I hadn't, I wouldn't be here right now."

She'd been so busy not believing the basic facts of his story, she'd almost forgotten the details. "Kurt? Was that his name?"

Sam nodded. Traveling through time seemed so unreal, she laughed nervously. Just imagine what people would say if they knew. The press would have a field day. He'd become the object of a media circus. Doctors and scientists would swarm the town, wanting a chance to examine him and experiment. There'd be movie offers and magazine interviews. A cold chill scurried up her spine and made the hair on the back of her neck stand up.

Just imagine.

She studied Sam for a long moment, trying to decide what was best for all of them. "How did Kurt react to jumping through time?" she finally asked. "Physically, I mean. Did it have any long-term effect on him?"

"Not that I know of, but then I wasn't around for long. Why?"

"I'm just wondering if it puts your body into some kind of stress."

"I was pretty sore for a day or two. That's all I know." He rubbed his arm as if thinking about the experience brought the pain back.

"Has the soreness gone away?"

"Pretty much."

"But not completely?"

"Not entirely."

Taylor argued with herself for another few minutes. She didn't want to turn Sam's life into a media event, but if the time travel had hurt him in some way, they should know about it. "Would you do one thing for me?"

"What's that?"

"I'd like you to see a doctor."

"A doctor?" Sam pulled back and stared at her. "Why?"

"Because we don't know what effect the time travel had on you. I think it would be smart to make sure."

"*I'm* sure. I feel fine."

"You *feel* fine, but how do we know you are? The time travel might have damaged your heart or weakened you in some other way."

"There's nothing wrong with me, Taylor. I guarantee it."

"You can't make a guarantee like that. I wish you could, but—"

Sam touched her chin lightly. "You'll feel better if I go?"

"I would."

"Fine." He squeezed her hands gently. "Then I'll go."

"You'd go just because I want you to?"

"Why not? I guess I'm a little curious, myself."

She stood on tiptoe and kissed his cheek. "Thank you."

He pulled her close again. "If that's the reward for a simple yes, I plan to be *very* agreeable in the future. That alone was worth the trip."

Taylor laughed softly, but the shadow in his eyes made her think about everything he'd told her. "Your friend owes you a great deal for jumping into the future so he could stay with the woman he loved. Did you know her?"

"She was my closest neighbor." There it was again, that slight tightening of his lips and the shuttering of his eyes.

For the first time, Taylor wondered if Olivia had meant more to him than he'd let on. An inner voice urged her to leave well enough alone, but the need to know everything got the best of her. "Will you tell me about her?"

"About Olivia?" He pulled his arms away completely. "There's not much to tell."

"I think that's the first lie you've ever told me." Taylor tried to keep her voice light, but the specter of the unknown woman stood firmly between them. She could feel Olivia's presence as surely as if she'd materialized before Taylor's eyes.

Sam leaned against the oak tree, long and lean, dangerously handsome. "You think I'm lying?"

"I think Olivia meant more to you than you're telling me."

"She meant a great deal to me once. But that was a long time ago." He grinned and added, "A hundred years or more."

"Was she beautiful?"

Sam shrugged casually. "I thought so."

The admission knifed Taylor's heart. She knew she was being foolish. After all, she had a past of her own. She had no right to envy Sam's. But Nate truly had been a long time ago. Technically, Sam had left Olivia only a few days before. "Did you love her?"

"I thought so for a time."

Taylor tried to find comfort in that, but peace and security eluded her. Sam had loved and lost. He'd sacrificed himself and his future for the woman who held his heart in the past.

The next morning Taylor watched the world go by from a booth at Deke's Restaurant. Holiday traffic clogged the streets and tourists jammed the sidewalks, but she couldn't work up any enthusiasm for heading into the crowd.

She couldn't stop thinking about the way Sam had looked with the moonlight in his eyes. She couldn't stop reliving the feel of his lips on hers. Her mind had been running on high all night—so high, she'd barely slept. She was in danger of losing her common sense. Even reminding herself that he loved someone else couldn't calm the butterflies in her stomach when she thought about him.

What kind of fool would let a tiny twinge of envy over Irene's interest in him get the best of her? What kind of idiot would let moonlight and stars turn her into a silly, romantic fool and wipe out every painful lesson she'd learned at Nate's hands?

She needed to keep her mind on what was real and im-

- portant—Cody, Charlie, her career, and the campaign. She *needed* to get real.

Taking a deep breath, she tried to push Sam out of her mind once and for all. Cody still wasn't acting like himself. She'd woken him early this morning just in case, but he'd flatly refused to go on the camp out with his friends. Charlie had promised to watch him today—which was a worry in itself.

While she sat there, the door opened and street noise came inside along with DeWayne and Kip. They made a beeline for her table, scowling, swaggering, and sporting bruises beneath their sunglasses.

Kip's face was still shadowed with the night's growth of whiskers. DeWayne pulled off his hat as they scooted into her booth. The acrid scent of stale cigarette smoke followed them.

"All right," Kip said before they even got settled. "Tell us."

"Tell you what?"

"About your friend and that stunt he pulled yesterday."

DeWayne turned his cup over in its saucer and motioned the waitress over. "I want to know why you let him get away with it."

She shrugged and followed up with a smile. They were friends, but she wasn't about to tell the truth. "It was a misunderstanding. No harm done."

Kip shoved his empty cup out of the way. "*What* misunderstanding? He came in there like Wyatt Fricking Earp, ready to take off both our heads. We're damn lucky the rifle was loaded with blanks."

"He wouldn't have hurt you," Taylor protested. "He didn't realize it was an act, that's all. He didn't want anyone to get hurt."

DeWayne snorted a laugh as the waitress filled his cup.

Kip touched his purple eye again. "Right. Didn't want anyone to get hurt. Come on, Taylor. How could he *not* know it was an act? It's corny and stupid and completely obvious."

"They don't do things like that where he comes from."

Kip leaned his arms on the table, and his thick brows formed a "V" over his nose. "And where is that?"

"Colorado."

"They don't have staged shoot-outs in Colorado?" DeWayne leaned back in his seat and folded his arms. "I smell a story, Taylor. We've been friends too long for you to hold out on us."

Guilt plucked at her, but she ignored it. On the scales of justice, the balance between a man's entire life and an omission of the truth was tipped heavily in Sam's direction. "I'm not holding out. There's nothing to tell." Taylor lifted her coffee cup so that it would hide at least part of her face. "He's a friend of Charlie's. He misunderstood what was happening yesterday. That's all there is to it."

DeWayne and Kip shared a look. "Hutton Stone doesn't think that's all," Kip said. "I heard he's calling for an investigation."

Taylor's cup nearly slipped out of her hand. "Into *what*? Nothing happened."

DeWayne touched his face and winced. "Something happened."

"Nothing serious." Taylor sat her cup on the table too hard, and coffee sloshed onto her fingers. She shook her hand and searched for a napkin. "You two have come home from the Moosehead in worse shape."

DeWayne reached over the bench and pulled a napkin from the booth behind them. "We all know that Hutton'll do anything to shoot you down," he said, handing the napkin to her. "Sam just handed him the ammunition last night."

Taylor wiped her hand and crumpled the napkin on the table. When she realized that her hand was trembling, she slid it beneath her leg. "This is ridiculous. Who does Hutton think he is, anyway?"

"We all know what he wants to be," Kip said quietly. "He made an announcement this morning that he's not going to stand by while you turn Heartbreak Hill into—What did he call it?"

"Sodom and Gomorrah," DeWayne said. "From the Bible."

"I know where it's from," Taylor said. "This is unbelievable. Hutton Stone doesn't even go to church. His wife's the only real religious person in that family. As far as I'm concerned, Hutton's an idiot who has *far* too little to do."

She slid out of the booth and stood, so angry that every inch of her body trembled. She jammed her uniform hat over her hair, tossed enough money onto the table to cover her bill and the tip, and turned toward the door. Only then did she realize that her voice had carried and that every eye in the place was on her.

Chapter 10

THE INSTANT SAM saw the fresh-faced kid who claimed to be a doctor, he began to have second thoughts about keeping his promise to Taylor. He didn't look much older than Cody with that pair of glasses riding his nose and the shock of sun-bleached hair sticking out all over. He wore a white jacket casually opened over a red shirt and a pair of faded jeans so tight Sam wondered how he could even breathe.

He called Sam from the waiting room as if they'd been friends for a lifetime.

Sam followed him along a long, airy hallway into a narrow, sunlit room filled with charts and pictures on the walls, a long, narrow metal bed, a short metal counter with sink, a contraption hanging from the wall spitting brown paper towels, one squat plastic chair, and a short round stool. There wasn't an ounce of comfort in the whole room.

The doctor held out a tanned hand and grinned like a little boy with a new toy. "Dr. Lipton, Sam. I've heard a lot about you."

"From who?"

"People. It seems you've been stirring things up a bit since you came to town."

"Not intentionally."

"Of course not. But you are the subject on everyone's lips these days." He waved Sam toward the metal bed. "Go ahead and undress. I'll be back in a couple of minutes."

"Undress?" Sam scowled. "Why would I need to do that?"

The doctor tapped his clipboard. "It says here you want a complete physical. Can't do that if you're dressed, can I?"

"Why not?"

"That's not how things are done, Sam." Dr. Lipton perched on the small round stool and rocked it back and forth. "My notes say you've recently done some extensive traveling and that you're concerned about how that's affected you."

"I'm not concerned," Sam told him. "Other people are. *I* know I'm fine."

"Okay. But unless you get undressed, I can't listen to your chest or check reflexes. I can't check anything, really." Dr. Lipton consulted his clipboard and flipped a couple of papers. "When did you last have a complete physical, Sam?"

"I don't remember." The truth was, he'd never been seen by a doctor. Never had the need.

Dr. Lipton scowled in concentration. "I don't seem to have any medical records here. Where was your last doctor?"

"Colorado."

"If you're going to be staying in Heartbreak Hill, I'd like to have your records transferred up here."

"I don't think that would be possible," Sam said honestly. "Dr. Parsons is long dead."

"But surely his records are still intact. Who took over his practice?"

"I'll check. Right now all I need is a clean bill of health so people will stop worrying about me."

The doctor laughed through his nose. "Well, I can't make promises. We won't know how you are until I can get a look at you. And for that, you need to disrobe."

It was on the tip of Sam's tongue to refuse, but he

stopped himself. If most folks got undressed for the doctor, well then, that's what he'd do. "How undressed do I need to get?"

"Take off everything but your shorts. If you're worried about modesty, you can put on that robe when you're ready."

"Robe?" Sam glanced at it, shrugged, and tried to look as if he got undressed in front of strangers every day. "Well in that case, sure. Fine."

The doctor gave him an odd look and left the room, shutting the door behind him. Sam undressed quickly, but when he got down to his fancy new shorts—which he still wasn't quite used to—and started searching for that robe the doctor had told him about, he started thinking he'd been tricked. The closest thing to a robe anywhere in the room was a little shift made of something that felt like paper. It wasn't even big enough to go all the way around him.

Sam snorted in irritation and reached for his clothes. Before he could get back into his shirt, the door opened and Dr. Lipton slithered into the room. "All ready?" He didn't even wait for an answer. "Great. Now, why don't you hop up on the examining table and we'll get started, all-righty?"

"Just what are we going to get started *with*?"

"Your physical, Sam." Dr. Lipton laughed again. "The way you're acting, you'd think you'd never had one before."

Sam didn't want to give that impression, but he wasn't ready to trust the doctor yet. "I have. It's just been a while. Remind me what's involved in a physical."

"Why don't you just sit back and relax? Let me do my job, okay? I don't come in to your job and tell you what to do, now do I?"

"I've never done a job that required you being nekkid on a table."

"You're not 'nekkid,' either." Without warning, Dr. Lipton slapped a cold piece of metal onto Sam's back. "Take a deep breath."

Sam gasped at the shock and jerked away.

Dr. Lipton grabbed his arm and pulled him back into

place. "Breathe *slowly*, please. I can't tell anything if you're jumping around like that."

Sam clenched his fists and took a slow, deep breath. The doctor moved all over Sam's back and chest, thumbed here, prodded there, poked a stick into Sam's mouth and looked into his nose and ears, and he damn near blinded Sam by shining a light in his eyes.

Finally he set aside his tools and leaned back so far on his little stool, Sam expected him to fall off. "How about blood work?"

"It works fine. Thanks, anyway."

"You have a very droll sense of humor, Sam. Very droll." He pulled a needle attached to a thick tube from a box and dug in a drawer for a tourniquet. "We really should check blood levels."

"Look, Doc, all I want to know is if my heart works and I'm breathing. Prove that to Sheriff O'Brien, and everyone will be happy."

"Please," the doctor said as he snapped a thick piece of rubber on Sam's arm and thumped around. "Let me do what I do, okay?" Without warning, he jabbed the needle into Sam's arm and began draining blood. Sam fought the urge to rip it from his arm, and vowed again that if everyone could put up with this, so could he.

"That wasn't bad, was it?" Dr. Lipton asked when he'd finished. He handed Sam a wad of cotton and showed him where to hold it. "There's just one thing left."

Thank the good Lord for that.

The doctor tossed away one set of thin gloves and snapped another over his hands. "I just need you to bend over the table, there."

"Bend over?"

"That's right."

"You mind telling me why?"

"Please, Sam. It's the last part of your physical. Let me do this and you're finished."

Sam had been remarkably patient up till now. Only remembering the worry in Taylor's eyes got him to turn around and only the memory of that kiss got him way over the table.

"There now." The doctor put one hand on Sam's back and kept his voice soothing. "I'll want you to turn your head and cough. This will be over in a minute. . . ."

Taylor was in the middle of an argument with Donald when the door to her office slammed open and cut her off mid-sentence. Dr. Lipton loomed into the doorway, puffing and out of breath, his face purple with rage. One eye had puffed shut, his nose was swollen and ugly, and his white coat was torn at the collar.

"That man is a maniac," he said with a jerk of his arm toward the street. "I want you to lock him up this minute, and I hope to God you'll throw away the key."

Taylor stood slowly, trying to convince herself that the timing was nothing more than coincidence. "What man?" *Please let him say it's a leftover tourist. Anyone but—*

"Sam Evans. He's crazy. Crazy and dangerous."

"I told you," Donald said smugly. "I told you he was a menace."

"A menace is right." The doctor touched his eye gingerly and winced. "He should be put away somewhere."

Donald put one foot on the chair in front of Taylor's desk. "Didn't I tell you? Didn't I—?"

"Oh, shut up, Donald." The words snapped out before Taylor could stop them, but she was already so frustrated she could hardly see straight.

Donald pulled back sharply. "Shut up? Shut *up*?"

"I'm sorry, Donald. But obviously we have a problem here, and—"

"And I warned you this would happen, didn't I? I warned you."

"Yes," she snapped. "You warned me. But that's not the issue right now, is it?" She turned back to the doctor, trying desperately to keep a pleasant expression on her face. After all, she was a public servant, sworn to protect the people of this community. Like it or not, Dr. Lipton looked as if he could use some protecting. "Why don't you have a seat and tell me what happened?"

"Isn't it obvious?" The doctor waved a hand toward his swollen face. "Can't you see what he did?"

"You can't mean Sam did this to you. He's not like that."

Dr. Lipton took a couple of jerky steps toward her desk and sagged into a chair. "It was a physical. That's all. Just a routine physical." He looked to Donald for support. "I didn't do anything I haven't done to a hundred other men in this town, but he went off on me like some lunatic." He leaned both hands on her desk, winced, and pulled one away to shake it. "I want justice done."

"Let's not get overly excited. Tell me exactly what you did before he hit you."

Donald coughed nervously and turned away.

The doctor sent him a thin-lipped look of disapproval. "It's a part of the physical, Sheriff. For men."

Taylor blinked, blushed slightly, and nodded. "I see. Did you explain what you were going to do before you did it?"

"Not in graphic detail."

"Maybe you should have. Maybe if you'd warned him—"

Donald muttered something. The doctor glowered. "I did what I always do, Sheriff. My male patients may not like it, but they don't attack me."

"No. No, of course they don't."

"I *want* him locked up, Sheriff. I want to press assault charges."

"Exactly what I say," Donald murmured over his shoulder.

Taylor took a deep breath and let it out slowly. "I understand why you're upset, Doctor. But let's not do anything rash."

"*Rash?*" Dr. Lipton bolted to his feet. "I've been assaulted, Sheriff. Are you going to do your job or are you going to let your *boyfriend* run around doing whatever he feels like, attacking anybody he wants to?"

"He's not my boyfriend. He's a friend of Charlie's."

"Let's not quibble over semantics. The question stands."

"I'll talk to him."

"You'll *talk* to him?" Dr. Lipton snorted softly. "Maybe you can give him a slap on the wrist while you're at it. Dammit, Sheriff, he's a danger to the community."

"He's not dangerous, Dr. Lipton. I'm sure it was a simple misunderstanding. In fact, I'd stake my reputation on it. Sam's . . . different. He's old-fashioned."

"He's violent," Donald put in.

"A lunatic." Dr. Lipton planted both fists on her desk. "If you won't take my complaint, I'll go over your head."

Taylor's nerves felt as if someone were holding a flame to them. She couldn't ignore this, but she couldn't punish Sam for something that wasn't his fault. She didn't look away, even though Dr. Lipton's expression made her uncomfortable. "I know Sam," she said. "He's not violent. With both you and Donald, he was only trying to keep another man from . . . well, in his mind, from getting fresh."

Donald's face flamed. "I wasn't getting fresh with him and you know it. I was frisking him."

"And I was giving him a medical exam. "There was nothing inappropriate about what I did."

"I'm sure there wasn't. Still . . ." She spoke slowly, thoughtfully, slanted a glance at the two men as if she were seeing them for the first time. Taylor battled a wave of guilt. She didn't like fighting dirty. It left a bad taste in her mouth. But she had to do something.

"Still nothing!" Dr. Lipton shouted. "*I* am not a pervert."

Donald looked as if he wanted to punch him. "Oh, and *I* am?"

"Calm down, Donald. I didn't say that. But I can't speak to your incident. I can only speak for myself."

Taylor looked from one to the other and crossed her legs. "You see how quickly suspicion spreads? One tiny question is all it takes."

Dr. Lipton clamped his mouth shut on his next argument and scratched the back of his head. "She's right."

Donald's eyes flashed with anger and his face turned a mottled red. He jammed his hands into his pockets and lifted one shoulder. "It's bull, and you know it."

The doctor touched the swollen skin around his eye again. "Maybe, but you know how people are. If there's even a hint that I did something wrong, I'll be finished. People don't take their children to doctors who . . . who . . ." He waved his hand ineffectually and left them to fill in the rest.

Taylor put a hand on his shoulder and tried desperately not to look relieved. "As far as I'm concerned, this can stay between the three of us. It doesn't ever have to leave this room."

Dr. Lipton allowed her to lead him to the door and slipped outside. Donald turned his back on her and kicked the filing cabinet.

Taylor battled one more wave of guilt and shut the door behind the doctor and let out her breath slowly. Just like the shoot-out, this wasn't over with yet.

It had been two weeks since Taylor's last visit with Mrs. Wilson when she found herself at the school again. The message Donald had left on her desk had been disturbingly vague—a request from Mrs. Wilson to meet with her for ten minutes, if possible, around noon.

What could be wrong now?

Mrs. Wilson was waiting for her when she knocked on her door. "Thank you for coming," she said as she ushered Taylor into the classroom. "This should only take a few minutes, but I thought you should be aware of the latest developments."

Taylor made herself as comfortable as possible on the kid-sized plastic chair. "Is there a problem?"

"I'm afraid so. I was really hoping that we'd put an end to Cody's wild stories, but I'm afraid we haven't. He's stopped making up tales about his father, but he's transferred his attention to your father's houseguest."

"To Sam?" Taylor nearly fell off the molded plastic chair. "What is he saying?"

Mrs. Wilson linked her hands together on her desk. "He's claiming that Mr. Evans is a gunslinger who traveled through time from the Wild West days." She shook her head sadly. "Cody's imagination is vivid, I'll grant him that. If only we could channel it into productive areas. . . ."

Taylor sank back in her chair. If she denied the story, she'd be painting Cody as a liar. What kind of mother would do that? If she didn't, the whole family would look crazy.

"Sam's a colorful character," she said at last. "And he loves to tell tall tales after dinner. The line between real and imaginary probably got blurred for Cody, but I'll talk with him this evening and make sure he understands."

Mrs. Wilson nodded slowly. "That would help, I'm sure." She unclasped her hands and drew them along the desktop. "There's one other thing you should be aware of."

Taylor tried not to look panicked, but what else could possibly go wrong? Forget she asked. She didn't want fate to show her.

"Against my recommendation," Mrs. Wilson said, "the school is planning their usual father-son activity for next month." She shook her head in disgust and stood. "They're also still planning that mother-daughter tea, but that's not the issue here. I don't know why some people have such a hard time understanding why parent-specific activities are difficult for some children. No matter how many times I try to explain that many of our students come from non-traditional families, they don't seem to get it."

She folded her arms and perched on the corner of her desk. "I'm afraid this may be what's behind Cody's latest episode of storytelling. He was obviously affected when the announcement came over the loudspeaker—as were several other boys whose parents are divorced or separated."

Taylor's spine lost its starch and she worried for a second that she'd slide off the chair and land in a puddle on the floor. "What did he do?"

"Nothing at the time, but the look on his face spoke for itself. Later, he and several other boys started making fun of the boys whose fathers live with them."

"They probably wanted to get the jump on them this time," Taylor said. The words tasted bitter as she spoke, but she couldn't seem to stop them. "They're probably sick and tired of being teased for things that aren't their fault."

"You're right, I'm sure. But I can't condone any sort of teasing."

"So Cody's being punished?"

"Mildly." Mrs. Wilson picked up a piece of chalk and rolled it between her fingers in a gesture Taylor remembered from years past. "He and the other boys are being kept in during recess for a day."

"Do the other kids receive the same punishment when the tables are turned?"

"Of course."

"I'm sorry. It's been a rough few weeks. I'm a little jumpy and far too touchy."

Chalk dust drifted from Mrs. Wilson's fingers onto her desk, but she didn't seem to notice. "Can I help?"

"I don't think anyone can help."

"I'm an excellent listener."

"You always have been," Taylor said, pushing to her feet and readjusting her duty belt. "But you have thirty-two children to keep your hands full. I'm sure you don't need parents adding problems."

Mrs. Wilson laughed softly. "I don't encourage *every* parent, but there are a select few I wouldn't mind helping. Even if I do nothing more than act as a sounding board."

"It's the campaign," she said weakly. "It's affecting everything."

"I'm sure it is, and things will only get more hectic from here on. Running against Hutton must keep you hopping."

Taylor smiled wryly. "That's one word for it."

"I was so surprised when he came by—"

Taylor sat up straight. "He came by here? Why?"

"To pick my brain, no doubt. He tried to be clever, but it was obvious he wanted me to tell him some dark secret about—what's his name? Sam?"

"Sam." Taylor clenched her teeth so hard, her mouth hurt. "Did he ask about Cody?"

"No, he didn't. And even if he had, I wouldn't have told him anything."

"What kinds of questions did he ask?"

"Like I said, they were all about Sam. Whether or not I'd ever met him. What I knew about him. Whether Cody had ever mentioned where he came from. You must admit, the town's introduction to him was a bit unorthodox."

"Yes. Yes, it was." Taylor tried to rub a knot from the back of her neck. "Do you know if Hutton's talked to anyone else?"

"I don't know for certain, but I'd guess that he has. He's determined to get your job."

Taylor stood slowly. "Thank you, Mrs. Wilson."

"Don't worry, dear. I'm sure things will be better soon."

Taylor laughed and turned away. "I'm not going to count on that. I have the feeling things will just keep getting worse—at least until November."

Sam watched Taylor carefully as she showed Cody how to fold brochures. A too-bright light glared into the small office, creating shadows against the wall as people moved. Ruby stood across the room arguing mildly with Charlie, who'd moved something she didn't approve of. Sam couldn't be sure, but he thought their arguments might be growing milder as the weeks crept by before the election. There wasn't much heat in tonight's disagreement, anyway.

So why was Taylor so agitated?

Her movements were broad and jerky, her voice and shoulders tense. Her gaze flitted from one thing to another, never quite landing on any one thing long enough to actually see it. When Cody folded a short stack of brochures wrong, she let out an agitated sigh and set about showing him again.

Sam waited until she'd finished, then left the pile of envelopes he'd been assigned to label. He followed Taylor into the dimly lit back room and blocked the doorway so she couldn't get past him.

"You want to talk about what's bothering you?"

She whipped around from the box she'd been digging through and brushed hair away from her forehead. "What makes you think something's bothering me?"

"Other than the fact that Charlie's avoiding you, Ruby's

walking on eggshells, and Cody's almost in tears?"

She turned back to the box and yanked something from inside. "I'm just tired, that's all."

"Okay." Sam leaned against the doorjamb and folded his arms. "Go home and rest."

"I can't. These brochures have to go out before the end of the week."

"The rest of us can get them out on time."

Taylor jammed the lid back onto the box and hoisted it onto the top of a teetering pile near the window. "It's *my* campaign. I'm not going to dump the work on the rest of you."

"We wouldn't be here if we didn't want to help."

She nudged another box with her knee and blew dust from its top. "I'm fine, Sam. Don't worry about it."

"If it's something I've done, I hope you'll tell me."

"It's not."

"Cody?"

She rounded on him and her eyes burned. "I said it's nothing. Why can't you leave it at that?"

"Because you're lying, and I don't like being lied to."

She tried to get past him, but he refused to budge. She fell back a step, clutching a stack of papers to her chest. "You want the truth? Fine. I'm in a very bad mood. Does that make you feel better?"

"Not particularly. I was asking for information I didn't already know."

Her bangs fell into her eyes again. She blew them out of the way and dropped heavily onto a nearby box. "I'm sorry I'm so ornery, but I'm completely overwhelmed. I feel as if I'm swimming upstream all the time."

"Then let someone else help."

She shook her head and looked away, as if she couldn't bear the idea of accepting help.

Sam pushed away from the door frame and hunkered down in front of her. "This might surprise you, considering how my life is at the moment, but there was a time when I carried a lot of responsibility on my shoulders. I can do it again if you'll let me."

Her gaze flickered to his face and darted away again. "I appreciate the offer, but—"

Impulsively Sam took the stack of papers from her, set them aside, and pulled her to her feet. "Come on," he said as he tugged her toward the door to the alley, "let's get out of here."

She dug her heels in. "And do what? Go where? Cody and Pop are out there—*and* Ruby. They'll all come looking for us. They'll wonder where we—"

He stopped her the only way he knew how—by covering her mouth with his. She resisted for half a breath, then softened and leaned against him, giving herself to the moment until they were both gasping for breath.

He could have gone on that way forever, but he'd never solved a problem by ignoring it. Ending the kiss reluctantly, he cupped her face in his hands. "Now, tell me what's got you so tied up in knots. Is it Cody?"

She shook her head and gently moved away from him. "Not this time."

His arms felt suddenly empty and cold. "Charlie?"

"No."

"I don't think I like the direction we're headed." He held open the back door for her, then followed her into the alley. "Tell me it's the job or that the campaign's failing, or *something*."

A shadow from the neighboring building swallowed her. Her voice drifted toward him from the darkness. "I guess it's a little bit of everything."

"Go on."

"It's not easy to tell you this."

"Just say it."

She took a deep breath and let it out slowly. "I met with Cody's teacher again today. She's worried because Cody's telling stories about you being from the past."

"Can't fault the boy for telling the truth."

"In this case, the truth could cause trouble. You know that Donald wants me to lock you up and throw away the key. I had to practically blackmail Dr. Lipton to drop the charges after you hit him. And Hutton Stone's been snooping around, trying to find something about you he can use against me."

Sam felt his shoulders slump and the blood drain out of his hands. It was a miracle she hadn't asked him to leave. "I'm sorry. I—"

She moved closer to put her fingers to his lips. Light spilling into the alley from the next building illuminated her face. "It's not your fault. At least, most of it isn't. I understand why you punched Donald and belted Dr. Lipton. I know why you thought DeWayne and Kip were robbing the stage. But this isn't the nineteenth century. There are laws against hitting people—even *with* provocation. We've been lucky so far, but I might not be able to smooth the waters next time. And I'm afraid of what will happen if I can't."

He felt so low, he'd have to look up to see a snake's belly. "I didn't mean to put your election in jeopardy—"

"The election is the least of my worries."

"I'd never purposely do anything to hurt Cody or Charlie—or you, either."

She took his hands in hers, but he couldn't find any comfort in her touch. "I know you wouldn't do anything purposely. But you're going to have to try harder to fit in or we're going to have a disaster on our hands. Just promise me that you won't hit anyone else."

"I won't even make a fist."

Taylor's lips curved into a smile. "And you'll blend in?"

"I'll be so damn normal, nobody will even notice I'm here."

Taylor scowled playfully. "I don't think you could ever be *that* normal. You're not exactly easy to ignore, you know."

"I will be from now on. I'll blend right in with the woodwork. I'll be downright invisible if that's what you want."

Taylor giggled—an honest-to-God schoolgirl giggle that made Sam's heart soar. "I don't think I want you to go that far."

Sam laughed with her, overwhelmed by the unexpected urge to dance until his feet hurt and sing until his voice grew hoarse. He settled for sweeping her off her feet and spinning her around that narrow alley, as if they were in a grand ballroom.

He had the sudden, intense longing to spend the rest of his life doing this very thing. And he wondered if Taylor was the reason he'd come to Heartbreak Hill.

He knew for damn sure she was the reason he wanted to stay.

Chapter 11

SAM CLOSED THE door of the men's clothing store and crossed off the last name on his list. Cody had been right about the prospects of finding a job now that summer was over. Nobody wanted help—especially, it seemed, help from someone who occasionally defended his honor by administering a solid pop in the nose. To make things worse, employers wanted references and Sam had none.

He took a few steps away from the clothing store and gazed out over the town. He was growing more used to the frantic pace of modern life. The never-ending noise didn't keep him awake all night any longer. But how in the hell was he supposed to fit in if he couldn't find a way to support himself?

His failures were making him think—about the Cinnabar, about Jesse and Elizabeth, Kurt and Olivia, and the friends he'd left behind. Going back wasn't an option, but there were times when he wondered if he'd ever succeed here, or if he'd have to spend the rest of his life sponging off Charlie.

He shook his head and headed toward the corner. No way would he spend his life being a burden to someone else. There had to be work somewhere. *Something* he could do. Someone willing to take a chance on him. He just had to keep looking. If he couldn't find a job in Heartbreak Hill, he'd have to move on.

But that prospect didn't set well, either. He was falling in love with Taylor. Cody was quickly worming his way into Sam's heart. And Charlie was one of the finest men he'd ever met. How could he leave them?

He stopped at the corner and waited for a truck to roll past. When the intersection was clear again, he caught a glimpse of Charlie halfway down the next block. Charlie looked up and saw Sam, waved, and hurried toward him.

"I wondered where you'd gotten to this morning," he said when he drew closer.

"I've been looking for work." Sam crumpled his list and shoved it into his pocket. "With no luck."

"You'll find something. Persistence is the name of that game." Charlie started walking slowly.

Sam laughed harshly and fell into step beside him. "I hope you're right."

Charlie sent him a sidelong glance. "You're down in the mouth this morning. Anything I can help with?"

As if he wasn't already doing enough. Sam shook his head and stuffed his hands into his pockets. "Thanks, but I'll be fine." Eventually.

"That's not what I asked."

Sam let out a weak laugh. "There's nothing you can do, Charlie. It's just a bad day, I guess. I can't stop thinking about all I left behind. Wondering what happened to my brother and his wife, my friends, the ranch. Questioning whether I'll ever build a life for myself here."

"Sure you will. You're smart, strong, honest. You have a place to stay as long as you need it. You've only been here a little while. Don't be so hard on yourself." Charlie gave Sam's shoulder a fatherly squeeze. "As for your family . . . There are ways you could check."

"Cody already checked on that com-puter of Taylor's. He couldn't find anything."

"The computer's not the only place to look. Not by a long shot. If it was me, I'd spend some time in the library."

"I didn't realize you have a lending library here."

"We have a good one since we're the only town of any size for quite a ways in any direction. The county put in some new computers a few years ago, and they're always bragging about how a person can find anything they need without setting foot outside the city limits."

Sam followed Charlie into the street to avoid a crew of men removing extra trash cans from the boardwalk. He nodded back toward the crew. "I could do something like that, if only someone would give me a chance." He took a deep breath and tried to shake off his mood. "If I can't find work, maybe I can keep myself busy searching for news of my family. Could you show me where the library is and how to use it?"

"I can show you where it is," Charlie said, "but you'd better get someone else to show you around. I know how to get myself a book when I want one, but research is another matter entirely." He waved to a man who stepped out of a building across the street and took another long look at Sam. "Is that the only thing on your mind?"

Sam shrugged, but he was surprised to find that being in the presence of a friend helped drain away some of his tension. "The whole point of leaving Cortez was to test myself. I wanted to find out just what I'm made of. I don't much like what I see."

"What's wrong with what you see?"

"I thought I had more steel in my backbone. I thought I had what it took to make my own way. I'm no better now, taking your charity, than I was living off my pa's accomplishments. Maybe I don't have what it takes."

Charlie ran a hand across the back of his neck and let his gaze drift out over the street. "I'd argue that point, but if you're determined to find fault with yourself, I guess you will. So I'll just keep my eyes and ears open for work you can do. Then you can stop feeling sorry for yourself and get on with what you came here for—falling in love with that daughter of mine."

"I can't afford to fall in love," Sam muttered. "Not yet."

Charlie stopped beside a post and turned to face him squarely. "Is that right?"

"Taylor's wonderful," Sam said, hoping he hadn't inadvertently offended Charlie. "She's beautiful and intelligent, and she'd keep a man on his toes for the rest of his life. If I could fall in love with anyone, it would definitely be her. But I can't ask for permission to court her when I have no prospects of ever supporting a wife."

"You're just in a temporary slump," Charlie assured him. "I just wish I knew why some people find it so easy to shut the door on love when it comes knocking. You're as blind and stubborn as that daughter of mine—and if you both don't wake up and smell the coffee, you'll end up alone and miserable when you could have been happy together. How smart is that?"

"Are you telling me you want Taylor to get involved with a man who can't even hold his own weight?"

"I want her to be happy. I don't know how much she's told you about Cody's father . . ." Charlie's gaze drifted, avoiding eye contact.

"She's said a little."

"That's all she ever says. She likes to pretend it never happened, I guess." Charlie let out a deep sigh and scuffed his feet on the boardwalk for a while. Just when Sam figured they'd left that subject behind, he started up again. "After Nate ran off, Taylor closed her heart to men. I guess she figured all men were made of the same stuff."

"Can't blame her. She was hurt."

"Hurt bad." Charlie smiled uneasily. "Broke my heart to watch her. And I hate to see her carrying a grudge all these years later. She's a good girl, Sam. She has a whole lot of love to give. I'd like to see her happy."

"She seems content with her life the way it is." Sam didn't know if that was entirely true, or if maybe he was trying to make himself feel better for ignoring the attraction between them? "She has a job she loves and people seem to like her."

"Friends are fine as far as they go," Charlie said, "but they can't always fill the lonely spots in a person's heart."

"And you think Taylor has lonely spots?"

"I know she does. I'm her father." Charlie smoothed a

palm across his hair. "She's gettin' by, Sam. She's gettin' by fine. But a man has hopes for his children. Wants to see them truly happy. Loved." He lifted his gaze again. "There's not a finer thing in this life than to be loved."

"You might be right," Sam said, "but I wouldn't know." He stopped walking, surprised by the bitterness in his tone, staggered by the realization that he'd never felt truly loved. Not by his father, who'd only wanted someone to take over the ranch when he died. Not by his mother, who'd resented Sam and Jesse for tying her to a life she hated. Not by the one woman who'd captured his heart in the past. His brother was the only person who'd truly loved him—and Sam had turned his back on Jesse when he jumped into the future.

His stomach knotted painfully and for a few seconds he worried that he might be sick. He'd spent hours missing Jesse and feeling sorry for himself. But he'd never really considered that Jesse might have been hurt by his disappearance.

If a man couldn't even be a decent brother, he had no business thinking about marriage or fatherhood.

As the afternoon wore on, Sam found himself wishing he'd never had that conversation with Charlie. The more he thought about it, the emptier he felt. He reminded himself that plenty of people went through life without ever giving or receiving love, but it didn't make him feel better.

He tried to shake off his low spirits, and when someone passed him carrying a cup full of soda and an order of French fries, he decided that hunger wasn't making his mood much better. He had a five-dollar bill in his pocket. Charlie had pressed it into his hands earlier. Might as well find something to eat and see if a full stomach would help.

He walked the two blocks to High Mountain Burgers and placed an order for french-fried potatoes and a slab of beef on a round piece of bread. To prove to himself how well he'd adjusted, he added a Coke and leaned against the counter to wait.

The clerk, a spotty girl with a round face punched buttons on her machine and smiled up at him with a mouth full of metal when she'd finished. "That'll be seven eighty-five."

"*How* much?"

"Seven eighty-five."

"Ridiculous. Where I come from, a man could live for a long time on that much money."

The girl ran her tongue across the metal on her teeth. "Funny." She held out her hand and bounced a little on one leg. When Sam didn't immediately hand over the cash, she shifted and started bouncing on the other. "Do you want your food or not?"

He didn't want to admit that he didn't have enough money, and he was still in shock that a simple meal could cost so much. Before he could decide how to extricate himself without embarrassment, a soft, round woman with a head full of brown curls and a warm, welcome smile, slid up to the window beside him.

"Is there a problem, Mandi?" The woman's breasts peeked out over the top of her blouse.

Her legs and arms were completely bared.

In fact, Sam could have sworn she was wearing nothing but her undergarments.

Mandi worked her lips over the metal and jerked her head toward Sam. "Only that he doesn't want to pay for his food."

"I didn't say that," Sam protested. "The price just seems a little steep, that's all."

The dark-haired woman looked him over slowly. "You're Sam Evans, aren't you?"

"I am, but I don't believe I've had the pleasure."

"Irene Beers. I'm a friend of Taylor O'Brien's."

"My pleasure." He turned his attention back to Mandi, who was busy rolling her eyes at a man who'd started muttering about having to wait. "How much for just the potatoes and the drink?"

Mandi gave him a look that could have bent a horseshoe. "You want to forget the burger?"

"I might. How much?"

Irene leaned one arm on the counter and her breasts squished together. "Can I buy your lunch?"

Sam half-expected one to flip out of her blouse. "I don't think so, but thank you for offering."

"No, really. I'd love to." She dug a bill from her purse and pushed it toward Mandi. "Give us two of whatever he ordered." She gave a little jiggle and smiled up at Sam. "I've been dying to meet you, and this will give us a chance to get to know each other."

It was bad enough that Charlie was supporting him. Sam couldn't accept charity from a woman. He was just about to refuse again when the man behind him muttered something sharp and angry.

"Call me when our lunch is ready," Irene sang out to Mandi, and tugged Sam away from the window.

"Thanks," Sam grumbled. "I'm not used to having ladies buy my lunch, but I suppose there's a first time for everything." *And a last.*

"That's exactly how *I* feel," Irene said with a laugh and another jiggle. "I'm *so* like that. If every day isn't an adventure, what's the point?"

What, indeed?

She flounced into a chair and arranged her breasts to their best advantage. "Taylor tells me you're staying with Charlie. How long will you be in town?"

"Hard to say." Sam kept his eyes riveted on hers. He refused to let them drop to her chest. "I guess that'll depend on whether or not I can find work."

"Oh? What kind of work are you looking for?"

"Anything I can get. I've done some ranching in my time, so I was hoping I'd find something along that line."

Her lips pursed in what Sam would've sworn was an invitation. "My brother runs the hardware store here in Heartbreak Hill. He told me last night that he's looking for someone to help out."

Sam sat a little straighter. Maybe this lunch wasn't such a disaster, after all. He knew hardware. At least, he had once. And what he didn't know, he could learn. "If you'll tell me where to find him, I'll see what he's got."

Irene bit her bottom lip and smiled seductively. "I'd be glad to introduce you."

"I don't want to take you away from . . . whatever you have to do."

Irene beamed and rotated one plump shoulder. "Don't be silly. What are friends for? And I *do* hope we're going to be friends."

"I'm sure we will be." What *else* could he say?

She reached across the table and touched his hand. "You'll tell me if I'm overstepping my bounds, won't you? Taylor told me the two of you are only friends. That's right, isn't it?"

Sam would've been happy to claim more, but he didn't want to jeopardize Taylor's reputation, especially since he couldn't state his intentions. "That's right. Only friends."

Irene's hand moved softly across his, but the contact brought him no pleasure. He drew away, pretending his nose needed scratching.

"I can't say I'm disappointed." Irene's voice dropped dramatically and began to sound downright sultry. "But imagine having a big, strapping, handsome man like you living right next door and not being interested."

Imagine.

"But, then, Taylor hasn't really gone out with *anyone* since Cody's father. And I guess I don't blame her. She went through hell when she found out she was pregnant. I remember." Irene broke off and covered her mouth. Her eyes widened and her shoulders sagged. "I can't believe I just said that. But if you and Taylor are friends, you already know, don't you?"

"I know a little." Sam didn't know what else to say. Luckily, Mandi showed up carrying a tray of food and gave him a short reprieve. He unwrapped his burger, pulled off all the trimmings, and tossed the bread onto his tray. But he felt like a cad letting a slight to Taylor's reputation go unanswered. "I was under the impression that the problem with Cody's father happened a long time ago."

Irene's gaze faltered. "Well, yes, it did. And I didn't mean to sound like I'm gossiping about her. I like Taylor a lot, even if I don't understand her." She ate a french fry or two, and she seemed so honestly distraught, Sam decided maybe she wasn't so bad. He wondered if Taylor knew how far the gossip had spread.

"You know," Irene went on after a minute, "I haven't thought about Cody's father for years, but for some reason he's been on my mind lately. And Shauna Parsons was talking about him at the Beauty Spot the other day. I just can't imagine why *she'd* be talking about him, either."

"Hutton Stone," Sam said around a mouthful of beef.

Irene's eyes widened. "You think he'd stir up talk about her?"

"Who else has reason to?"

Irene popped another couple of fries into her mouth and let out a heavy sigh. "Nobody, I guess. But that's so . . . *nasty*. This is Heartbreak Hill. We're not supposed to have ugly things like that going on."

"Ugly things go on no matter where you live. It just takes the right kind of people—or should I say the wrong kind?"

"I know, but—that's just wrong. Poor Taylor."

Taylor's image floated in front of him, soft and vulnerable and easily hurt. He felt like a cad for adding to her problems, even for a minute. He'd give anything to help instead of heaping more worries on her shoulders.

Irene squeezed something from a red container and stirred it listlessly with a french fry. "The problem with Hutton Stone is that he's such a paragon of fricking virtue, you know? And his wife is just as bad. They never do anything really wrong, and they're not very nice to people who do."

Sam thought about what she'd said as he polished off his lunch, and by the time he and Irene started toward the hardware store, he'd made a decision.

It was time to pay Hutton Stone a visit.

Irene bounced and jiggled and chattered all the way through town to her brother's hardware store. It didn't seem to matter what she said, as long as she was saying something. Sam wondered if she ever tired of the sound of her own voice. *He* was certainly growing weary of it.

"And that over there," she said, waving a hand toward something across the street. "That's where I have my hair done. You probably won't believe this, but this isn't my natural color. . . ."

Sam smiled as if he cared and followed her hand when she wagged it toward a sad-looking woman trying to get a passel of kids to follow her out of the food store.

"That's Lisa Mooney," Irene whispered when they were out of earshot. "Her husband? Joe? He lost his job a few months ago, and I've *heard*, but I don't know if it's true, that their marriage is in trouble because, you know, of all their kids and the bills. Not that I'm gossiping." Irene's hand fluttered over her breasts. "I just like to *know* what's going on with friends and neighbors so I don't accidentally say the wrong thing when I meet them."

Her hand took flight again and aimed at a group of men on a bench in front of the feed store. "That's who you want to watch out for when it comes to gossip. I don't know why people say women like to talk. Men can be a hundred times worse."

Before Sam could even get a look at them, she was pointing at something else. "See that building? The one with the dark wood? That's the Moosehead Lodge. If you ever want to go out for a drink, that's *the* place to go unless you're a tourist." She beamed and added, "Come to think of it, I'd be glad to take you to the Moosehead and introduce you."

Sam tried to work up a regretful smile. "Maybe someday. I'm still trying to adjust to being here."

"Oh. Sure. Taylor said you'd been through some rough times. I want you to know that I'm an excellent listener—if you ever want to talk about it."

"I'll keep that in mind."

"Seriously, I love listening to friends. I'm very empathetic." She tucked a hand beneath his arm and brushed against him. "And I know how to help a man feel better."

Sam drew away and put some space between them. "I'll keep that in mind, too. How much further to this hardware store?"

"Just up the street." She pointed to a low-slung cinder-block building on the next block. "I know DeWayne will hire you if I ask him to."

"DeWayne?" Sam ground to a halt. "DeWayne from the shoot-out?"

Irene giggled. "Don't worry about that. DeWayne's not the type to hold a grudge."

Sam hoped she was right. He was running out of options.

Five minutes later Sam stood stock-still while DeWayne Beers walked around him on the sidewalk outside his store. Irene had made herself comfortable on the trunk of a nearby car.

DeWayne crushed a cigarette with the toe of his boot and blew out a cloud of smoke. "You want a job, huh?"

"I could use one."

"You know your way around hardware and tools?"

"Pretty much."

DeWayne gave him a long, slow look with one eye. "Where else have you worked?"

Irene shifted herself to a new position and dangled one leg provocatively. "Lighten up, DeWayne. Just hire him, okay?"

Sam appreciated her backing him, but he didn't want to owe her more than he already did. "I ran a ranch back in Colorado for a spell."

"A spell? How long is a spell, exactly?"

"A few years."

DeWayne tapped another smoke out of his pack, caught Irene's quick frown, and tucked it behind his ear. "How many is a few?"

"Several. It was a family-run business. I spent most of my life there."

DeWayne stopped circling. "Why'd you leave?"

"I wanted to start fresh somewhere I'd never been before."

DeWayne nodded slowly. "You dependable?"

"As the sun."

"And you expect me to hire you after what you did at the shoot-out?"

Sam smiled sheepishly. "Sorry about that. It was a misunderstanding. Hope I didn't hurt you."

DeWayne squared his shoulders and laughed through his nose. "Hell, no. Just surprised me and Kip a little. We weren't expecting the Lone Ranger to show up."

"It was an honest mistake," Sam assured him. "Hope you're willing to treat it like one."

DeWayne appraised him for a few more seconds, then dipped his head once. "Why not? Taylor seems to like you, and so does Irene. Guess I'll give you a chance."

Sam thought the relief might knock the legs out from under him. "You won't be sorry."

"I hope not." DeWayne rested one foot on the car's bumper. "I'll need you here every morning before eight."

"That's not a problem."

"The pay's not much."

"Can I live on it?"

"If you're careful."

"Then it sounds fine. When do you want me to start?"

DeWayne looked at Irene, pulled the cigarette from behind his ear, and lit up. "Tomorrow too soon?"

"Tomorrow's fine."

"Eight o'clock." DeWayne scowled in response to Irene's delighted smile and tossed his barely touched cigarette into the gutter. "Don't be late."

Irene tagged along with Sam as he walked back through town, still chattering like a magpie. Never in his life had he heard a woman so in love with the sound of her own voice.

When a person didn't notice her right off, she'd find a way to get their attention. Sam had started wondering if she *wanted* people to see them together. And that made him even more anxious to part company. He owed her something for introducing him to DeWayne, but she wasn't the kind of woman he wanted to keep company with.

After what felt like hours, they made it back to the burger stand and Sam stopped walking. "Well, here we are. Right back where we started."

"So soon?" Irene sagged with disappointment, but she perked up again almost immediately. "Would you like to see my store?"

"Afraid I can't right now. Some other time, maybe." When he could bring Charlie or Cody—or even Taylor along.

"It's just right here." She slipped one hand beneath his arm and tugged him around toward a small store about two steps away. "I'd love to show you around."

Sam disengaged himself casually. "Sorry. I can't. I have a few more things to take care of before I head back to Charlie's."

"Oh, I see." Irene gave her hair a fluff with one hand. Her face creased in thought. "You could always run your errands and then come back here. I'd be glad to give you a ride home."

Sam backed a step away, trying not to look anxious to be gone. "Another time."

He put a few more feet between them, waved in response to the finger-wriggle she aimed at him, and turned away before she could stop him. He didn't relax completely or slow his pace until he'd put a couple of blocks behind him.

He was starting to recognize landmarks in town. He was growing used to the weathered wood on each of the buildings, the rich scent of the ice-cream parlor, the sweetened air of the candy shop next door, the strange smell that wiped out everything else by the photo shop.

He could get used to this in time.

He slowed a bit further and paid particular attention to the storefronts he'd never noticed before, looking for Hutton Stone's real estate business. After several minutes he saw the sign he was looking for swinging gently in the breeze ahead. Smiling grimly, he adjusted the angle of his hat and stepped into the office.

It took a few blinks for his eyes to adjust after being outside for so long, and by the time he could see, the man was almost upon him. Tall, though not as tall as Sam. Portly, with an insincere smile and quick, darting eyes that seemed to see everything at once.

He held out a pudgy hand and gripped Sam's before Sam could react. "Well, well, well. The mountain comes to Mohammed."

"Excuse me?"

"The old saying. If you can't make Mohammed go to the mountain . . ." He wagged his hand as if Sam was supposed to know the rest and perched his ample bottom on a spindle railing that ran the length of the office. "Mr. Evans, right? To what do I owe this pleasure?"

Sam gave Hutton a long, slow, deliberate once-over. "You're Hutton Stone?"

"I am."

"And you're running for sheriff against Taylor O'Brien?"

"That's right." Hutton flicked something from the knee of his black trousers. "But I suspect you already know the answers to both of those questions or you wouldn't be here."

Sam acknowledged that with a nod.

Hutton smiled again, a thin, unfriendly curve of the lips. "Obviously, you're a man of few words, so we'll cut to the chase. What do you want?"

"I've been hearing talk around town. I figure it's coming from you."

"Is that right?" Hutton shrugged eloquently. "We're in the middle of a campaign. Talk is inevitable. If Taylor can't stand the heat, maybe she should get out of the kitchen instead of sending a goon to intimidate me."

Sam didn't have to understand the word to know he'd just been insulted. "She didn't send me," he said, letting his gaze move slowly through Hutton's office and then, finally, slip back to the man's pudgy face. "She doesn't even know I'm here. I just wanted to see what kind of man is so afraid of losing that he'd resort to stirring up things long forgotten."

Hutton laughed sharply. "I assure you, Mr. Evans, I haven't done a thing. And I'm certainly not afraid of losing this election to Taylor O'Brien."

"Is that right?"

"One-hundred percent right." Hutton stood, but Sam

thought he seemed a touch less certain. "She's totally ill-suited to the job. Voters are beginning to realize that. If they're stirring up old gossip, I can't be held responsible for that."

"Unless you're behind it."

"Which I'm not."

Sam could feel the lie hovering between them, but he had a firm rule about not acting without proof. "Glad to hear it. I'd hate to find out otherwise."

"And if you did?"

Sam had another rule, this one learned at his father's knee. *Never let the enemy know your next move.* He shrugged. "I guess we'll never know, will we?"

"I guess not." Hutton folded his arms and regarded Sam slowly. "Just who are you, Evans? Where did you come from, and why are you in Heartbreak Hill?"

"That's my business."

"Maybe." Hutton propped his hands on his hips and smiled ice. "And maybe we all deserve to know who's exerting influence over our sheriff."

Sam laughed. "If you think anyone influences Sheriff O'Brien, you don't know her very well."

The ice crept into Hutton's eyes. "I only know what I see. She's let you get away with three counts of assault. I wonder why."

The scoundrel's meaning was clear enough. Sam balled his hands into fists but forced himself to leave them there. "And I wonder how any man who elevates himself by defaming an innocent woman's reputation can look himself in the mirror." He yanked open the door and started through it. "Just keep the fight fair, Stone. That's all."

"Or?"

"You can find out if you want to. It's up to you." He tugged at his hat brim and grinned. "Nice meeting you, Mr. Stone. I'm sure I'll be seeing you around."

He let himself outside and closed the door before Hutton could respond, tipped his hat so he could feel the afternoon sun on his face, and whistled all the way to Charlie's house.

Chapter 12

SAM SAT ON Charlie's back steps, feeling better than he had in days. The hardware store might not be the answer to his dreams, but at least he had work. He might not have solved all of Taylor's problems, but he'd made his presence felt.

He stared at a section of loose boards for several minutes before it dawned on him that he could do something for Charlie, as well. Whistling softly, he dug around in Charlie's shed until he found a hammer and some nails, then carried them back outside just as Cody came flying down the driveway on his way home from school.

The boy skidded to a stop, his hair flopped into his eyes, and his mouth stretched into a wide, delighted smile. He brushed back his hair and glanced at the tools in Sam's hands. "What are you doing?"

"Thought I'd fix some of those boards on your grandpa's fence."

"Cool. Can I help?"

"You know how?"

"Heck, yeah. I'm good with tools. Just ask Grandpa if you don't believe me."

Sam rested the hammer on his shoulder. "Why wouldn't I believe you?"

"I don't know. You might not. Sometimes people don't."

"I don't doubt someone's word unless they're in the habit of lying. Have you ever lied to me before?"

Cody's gaze flickered away. "No."

"You plan on lying to me in the future?"

"No."

"You plan on lying to anybody else?"

Cody's cheeks reddened and his gaze locked on his toes. "No."

"Well, then, I guess your word is good enough." Sam put a hand on Cody's shoulder. "What about schoolwork? Do you have any?"

"Only math, and I can do that later."

Sam quirked an eyebrow. "Is that right?"

"Sure. I don't have much. I can get it done in fifteen minutes, maybe less. I'll just do it after dinner."

"And your mother won't care?"

"Nope." Cody's gaze faltered again. "As long as I get it done."

"I have your word on that?"

"I *think* so."

"Maybe you should ask your mother to make sure." At Cody's disappointed scowl, he added, "I'll wait."

Cody hopped up the stairs and disappeared into the house. Sam barely had time to walk to the end of the driveway to see if anything else needed fixing before the boy was back again. It had been a long time since anyone wanted to be around Sam quite so much. Not since Jesse was a kid and thought the sun rose and set on Sam's shoulders had anyone been quite so delighted in his company. Truth to tell, it was pretty damned hard to resist.

The soles of Cody's shoes slapped the driveway as he caught up with Sam; two bright spots of color flamed on his cheeks. "Mom says it's okay for me to help you as long as I don't bug you. I told her I'm not going to *bother* you, I'm going to *help*."

"You're darn right you're going to help." Sam jerked his head toward the shed. "Bring out that little ladder of your grandpa's and carry it around to the backyard. Can you handle that?"

"Can I!" Cody raced off as if he'd been given a rare treat, and Sam watched him go with a fond smile.

Cody banged out of the shed with the ladder, one end screeching as it dragged along the driveway. "Where do you want it?"

Sam bit back a smile and waved him toward the far corner. "Just put it in the corner while I check some of that wood piled behind the shed to see if there's any we can use."

The ladder bumped along the lawn while Cody dragged it into place and broke the silence with a loud clatter as the boy dropped it. "Sam?"

Sam hunkered down in front of the woodpile and started sorting. "Yeah?"

Cody came up behind him and leaned against the wall of the shed. "Does it count as lying if you just don't tell somebody something?"

Sam paused with a rotting piece of timber in his hands. "I don't know if that counts as a lie, but sometimes you've got to take other things into consideration. Will not telling hurt someone?"

"Maybe. But telling might hurt more."

Sam lowered the wood to the pile and brushed his hands on his pant legs. "Suppose you tell me what it is. Maybe I can help you decide what to do."

"Will you tell?"

"Not if you don't want me to."

"Promise?"

Sam nodded and pushed to his feet. "What is it, boy?"

"Well . . . see, it's about my dad. First of all, I kinda lied to you when I told you that he died."

"You did?"

"Yeah. But that was before I knew you. I mean, you were in jail, you know? I haven't lied to you since then."

Sam found a place to sit on the woodpile and gestured for Cody to join him. "Okay. We'll count ourselves square as long as it doesn't happen again. What else are you worrying about?"

Cody climbed onto the pile of wood and mirrored Sam's position. "It's my mom. I'm afraid that if I tell her what I've done, she'll be mad at me."

"What have you done?"

"Well, you know the Internet? There are places there where you can look for people who are still alive, you know? And I kinda . . ." His gaze traveled to his toes again. "I kinda posted that I was looking for my dad."

"And your mother doesn't know?"

"Are you kidding?" Cody's gaze shot back to Sam's face. He looked horrified. "She'd be royally pissed if she knew. But she doesn't get it, you know? I mean, somewhere out there I have a *dad*. I just want to know who he is and see if maybe he wants to know me."

Sam linked his hands over his knees. "Have you heard anything from him?"

The excitement in Cody's eyes died away. "Not yet. I probably haven't found the right places yet."

"How will you feel if he doesn't contact you?"

"I don't know."

"Well, for what it's worth, he's a fool if he doesn't. Any man would be damn lucky to have you for a son."

Cody blinked up at him. Smiled. Ducked his head again. "I want to keep looking, but you know what you said about lying. It's not that I want to lie to my mom, but she won't let me do it if she knows."

Sam wished the kid hadn't felt compelled to tell *him*. How could he keep this secret from Taylor? How could he break his word to Cody? He took a deep, steadying breath and stroked his moustache thoughtfully. "There's one thing I've learned about secrets," he said after several minutes. "They're hard to keep. Sooner or later they always catch up with you."

Cody's expression fell. "Nuh-uh."

"I'm afraid so. It never fails."

"I don't want my mom to find out."

"She will." Sam put a hand on the boy's knee and stood.

"Telling the truth isn't always easy, but in the long run it's always easier than dealing with the trouble a lie can bring." He adjusted his hat and ruffled the boy's hair. "But that's something every man needs to figure out for himself. I'm sure you'll make the right decision."

He walked away slowly, whistling, checking the sky for signs of an approaching storm, and listening until he heard Cody scramble off the boards to come after him.

Taylor leaned back in her chair and fingered the envelope that had just arrived by courier. The fax had come in while she was on patrol—a set of tiny pictures so grainy she hadn't been able to distinguish anyone's features. Even so, she knew that Sam was the tall man in the first picture and that Olivia was the woman whose delicate, beautiful face peered into the camera in the second photo. Even with the poor fax quality, Taylor knew she'd never be a match for Olivia Hamilton Richards.

She slit the envelope and slowly pulled out the copies Detective Sweeney had sent her. Sam's deep scowl as he posed beside his brother was lightened by the glint of humor in his eyes. His hand rested on his brother's shoulder, and even with their stiff poses and serious expressions, she could sense the deep affection between them.

She touched Sam's face and traced her finger along the curve of his mustache, then set the copy aside and forced herself to look at the second picture. Hard as it was to see Olivia, maybe it was for the best. It certainly put a quick end to any fanciful thoughts she'd been having.

Olivia's posture was absolutely perfect, her eyes deep and dark, her lips full and perfectly curved. Her hair thick and brown, and her smile secretive and alluring. It didn't matter that she'd married the good-looking guy in the picture with her. Olivia's heart wasn't the one in question. Olivia might have chosen Kurt Richards, but Sam had chosen her. How could Taylor—a plain Jane at best—*possibly* compete with a woman who looked like this?

She set the picture aside and started to run her fingers through her hair, caught herself and pulled her hand away.

Why was she even thinking this way? She didn't *want* to compete with Olivia Richards or anyone else. She didn't want a man in her life—not right now, anyway. She and Cody had enough to deal with.

She slipped the pictures back into the envelope and tucked the envelope into her top drawer, made it halfway across the room, and doubled back to grab the envelope. The photos had no meaning for her, and Sam would probably treasure them—even if they were only copies of the originals.

She let herself out of the office, locked it behind her, and started down the boardwalk. She felt better now that she'd made a decision, and she could hardly wait to give him the pictures. It would prove, not only to Sam but to her self, that she had no interest in Sam beyond friendship.

A storm had started moving into the valley, and the sky was low with moisture-laden clouds. They moved quickly across the horizon, hit the mountains, and bunched there. They matched her mood exactly, though she didn't understand why it should matter so much that Sam was in love with someone else. Yes, she was learning to like him— maybe even a little more—but she certainly wasn't falling in *love* with him. It had been so long since she'd had any attention from a man, she was probably overreacting.

That was pathetic. And Taylor refused to be pathetic.

She decided to leave the patrol car and walk off her mood. Two blocks later she regretted her decision. The wind picked up and flung bits of leaves and dirt along the street. She ducked her head as she passed Bissell's Drugstore, but by the time she reached the corner, stinging pellets of rain slashed at her face.

She turned back quickly. She'd have to take refuge inside and hope the storm wouldn't last.

Inside Bissell's the overhead lights looked almost too bright against the darkening sky. Several laughing groups of people clustered near the windows to keep an eye on the storm. Taylor wasn't in the mood for making small talk, so she ducked down the far aisle and headed toward the back of the store, where Hyrum Bissell kept chairs for customers waiting for prescriptions.

She'd only gone a few steps when she realized Lisa Mooney and her husband were at the far end of the aisle. Three of their children stood slightly to one side, but Cody's friend Justin wasn't one of them.

Taylor couldn't hear the conversation between Joe and Lisa, but the way Joe loomed over his wife, and Lisa's self-protective posture, urged Taylor closer. She smiled as if she wanted only to say hello or comment on the weather.

Joe broke off whatever he'd been saying and jerked away from Lisa. "Sheriff."

"Evening, Joe. Lisa." Taylor turned her smile on the children, but only the youngest, Jasmine, who must have been about five, smiled back.

Lisa hunched her shoulders and sidled away from her husband. "Evening, Taylor."

Taylor checked quickly for visible bruises—not that she'd seriously thought Joe would batter his wife. But anyone might be capable of anything if they were pushed hard enough, and five children and no job might be provocation, even for Joe. He certainly looked more volatile than she'd ever seen him.

"Quite a storm, isn't it?" She kept her tone light and easy.

Lisa nodded and tucked a lock of hair behind one ear. "It won't last long, though. Summer storms never do."

Joe shot Lisa a look so full of venom, Taylor couldn't pretend she hadn't seen it. "Is everything all right?"

"Everything's fine," Joe said. "Just perfect." The words came out clipped. Harsh. Bitter.

"You seem upset, Joe. Do you want to talk about it?"

Lisa put a few more inches between herself and her husband. "It's okay, Taylor. Just a family disagreement. We'll be fine."

"Are you sure? I'd be glad to give you and the kids a ride home." *And give Joe a chance to cool off.*

"She said it's fine," Joe snapped. "Why does everybody

in this town think they have the right to butt in to a man's business?"

"Nobody's butting in," Taylor said evenly. "I just want to make sure that Lisa and the kids get home okay."

"The kids will be fine. And Lisa's a big girl. I'm sure she can get herself wherever she wants to go." Joe waved a hand toward the kids, who bolted down the aisle like rabbits. Tossing one more loaded look at Lisa, he followed.

Lisa laughed uncomfortably when he'd gone and smoothed her hair with one trembling hand. "It was really nothing, Taylor. Things have been a little strained since Joe lost his job, that's all. Please don't make this into something it's not."

"I hope you're right, Lisa. But promise me that if things get worse, you'll call me. I don't want anything to happen to you or the kids."

Lisa's eyes rounded in shock. "Joe wouldn't hurt us. He's not that way."

"For your sakes, I hope not."

Lisa laughed again and shook her head again. "Really, Taylor. Joe would never hurt me. The worst he'd do is punch a hole in the wall. Please, just forget about this."

Taylor nodded reluctantly. She'd drop it for now, but she wouldn't forget. When Lisa left, she spent a few minutes trying to calm herself, but nervous energy kept her moving up and down the aisles.

When she strolled down the makeup aisle, the picture of Olivia still tucked beneath her arm made her hesitate instead of curling her nose and passing by.

Maybe Charlie was right. Maybe she did need to pay a little more attention to her appearance. She wasn't talking about a *lot* of makeup. Certainly nothing elaborate. But it might not hurt to accentuate some of her better features.

The trouble was, she didn't even know where to begin. Oh, she knew the basics. Foundation ought to be foundation, but there were at least a dozen varieties hanging from hooks on pieces of cardboard with all sorts of features blazoned on the front to convince her to buy this one instead of that. She had no idea whether she wanted a light translucent base or something thick and heavy to cover the freckles on her nose and cheeks. And what about eyeshadow? Liquid or powder, or the kind that could be either? And that didn't even touch the question of color, or blush, or powder, or mascara.

"Taylor?"

A wave of Eternity hit her and she hunched her neck instinctively, just as Lisa Mooney had a few minutes before.

"Don't try to hide. You're the only woman in town who wears a uniform." Ruby pulled Taylor around to face her. "You were looking at makeup, weren't you?"

"Looking, not buying."

Ruby's eyes flickered down to her hands, empty except for the envelope. "I can see that. But you don't usually look. Is there some special occasion you haven't told me about?"

"No." Taylor lifted her chin, but the look on her friend's face tore through the layer of self-protective bristle. "Yes. Not a special occasion, exactly, but . . ." She held out the envelope miserably. ". . . this."

Ruby pulled out the photocopies and looked the first one over. "What is this?"

"A picture of Sam—taken around eighteen eighty-five. That man with him is the brother I told you about."

"But—" Ruby's eyes flicked back and forth between the picture and Taylor's face. "But—"

Taylor nodded miserably. "I know, I know. Impossible. But true. Look at the second picture."

Ruby looked, but she obviously didn't understand. "So, who are Kurt and Olivia Hamilton Richards? What do they have to do with this?"

"Not *they*," Taylor whispered. "*She*. She's the woman Sam's in love with. The one he left behind when he came here."

"Okay. So?" Ruby studied the picture for another second or two before the realization slowly began to dawn. "Oh. *Oh!* You're jealous?"

"I think so."

"Of a woman who must have been dead for . . ." Ruby checked the caption of the picture and did a quick calculation. ". . . for at least seventy-five years?"

Taylor motioned for her to lower her voice. "Whether or not she's dead, or for how long, isn't the point. The point is, she was very much *alive* when Sam left Cortez."

"Okay. She's lovely. But so are you."

Taylor laughed in disbelief. "I can see myself, Ruby. I can't even begin to compare."

"Why are you so hard on yourself? You're just as beautiful, only in a different way. It's like comparing apples and oranges. If you're falling in love with this guy—"

"I'm not falling in love. I just have a mild crush, that's all. It'll be over in a few days. A week at the most."

"And in the meantime, for this temporary crush, you're looking at *makeup*? That doesn't sound like a crush to me."

"Well, it is." Taylor snatched a card of foundation from the rack beside her. "And besides, Sam isn't the only reason I'm looking."

Ruby took the foundation away. "That's not your color. You'd look like a dead lemon with that on." She replaced it with another color. "If you insist on changing yourself, at least let me help."

"I don't want to look ridiculous."

"You won't. Trust me. Sam will fall all over himself when we're done with you." Ruby began pulling things from the racks, holding them up to Taylor's face as she talked. "Maybe one of these days you'll explain why you had to pick *now* to start being interested in men again."

"I will," Taylor vowed, "just as soon as I understand it, myself."

Taylor was so uncomfortable as Ruby drove her home an hour later, she could have been sitting on hot coals. Ruby hadn't let her peek while she worked, so Taylor had only seen herself a few minutes earlier. Her eyes looked bigger, her cheeks more sculpted, her lips fuller, but she still wasn't ready to go up against Olivia in a beauty contest.

She ran her fingers across the envelope on her lap and grimaced. "I don't think I can do this."

"Of course you can. Your coloring is spectacular. Your features are absolutely perfect. You look like a day in autumn with your hair and eyes. The only thing you need to do is start wearing the right colors for your complexion; your face would really come to life."

Taylor didn't want to get her hopes up too far, but if something that simple would make a difference, maybe she could think about it. "You're talking about buying a whole new wardrobe."

Ruby grinned. "Yes, isn't that horrible? I suppose," she said with a little sigh, "if you need to do *that*, I'd be forced to help."

"I'm quite sure you'd have to."

"And I'd probably have to buy a few new things for myself." Ruby sighed again, but her eyes danced with mischief. "And we'd probably have to spend hours and hours poring through all my mail-order catalogs."

"Yes, I guess we would."

Ruby put her hand to her forehead dramatically. "I don't know if I can hold up under the strain."

"Maybe we should forget it, then. I wouldn't want to cause you any pain."

Ruby dropped her hand and scowled as she pulled into the driveway. "If you *dare* try to deprive me of a perfectly justified shopping binge, I'll never forgive you."

Taylor smiled, but her heart wasn't in it. "I wish I could be as certain as you are that a few new clothes would make a difference."

"Oh, they will. But what would make an even bigger difference is if you stopped seeing ugly when you look in the mirror and started seeing the truth."

Taylor reached for the door handle so she could put an end to the conversation. "I do see the truth, Ruby. I don't see ugly when I look in the mirror, but I don't see beautiful, either. I'm okay, but I'm nothing to write home about."

"What on *earth* gave you that idea?"

Taylor smiled bitterly. "Think about it, Ruby. If I was

such a stunner, wouldn't *someone* have noticed me during the past eleven years? Wouldn't some man have been even mildly interested?"

"Not necessarily. You haven't wanted anyone to notice you until now, remember? If some unlucky soul had paid attention to you, you would have made his life miserable."

"You make me sound like an ogre. Have I really been that bad?"

"Not to *me*. But, then, I'm not a man." Ruby flicked her little finger across her lipstick and grinned. "As your campaign manager, I'm not sure this Sam thing is smart. But as your friend, I think it's about time. So quit selling yourself short. Get over there and strut your stuff."

Taylor hugged her friend, wondering if she'd have been so inept with feminine things if her mother had lived. "Thanks, Ruby. I mean that."

Ruby waved a hand between them. "For nothing."

Taylor grabbed the envelope and the bag holding all her new makeup treasures, and climbed out of the car. She left the bag on her back step, squared her shoulders, and headed toward Charlie's house. Her uniform ruined the effect Ruby had worked so hard to achieve, but she didn't dare change or she'd smudge her makeup and ruin her hair.

She found Sam and Cody in the backyard replacing boards that had been loose for so long she couldn't remember them any other way. She stood just inside the gate, clutching the envelope in front of her, arguing silently with herself about changing her mind.

She didn't want to give Sam the pictures and remind him of Olivia, but she couldn't keep the pictures from him. She had no right to even think about it.

Just then, Cody reached for something on the lawn and saw her. "Hey, Mom, come and look at this. These boards are practically rotted all the way through. Sam thinks we're going to have to replace the whole fence."

Sam stood and brushed his hands on the seat of his pants as he came toward her. "The rest of these boards will hold for a while, but it would be a good idea to . . . replace them. . . ." His voice trailed away completely and he looked her over slowly. "You look different. Nice. Not that you don't always look—I mean—"

Taylor laughed at his obvious confusion. "Thanks for the compliment—I think. Maybe you'd better stop while you're ahead."

Cody trotted across the lawn. He couldn't seem to let more than a few feet separate him from his new hero. "Ahead of what, Mom?"

"Before he says something he'll regret." Taylor turned the envelope in her hands. "Listen, sweetheart, could you go inside with Grandpa for a few minutes? I need some time alone with Sam."

Cody's smile drooped. "Why?"

"Please? I'll explain everything to you later, okay?"

Cody didn't move until he'd looked to Sam for direction and gotten the nod. Taylor tried not to let it bother her, but a tiny voice in the back of her head warned her that Cody just might be growing too attached.

Even with Sam's nod of approval, Cody didn't move very fast. He strolled across the lawn, head down, hands in pockets, shoulders slumped. Even though she could feel Sam watching her, she didn't speak until Cody finally let himself in the back door and, with one last, hopeful glance in case they'd changed their minds, closed it behind him.

"Don't tell me I did something wrong again." Sam asked as soon as the latch clicked.

"No, not at all." She shoved the envelope at him before she lost her nerve. "I thought maybe you would want these."

He took it with a quick glance and turned it over in his hands.

"I asked for them a few days ago," Taylor explained. "When I was still trying to prove you couldn't possibly be who you say. They came this morning."

Sam patted the envelope with one hand. "It's not thick enough for handcuffs," he said with a grin.

She tried to smile back, but her mouth felt tight and stiff. "Not handcuffs."

He reached into the envelope and slowly drew out the

photocopies. It seemed to take forever for him to look down at them, to focus, and for his eyes to dart back to her face when he realized what he was looking at. "Where did you get this?"

"The sheriff's department in Cortez."

He looked back at the photograph and touched it reverently. She couldn't be sure, but she thought she saw tears shimmering in his eyes. "This is my brother, Jesse."

"I know. That's why I thought you should have it." She swallowed thickly. "There's another one there, too."

Sam switched pages and his expression changed. A hint of a smile hovered near his lips and affection glittered in his eyes. "Why, look at that irascible old fool."

"Who?"

"Kurt. This picture was made about five years after I left. He looks like an old country farmer from way back."

What about Olivia?

"Olivia?" He looked at Taylor quickly, and she realized too late that she'd voiced her question aloud. "This is her, all right. She looks well, doesn't she?"

She looked more than "well" and he damn well knew it. "She's beautiful."

"Well, yes, she always was." He looked the picture over and sighed. Did it sound wistful? "I'm glad to see she and Kurt got married. It would've been a shame if I'd gone to all the trouble to move a hundred years away for nothing." His eyes turned the color of twilight, and he swallowed thickly. "Thank you, Taylor. These mean the world to me."

Of course they meant the world to him. She'd known they would. That's why she'd brought them. She thought about the bag full of makeup she'd left sitting on her back porch and laughed silently at herself.

What a waste of time and money that had been. She should have known better than to try to make herself into something she wasn't.

Chapter 13

TAYLOR FORKED A bite of salad into her mouth with one hand and swatted away a swarm of gnats with the other. Usually, she loved eating outside, but at the moment everything bothered her. Maybe it was the makeup that drew the bugs to her. Maybe they always buzzed around her face this much. And maybe she was still feeling the sharp sting of loss—not of Sam, actually, but of something she'd started to wish for.

It was ridiculous, she told herself. She didn't *really* want someone in her life—especially not someone who'd zapped here from another century and was in love with another woman.

She swatted another swarm of gnats and tried not to listen to the sound of Sam talking with Cody, laughing with Charlie, telling stories about his life in Cortez—the life he missed, the woman he loved. A deep discontent began in her center and spiraled outward. Discontent. Jealousy. Pain.

She couldn't be falling in love with Sam. She *couldn't* be. It was all wrong. Wrong, wrong, wrong. She didn't want to do this again. She'd been so madly in love with Nate Albright she couldn't see straight, so desperately in love she'd lost all common sense, so urgently in love that she'd actually thought she could love him enough for both of them.

Well, she wouldn't go through that again. She wouldn't *let* herself love Sam.

Really, it was a good thing she'd caught it this quickly. Before her attraction for him got out of hand. Before she lost control. She wasn't seventeen anymore. She knew how to keep her wits about her, how to keep her emotions under control—especially since she had more than herself to consider this time.

From the corner of her eye she caught Charlie sending her a look and realized that she hadn't been paying attention to the conversation around her. Cody had been chatting happily for the past several minutes, and all she knew for sure was that it had something to do with the computer.

". . . and they have chat rooms," he was telling Charlie, "and bulletin boards where you can post messages. So I thought maybe that would be the best way to find him."

Taylor drizzled a little more dressing over her salad. "Find who?"

"Nate Albright," Charlie said, his voice brittle. "Cody's decided to look for him on the Internet."

Taylor's fork slipped from between her fingers and clattered to the patio floor. "Nate Albright? Why?"

Cody lifted one shoulder and stuffed his mouth with hamburger. "He's my father, isn't he?"

"Well, yes, but—"

"So, I want to know him. I want to at least *meet* him before I'm an old man."

"You're nowhere near in danger of that," Taylor said with a thin laugh. "You've got lots of time."

"But I want to meet him *now*."

"Cody, sweetheart . . ." Taylor bent to pick up her fork and struggled with her response. She didn't want to encourage him, but discouraging him would only make him more determined. "I don't think it's a good idea right now. Maybe later."

"Later when?"

"When you're a little older and better able to handle whatever happens."

Charlie nodded thoughtfully. "She's got a point, son. There's no tellin' how Nate Albright would react to having you come looking for him."

"He might be thrilled," Taylor said quickly, not because she believed it but because she couldn't stand to see the hurt on Cody's face. "He *should* be thrilled. But people don't always react to things the way they should."

"Yeah, but if I don't try, I won't ever know."

"I'm not saying you shouldn't try." Taylor reached across the table to touch her son's hand. "Just that you should wait until you're older."

Cody jerked away from her. "I can't wait. I've already started looking. And I'm not gonna stop just because you want me to. I'm not a baby."

Sam spoke for the first time. "Maybe the boy's right. Sometimes knowing—no matter what you find out—is better than not knowing."

"That may be true for adults," Taylor said evenly, "but Cody's a child."

"He's all set to become a man."

"Where you come from, maybe. Here, he's a child."

Cody jerked to his feet, knocking his plate to the ground. "I'm *not* a baby, Mom. I'm almost eleven. And you don't have any right to stop me from looking for my dad just because you don't want to see him."

She stood to face him, stinging from the pain in his eyes, the anger on his face. "I have the right to protect you," she said firmly. "I have the responsibility to protect you."

Cody's lip curled. "It's not *me* you want to protect, it's *you*."

Taylor recoiled as if he'd slapped her. She would have preferred that he had. Her heart felt as if it would shatter into a million pieces. "That's not true. You're more important to me than anything in this world."

"The campaign's all you care about!" Cody shouted. "It's the only thing you care about. You're never home and you don't even think about anything else. Well, guess what,

Mom. I hate the stupid campaign, and I hope you lose." Cody kicked his plate out of the way and took off across the yard.

Taylor raced after him, but he was too quick. By the time she reached the front yard, he'd already disappeared. She stood there, panting and breathless, trying to decide which way to go search for him.

"Let him go, Taylor."

She whipped around to find Sam a few feet behind her. "I can't. He's too upset."

"He'll be back. He just needs to blow off some steam."

"He could get hurt. He could—"

"He could. But he probably won't." Sam narrowed the distance between them. "Whether you want to believe it or not, he's right on the threshold of manhood. Give him some dignity."

"If he wants to be treated like an adult," she snapped, "he should behave like one."

Sam took a long look up the street and hooked his thumbs in the waist of his jeans. "When I was back in Cortez and my father was alive, I had a dream of making it on my own somewhere. Every time I started making plans, the old man derailed me. I know he meant well. He was afraid I'd make a mistake, and maybe I would have. But it would've been nice to find out."

"There's no comparison between that situation and this."

"Are you sure about that?"

"He never even asked about his father until last week."

"That doesn't mean he never thought about him." Sam stared straight ahead. "You can't choose the boy's dreams for him, Taylor. You can't change what he wants."

"I'm not trying to."

"No?"

"No."

Sam let his gaze slip over to hers for no more than a heartbeat, then turned back toward the house and left her alone.

• • •

Taylor lifted one slat in her blinds and checked out the window. Cody had been gone for more than an hour, and she was beginning to regret listening to Sam. The self-enforced delay ate at her patience until her skin felt as if something was crawling across it.

She'd kept busy. Idleness only made her imagination run in circles. During the past hour she'd cleaned her kitchen counters, mopped the floor, and filled the trash can with the junk mail she'd been ignoring for weeks.

And there was still no sign of Cody.

A dog darted out from a house across the street, and the unexpected movement caught her off guard, sent her heart ricocheting in her chest and sucked her breath away. When a neighbor's door slammed, she felt it all the way to her toes.

She opened the window partway so she could hear, but the only sounds that reached her were leaves rustling in the light wind. The sky was overcast with clouds left over from the afternoon's rainstorm, dark gray and ominous.

This was ridiculous. Why was she waiting? Sam knew nothing about raising a child. He'd come from a safer time. A quieter time. A time when parents didn't have to wonder if their child might be snatched from their own front yard if they turned their backs.

Dropping the blind, she hurried to the counter and snagged her keys. She grabbed her purse and pushed through the door, cursing herself silently as she raced toward the car. She struggled to fit the key in the car door, but her fingers refused to work. She'd never forgive Sam if anything happened to Cody.

She'd never forgive herself.

She heard the sound of a footstep behind her, and she turned quickly, fully prepared to argue with Sam or tell Charlie to mind his own business. Instead, she saw Cody at the end of the driveway, his tiny shoulders stooped. That blessed, beautiful, stubborn lock of hair fell over his forehead and covered one eye, which wasn't looking at her anyway.

She let out a cry of relief and ran to him. She pulled him

close and kissed his cheek. "I've been so worried about you, sweetheart. Are you okay?"

He squirmed in her embrace, planted his hands on her shoulders, and pushed her away. "Jeez, Mom. Don't *do* that. I told you, I'm not a baby anymore."

Stung, Taylor dropped her arms and took a step backward. "Where have you been?"

Cody lifted one narrow shoulder. "Around."

"Around *where*?"

"Just around. Thinking." He started to walk past her, as if this were an ordinary afternoon and he were just coming home from school.

Taylor pulled him back to face her. "Don't walk away from me, young man. I've been worried sick. I was just coming to look for you."

"Why? I was okay."

"You knew that. I didn't. I've been going crazy wondering where you were and what you were doing—"

His face grew stormy, his eyes clouded. "Sorry if you couldn't think about the campaign."

"This doesn't have anything to do with the campaign. How many times do I have to tell you that?"

Cody shrugged again. "Okay. Sure. Can I go inside now? I'm thirsty."

His cavalier attitude grated on her nerves. "You most certainly *can* go inside, and you can stay there for the rest of the evening. You and I have some things to talk about."

"Like what?" His chin lifted and anger snapped in his eyes. "All you're going to do is tell me I can't find my dad."

"You're right. I am. There are things you don't understand. Things you *can't* understand."

Cody tried to jerked his arm away, but she held firm. The look on his face was filled with such anger, it left her numb. "Fine. So I'm stupid."

"I didn't say you were stupid, Cody."

"Well, you must think so."

"No, I don't. You're just too young to understand—"

"I'm *not* too young," he interrupted. This time he yanked

hard enough to break her grasp and backed away quickly
so she couldn't grab him again. "I know exactly how you
ended up having me, and you know what? My dad wasn't
the only one who didn't want me."

Taylor stared at her son in disbelief. "You can't believe
that. Of course I wanted you."

"You got pregnant by accident, Mom. Don't lie."

"Cody—" She reached for him, but the pain was so
sharp, she couldn't catch her breath and her arms felt sluggish and heavy.

"Don't lie, Mom. You didn't want me, either. You just
couldn't get away."

"That's *not* true. I love you. You're my whole life—"

"If you loved me," Cody shouted, his face twisted with
pain and anger, "you'd stop treating me like a baby." He
jumped onto the back step and jerked open the door. "If
you loved me, you'd *help* me find my dad. But you won't,
will you?"

Taylor started after him, but he slammed the screen door
between them. "Just leave me alone, Mom."

His bedroom door slammed before she was halfway
through the kitchen, and the sound echoed in her heart. She
leaned against the wall and fought back tears. She didn't
have time for weakness right now. Later, maybe.

When had Cody started to feel this way? Why hadn't he
said something before now? She took several deep breaths,
hoping to slow the too-fast beating of her heart.

Loud, heavy music started up in Cody's room, the vol-
ume so high she could feel it through the wall. The picture
frames beside her buzzed softly in rhythm with the angry
sounding rap that burst from beneath Cody's door and filled
the house.

Taylor wanted desperately to talk with Cody, but he
wouldn't listen if she tried, and she'd only make things
worse if she pushed.

At least he was home. She was grateful for that.

As she walked back into her kitchen, the strangest urge
came over her to talk with Sam again. He seemed so certain, so confident. Even when she was frustrated with him,

he had a calming effect—as if he knew the answers to every question she might ever have to ask. But the idea of being dependent on him for anything, even peace of mind, left her cold. It went against everything she'd ever wanted, ever worked for, ever hoped to be.

She stood at the back door for a long time, looking at Charlie's house across the driveway and letting Cody's music vibrate through her. One minute she wished Sam would feel her need and come to her; the next, she hoped he'd stay away.

Finally, as dusk settled over the valley and lights began to glow in neighbors' windows, she turned away and closed the door.

Sam started off early the next morning in case it took him a while to find the hardware store again. Sunlight hovered at the crest of the mountains and spilled into the valley in places, making yesterday's storm nothing but a memory. He whistled softly as he walked, trying not to think about the confrontation he'd witnessed between Taylor and Cody the previous evening.

They'd both been so hurt and angry, Sam had ached for them. For hours after they disappeared inside, he'd fought the urge to go to Taylor. But he couldn't have done anything to help, and he didn't think she'd have welcomed his interference.

He turned his gaze to the mountains again, hoping the changing leaves on the hillsides would keep his mind off Taylor and Cody. Autumn would come early at this altitude, and the change in seasons made him feel as if he'd been in Heartbreak Hill for months instead of weeks. But those pictures Taylor had brought made him wonder if he'd ever fill the empty places inside him.

He dodged the spray of water on someone's lawn, and stopped at the corner to check for traffic. Just as he stepped off the curb, he heard someone call his name.

Taylor came up behind him and tried to smile, but her heart obviously wasn't in it. "What are you doing out so early?"

"I found work yesterday. Figured I'd get an early start, just in case I get lost."

"Oh, Sam, that's wonderful. Where are you working?"

Her eyes caught the sun and turned deep, sea green. They seemed bigger this morning, and her lips looked moist and inviting. Sam stepped off the curb again and she fell into step beside him. "A fella named DeWayne Beers took me on at his hardware store."

"DeWayne?" Her eyes darkened slightly. "That's interesting. How did you meet him?"

For some reason, Sam couldn't get the words out to tell her about Irene's part in his good fortune. He gave up with a shrug. "I had some time on my hands yesterday. You know DeWayne?"

"All my life. But—" She cut herself off and gave him another of those weak smiles. "Did you recognize him from the shoot-out?"

"He made sure I knew who he was."

"And everything's all right between you?"

"Is there some reason it shouldn't be?"

She shook her head and glanced away. "No. Of course not. DeWayne's a good guy."

"Glad to hear it." A few minutes of silence fell between them, but it didn't take long for the holes in the silence to make Sam uncomfortable. There were too many things unsaid. "I saw Cody come home last night. Did things get better after you went inside?"

Her eyes shot to his, then away. "He's not even speaking to me."

"He will. He just needs time to be angry before you talk to him."

"I hope you're right. He wouldn't even look at me this morning. I wish I knew what's put all this into his head. Why does he suddenly want to find Nate, and how could he believe, even for a second, that I didn't want him? He's everything to me."

"He's been thinking about his pa for a long time, Taylor."

"He's never said a word about it until now." She

wrapped her arms around herself, and Sam had to fight the urge to follow her arms with his.

If they'd been alone, he might have let himself go, but he could almost feel curious eyes peering out of the nearby houses, and he wouldn't compromise her in front of her neighbors. "That doesn't mean he hasn't been thinking," he said. "Any boy in Cody's circumstances would."

Whatever had been holding her up seemed to collapse, and she sagged without it. "I know you're right, but I'm so hurt that he didn't talk to me about it. His teacher tells me he's been making up outrageous stories to explain why his father isn't around. I just don't understand why."

Before Sam could respond, she stopped walking altogether. "That's not true. I *do* understand. I just never wanted Cody to be hurt by my choices. There are so many single-parent families around, I didn't think not having a father would to affect him so much. I've done my best to be everything he needs—"

"Nobody can be everything to another person," Sam said. "That's asking too much of yourself."

Taylor took a shaky breath and let it out slowly. "I know I don't always react the best way, but please don't let that stop you from telling me something if it will help Cody. I flare up easily, but I've never been able to stay angry for long." She started walking again slowly. "In one way I'm jealous that Cody will talk to you since he won't talk to me. But in my rational moments, I'm thankful you're here for him. At least he's not keeping everything locked up inside."

Sam matched her pace again and kept his hands linked behind his back. "I don't know how much help I'll be."

"You help just by listening to him when he talks."

"That's easy enough to do. I like having him around."

"He doesn't bother you?"

"Not a bit. My kid brother used to tag along with me when he was younger, so it's like a bit of home."

"Do you miss home horribly?"

"Not horribly," he lied. "Some days I don't even think about it."

"Is that true, or are you trying to sound strong, noble, and brave?"

Sam laughed and glanced away. "Am I that obvious?"

"No, but I know how hard it would be to leave everyone I loved behind. I'm not sure I could do it."

Sam cleared his throat cautiously. "Well, there's not much I can do about it now."

"Yes, but don't you have regrets?"

Sam could feel his throat closing off. Those damn tears that bothered him in quiet moments burned his eyes. "I don't believe in regrets," he said gruffly. "They don't accomplish anything."

Taylor looked as if she was about to say something else, then thought better of it. But her expression remained thoughtful and something hovered just behind her eyes until they parted company.

That conversation set the tone for Sam's entire day. He made it to work as DeWayne opened the store and spent a few minutes looking around, but other than a few recognizable items in the bins, most of the parts and tools were unfamiliar to him.

He fumbled everything he touched, botched the few pieces of advice he actually felt qualified to give, and jammed the cash register when DeWayne left him in charge for two minutes. DeWayne couldn't ring up sales for three hours until his repairman came, and he spent the rest of the afternoon glowering whenever Sam crossed his path.

To put icing on an already ruined cake, Irene Beers sashayed into the store a little before closing time, her eyes shadowed heavily with some color that wasn't natural on a woman, her lips so coated with bright red they looked as if they were in danger of sticking together. She'd painted her fingernails, as well—long red daggers to match her lips—and on the very tips, little round gems flashed light every time she moved.

Sam saw her coming through the door and ducked down an aisle to escape notice. She came after him as steadily as if she were part bloodhound and greeted him with a huge, white smile. "Sam! I was hoping you'd still be here."

She wore tight-fitting jeans and a blouse unbuttoned so low Sam could see the lace of her undergarments. "I don't get off work for another fifteen minutes." A fact he suspected she knew very well.

She slipped her hand beneath his arm and batted her eyelashes. "Well, now that I've found you, I was hoping that you'd agree to have dinner with me."

"Afraid I'll have to pass. I haven't been paid yet."

"That's not a problem. It would be my treat." Irene pursed her lips as if she thought he might be enticed by them. "I thought you'd like to see something of Heartbreak Hill and meet a few people while you're at it."

"Taylor and Charlie have shown me around some. So has Cody, for that matter. And I've already met so many people I can't remember all their names."

"Forget meeting people, then." She squiggled a little closer, brushing her breasts against his arm. "I'd like a chance to get to know you better. A person can't have too many friends."

"You have a point, there," Sam said. He pulled away and pretended a deep interest in a bin full of nails. "I appreciate the offer, Irene, but I'm dog tired." It *was* the truth—just maybe not the whole truth.

"Oh." She pulled back a little and almost lost her smile. "Oh, well, of course you are. I wasn't thinking. Some other time, then?"

"Some other time."

She let go of his arm and started away, then whirled back, beaming. "If you're that tired, the least I can do is offer you a ride home. You don't *have* a ride already, do you?"

"Not exactly."

"Well, then. That's settled. I'll just pop over and say hello to DeWayne. Maybe I can even talk him into letting you off early." Irene swung off, swiveling her hips slowly and looking back over her shoulder just before she disappeared from view.

Sam held back a groan. He didn't have the energy to

fence with Irene, but he couldn't think of a graceful way to escape. He spent the next few minutes sorting nails into bins by size, contenting himself with mindless work until Irene came back, click-clicking on her heels across the floor and flicking her tongue across her lips.

"DeWayne says you can go on home for tonight. Are you sure you don't want to have dinner with me?"

Sam shut the bin drawers and straightened. "It's kind of you to ask, ma'am, but I'd better not." He ignored her pout of disappointment and gathered his things, then followed her into the bright afternoon sunshine.

She led him to a tiny car as red as her lips and looked at him as if she expected some reaction. "It's one of those new VW Bugs," she said, motioning him toward the driver's side. "If you want to drive, I don't mind."

Sam held up both hands and backed away. "No, thanks."

"Oh, come on. Really." She dangled the keys at him across the top of the car. "My dad always did the driving in our family, so I feel funny driving when there's a man around to do it for me."

Sam shook his head and backed up even farther. "You're going to have to. I don't know how to drive."

"You don't—" Irene gaped at him. "You're joking, right?"

"No, ma'am."

"How can you not know how to drive?"

"Never learned."

"Not even in school?"

"No, ma'am."

She took a few seconds to process that idea. "I could teach you."

"I don't think so." He was barely getting used to riding inside the damn things; he wasn't ready to take control of one.

"But you *have* to know how to drive. You can't get around if you don't."

"I get around fine on my own two feet."

"Well, yes. You can walk around Heartbreak Hill. But everybody knows how to drive out here. Cars are practically a part of us. What if you need something you can't get here in town? The nearest big town is, like, two hundred miles away."

"I'll deal with that if I have to."

"Or what if you want to go up into the mountains," she said as if he hadn't answered, "or if DeWayne asks you to pick up something for the store or make a delivery? You have to know how to drive, Sam."

Sam cast a glance at the gleaming red automobile. He still wasn't sold on the idea, but if learning to drive would help him fit in, maybe he should try it. "Is it hard to learn?"

Irene waved a set of red claws at him. "It's the easiest thing in the world."

"How long would it take?"

"Three or four lessons and we'd have you driving like a pro."

He eyed the car carefully, looked inside at the controls, and pushed aside the little voice that questioned what Taylor would say about this idea. "If you think you can teach me, I'm willing to try. When do you want to get started?"

"Right now. Or are you too tired?"

Sam started to refuse, then realized that the idea of doing something new and different had given him a second wind. "Now's perfect."

She scowled thoughtfully and glanced up the street. "We'd better not start here in traffic. We don't want an accident." She waved Sam toward the passenger door. "I know the perfect place. We'll go to the old tannery on the edge of town. We can't possibly get into trouble out there."

Chapter 14

SAM GRIPPED THE steering wheel and tried to get his feet positioned in the cramped space so he could work the pedals. Three pedals for two feet didn't seem quite right. But if everyone else could do it, by damn, so could he.

Irene rolled down her window and let in the scent of pine and sage. "You've got your left foot over the clutch?"

"If this bitty thing down here is the clutch, then yes."

"And your right foot's over the gas and brakes?"

Sam nodded and looked skeptically at the dozens of knobs and buttons in front of him. "What do I do with all these?"

"Nothing yet. First things first." She checked all around them, seemed satisfied with what she found, and leaned back in her seat. "Now, push in the clutch with your left foot and gently press on the gas pedal with your right. As you put on the gas, ease the clutch out. Does that make sense?"

"Not a bit."

She smiled at him as if he was a newborn pup. "Push in that pedal over there with that foot. Now, step on this pedal . . . gently."

He gave the second pedal a gentle nudge with the toe of

his boot. The car let out a high-pitch whine. "Sounds like a dying animal."

"It'll be fine. Just let out that pedal over there while you're pushing on this pedal over here."

One foot in, one foot out. That made sense. Sam did what she told him. One foot in, the other foot out. Simple enough.

They jerked forward so fast, both feet slipped off the pedals. The car bucked, lurched, coughed, shuddered, and died several feet from where they'd started.

Sam sent Irene an embarrassed smile. "Not quite right?"

She brushed a lock of hair out of her eyes. "Not quite. Do it *gently* next time."

"I thought I did."

"You need to be a little *more* gentle. Get your feet in position and start the car again—and this time pretend you're making love to a woman. *That's* how gentle I want you to be."

Sam scowled doubtfully. He didn't think the two things could be compared, but he didn't want to debate the question with Irene. He worked his feet into place, held on to the wheel while Irene turned the key, and tried hard to make the switch with his feet.

The car roared, whined, shivered as if it was alive and anxious to get moving. The next second they'd bucked several feet away and the car jolted to another shuddering stop.

"That was better," Irene said brightly. "The third time's the charm. You're going to do it perfectly this time. Ready?"

Sam planted his feet again, nodded, and began the ritual once more. To his surprise, the car didn't buck; it gave just one little lurch and then shot across the pavement. The only trouble was, it was heading straight for a redbrick building that had been on the other side of the lot only seconds before. Now, it loomed in front of them and the car showed no signs of stopping.

"The brake!" Irene shouted. *"Put on the brake!"*

If he'd been on a runaway horse, Sam would've known what to do. A runaway car was a different matter entirely.

He worked instinctively, jerking the wheel as he would've done with reins, and guiding the car away from its head-on path with the building. But the damn thing still didn't show any sign of slowing down.

Sam held on for dear life, vowing never again to ride something that wasn't alive. The car circled around the lot several times until Sam could think clearly enough to figure out he needed to make an adjustment.

"Stop!" Irene's foot came flying across the bump on the floor that separated them. She must've been trying to work the brake, but she caught the toe of Sam's boot instead and brought his foot down on the gas pedal.

They shot forward so fast, Sam thought his neck would break. While Irene screeched, he swerved to the right to miss the fence, yanked the wheel to the left to avoid a ditch he saw looming on the other side, and finally got the car going straight in the direction that seemed safest—back down the long driveway that led to the road.

The engine let out an unhappy screech as they shot out of the parking lot, and Sam had to use all his strength to get the car heading down the road. Irene fought with the belt that held her strapped and Sam caught a glimpse of another car in the mirror.

His hands grew clammy and his heart leaped into his throat, and he was hardly aware of Irene kicking his boot. The familiar red and blue lights begin to spin on the car behind him, and Sam's concentration was shot. Irene's car careened off the pavement, spun on gravel, and finally nosed down into a ditch.

Sam shot forward and back again, and he thought his neck would snap from the impact. Irene let out a scream and slid in a heap from the seat onto the floor.

Dust billowed up around them and blocked Sam's view of the patrol car. Irene's Bug coughed twice and died with a heavy shudder. And for a second or two everything was so silent, Sam wondered if maybe he'd passed on to the other side.

He didn't have to wonder long. Irene let out a moan and one of her legs moved.

He leaned to one side and tried to get a good look at her. "Are you all right?"

"I'm fine, but my car—" She somehow got herself flipped around and held out a hand for Sam's help. "My car."

"I'm real sorry about that—"

"Sorry?" Irene struggled onto the seat and used both hands to smooth her hair away from her face. She tried to open her door, but the ditch banks kept the door from opening more than an inch or two. "Try your door," she demanded. "See if we can get out your side."

Sam gave it a try, but the door wouldn't budge. He tried again, shoving with his shoulder. Still no luck. A sound near the window caught his attention, and two tan-clad legs appeared on the edge of the ditch just as Irene began a frantic scramble across his lap toward the open door.

A strange hissing sound filled the air, and Irene slapped his shoulder in frustration. "My new car. My *brand-new car*. I'll never get it out of here." She stopped with her hips smack in front of his face and looked back at him. "What's that noise? What's wrong with my car?"

Dust clogged Sam's throat and crawled up his nose. He sneezed, coughed, and tried to keep his eyes off the rounded backside in his face. The only other thing he could see was a pair of shiny boots and the hem of tan uniform trousers. Deputy Donald or Taylor? He didn't know which was worse.

The boots shifted, came downhill stirring another cloud of dust, and the uniform hunkered down to window-level. Taylor's face showed no expression as she looked from Sam to Irene's backside and back again. "Am I interrupting something?"

"Get me out of here," Irene demanded. "He almost killed me."

Taylor obligingly held out a hand and gave Irene a little tug. "I don't think it was quite that bad, but only by sheer luck. If you'd kept going half a mile to the switchbacks, you might not have been so lucky."

When Irene had scrambled out of the car, Taylor held

out a hand to Sam. He ignored it and made it out on his own, scuffing his knee and skinning his back in the process—but a man had to have *some* pride.

Taylor waited until he could stand, then propped both hands on her hips and looked him over slowly. "What on earth were you doing?"

"Learning to drive."

"Do you mind if I ask why?"

"It seemed like the thing to do at the moment." He reached back inside the car for the hat he'd left on the backseat and nearly lost his balance in the process.

Taylor took Sam's arm and dragged him to the top of the ditch. "Do you mind my asking why you asked Irene to teach you?"

"I didn't ask, she offered." Sam dusted the seat of his pants and put his hat on to give himself a little confidence. "I couldn't see any reason to refuse."

"Irene has no way of knowing how foreign all this is to you." Taylor watched Irene scramble across the side of the ditch toward the back tire and winced when she let out a low moan. "I didn't realize you and Irene were such good friends."

Something in the tone of her voice made Sam take a good look at her. Had he imagined that knife-edge on her words? "We're not. Not really. I know her slightly, is all."

Irene mumbled something unintelligible and disappeared behind the tail of the car.

Taylor's jaw clenched and unclenched a time or two. "You don't need to do this, you know. Charlie or I can take you wherever you need to go."

"Not forever."

"For a while. Until you get used to things."

"Thanks, but I'm not big on taking charity. Besides, I thought knowing how to drive would help me fit in. Isn't that what you wanted?"

"Well, yes." She turned a set of huge hazel eyes on him. "But you're not ready for this, Sam. You're lucky neither you or Irene were hurt."

"Nothing but my pride."

"Well, you're lucky," she said again. She fidgeted with her fancy holster and sighed, waved one hand toward Irene's car and started back up the bank of the ditch. "You'd better hope she has good insurance. I have a feeling she's going to need it."

Not surprisingly, Taylor couldn't sleep that night. Cody had spent the evening slumped in front of the TV rather than locked in his room. That was the best thing that had happened all day.

Every time she closed her eyes, she saw Sam and Irene together in that car. She wanted to convince herself that she didn't care, but she couldn't lie. She cared—a lot. Far more than she wanted to.

She'd never been the jealous type before. She'd never envied anyone or coveted a single thing that belonged to someone else. Now, it seemed, she was going to lose sleep over every woman Sam came into contact with.

Pathetic.

She lay in bed for a while watching shadows dance on her ceiling and listening to the refrigerator turn on and off until she thought she'd go crazy. Finally she gave up on sleep, pulled on her robe, dug in the fridge for a Sprite, and carried it outside to the back porch.

She had nothing against Irene. But Irene wasn't exactly shy and retiring. She certainly wouldn't sit around and twiddle her thumbs, waiting for Sam to get over Olivia. Irene loved men and she made no bones about it. She drew them like moths to a flame—young, old, short, tall, thin, heavy, it didn't matter to Irene. All her men had one thing in common—a spark that transcended looks.

If anyone had that quality, Sam did. There was something about him that seemed larger than life, some restless energy that filled the air around him even when he was sitting still.

That's what worried Taylor.

Sam still thought women were gentle creatures who needed to be taken care of by a big, strong man. He had a lot to learn before he was ready to go up against someone like Irene.

Taylor took a long drink and set the can aside, tilted back her head, and let the cool breeze ruffle her hair. Overhead, stars filled the sky—tiny pinpricks of glittering, winking light that soothed her and reminded her that, by comparison, her troubles and concerns were inconsequential. Speed bumps on the road of life, nothing more.

In the blink of an eye, this moment would pass and with it the pain or worry or fear. She'd learned to put things in perspective this way after her mother's death, and the trick still worked now that she was an adult and life sometimes threatened to overwhelm her.

When she heard the soft sound of footsteps from the other side of the hedge, she knew she'd been waiting for this. Her heart took off at a dead run and her nerve endings began to tingle.

Sam looked over at the porch as he passed. His step slowed and he pivoted toward her, walking so slowly it almost hurt to wait. Each step made her heart beat harder, until she was quite sure he'd be able to see her chest thumping if he looked hard enough.

"Well," he said as he drew even with her, "fancy meeting you here."

She moved the can and shifted slightly so he could sit if he wanted to. "It's a nice night." No matter how much she wanted to see him, her natural defensiveness always rose to the surface and came out in her voice. She tempered her answer with a thin smile and added, "Would you like to join me?"

Sam's eyebrows rose in surprise, but he didn't waste even a second accepting her offer. Before she knew it, he was sitting on the step beside her, so close their thighs brushed. She longed to lean against him, to feel the heat and strength of his body, but she wouldn't let herself start behaving like Irene. Holding herself rigid, she clasped her hands between her knees so they wouldn't wander.

Sam glanced at the can on the porch beside her. "More of that soda you like so much?"

She laughed softly. "Yes, just a different kind. Would you like one?"

"Lord, no. I still can't get used to the stuff."

"What do you drink when you're hot and thirsty?"

"Back home we had water from the well. Once in a while if we were lucky, we'd have lemonade."

"I can't imagine having to pump water every time I needed it."

His mustache twitched. "It's a far sight better than hauling it half a mile from the creek." He rested his hands on his knees and looked wistful. "I remember when my father had a pump installed in the kitchen for my mother. The men in my family thought life couldn't get much better, but it didn't impress my mother. She knew how backwater we really were."

Taylor regretted not paying more attention to his stories when he first came, and she found herself hungry for details now. "Your mother didn't like Colorado?"

"That would be putting it mildly. She hated the Cinnabar. Absolutely detested the roughness and seclusion. By the time she died, she'd turned all that hatred onto my father, and there were plenty of times when it spilled over onto Jesse and me." He shook his head sadly. "I loved her, but she was the most miserable person I ever knew. She never let go of anything."

"Some things are hard to let go of," Taylor said softly. "Some things are almost impossible to let go of."

Sam turned to look at her. "Are you talking about yourself now?"

"I suppose I am." She laced her fingers together and pressed harder with her knees. "Sometimes I think I let people use my past as a weapon against me. It's just that people were so cruel when I was young and alone and pregnant. If it hadn't been for Charlie, I don't know what I would have done."

"Everyone was cruel?"

She smiled halfheartedly. "Not everyone."

"Then you can't believe that everyone will listen to Hutton Stone now?"

She shook her head slowly. "I guess not."

"Tell me, besides the election, why does it matter so much what people think of you?"

"It doesn't." She jerked her hands from between her knees. "It doesn't matter to me. But Cody—"

"Cody's going to react exactly how *you* react," Sam said gently. "He's going to take his cues from you. If it matters so much that you'll give up what you want most, it'll matter to him, and it'll take something big and probably ugly and painful to shake him from that belief when he's older."

"That didn't happen to you," she protested. "You say your mother was miserable, but you're not miserable."

"I was." His eyes met hers slowly. "I was before I came here. I just didn't know it."

"How can you not know you're miserable?"

Sam made himself more comfortable, brushing against her side as he slid his legs out in front of himself. "What my mother taught me without knowing it was that obligation came before anything. She'd married my father, and even when she realized that she hated the life she'd married into, she stayed put. That was good, I suppose. I learned not to run from tough times. But we were a duty to her, and not much more. No matter how miserable *she* was, she wouldn't make changes."

He crossed one foot over the other and stroked his mustache with his thumb and finger. "I ended up doing the same thing my mother did, just in a different way. My father left me the Cinnabar when he died and told me to take care of Jesse. I took on the responsibility for looking after Olivia when her husband died."

Olivia's name knifed through Taylor, but she tried not to show it.

"I was all set to spend the rest of my life on the ranch— even had myself convinced I was supposed to marry Olivia. But then Jesse threatened to leave and Olivia turned me down."

"You . . . you proposed to her?"

Sam chuckled. "Several times. Couldn't get it through my thick head that she didn't love me. She was smarter than I was, that's for sure." He turned those deep gray eyes toward her and his smile faded. "The day I saw her and Kurt together and knew they were in love was the day that changed my life."

Taylor's stomach lurched. The logical side of her brain didn't want to hear this; the other side needed every detail. "It must have hurt."

Sam nodded, plucked a blade of grass from the lawn beside him. "You'd think so, wouldn't you?" He smoothed the grass on his knee methodically, as if the world would stop spinning if he didn't. "The truth is, that's the day I realized Jesse was right. He'd been telling me that I needed to find some happiness for myself, but all I could think about was my duty. Once I faced the truth, the solution was so simple it's almost embarrassing. That's when I decided to leave the Cinnabar and start over in Montana."

"I thought you said you ran into that time warp on impulse."

"I did. My plan was to pack my things and travel up here by horseback, by train, by stage. I wasn't expecting any other options. But then the opportunity to leave another way presented itself and I took it."

"You mean you'd already decided to leave Olivia *before* you jumped through the time warp?"

"I had."

"Then you aren't . . . I mean, you don't . . ." For some reason the rest of her question lodged in her throat and stayed there. When Sam just quirked an eyebrow and waited, she forced the words out. "You're not still in love with her?"

Sam's expression changed subtly, slowly. From confusion to enlightenment one muscle at a time. "Did you think I was?"

"Well, yes. Of course."

His eyes roamed her face. "Did that bother you?"

"A little." She felt her defenses slipping back into place, but the moment was too important. She couldn't hide from it. "Yes, of course it did. Just like seeing you with Irene Beers this afternoon bothered me."

Sam grinned like a little boy who'd just been handed a new puppy. "Well, hell, *that* was nothing. I was just trying to fit in better."

"I'm sorry I told you that. You're fitting in just fine. Better than I would if our situations were reversed."

"I don't know about that. I have a feeling you'd take to life in my time."

Taylor tugged the edges of her robe across her legs. "Speaking of fitting in, how did the job go?"

"You want my version or DeWayne's?"

"Not well?"

"Not even close. Turns out I don't know a damn thing. But I'll get it."

Taylor studied him for a long moment, thought about everything he'd told her, and realized how difficult this transition must be. "I think you're making a mistake working for DeWayne," she said impulsively. "I think you're wasting your talents."

Sam let out a sharp laugh. "What talents would those be?"

"I'm not sure," Taylor admitted, "but I am sure fate didn't sweep you up and drop you here so you could sell nuts and bolts. There must be something you can do that's more you."

"Hell, woman, I'm just a cowboy."

"Well, then *be* one." Taylor's vehemence surprised her as much as it seemed to stun Sam. But now that she'd said it, it seemed exactly right. "You don't belong in this town, Sam." She waved a hand toward the mountains. "You belong out there somewhere on the back of a horse."

"And leave you?"

Taylor held herself rigid and forced out the words she knew she had to say. "If it would make you happy."

"It wouldn't. Now, if I could have both worlds, that would be heaven. The feel of a horse beneath me would be a mighty fine thing."

"Are you unhappy here?"

"No. But this is the longest I've ever spent in a city. And

Jesse'd fall over backward if he knew I'd been out of the saddle this long."

"I wish I could have met him."

"So do I. He'd have liked you."

"Really?" The simple statement made her heart soar. "Why?"

"Well, for one thing, you put up with me. He was beginning to despair of me ever finding a woman who could do that. Even with all the doubts and the mistakes, you haven't sent me packing yet." He cupped her cheek and his hand felt warm, solid, and huge against her face.

She leaned into his touch, wanting to freeze this moment in time so she could remember it always. She wanted to memorize his scent, the look in his eye, the feel of him beside her. She wanted to look back on this moment and draw on every detail when she needed it.

He leaned closer and kissed her, and she could have sworn the world stood still. The breeze died, the cricket song stilled, and lights faded away. He slid one arm around her and drew her closer. Fire ignited low in her belly and that old familiar longing—the very one she'd run from for so long—began to move through her.

Her first instinct was to pull away, but she couldn't. She belonged in this man's arms. The years she'd spent alone had been leading her to this moment. She slid her arms beneath his and gripped his shoulders, arching her neck and moaning when his mouth left hers and trailed kisses to her throat.

He whispered against her skin, and the cool brush of air against the moistness where his lips had been sent delicious shivers in every direction.

She worked her fingers into his hair and held him there, kissing his temples and the side of his jaw as his mouth lifted to hers again. A hard corner of cement jabbed into her back, but she didn't care.

And when he lifted his mouth and looked deep into her eyes, breathing out her name as naturally as if he'd been saying it his entire life, even the sharp corner of the step disappeared into that vapor of desire that surrounded them.

He could take her right then and there and she'd have been helpless to resist.

Her hands slid across his back and her hips arched in silent invitation. He breathed again, a sigh that was either unspeakable pleasure or regret, and smoothed his hands along her hips. "If I don't stop now, I won't stop at all."

"You don't have to stop," Taylor whispered back. "We can find somewhere to go."

Sam leaned back and looked into her eyes. *"Now?"*

She quirked a smile as she struggled to catch her breath. "That's kind of what I had in mind."

"Do you know what a temptation that is?"

"Well, I *hope* so. What a disappointment to find out otherwise."

He kissed her again, lightly, and moved away. Even in the warm September night, her overheated skin felt cold when he left her. "Much as I want to, I can't take advantage of you that way. It isn't right. I've already gone too far."

Taylor would have given him anything in that moment. The *last* thing she thought she wanted was for him to pull away and turn her down. And yet . . . something she couldn't understand or explain rejoiced in the fact that he did just that.

She put her hand on his, marveling at how right it felt to be here with him, how wonderful to be respected. Maybe that was it. Nate had been so eager to get her into the backseat of that car, and so quick to leave her afterward. The pain had scarred her for years.

But maybe this old-fashioned man was all her heart had ever needed.

Chapter 15

AFTER TWO WEEKS at the hardware store, things weren't much better. Sam had learned a few things, but he couldn't help the customer who wanted help winterizing his cooler or the one whose dryer wouldn't work. He could feel DeWayne watching him like a hawk, circling closer, hovering every time Sam opened his mouth.

By midmorning Sam had annoyed half a dozen customers and was beginning to doubt that he'd ever be able to hold his own. He watched DeWayne bag an electric timer for a customer and punch buttons on the cash register. "Thanks, Mr. O'Donnell. Sorry about"—he glanced at Sam and lowered his voice—"the confusion."

Mr. O'Donnell's gaze followed DeWayne's and his smile wavered. "No problem, *De*-Wayne. Just glad *you* knew where to find it." He tucked his purchase under his arm and limped toward the door.

DeWayne waited until he was gone, then turned slowly toward Sam. "You don't know the first thing about hardware, do you?"

Sam set aside the bag of newfangled doodads he'd been sorting. "I know it doesn't seem like it, but I do know basics."

DeWayne took a sip from the dirtiest coffee cup Sam

had ever seen. "Earlier today, Keith Potter needed some electrical tape. *That's* basic. You didn't even know what it was."

Sam brushed his hands on the legs of his trousers. "I know now."

DeWayne's eyes narrowed so far Sam wasn't sure he could actually see. "How can you *not* know what electrical tape is? That's what I don't understand. Hell, my *kid* knows what it is, and he's six."

Sam hated being made to feel stupid, but he managed not to lose his temper. "You wouldn't believe me if I told you."

DeWayne's narrow mouth curved into a deep scowl. "Try me."

"It's complicated."

"Look—" DeWayne fiddled with the pack of cigarettes in his sleeve. "You *said* you had experience. You *said* you knew your way around. That's why I hired you. Now I'm starting to wonder. Just what do you have experience *in*?"

Sam considered telling him the truth but decided against it. He didn't think DeWayne would believe him, but he'd probably share the story with other folks in town. People would think Sam was crazy, and Taylor, Charlie, and Cody would suffer.

"I do have experience," he said, "but it was different. I guess what I know doesn't translate well."

"You can say that again." DeWayne rested his elbow on a shelf and scratched his head. Took another sip and set his cup aside. His hair curled gently down the back of his neck and brushed his collar, but left a gaping bald spot in the center of his head—an island in a sea of curly brown hair. "I don't want to cut you short or anything, but you've been here two weeks now and things aren't getting a whole lot better. If all you can do is sort nails, it's just making more work for me. I need someone who knows what he's doing."

Sam tried to keep his head up, but never in his life had he felt like such a failure. An abject, utter failure. In all the times he'd fantasized about carving out his own life, he'd never once considered that he might fail. And the fact that he was failing at something that should've been so simple galled him.

If DeWayne fired him, Sam could forget his dreams for a good, long time. "I know you're disappointed in me," he said, "but I really need this job. Tell me what I need to do, and I'll do it."

"That's the trouble. I don't know what to tell you." DeWayne jerked his head toward the door. "Let's go outside for a second. I need a smoke."

Outside, DeWayne leaned against the wall and lit up. "I don't want to be too hasty," he said through a cloud of smoke. "Other than not knowing a damn thing, you're a great employee."

"Thanks. I think."

"You're dependable—always here before me and willing to stay late. But I need to be able to leave the store once in a while, and so far I can't do that." He took a deep drag and exhaled into the early fall sunlight. "Today's a prime example. I need to get out of here early. I promised my friend Kip that I'd help with his Mustang, but—"

"A mustang?" Sam's spirits took a decided upswing. "Now that's something I can help with—if you want help, that is."

DeWayne peered at him through the cloud he was creating. "You know Mustangs?"

Did Sam know horses? He struggled not to laugh out loud. He wasn't in the habit of bragging about himself, but this wasn't the time for false modesty. "I was one of the best where I came from. People said I had a way with 'em."

DeWayne crushed out his cigarette and looked away down the street. "Neither Kip or I can figure out what the problem is."

Sam was confident for the first time in weeks. "No problem. I can just about guarantee it."

DeWayne dragged his gaze back. "Okay, then. I'll let Kip know I'm bringing you along."

Sam let out a silent sigh of relief. He'd bought himself some time. Now, if his luck would just hold. . . .

•   •   •

Sam sat in the passenger side of DeWayne's truck, one arm out the window, and whistled softly. If he ever got on his feet, he'd think about buying a truck like this one. He liked sitting high enough to see the land around him, and he liked the way the truck moved as DeWayne negotiated the curves in the road. It was, Sam thought, the next best thing to being on a horse.

He strained against the seat belt as city gave way to country, excited to get his hands on a horse again. Sam didn't worry about the mustang. He'd never seen a horse he couldn't gentle. It was all just a matter of respect. If you respected creatures, they respected you right back.

He took a deep breath of the clear mountain air, relishing the scents of pine and sage, the loam of needles carpeting the earth, and the tang of something wild and bittersweet. This was heaven right here on earth.

DeWayne smoked one cigarette after another, silently, almost sullenly, as if he'd already had more conversation than he could handle. Sam didn't mind. He enjoyed the silence. If not for the hum of tires on the road and the speed they traveled, he could almost imagine himself alone on horseback.

It didn't take long to reach the turnoff to Kip's place, hidden deep in the trees. They veered onto an unpaved road and the smell of dust stirred Sam's memories. They passed through thick forest and meadows of wildflowers—some Sam recognized, some he didn't—and a profound hunger began to fill him.

He imagined riding at Jesse's side, laughing, joking, even arguing. How would he ever reconcile the soul-deep missing of his brother with his growing hopes for the future?

It didn't matter, he supposed. He had no way back. But he worried that his regrets might one day destroy what he and Taylor were building. The last thing he wanted was to re-create his parents' lives, to hurt Taylor by wanting something he couldn't have. He couldn't go back; but knowing that, why couldn't he forget the past and get on with his life?

"You're awful quiet," DeWayne said at last.

"Just thinking." At DeWayne's arched eyebrow, he added, "Thinking about my kid brother. We used to spend a lot of time in the country together."

"I didn't realize you had a brother." DeWayne pulled something from his tongue with two fingers. "Come to think of it, I don't know much about you at all. You have family, then?"

"A brother. My parents are both gone." The tart scent of wild grass floated in through the window, and Sam drew it in greedily.

"What made you decide to come here?"

Sam shrugged. "Hard to say. I sort of went where the wind blew me."

"Does that mean you'll be blowing away again when the mood hits?"

"Don't plan on it."

DeWayne looked away from the road, and the truck jounced over a series of ruts. "You know Taylor's a friend of mine. Has been since we were kids."

"So she tells me."

"You seem like a decent guy, so I almost hate to say this, but I think you should know that there's a whole town full of people who'd be only too glad to take you apart limb by limb if you hurt her."

"I'm glad to hear it. I wouldn't have expected anything less."

DeWayne smiled slowly. "You're a strange case, you know that?"

Sam laughed. "So I've been told."

DeWayne shifted his eyes from the road for a second and grinned. "You remind me of my grandpa in a weird way. I don't mean that to sound rude. My grandpa was one helluva guy. He died last year."

"Sorry to hear that."

"Yeah. We were real close." DeWayne shook out another cigarette and flicked his lighter. "He was just who he was, you know? No pretense. No masks. Just himself. He didn't care who liked it and who didn't." He laughed fondly, remembering. "That's probably why Taylor likes you. She's not into head games and bullshit. She's the most honest woman I know."

Sam acknowledged the compliment with a dip of his head. "Must be why she likes you, too."

DeWayne chuckled. "You're all right, Sam. I just wish I knew what to do with you at the store."

"If I'm not working out, let me go. I've never been one to stay where I'm not wanted."

"We'll see." DeWayne turned the wheel to round a bend, and they bounced over another series of ruts. The truck dipped into a swale, swallowed whole by shadows, and crested on the other side in a wide meadow circled by trees.

A small log house took up one side of the clearing and brought up another wave of Sam's increasing homesickness. Log walls. Wooden doors and floors. A sagging, unpainted barn sat nearby. Near that, an unused chicken coop with the roof caving in.

Sam cleared his throat and envied the man who lived here. Only the vehicles scattered about the yard gave any sign that they were in the twenty-first century. DeWayne shut off the engine, and Sam scanned the clearing for a corral so he could take a look at the mustang he'd be working with. But he couldn't see hide nor hair of any horses. Only cars and trucks scattered about at intervals and between them rusting spare parts.

DeWayne nodded toward a red car with no tires, held off the ground by cinder blocks. A pair of feet stuck out from beneath it and moved in time to music coming from a nearby radio. Something clanked beneath the car, the sound of metal on metal.

"Well, that's it," DeWayne said around an unlit cigarette.

The bottom fell out of Sam's stomach. "That's what?" he asked, praying he hadn't made another mistake.

"There it is. It's a sixty-four. Beautiful, isn't it?"

Ah, hell.

Sam nodded slowly. "Sure is."

DeWayne started toward the car. "We've put in a new battery, checked the carburetor, and replaced the starter motor. We've checked all the wiring, and we put in a new alternator last week. It's finally holding a charge, but we're still having trouble getting it to kick over."

Sam looked from DeWayne's expectant smile to Kip's dancing feet. He skimmed a glance at the car and noticed the tiny metal mustang galloping on its hood. His stomach knotted and he broke out in a cold sweat.

Kip slid out from beneath the car and stood, brushing at his Levi's. "Think you can help?"

Sam swallowed hard. He'd never been an overly religious man, but a little help wouldn't go amiss. He tried a quick prayer. Heard only a resounding silence in response.

He imagined Taylor's face, saw Cody looking up at him as if he held the world on his shoulders, and thought about everything Charlie'd done for him. And he knew he couldn't just throw up his hands and admit defeat. "I can try," he said, wiping his sweaty palms on the back of his pants. "Won't make any promises, though."

"That's fair enough. You want to look under the hood or see what's underneath her first?"

"I'll get underneath." Sam took Kip's place on the tarp and inched beneath the car. He didn't have the foggiest notion what to do with any of the pipes and doodads over his head, but if he pretended long enough and made enough noise, maybe they'd believe he'd done his best.

Kip and DeWayne couldn't fix the car—they couldn't get upset if Sam failed.

He picked up a tool and banged something. He clanked something else and felt a wash of relief as the two men stopped paying attention to him and started talking about something else. Growing a little braver, he toyed with a couple of nuts and bolts, banged around a bit more.

After a few minutes of nothing, he realized that the wrench beside him fit perfectly around a nut directly over his head. Couldn't hurt to loosen it and tighten it again. It would put grease on his hands so that DeWayne and Kip would believe he'd really done something.

He moved to a better position, fit the end of the tool over

the nut, and yanked. The nut gave a satisfying turn and grease smudged his fingers.

Perfect.

He gave it another turn, feeling mighty proud and enjoying himself, even if he didn't know what he was doing. One more turn . . . the nut twisted and Sam's smile broadened a split second before something thick and dark poured out of the contraption.

Sputtering, spitting, cursing, Sam scrambled out from beneath the car. The taste filled his mouth and nose, the slimy liquid slithered down his neck and into his shirt. He looked for something to clean his face with and caught DeWayne and Kip staring at him.

"What in the hell—?" Kip began.

DeWayne wagged a hand at him and took a step toward Sam. "It seems," he drawled, "that you know as much about cars as you do about hardware."

"It seems so," Sam admitted reluctantly.

Kip muttered something under his breath and offered Sam a grease-stained rag.

Sam took it gratefully and mopped his face.

When he looked up again, DeWayne was standing directly in front of him. "Do you want to tell us the truth about who you are and what's going on? I've about had it with the games."

"No games," Sam said as he wiped away some of the slime. "When you mentioned a mustang, I thought you were talking about a horse. I know horses, and that's the God's honest truth."

"I suggest you tell us the *rest* of the truth."

"I wish I could," Sam said, working the rag between his fingers. "You've been decent to me, and this is no way to repay you. If Taylor says it's all right to tell you everything, I'd be mighty happy to do it. Until then, I'm honor bound to keep my mouth shut."

Kip snorted softly. "We'll just ask Taylor, then. She'll tell us."

Sam set the rag aside. "I hope she does. Meanwhile, how can I help clean up this mess I've made?"

"You," DeWayne said, giving his pants a hitch, "can sit in the truck and watch. Kip and I will take care of this." He turned away, then back so quickly he almost lost his balance. "And don't touch anything."

Sam couldn't remember when he'd felt so low. He'd sat at Taylor's kitchen table for two hours, trying to feign an appetite and struggling to show an interest in the family's chatter over dinner. His mind had wandered continually, thinking back over the day's disaster. He'd been so distracted, even Cody had stopped trying to engage him in conversation.

Now, hours later, his mood had dropped even lower. He'd probably offended Taylor by being so distant. Probably hurt Cody's feelings, as well. And Charlie had been watching him like a hawk since they came home again.

He poured a cup of hours-old coffee and carried it onto the patio to think. A stiff breeze rustled leaves overhead and carried the scent of autumn from the mountains.

"You want to tell me what's bothering you?"

Sam looked over his shoulder at Charlie. "I didn't hear you come outside."

"Not surprising." Charlie pulled on a light jacket and dropped into a chair beside Sam's. "You've been a million miles away all evening. Anything I can help with?"

Sam wrapped both hands around the warm cup and sipped. "I don't think so."

"Sometimes it helps to get troubles off your chest." Charlie zipped his jacket and stuffed his hands into the pockets. "I'm a good listener."

Sam laughed softly. "You're a good man, Charlie O'Brien. I'm pleased to know you, and I already owe you more than I can ever repay."

"You've repaid me already. A man can't put a price on friendship or his family's happiness."

Sam shook his head and looked away at the mountains shadowing the darkness. "I wish I could take credit for Taylor and Cody's happiness. It might help."

"You can." Charlie pulled a cigar from his pocket and

dug around for a lighter. "Cody's a sight happier since you came along. He hasn't been in trouble in weeks." Charlie grinned wickedly, touched the flame to his cigar, and puffed vigorously for a few seconds. "Taylor's a different woman these days," he said when he had the cigar lit, "and I'm a whole lot happier because she doesn't concern herself nearly so much about what I'm up to."

Sam chuckled. "Well, in that case—" He couldn't lie to Charlie. The man had been too good to him. His smile slipped away slowly and he set his cup aside. "I lost my job today."

"Did you quit?"

"DeWayne fired me. I don't blame him. I didn't know a damn thing, and customers were getting upset." He shrugged and added, "Course, I think the final straw was when I accidentally emptied the oil from his friend's car."

Charlie let out a whoop. "That old car of Kip's?"

Sam nodded, realized he felt a little better already, and grinned. "His Mustang. I thought they were talking about a horse."

Charlie leaned back in his lawn chair and released a cloud of smoke into the sky. "I can't say I'm surprised. Those two boys never were all that bright. Neither one of 'em would know a good thing if it bit 'em in the butt." He slid his gaze to Sam's face. "But I guess you're not happy about it."

"Not exactly. I still don't have any means of supporting myself, much less—" Sam broke off, wishing he could kick himself for the slip.

"Much less a family?"

"I'm not in any position to take on a family," Sam muttered. Too agitated to sit still, he shot to his feet and paced to the edge of the patio. "I was hoping that within a few months, I could ask you for permission to court Taylor. At the rate I'm moving, I'll never be ready."

Charlie took another few puffs, formed a smoke ring, and watched it drift into the night sky. "Things aren't like they were in your day, son. First of all, men don't ask the father for permission to come courting any longer. It's Taylor's choice—and it seems to me that she's made it. Second, work's not always easy to get, and it doesn't always pay enough when you do get it. These days men and women work together to make ends meet."

"Together is a whole lot different than a woman supporting her husband."

"Sometimes it works that way, too."

"Not for me."

Charlie lowered his cigar and looked Sam over slowly. "No, I guess you're probably right. You probably couldn't be happy that way, could you?"

"I couldn't look myself in the mirror if I let a woman support me."

Charlie leaned a little closer and dropped his voice. "I understand one hundred percent. But let me give you a word of advice—don't let Taylor hear you say that. Women these days don't always understand how a man's pride works. Some of 'em are awfully quick to take offense when they hear something like that."

"Thanks. I'll keep that in mind."

Charlie waved his cigar between them. "I know you don't want me to tell you want to do, and I won't insult you by trying. You're a smart man, Sam. If you want Taylor and Cody, I'm sure you'll figure something out."

Sam laughed sharply. "I wish I had as much faith in me as you do."

"It's a whole lot easier to have faith in someone else than in yourself." Charlie pushed to his feet and ground out his cigar. "But you'll get there. That's what you came here for, isn't it?"

Sam nodded slowly. "I suppose it is."

Charlie let himself back into the house and grinned. "Well, then, I suggest you get to work on it."

Taylor smoothed the folds in a stack of brochures and pushed them across the table toward Sam and Charlie. Soft music played on Ruby's portable CD player on the other side of the room, but it was beginning to grate on Taylor's nerves. They'd been folding, stuffing, sealing, and labeling for hours, and it didn't feel as if they'd made a dent in the job.

Cody had already grown tired of helping. He sat at Ruby's desk playing a hand-held computer game, dipping into a bowl of popcorn and a bag of chips. Taylor checked the clock, promised herself that she'd leave in half an hour to get him home, and turned back to study Sam.

He'd had been withdrawn and quiet for days, and Taylor was growing worried. He'd left the table the instant dinner was over and had responded to every question she'd asked with answers of one syllable.

When he picked up a stack of envelopes and carried them to the small storage room in back, an air of disquiet seemed to go with him. And when she heard the soft click of the outside door, she leaned across the table and whispered to Charlie. "I'm worried, Pop. Sam's not acting like himself at all."

Charlie wiped a damp sponge across an envelope and pressed the seal. "You know why."

"I never thought that job was right for Sam, but I could wring DeWayne's neck for firing him. And I could kick Kip in the seat of the pants, too. I have half a mind to talk with both of them."

Charlie pulled another stack of envelopes from the center of the table. "And say what?"

Ruby set an armful of freshly printed brochures on the table and wiped her hands on the back of her pants. "You can't tell them the truth. Kip can't keep a secret to save his life."

"But this is ridiculous. It's not as if Sam's helpless or stupid. There must be *something* he can do."

"There is." Charlie patted the seal on another envelope. "And he'll find it one of these days."

Taylor leaned her chin on her hand. "What if he doesn't?"

Charlie flicked a glance at her. "He will."

"But what if he *doesn't*? I can't stand to see him like this. Even Cody's staying away from him."

"He'll work it out."

Taylor shot to her feet. "How can you just *sit* there? Don't you care?"

"Of course I care."

"Then *do* something."

"I am." Charlie patted the stack of brochures on the table in front of him and found a piece of beef jerky he'd misplaced. "I'm letting him work it out."

"But he needs help."

"Maybe. But he doesn't want it."

"So what are you saying? That I should let him be miserable because he's got some macho need to do everything himself?"

"Pretty much."

"Well, that's just stupid." Taylor let out a frustrated growl and pushed away from the table. She crossed to the window where she could see Sam standing near the edge of the boardwalk, studying the night sky. "Look at him, Pop. He's moping around here like the world's about to come to an end."

"He thinks it is."

Taylor leaned against the wall and looked to Ruby for help. Surely, Ruby could hear how ridiculous Pop's advice sounded. But Ruby looked at her with deep brown eyes full of pity—as if *she* was missing some vital piece of information.

She started toward the door, but before she could open it, Cody's voice stopped her. "Leave him some dignity, Mom."

She froze with her hand on the doorknob and turned slowly back to face him. "What?"

Cody's cheeks flushed and his eyes glittered. He plucked at the leg of his jeans and fidgeted with the bowl beside him. "You've gotta leave him some dignity, Mom. You've gotta let it be his idea."

"Let *what* be his idea?"

"Whatever his idea *is*." Cody shoved the bowl out of his way.

"The boy's right," Charlie said. "Sam'll find his way out of this. He has to, don't you see?"

"No, I don't see."

"He came here to discover something about himself," Charlie said softly. "If you help him, what he'll discover is that he can't make it on his own, and for the rest of his life he'll be half a man and miserable."

Taylor sagged against the door. "Men are weird."

"Not so weird, Sweet Pea. This is no different from you insisting that you live in your own house and pay your own way in life. You needed to know you could stand on your own two feet. It was important to you. Well, Sam needs the same thing. And there's only one way for him to find it."

Taylor pushed away from the door with a groan and gave in when Ruby tugged her back to the table. But she remained acutely aware of Sam as she worked, and she realized all over again that it was much easier to go through a struggle personally than to stand by helplessly and watch.

Chapter 16

SAM LOOKED UP from the pile of books he'd been studying and rubbed his eyes. Dust motes danced in sunlight that streamed through the library's high arched windows. The scents of paper and dust, of leather and glue and wood mingled together and tickled his nose. His legs were cramped and nervous from sitting in one position too long.

After feeling sorry for himself for two days, he'd pulled himself up by the bootstraps and decided to do something—anything. That's when he remembered the lending library.

He'd been coming every day since then. He'd poured through every book the library had on Cortez in the nineteenth century. He'd searched so long, his eyes burned at the end of every day. But he still hadn't found more than a passing mention of Kurt and Olivia, and next to nothing about Jesse.

He knew Jesse had lived to a ripe old age. He knew he'd still owned the Cinnabar at the time of his death and that he had three sons and two daughters. But that was it.

What had happened to the ranch after Jesse died? Had his sons kept it?

Was it still there?

The question sat him back in his chair so hard the wood groaned in protest. Why hadn't he considered that before?

The Cinnabar might still exist. How could he find out?

He closed the books one by one. The sound of leather slapping shut cracked in the silence of the library and caught the attention of the librarian. Smiling, she pushed away from her desk and crossed the long, high-ceilinged room toward him in a swish of fabric and accompanied by the *tat-tat* of heels on hardwood floor. "No luck?"

"Not so far."

"If you'd be more specific about what you're looking for, I might be able to help. Is there something specific you want to know about Cortez in the nineteenth century?"

Sam pushed the stack of books out of his way. "Actually, yes. I'm looking for information about two families—Evans and Richards. And the Cinnabar Ranch. How would I find out if it's still there?"

"The Cinnabar Ranch?" Helen pulled out a chair and sat opposite him. "That should be easy to find out. I'll just call directory assistance."

Easy for her to say. Sam didn't let himself get too excited about the possibilities. He didn't want to be disappointed.

"As for those two families, we might find them in the directory as well. And if you're interested in their history, maybe the best thing to do is access a genealogy Web site. I can show you how on the computer if you'd like."

Sam was so hungry for a connection to his past, his heart just about jumped out of his throat. He forced himself to remain calm. Even if he could find descendants of Olivia and Kurt and relatives of his own, that didn't mean they'd be interested in hearing from him.

What would he tell them? How would he explain himself?

He wouldn't worry about that now. He'd just find out of they existed.

He followed Helen through the hushed stacks of books to the computer and pulled up a chair to watch as she pushed buttons, pointed and clicked faster than he could follow. "Now then, what were those names?"

"Try Jesse Evans first."

"Date and place of birth by any chance?"

"April 14, 1863, born on the Cinnabar Ranch outside Cortez."

Helen typed, clicked and blinked up at him while the screen changed. "Some ancestor of yours, I assume?"

Sam grinned. "That's right. A real old codger."

Helen nodded appreciatively. "I love seeing people show an interest in their families. Genealogy is one of my passions. I could spend hours looking things up, so I'm always glad for an excuse to dig around." She glanced at the screen and smiled in satisfaction. "Here he is. Jesse Randolph Evans? Is that the one?"

"That's the one." And there it was, one tiny blue line listing Jesse's name and the dates of his birth and death. Sam's spirits sank again. "It's sad to think a person's whole life can be reduced to one short entry on a computer screen."

"It's probably more than one short entry. This site provides pictures if there's one available, and it looks like we have a link here." She touched the arrow to Jesse's name and clicked, and before Sam knew what was happening a picture of Jesse began to appear on the screen.

At least he *thought* the old man was Jesse. If it hadn't been for that grin and those devilish eyes behind the spectacles, Sam wouldn't have known him.

"He looks like an old rake," Helen said with a laugh. "Thoroughly mischievous. As if he knows a secret and he's not telling anybody."

Sam watched the picture form, line by line and slowly grow clearer. The collar of Jesse's shirt, the rough tweed of his jacket, the ledger in his hand. Jesse had always been more partial to keeping books than Sam, but Sam couldn't imagine having a picture made holding one.

It took a few seconds for Sam to realize that the ledger had a label on it. Curious to know what had been so important to his brother, he squinted and leaned closer to the screen. "Can you make out what that says?"

Helen lifted her glasses, then dropped them into place again. "To . . . be . . . kept." She leaned a little closer and peered at the label. "To be kept for Sam Evans?"

Sam's ears buzzed and his mouth dried. A tingle started in his toes and raced to his shoulders. "Are you sure?"

"As sure as I can be. Do you want me to enlarge the picture?"

"Please. But can you print it this way first?"

"Of course." Helen pushed a button or two, clicked once or twice, and the ledger filled the entire screen. "That's what it says, all right. 'To be kept for Sam Evans.' " She grinned at him. "Do you suppose that means you? Or were you named after someone else?"

He shook his head in disbelief. "I have no idea."

But he *did* know. Olivia and Kurt must have told Jesse what happened to him. He could hardly breathe for thinking of the possibilities. Had Jesse known that Sam would stumble across this picture some day? He must have suspected he would, and he'd sent Sam a message.

Stunned speechless, Sam sank into the chair beside the computer and took another look at the screen. "Is there—" His voice caught on the two simple words. He cleared his throat and tried again. "Is there anything else?"

Helen clicked again and shook her head. "Looks like that's it for him. Do you want to try the others you mentioned?"

Sam pulled a scrap of paper and a nub of pencil from the wooden box in front of him and wrote names quickly. "You bet I do. Let's see what the rest of these folks have to say."

Taylor couldn't shake the feeling that seemed to follow her wherever she went. Like a storm hovering on the edges of her mind, disquiet flowed through her with every heartbeat. She followed her usual routine, stopping to chat with friends, smiling and waving as acquaintances passed. As if it were an ordinary day—an ordinary month. As if that strange, prickly feeling wasn't inching up her spine and she wasn't whipping around at the slightest sound to see what was creeping up on her.

Taylor loved this time of year—the quiet after the summer storm. She loved the long, lazy days when people laughed more and the town took on a languid feel as folks wound down and went about their own business for the first time in months.

Except this year, there was an election coming up. And for Taylor, at least, things wouldn't quiet down. The next few weeks would be sharp-edged and frantic. Until Sam came, she'd been looking forward to the fight. Now she wanted it to be over with so she could get on with her future.

She turned a corner and saw a small crowd of people collected near Broward's Bagelry. Mildly curious, she set off to see what could be attracting them. The scent of fresh bagels reminded her that she'd skipped lunch, and a sun-dried tomato bagel with cream cheese sounded like a slice of heaven.

As she neared the crowd, Rosie Garcia slipped away from the group. Her long dark braid hung over one shoulder and her petite body stooped, as if she were sneaking out of school.

"Morning, Rosie."

"Taylor." Rosie stopped, shot a glance over her shoulder, and looked back, wide-eyed. "Taylor. Good morning."

"What's going on at the Bagelry?"

"That?" Another quick glance, another weak-lipped smile. "Nothing. It's just. It's just—" Rosie's shoulders tensed and the braid zinged through the air as she looked over her shoulder again. "It's nothing. What's been going on, anyway? I haven't seen much of you lately."

The prickly sensation between Taylor's shoulders grew stronger. "What's going on at the Bagelry, Rosie? Is it something I should know about?"

"No. No." Rosie brushed her braid over her shoulder and shook her head with wide-eyed innocence. "It's nothing, really. Nothing important, anyway. Just Hutton yapping. You know how he is."

Taylor's heart sank like a stone. "What's he yapping about?"

"Just stuff. Nothing important." Rosie forced a tight laugh. "You know how politics are. I mean, you *should*."

Taylor watched as Jay Carter broke away from the crowd, saw her standing there, and crossed the street to avoid running into her. "What's Hutton saying about me, Rosie?"

"It's just *junk*, Taylor. Nothing important. Nothing *real*. Nobody's really listening to him."

Taylor didn't believe that for a second. "If you don't tell me, I'll find out for myself." Bluff. Pure bluff. The last thing she wanted to do was present herself in the middle of that crowd while Hutton Stone did his thing.

"You don't want to go down there, Taylor. You really don't. It's all ridiculous, anyway."

"Then tell me what he's saying."

Rosie hesitated, finally nodded and took Taylor's elbow to lead her around the corner again. She shifted her weight from foot to foot and let out a sigh. "First, let me ask you a question. Who is this guy you've been seeing?"

"Sam? He's a friend."

"Where did he come from?"

"Colorado."

Rosie touched her arm gently. "How much do you know about him?"

"He's a wonderful man, Rosie. Kind and gentle and wonderful with Cody. Charlie adores him—"

"Is it true that he attacked Dr. Lipton a few weeks ago?"

Everything inside Taylor turned to ice. She'd known they weren't through with that incident, but the question still caught her off guard. "There's an explanation for that," she said, though just what explanation she could offer the general public, she had no idea.

"Then it's true?"

"*Attacked* is too strong a word," Taylor said desperately. "If you ask Sam, he was defending himself. There are always two sides to every story."

"Hutton says he attacked Donald before that. And we all heard about the shoot-out."

"There again—" Taylor said weakly.

"And he threatened Hutton?"

"*That's* not true. Sam's never even met Hutton."

"Who *is* he, Taylor? Where did he come from? Hutton's been trying to find out, but he can't find any information. There's no record that he even exists. Hutton says it's as if he just appeared out of nowhere."

Taylor thought she might be sick. "I told you, he's from Colorado."

Rosie darted a glance around the corner, came back with a scowl. "Then Hutton's lying?"

"Maybe he doesn't know where to look."

"Well, Hutton says Sam must be trying to hide his past—and you're helping him. He says you're letting criminals have the run of Heartbreak Hill."

"Sam is *not* a criminal."

"Look, Taylor, *I* believe you. And I'm sure a lot of other people will, too. But the thing is—" Rosie took a deep breath. "The thing is, Hutton's implying that you're falling victim to this guy because you're . . . well, because you're desperate. And he's saying that this wouldn't be the first time you've made unwise choices just because some man wanted . . . whatever."

The iciness spread through Taylor's limbs and into her chest. Hot on its heels, a burning fury. "How *dare* he!"

Rosie smiled sadly. "You know Hutton."

"Yes, I'm afraid I do." But he had credibility with most of the people in town. The only way to fight him would be to tell the truth about Sam, but that would ruin Sam's life—and shatter the peace Cody seemed to have found with Sam around. Not to mention how much it would hurt Charlie.

She couldn't throw Sam to the wolves. She couldn't allow Hutton to continue speculating aloud about Sam's background. The speculation could destroy Sam's chances for happiness here in Heartbreak Hill.

The only solution was for her to back out of the campaign. But it made her sad in every cell of her body. Life was so unfair. So terribly, terribly unfair.

Taylor could hardly breathe as she hurried to the campaign office. She was too hurt and angry to think straight, but Ruby would know what to do. She tried not to notice the way her supposed friends and neighbors looked away as she approached and tried not to care that they found it so easy to believe the worst of her.

She shouldn't be surprised, she told herself bitterly. This was exactly how they'd behaved when she got pregnant with Cody. They'd judged her and found her wanting, and they were only too willing to do it again.

Tears stung her eyes, but she refused to give in to them. She wasn't a kid any longer. She wasn't weak. She didn't care what they thought.

It seemed to take forever to reach campaign headquarters. She ducked inside gratefully and turned the lock on the door behind her. Ruby had one ear glued to the telephone and a can of soda in front of her. Her feet were propped on a stack of old newspapers.

She waved Taylor inside and covered the phone with one hand. "You look awful. What's wrong?"

Taylor wagged a hand. "I'll wait until you're off the phone."

"If you really want to feel great, take a look at the flyers."

Taylor wandered to the smaller desk and picked up one of the flyers they'd ordered from a printer Charlie had found on-line. They looked as if someone had soaked them in Pepto-Bismol, and the printer had managed to spell Taylor's name wrong. She sank into a chair and trailed one finger across the banner:

REELECT TAILOR O'BRYAN

"I wonder if it would have been too much trouble for them to spell *one* of the names right?" she asked, crumpling the flyer in her fist.

Really, this whole thing was turning into a joke. A big ugly, hurtful joke.

"No!" Ruby shouted into the telephone. "I've already been holding for ten minutes. Don't you—*Don't* put me on—" She sighed heavily and lifted the phone away from her mouth. "I'm calling the credit card company to see if

I can get the charge reversed, but I don't know how long it'll take to get those replaced."

"Maybe it doesn't matter." Taylor propped her elbows on her knees and cradled her head in her hands. "Have you heard the latest?"

"*What* latest?"

"Hutton Stone's out there right now claiming that Sam's a criminal and that I'm helping him conceal his past."

"Well, in a way you are."

"Yes, but he's not a criminal. Hutton's going to ruin him."

"Then go out there and tell the truth."

"I can't. You know that. We all know what would happen to Sam if I did."

"If Hutton's digging into Sam's past, he's going to find out."

Taylor let out a bitter laugh. "*What* will he find out? That Sam traveled through time? Get serious, Ruby, there's no *way* he'll figure that out. There's no proof anywhere. Hutton may jump to other conclusions, but I doubt the truth will be the first thing he thinks of—or even the twentieth."

"I know Hutton. He'll just come up with worse explanations."

"Worse than what he's already suggesting? I doubt that."

Ruby rolled her eyes and hung her head for a second. "My God, that man's imagination is frightening. You're going to have to figure something out soon or you won't stand a chance of being reelected."

"I don't care about getting reelected. Not if it's going to cause misery for another person."

Ruby moved the mouthpiece higher over her head. "Don't give me that. Don't even start. You're going to give up all your hopes and dreams because of this? That's just stupid." She took a long drink and tossed her can away. "How can Sam let you do that?"

Taylor averted her gaze, and Ruby let out her breath on a long sigh.

"You haven't told him, have you?"

"No, and I'm not going to. He'll feel guilty, and then

he'll do something foolish like come forward with the truth. I know him. He's too honorable."

"So you're going to take the high road and protect *him* so he won't try to protect *you*." Ruby dabbed a speck of lipstick from the corner of her mouth. "All this honor floating around is making me nauseated. Meanwhile, if we could come back to earth for a minute . . . I think you're taking the easy way out."

Taylor gaped at her. "What's easy about this?"

"What's easy about quitting? If you back out, you don't have to risk losing. You don't have to stand up for what's right. You don't have to face down someone who'd rather lie than breathe. You don't have to do *anything*. You can just walk away and spend the rest of your life patting yourself on the back for being so damn *noble*." The last word came out as if it left a sour taste in her mouth.

Taylor's chest tightened and the unfairness of life and her situation singed her again. In all the years Taylor and Ruby had been friends, through all the arguments they'd had, Taylor couldn't remember one that had hurt so much or made her so angry. What did Ruby know about it? She couldn't feel the conflicting emotions that clawed Taylor like so many angry beasts, each demanding that it be honored.

"It must be wonderful to be so certain about everything," she said acidly. "But, then, I guess it's easy to be certain when it's not your decision to make."

Ruby banged the receiver down onto the cradle and stood to face her. "You're right. It's not my decision to make. I just wish you'd just make it already and quit sitting on the fence. One day you're gung-ho about the election, the next you're talking about backing out. You're my best friend in the world, Taylor. And I'm willing to do *anything* you ask if you're willing to put forth a little effort. But I really resent being kept hanging this way. Decide, Taylor. Tell me what you're going to do and then, for God's sake, *do* it so I can get on with my life."

The truth of what Ruby said echoed through Taylor, but she was too angry to admit it. Too hurt and angry and frustrated and confused. Ruby had devoted endless hours to her campaign, had put everything else on hold to help Taylor achieve her dream. And how did she repay her?

It seemed that no matter which way she turned, no matter which choice she made, she'd end up hurting someone she loved.

"What's wrong with Mom tonight?" Cody sat on the picnic table, his legs swinging in the air beneath him. "She's acting weird."

Sam lowered the lid on Charlie's barbecue and followed the boy's gaze to where Taylor was yanking onions from Charlie's garden as if she had a personal vendetta against them. "Your guess is as good as mine. I don't think she's said two words since she came home from work."

"Yes, she has," Cody said sullenly. "But she'd wash my mouth out if I repeated them."

"It must be the campaign," Charlie said, coming up behind Sam. His old face was wrinkled with concern, his eyes darkened with worry. "I stopped by headquarters this afternoon and Ruby like to took my head off just because the printing company made a mistake. I had a feeling there was more to it than just those flyers, but she wouldn't tell me what."

Taylor tugged on an onion that resisted, snapped it off at the neck, and moved on.

"Maybe I should talk to her," Sam suggested cautiously.

"Sure." Charlie backed a step away. "Great idea. Go ahead. Cody and I will . . . we'll . . ." He looked around quickly. "I haven't checked the mail today. We'll walk out to the mailbox and do that. Might be something important in there."

Cody jumped from the table and hurried toward the gate. "Your retirement check might be there, huh?"

"You never know." Charlie hitched his pants and moved after the boy as quickly as his old legs would move.

Sam watched them go, then turned back toward Taylor. Okay, so maybe he was taking his life in his hands. It wouldn't be the first time. He'd survived worse.

Maybe.

He hooked his thumbs into his back pockets and started across the lawn slowly, watching to see how she'd react when she realized she was about to have company. She didn't notice him coming—or pretended not to. She yanked, tugged, snapped, and swore at the onions as he crossed the lawn. Maybe she wouldn't welcome the interruption, but he couldn't stand seeing her so upset.

He moved to the edge of the garden, where his shadow spilled across her, and waited for her to look up. When she didn't, he hunkered down in her line of vision. "You want to talk about it?"

"There's nothing to talk about."

"Really? So why are you ripping the life out of those poor onions? What did they do?"

"I'm just in a bad mood, okay?" She shot a glance at him. Her gaze bounced off his face and landed in the dirt in front of her. "It's one of those days."

"It might help if you talk it out."

"There's nothing to talk about," she said again. "It was just an ordinary day."

Sam sat on the grass and stretched his legs out in front of him. "Why don't I believe that?"

"I don't know. Why don't you?" If she'd set those eyes on a pile of kindling, the whole town would have been in flames.

"Maybe because you're not a very good liar." He leaned back on his hands and crossed one foot over the other. "You're tense from head to toe, your eyes could bore holes in hardwood, and Charlie's not going to have much of a garden left when you're through."

"Well, excuse me for not being Little Merry Sunshine every second. I'm sorry if my mood bothers you."

"I didn't say it bothered me."

Her eyes finally landed on his face. "Well, then, I hope you're enjoying it."

"Didn't say that, either."

She tossed a dispossessed onion into the pile behind her. "Well, then what *are* you saying?"

"Nothing. Just observing."

She brushed hair away from her face with the back of her arm. A fine sheen of perspiration glowed on her nose and forehead. "If it's not too much trouble, would you mind observing something else? I just want to be left alone."

Sam shrugged as if it didn't matter in the least. "Sure. Maybe I'll see if Irene has time to give me another driving lesson."

That brought Taylor's head up sharply. "Is that a threat?"

"A threat?" Sam feigned innocence. "Why, no, ma'am. It's just that I've been wanting to tell someone what I found at the library, and you're obviously too busy to talk. And Irene said I could call her any time—"

Taylor propped both hands on her hips. "I'll just bet she did. All right, fine. You win. What?"

"What, what?"

"What did you find at the library?"

Sam stood and waved off her question. "No. No. I don't want to disturb you. You go on back to your onions. I'll just call someone else." He turned away and sauntered slowly, giving her plenty of time to catch up with him.

She grabbed his arm and spun him back around to face her. "I *hate* being manipulated."

"I'll make a note of that. *I* hate being shut out when someone I care about is troubled."

She kicked softly at the sprinkler near her feet. "I wish I could talk about this, but it's something I need to work through on my own. Are you going to tell me what you found at the library?"

Her answer disappointed him, but at least she seemed a little less ready to snap. He told himself to be content and pulled the picture of Jesse from his pocket. "What do you make of this?"

She unfolded it slowly, took a look, and looked up at him quickly. "Is this real?"

"Far as I know."

"It looks like a message of some sort."

"That's what I think, too. Kurt and Olivia must have told him what happened that night on Black Mesa. I'd like to find out if that book he's holding still exists."

"Of course. You have to."

"But if I know Jesse, he didn't leave it just lying around where anyone could find it. I think he probably hid it somewhere at the Cinnabar."

That doused the excitement in her eyes. "Oh. Well, yes, of course. I guess that means you're leaving?"

"Not forever. Just long enough to find the ledger. And I wasn't planning to go alone. I'd like you to come with me." He wanted to share his world with her—the place where he was born, the spot where his horse had thrown him into a patch of thorns, the first fence he'd ever built. Not that those things were still there, but the land was. Land lasted through anything.

"When do you plan to go?"

"Soon."

She looked crestfallen. "Oh, Sam, I'd love to go with you, but I can't."

Sam's smile slipped. "Why not?"

"It's this stupid campaign. Ruby would kill me if I left before the election."

Sam took her shoulders gently. "Is that the only reason?"

"Yes, of course."

"Then I'll wait."

"I can't ask you to do that."

"You didn't." Sam pulled her closer, needing all at once to feel her close, to hold her, to wipe away whatever it was that kept her apart from him. "You didn't ask," he said again. "I'm offering. I don't want to go back without you."

"Even to find your family?"

"Even then."

"But family's so important, Sam. I feel horrible keeping you from yours."

"You forget," he whispered against her temple, "even if I have family now, I don't know any of them. You and Charlie and Cody are more family to me than they are."

She leaned against him lightly, still not giving herself completely. "I can't ask you to stay here, either. Oh, Sam, the whole thing is such a mess."

"Tell me," he whispered. "Tell me what's making you so sad." She shook her head and started to pull away, but he didn't release her. He couldn't. "I can't help if you won't tell me what's wrong."

"You can't help, anyway."

Stung, he loosened his grip. "You still don't want me involved in your life?"

"It's not that," she said miserably. "I want you in my life. Of *course* I do. But—"

Sam touched her cheek, trailed one finger to her lips. "I love you, Taylor. I feel more for you than I've ever felt for any woman. I'd like to spend the rest of my life with you. But it won't work if you won't let me share the bad times along with the good."

"I can't tell you," she said angrily, "because I know what you'll do if I tell you. And I won't have that on my conscience."

He caught a glimpse of Cody peeking around the fence, disappearing again, and a second later he saw Cody and Charlie hurrying down the driveway.

Instinct told him to keep pressing. He knew he could break her. But he didn't want to break her. He wanted her to open up to him, to trust him, to tell him whatever it was on her own.

He slid his hands down her arms and slowly, slowly, pulled her toward him. "You'll tell me if and when you're ready." He brushed a kiss to her cheek and cradled her against his chest, surprised that she didn't pull away. "I'll just wait until you're ready."

"What if I'm never ready?"

"Well, I hope you are, but if you aren't, so be it. Far as I know, there's no law that says a woman has to tell the man in her life *everything*. As long as I know you'll eventually go to Cortez with me, I'll be fine."

She gazed up at him for a long, long time, then finally twined her arms around his neck and kissed him thoroughly. When she was finished, she whispered, "Thank you, Sam."

"Thank *you*," he said with a teasing smile. "I can wait a long time with incentive like that."

She snuggled against him, content, sweet, and looking so young he was half convinced his heart would break. But he couldn't help but wonder if he'd been absolutely truthful with her.

Would it be enough if that restraint remained between them? Or could that become a wedge between them?

Chapter 17

IT DIDN'T TAKE Sam long to find out what was bothering Taylor. The instant he and Charlie left the house the next morning, Charlie's neighbor, Mrs. Bacon, came waddling to the fence to make sure they knew.

She wore short pants, beneath which the plentiful skin around her knees bunched and buckled. Her arms waddled when she walked, and her pudgy toes squished in the dew-damp lawn.

"Good morning, Charlie." Her blouse hugged her body like a second skin, revealing bumps and bulges she must have thought were well-disguised. She turned an ice-cold imitation of a smile on Sam.

This wasn't the first time he'd been on the receiving end of a look like that. That didn't mean he liked it. For Charlie's sake, he forced a smile.

She responded with a slight flaring of her nostrils and turned back to Charlie. "I don't suppose you caught Hutton Stone's rally yesterday."

"Didn't know Hutton was having a rally."

"Oh, yes. Outside the Bagelry yesterday afternoon."

"And why would I care what Hutton Stone had to say?" Charlie asked.

"Because he made some valid points." Her nostrils flared

a bit further and her eyes darted across Sam's face as if she was afraid to look straight at him. "Some *very* valid points. He certainly made *me* think about things."

Sam forced himself to keep his mouth shut. Charlie had things well under control. He stuck his hands into his pockets and rested one elbow on a fence post.

"For instance," Mrs. Bacon said with a bob of her head, "how easy it is for a certain type of person to take advantage of decent folks."

It wasn't hard for Sam to figure out who she was talking about, and he was pretty damn sure she didn't consider him "decent folk."

"Well," Charlie said, "I suppose if anyone would know about taking advantage, Hutton would. Or have you forgotten that he hasn't always been the most ethical person in the world?"

"He's not unethical. He's a businessman."

Charlie snorted a laugh. "I wouldn't want him selling *my* house."

Mrs. Bacon sniffed as if Charlie had insulted her personally. "You might as well know," she said with a glare at Sam. "Hutton has *you* all figured out."

"Me?" Even though Sam had seen it coming, the attack still took him off-guard. "He has *me* figured out?"

"He certainly does."

"Do you mind if I ask just what he's figured?"

Her eyes slanted down at the corners and her mouth did the same. "He knows who you are, that's what. Or maybe I should say he knows who you *aren't*."

Charlie's eyebrows came together over his nose. "Hutton's been digging into Sam's past?"

"Well, he can't, can he? Since apparently, there's no past to dig in*to*. Heartbreak Hill doesn't need people like you around," she snarled at Sam, "and we certainly aren't going to elect a sheriff who'd let that sort of element take over our town."

Sam saw again the look on Taylor's face the evening before, heard again her agonized voice. *I know what you'll do if I tell you. And I won't have that on my conscience.*

How could she know when Sam had no idea what he wanted to do?

He balled his hands into fists, and his head felt as if someone had tightened something hot and metal around it. He wanted to find Hutton Stone and beat some sense into him, but that wasn't the answer. Hutton Stone wasn't the problem.

Sam was.

If he'd never accepted Charlie's hospitality, he wouldn't have gotten so involved with Taylor and her family, and she wouldn't be facing the scorn of her friends and neighbors now. He was destroying her chances of winning this election—the election that meant so much to her. It was a fine kind of love that would allow a man to ruin the woman he loved.

"Whatever my faults," he said to Mrs. Bacon, "Sheriff O'Brien and her family shouldn't be held accountable. It would be a shame if people were so closed-minded that they punished her just because she was kind enough to help a stranger."

"And let him have the run of the town." She turned to Charlie and added, "You'd better be careful, Charlie O'Brien. He's already gone after Donald and Dr. Lipton, and he's threatened to harm Hutton. You could be next."

She waddled away, and two swings of her ample hips were all Sam needed to make a decision. He whipped back toward Charlie's house and crossed the lawn in three strides.

"Where are you going?" Charlie called after him.

"I'm going to tell the truth."

"Don't be a fool." Charlie panted as he followed Sam up the steps. "You *can't* go public. Do you have any idea what would happen if you did?"

"People would think I'm crazy."

"Crazy?" Charlie grabbed Sam's arm and pulled him to a stop, then leaned over and grasped his knees as he struggled to catch his breath. "Crazy will be the least of it," he said when he could talk again. "You go public with your story and you can forget having a life. *Ever.* You'll spend the rest of your life in a mental hospital or hounded by the media—or both."

"I'll move. Start over somewhere new."

Charlie gave his head a brisk shake. "You wouldn't be able to move far enough. You've seen Taylor's computer. You've seen the television. If the wire services were to pick up your story—which they would—there wouldn't be a place on earth you could go to escape. No matter where you went, reporters would follow you. Ten years from now—*twenty*—they'd still be doing stories about you." He moved one hand slowly in front of him as if he was reading something. "Whatever happened to the crazy man from Heartbreak Hill? Where is he now?"

Sam didn't like the idea, but he liked destroying Taylor's life even less. "Fine," he growled. "If that's my lot in life, then I'll put up with it."

Charlie glowered at him. "It's not your lot in life, you damn fool. If you have a lot, it's Taylor and Cody. That boy worships the ground you walk on, and she does, too. You think the winds of fate brought you all the way to Heartbreak Hill so you could destroy your life? You think they dropped you here on a whim? I'm tellin' you, son, you're here because you and Taylor belong together, plain and simple."

Sam yanked open the door. "I'm ruining her life, Charlie."

"You're *giving* her a life, Sam. She doesn't need this job anywhere near as much as she needs someone she can love and trust to stand beside her no matter what comes her way. Maybe that's something both of you need to learn." Charlie drew himself up to his full height. "If you think the folks in this town have short fuses, just you *try* walking out on my daughter. You'll see what hell's all about."

"Are you threatening me?"

"You're damn right I am." Charlie met Sam eye-to-eye . . . almost. "I never figured you for the type to run away from a fight."

"I'm not running away. I'm backing off so that Taylor can get what she wants."

Charlie shook his head. "I never figured you for a fool, either. But you *are* a fool if you can't see that what she wants is you."

"If that's true, why didn't she tell me about this?"

"About *this*?" Charlie laughed without humor. "Because she knew you'd react exactly the way you're reacting now. And because she doesn't want you to destroy yourself to save her. Hell's bells, man, surely you can see that."

The fury inside Sam slowly began to dim, but he still wasn't completely convinced. "She could at least let me stand with her against the enemy." Even Olivia, who'd flatly refused his proposals of marriage, had granted him that much.

Charlie nodded slowly. "She could. And if she were another woman, she would. Maybe it's my fault. Her mother died when she was so young, and I didn't know a whole lot about raising a girl. So maybe I taught her to be *too* independent."

"It's not her independence that's the problem," Sam said. He rubbed the back of his neck and felt another bit of tension drain away as he tried to figure out how to explain. "It's just that she shuts me out. Like she has a door she opens and closes when the mood suits her. Sometimes I get a glimpse inside, but that's about all. She doesn't trust me. Maybe that's it. And I happen to believe that you can't love someone you don't trust."

Charlie took his elbow and started led him inside. "Well, now, I agree with you there. But if it's any consolation, I think Taylor trusts you as much as she trusts anyone—a lot more, in fact. She was so young when all that mess happened with Cody's father. Young and naive and so trusting you wouldn't recognize her. Just like her mother was when we met. My wife believed that people are good and that they mean what they say. Can't say I always agree with her."

"That's the way it should be," Sam said miserably.

"True enough. Too bad it's not always." Charlie pulled his hand away and linked his hands behind his back. "Nate Albright using Taylor the way he did drained a lot of that trust away. After losing her mother and then being left by that sumbitch, she started thinking everybody was going to leave her. And a few of the folks in this town did the rest of the damage, smiling at her out of one side of their mouths and passing judgment with the other."

"Are you saying she's afraid I'm going to leave her?"

"I think it's a safe bet, even if she doesn't know it. You've shut her out a time or two, yourself. And even if she did believe that you love her and want to stay . . . well, considering how you got here, you really can't make any promises, can you?"

"No more than the next man," Sam said. "I'm pretty sure I won't get pulled away from here, but I can't guarantee it. But, then, nobody can guarantee anything, can they? That's life."

"You don't need to convince me," Charlie said. "Taylor's the one you need to talk to."

"And I will. But just so you know, I don't plan to go anywhere." He slanted a grin at Charlie and added, "I don't want to see what hell's all about."

A cloud of dust flew around Taylor's office, tickling her nose and threatening to make her sneeze. She'd sent Donald back into the cells to sweep them out, and he was making his displeasure known.

She sighed softly and turned her attention back to the report of a fender bender she'd investigated that morning on the edge of town. Another puff of dust wafted through the open doorway and a loud clank followed. Donald's voice rose and fell on his long list of complaints that seemed to range from Taylor's offenses against society to the meat loaf his mother had served for dinner the night before.

Where *was* he finding all that dust?

She worked the fingers of one hand into her hair and tried to concentrate on the report. Before she'd filled in even three more blanks, the street door opened and a shadow fell across her desk. She lifted her eyes, surprised to see Sam standing inside the doorway, hat in hand.

Setting aside her pen, she shoved the report out of her way. "What are you doing here?"

"Can you take a break? We need to talk."

"Oh?" She didn't like the serious expression on his face. "About what?"

He glanced toward the door as another puff of dust floated into the main room. "I'd like to talk to you somewhere else, if that's all right."

She thought about leaving without telling Donald she was going, but considering Donald's current mood, she'd only create problems for herself if she did that. "Give me a second," she said to Sam. "I'll meet you outside."

He nodded solemnly and pulled the door closed behind him. Her stomach twisted as a dozen possibilities raced through her head. Cody had been hurt. No, if that were true, Sam would have just told her. Charlie had done or said something wrong. No, there again, Sam would have just said so. She discarded several other theories before she reached the door to the back room, but one thought kept racing through her mind. Sam had changed his mind about waiting for her. He was leaving.

And if he went to Cortez without her, he probably wouldn't come back.

She took a couple of deep breaths to steady herself, then poked her head into the back room. "Donald? Can you watch the office? I need to run out for a few minutes."

His narrow face pinched into a scowl, but he nodded. "Anything's better than this."

"Great." She tried for a cheerful smile, but her mouth failed her miserably. "Thanks."

"What do I do if your boyfriend decides to pop someone else in the nose while you're gone? Take him out to lunch?"

"The sarcasm's getting old, Donald."

"Oh. Well, pardon me."

Taylor gritted her teeth to keep from rising to the bait. "Just keep an eye on things, please. I'll be back as soon as I can."

Donald set the broom aside and trailed her into the front

office. "I'm serious, Taylor. What if something happens? Shouldn't I know where to find you?"

"I won't be gone that long."

"Keeping secrets isn't going to help, you know. People are talking."

"Good grief," Taylor snapped. "Can't I step out of the office for five minutes without getting the whole town in an uproar?"

"Not the way things've been going lately." He dropped into her chair and looked as if he might kick his feet onto the desk, then thought better of it. "It's not only you who's being affected, either. Have you ever thought about what I'm going to do if you're not reelected?"

"Well, of course I have. But let's not borrow trouble. I'm trying desperately to stay upbeat. If I run around thinking I've lost, or that I'm likely to lose, I probably will."

Donald scratched one eyebrow with the tip of a finger. "You're going to rely on positive thinking? Gee, why don't I feel relieved?"

Taylor could almost *feel* Sam waiting on the other side of the door. The last thing she wanted was for him to come back inside. "I'm not relying on positive thinking," she said. "No matter what you may think of me, Donald, I'm not a fool."

"Not a fool," he said, "just naive. I don't know who Sam Evans really is or what he wants, but it's obvious that he's using you for some reason. And all you do is run around with your head in the clouds."

Taylor battled one quick sensation of doubt before she shook it away and yanked open the door. "It really doesn't matter what you think, Donald. Or what anyone else does, for that matter. From now on, the subject is off-limits in this office."

"You can't tell me what I can and can't talk about."

"I can as long as you're on duty. What you talk about after work is completely up to you." She shut the door hard enough to make the windows rattle and looked around for Sam.

She found him two doors down, leaning against the railing of the boardwalk, his legs stretched out in front of him, his hands in his pockets. He looked so handsome, so dear, her heart did a little tap dance in her chest.

He stood when he saw her and started coming her way. Taylor hurried toward him, forcing a smile as if she could prevent him from delivering bad news if she could keep her spirits up.

"There you are." She kept walking, forcing him to turn around and follow. She trailed her fingers along the varnished pine railing and ignored the curious looks coming their way from just beyond the mirrored store windows. Either Donald was right or she was becoming paranoid, because it felt as if every eye in Heartbreak Hill was on them. "You look awfully serious. What's up?"

"You're damn right I'm serious. If you want to know the truth, I'm fed up."

Why did his voice always affect her like that? She could feel it in every cell of her body and its resonance set her nerve endings on fire. "Oh?" She sounded sickeningly chipper—and totally bogus. She dropped a little of the false cheer. "With what?" As if she couldn't have guessed.

"With the campaign, with the gossip. With everything."

"What's happened now?"

He shot a look at her, then glanced away. "Nothing in particular. I'm just tired of what it's doing to us."

Taylor stopped walking completely. "To us?"

"That's right. I'm tired of worrying and dodging bullets, and I'm tired of treating this campaign as if it were the most important thing in the world. I know it's important to you, Taylor, but one of these days it'll be over. Win or lose, we'll go on." He turned to face her, his eyes dark with an expression that made her pulse leap. "At least, I hope we will."

"I—"

He held up one hand. "Wait. I'm not finished. The fact is, it doesn't matter one bit to me whether you keep this job or find another one. You tell me it doesn't matter what I do for a living. Well, I feel the same way. I can live with whatever comes. What matters is finding out how you feel about me. I've been swinging in the wind for weeks, thinking you care about me one day, worrying that you don't the next."

She gaped at him. "You don't *know* how I feel about you?"

"How would I?"

"Well, it's . . . it's obvious. Everyone else can tell."

"I don't care about everyone else. I love you, Taylor, and I want to know whether I'm whistling in the wind here."

Taylor shook her head in disbelief, but the words stuck in her throat. Why couldn't she say them? Her heart was full to overflowing, her soul brimmed with it. So why did she have so much trouble voicing what she felt? "You know how much I care about you."

"I don't want you to *care* about me, Taylor. You can care about your friends, about your town, and even about your job. I want you to *love* me. I loved a woman once who didn't love me. I stayed around like a cur dog, waiting for her to toss me scraps of affection. She liked me fine. She *cared* about me. She just didn't love me. It's not an experience I'm eager to repeat."

He looked so miserable, Taylor suddenly didn't care who saw them or what they thought. She slid her arms around his waist and leaned her head on his shoulder. "Of course I love you, Sam."

"Do you trust me? Do you know that I'd do anything in the world for you and Cody? That I'd die before I hurt you? That I'd only leave you if you ask me to—and then I wouldn't go willingly?"

Tears burned her eyes, but she forced a tiny laugh. "Yes."

"Maybe it's my fault," he said. "I've kept silent because I wanted to *be* somebody before I spoke for you. But when I think about leaving here and starting over without you, when I imagine losing Cody or never spending another evening with Charlie, I realize how foolish I'm being. Being somebody alone doesn't have a whole lot of appeal."

"Oh, Sam—"

"I want to share your life, Taylor. I want to share the good things and the bad. I want to include you in every part of my life. But you have to trust me enough to *let* me share the tough things, or we have nothing."

Taylor slowly pulled away from him. "I'm trying, Sam. I tell myself every day that you're not Nate. I tell myself that you truly do love me and Cody, and you won't walk out on us."

"But you don't believe it."

"I *do*. I believe it logically, and I'm trying so hard to believe it in my heart. Don't give up on me. Once the campaign is over, things will be better. I promise. You and I have hardly had any time to be together. There's always something keeping us apart. What we have doesn't feel quite real, I guess."

"Then let's spend some time on us." He put his fingers over her mouth to keep her from protesting. "Let me finish before you give me all the reasons why you can't. I'm not asking for much. Just one day for the two of us. Can we do that?"

A dozen waiting tasks rushed through her mind, but she shook them away. "Yes," she whispered, "of course we can. My day off is tomorrow."

"We'll get away from town and everyone in it?"

She found herself warming to the idea. "It sounds wonderful."

"Where shall we go?"

She smiled slowly, remembering how wistful he'd sounded about getting back into the saddle a few weeks earlier. She'd meant to take him riding then, but one thing after another had diverted her attention. She didn't like knowing that she'd been putting the people she loved most way down on her list of priorities.

"How about if I surprise you?" she asked. "Will *you* trust *me*?"

"With my life."

Taylor laughed. "I don't think we need to go that far." She glanced at the clock on the corner and realized that more than a few minutes had passed. She'd rather stand here with Sam than go back to work, but once again, reality carried more weight than dreams. "I'd better get back before Donald comes looking for me," she said, standing on tiptoe and brushing a kiss to the side of Sam's jaw.

He nodded reluctantly and drew his arms away slowly. A minute later she watched him walk away and knew that she'd lost the battle to keep her heart safe. She'd fallen madly, deeply, helplessly in love with him.

Today, love made her heart light and laughter danced in her throat. She had the crazy urge to throw out her arms and spin until she couldn't stand or see or think. But she'd seen the other side of the coin and that terrified her.

If she lost Sam now, it would destroy her.

Morning dawned cloudless and cool, the sky the soft powder blue of early autumn. Taylor had been up since before the sun, packing a lunch of thick ham and cheese sandwiches, fresh fruit, chips, and raw vegetables. At the last minute she tossed in bags of trail mix in case they got hungry before lunchtime.

As the sun came up, Cody's alarm went off, and a few minutes later he scuffed into the kitchen, hair tousled and eyes puffy from sleep. Yawning, he rubbed his eyes, but when he saw the open picnic basket on the table, he came fully awake.

"What's this?"

"Lunch for Sam and me. We're going to spend the day together."

"Cool. Where?"

"I haven't told Sam yet, but I'm taking him into the mountains to ride horses."

Cody's face fell. "Without me?"

"You have to go to school."

"I could skip one day. Please?"

"Not today, sweetheart. Sam and I need a day for the two of us. Next time, okay?"

Cody slid into a chair and studied her thoughtfully. "Are you going to marry him, Mom?"

The abrupt question surprised her. She let out a nervous laugh. "Who's talking about marriage?"

"I am. I like Sam. I don't want him to go away."

Taylor poured a cup of coffee and sat across from her son. She forced herself not to give in to her instinct to evade the issue. "I don't want him to go away, either."

"So, are you going to marry him?"

She started to say that Sam hadn't asked, but honesty made her stop. "I can't make any promises, but that's one reason Sam and I need to be alone today. We still have things to work out."

Cody's brow puckered. "Like what? I know he loves you, and you love him, too. I can tell."

"I do love him. I'm just a little nervous still."

"Why?"

She sipped and glanced at the clock, trying to decide how much Cody needed to know, how much he needed to be shielded from. "That's hard to explain."

"Grandpa thinks you're afraid Sam will leave like my dad did."

Scowling, Taylor lowered her cup. "Oh, does he?" Grandpa talked too much.

"Yep." Cody got up and found a container of orange juice in the refrigerator. He pulled a glass from the cupboard and carried both back to the table. "He thinks you're afraid that Sam doesn't love you enough to stay. Or maybe that you think he'll go back through time and leave us. Do you really think that?"

He looked so honestly concerned, Taylor pushed her slight irritation with Charlie aside. "Sam doesn't think so. He says he filled the empty space his friend left."

"Do you believe him?"

Taylor shrugged carefully and watched as the sun began to slant across the table. "I think so. I certainly don't *want* to think he might be pulled back to his real life."

Cody took a swig of juice and mopped his mouth with his sleeve. "Why can't *this* be his real life?"

Taylor turned her cup slowly, wondering why she hadn't realized that deep inside she must believe that Sam belonged somewhere else. She glanced toward Charlie's house, where the lights were coming on and Sam would be getting ready to meet her. "Maybe it is his real life," she said softly. "I guess time will tell."

"I don't want time to tell. I want Sam to be my dad. He'd be the coolest dad, ever."

Taylor grinned, realizing she couldn't remember the last time Cody had talked about finding Nate. "He would be, wouldn't he?"

"The *coolest*. My friends are already jealous because he lives with Grandpa. Just imagine how they'd feel if he lived with *us*."

Taylor replaced the cap on the bottle of orange juice and carried it back to the fridge. *Just imagine how hurt Cody would be if Sam didn't stay.* She found cereal and a bowl and set them on the table in front of Cody. "What have you told your friends about Sam?"

Cody dug into the cereal looking for the prize inside. "Just stuff, why?"

"What kind of stuff?"

Cody stopped digging and glanced at her. "You mean have I told them about Sam coming from the past?" He frowned so hard lines formed over the bridge of his nose. "I'm not stupid, Mom."

"Oh, Cody, I know you're not." She ruffled his hair and kissed his forehead. "It's just so important that nobody ever finds out. Sam's life would be ruined. It would turn out like that movie we saw—you remember the one where that kid was an alien. . . ."

"And the scientists kidnaped him so they could study him?" Cody found his prize and set it aside. "Yeah, I remember. What they did to that kid was gross. So why would I tell? I want Sam to *stay*."

Taylor pulled a carton of milk from the refrigerator and handed it to him. "Sorry. Stupid question."

"Jeez, Mom. Have a little faith, wouldja?"

That seemed to be a constant complaint from the people in her life. "I'll try."

Cody poured cereal and splashed milk into his bowl and

onto the table. Before she could grab a dishcloth, he swiped it up with his sleeve and gave her long, slow look. "I'll make a deal with you. I won't bug you to let me go with you today on one condition."

He looked so grown up, Taylor's heart constricted painfully, but she couldn't help grinning at the expression he wore. "What condition would that be?"

"That you tell Sam you'll marry him."

"I can't promise that," Taylor said with an uneasy laugh. "But I will promise that I'll work on it."

Cody squinted one eye and twisted his mouth as he considered the deal. "Okay, I guess. But it'd be better if you did it my way."

Chapter 18

Damn, BUT IT felt good to be in the saddle again. The creak of leather, the earthy scent of the animal, the shift of haunches beneath him were like strong liquor to Sam—even if the horse did walk as if it was half asleep.

And the silence.

He didn't think he'd ever heard anything quite so beautiful. He'd been growing more used to the noise of living in modern times, but he still didn't know how people could stand the never-ending racket. Even at night the sound of a neighbor's television drifted in through his open window, the roar of a car engine or a door slamming, of a telephone ringing or some other unnatural thing broke the stillness.

A bird swooped overhead and something rustled through the bushes at his side. He glanced behind him to make sure Taylor was still all right. The breeze picked up and tossed her hair in the sunlight. Strands of fire shot out from it, burnished gold and russet, the color of the Colorado hills. The color of the changing leaves around them. It was all he could do to drag his gaze back and focus on the trail where webs of exposed roots and rocks made for slow going.

"When do you want to stop for lunch?" Taylor called.

"As soon as we find a comfortable spot. Are you hungry?"

"A little, but I can wait. I'm not ready to waste away yet."

He laughed and reined in, turning his horse on the narrow trail so he could see her better. "I could ride forever, but I don't want to go too far for you."

"We can go as far as you want to—as long as we can find our way back. I lost track a long time ago."

Sam chuckled. "We haven't gone far, and these horses are so tame, if we let go of the reins they'd have us back to the paddock in nothing flat." He patted his mount's neck and gave the horse some slack so it could nibble at the sweet grass at their feet. "I know the fella who owns these horses is a friend of yours, but I've gotta be honest with you. These horses aren't the healthiest or happiest animals I've ever seen. Their coats are dull and the spirit's all but gone out of 'em. Is this usual?"

Taylor nodded. "Unfortunately, when it comes to trail horses like these, it is. They have to be docile so they'll tolerate people who've never ridden before."

"People who've never ridden before take horses into country like this?" It was a recipe for disaster if you asked Sam.

"Well, yes." Taylor shifted in her saddle again. "It's one of the most popular things people do while they're on vacation. Harlan runs his string up here in the summer and takes them down to Arizona during the winters."

Sam watched her move in the saddle and scowled slightly. "You look uncomfortable. Do you want to rest here for a while?"

"If I get out of this saddle, I may never make it back into it."

"Sure you will. I'll make sure of it." The idea of helping her into the saddle made Sam warm in spite of the cool autumn air and deep forest shade. "And if you can't make it," he teased, "I'll just sling you over the back of my horse and get you back down the mountain that way."

Taylor laughed. "What a dignified way to make my return. It'd give people something to talk about for weeks."

"I'll only use that as a last resort," Sam promised. "If every other effort to get you into the saddle fails."

Taylor's expression sobered suddenly and her eyes softened. "Well, then, in that case I'll stop whenever you want to."

Looking into those bottomless eyes, Sam wasn't at all sure he'd be able to ride on. He dismounted and dropped the reins to let the horse eat, then crossed to Taylor and held out his hands to help her down.

She slid from the saddle slowly, brushing against him the whole way down in an act so utterly sensual, he couldn't breathe. As her feet touched the ground, he pulled her close and covered her mouth.

All thoughts of lunch slid right out of his head; the need to ride until he had his fill suddenly seemed trivial. All he wanted, all he needed in the world was right here in his arms.

She twined her fingers into his hair and melted against him. Lips, breasts, hips, hair, scent—everything about her was soft and alluring and utterly irresistible.

He released her slowly, knowing that it wouldn't take much to push him beyond control, fearing that would destroy what they had. When a soft moan of disappointment escaped her lips, he put a few inches between them. "I'm trying like hell to control myself, Taylor. I'm not sure I can."

"I'm not sure I want you to."

He pulled the blanket she'd brought from the pack on her horse and spread it on the ground. "Don't say that unless you mean it. I'm not going to touch you until I know you trust me. I don't want you to worry that I'm going to leave you."

She shivered slightly and rubbed her arms for warmth. Sam ached to warm her himself, but he forced himself to stay put.

"I know you won't leave me," she said after what seemed like forever. "It's not you I don't trust, it's me. It's hard to believe that someone as wonderful as you could love me, and it's hard to trust myself to be in a real relationship after all this time. I've never had a successful relationship, Sam. I don't even know what to do."

He shoved his hands into his pockets and leaned against the trunk of a tree. A shower of leaves fell onto his shoulders. "You think you're the only one in that boat? Hell, Taylor, I don't have the slightest idea what I'm supposed to do or how to do it. I only know that I love you."

Her eyes filled with tears. "And I love you." She closed the distance between them and slid her arms around his waist. "Cody adores you. He told me that you and I had better come home engaged. I'm not sure he'll let me in the door if we're not."

Sam couldn't resist. He wrapped his arms around her. "I wouldn't want to make the boy mad."

"Neither would I."

He kissed her quickly. He still wasn't ready to trust himself with more. "But I don't want to rush you into a decision like that."

"If you had any idea how much I want it, you'd be impossible to live with." She moved closer, stirring the scents of fresh air and autumn, of loamy soil and leaves. "I can't go through the rest of my life afraid, Sam. I need you."

His hands took on a life of their own, running to places he might not have dared to touch if he'd been capable of calling the shots. His need became urgent and painful, and he pulled her against him in near desperation.

He tried to speak, but need silenced him. Drawing breath was almost too much.

Her hands slid through his hair, worked magic on his shoulders, then made their way with agonizing slowness down his back to his hips. Was it possible that she could want as much as he did? That she could need with the same urgency? He would never have imagined it possible or dared to hope for it, but her eagerness drove him out of his mind.

He moved his hands tentatively to her waist, slid one beneath the soft fabric of her sweatshirt, and brushed the swell of her breast with his fingertips. She moaned and

tilted back her head, exposing the long curve of her throat
to his mouth.

He nipped softly and the fire inside him roared to life.
He should stop, he warned himself, before he reached the
point where he couldn't go back.

She ran her hands to his stomach, then inched them
slowly up his chest where she began to slowly, deliberately,
unfasten the buttons of his shirt. When she had the first two
open, she touched her lips to his chest and flicked her
tongue against his overheated skin.

He sucked in a breath and slid his fingers beneath the
lace that covered her breasts. The feel of her warm skin
beneath his fingers pushed him further toward the edge. He
forced himself to pull the sweatshirt over her head instead
of ripping it off, but he couldn't stop his hands from traveling to her jeans, unfastening the snap and working the
zipper. He told himself to hold back, even as he skimmed
her jeans down over her hips.

There in the dappled sunlight of the forest, with the fresh
air and breeze dancing around her, she stood tall and proud
in nothing but the navy pieces of lace that covered her most
secret parts from his hungry eyes.

He let his eyes linger for what felt like an hour, but it
couldn't have been more than a second or two before desire
and need took over again. He pulled her to him hungrily.

When she reached for the buckle on his trousers, Sam
knew he was lost. If someone had come out of the forest
at that moment and held a gun to his head, he wouldn't
have been able to pull away from her.

With the gentlest touch imaginable, she drew him onto
the blanket with her. The hillside may have been hard and
rocky, branches and roots surely protruded from the ground
beneath them, but Sam didn't notice and Taylor didn't complain. He was in heaven, as oblivious to everything around
him as he'd been when he traveled through time to get here.

She pulled him closer and kissed him, opening her mouth
beneath his and caressing his tongue with hers. Her breath
came in ragged gasps that drove him to a frenzy. She slid

her hands up his back and held him, moved beneath him, gently at first, then with more urgency.

Time had no meaning as they lay together. Fear had no power. There was only the need to become one soul in the only way possible. She was as much a part of him as breathing, as necessary to his survival as food and water. He kissed her everywhere—mouth, shoulders, breasts, waist. He couldn't seem to get close enough, or take enough, or give enough.

He rolled over and pulled her on top of him. A rock jabbed his shoulder, but when she leaned over him and kissed him, the pain faded to nothing. She was fire, warm honey, and satin—the other half of his heart, the other side of his soul. She worked magic until he was certain he'd die from pleasure.

When he knew he couldn't bear one more kiss, one more touch without exploding, he pulled her hands away and rolled her gently onto the blanket. Her sighs of pleasure, the tiny whimpers that escaped her lips finally drove him to the edge and he couldn't hold back anymore.

He began gently, but being with her was like stepping off a cliff into a bottomless pool. Sensation exploded and his breath stopped. Fire burst through his body, and then, at last, he fell helplessly into nothing.

Afterward, he stroked a lock of hair from her cheek and kissed her tenderly.

She turned those incredible eyes toward him, soft and green and flecked with brown, and stretched languidly, like a cat in the sun. "This has changed everything, you know."

He leaned up on one elbow so he could look at her. "You don't mind that I have nothing to offer you?"

She splayed her fingers across his chest and stroked the hair there lightly. "I don't need money, Sam. I don't need things. I need you. Just don't leave me and I'll be happy."

"I can't leave you," Sam said honestly. "It would kill me. I've just discovered the way I want to end every day for the rest of my life."

"Or start them." She traced one finger across his lips.

"Are you sure you don't mind taking on a ready-made family?"

"I want the whole thing, Taylor. You. Cody. Charlie. It's all part of the package, as far as I'm concerned."

She tweaked his nose and followed it up with another kiss, then lay back on the ground. "So do I."

Sam let out a whoop that bounced off the surrounding peaks and filled the valley with its echo. Creatures skittered away and birds took flight. The horses nickered softly and tossed their heads.

Laughing, Sam pulled Taylor to her feet. "Let's get dressed before someone gets curious and decides to check out what's going on."

Her eyes glittered. "I *dare* someone to come looking."

"We don't want that." Sam picked up her clothes and held them out to her. "If some other man came walking up right now and saw you this way, I'd be forced to kill him. A thing like that could ruin a whole day."

Taylor wished she could remain in the idyllic world they'd created that afternoon, but real life returned with a resounding crash when they got home. Ruby had left half a dozen urgent-sounding messages. Cody was dancing all over the kitchen, panicking over a report he'd forgotten even to start until Mrs. Wilson called on him to present it in class. Charlie was trying out a food processor he'd ordered through Betty D'Angelo at The Gadgetry. Taylor couldn't imagine why he needed one, but she didn't bother asking. She doubted he could have heard her over the sound of the motor, anyway.

While Sam brought in the picnic basket, she picked up the phone to return Ruby's calls and sat down at the table to thumb through the encyclopedias Cody had carried over from Charlie's house. She didn't waste time asking how Cody could have forgotten a major report in the first place. Badgering him wouldn't get the report done. But they'd definitely discuss it later.

While Ruby's phone rang, she got straight to the point with Cody. "What's your report supposed to be about?"

"Spain."

"Spain? The entire country?" Taylor rubbed her temple and closed her eyes. "This is a major report, isn't it?"

"I guess so. Can you take me to the library? Grandpa's encyclopedias are too old."

Ruby's answering machine clicked on. Distracted from Cody's question, Taylor left a message and turned back to Cody when she'd hung up again. "How long is the report supposed to be?"

"As long as it needs to be to cover all the information." Cody pulled a crumpled, torn piece of paper from his backpack and slid it across the table. "That's what we have to have in it."

Taylor scanned the list and felt the peace and contentment she'd found in Sam's arms draining slowly away. "There are at least nine sections here, and it's already six o'clock. There's no way you'll get this done tonight."

Charlie changed blades on his processor and started feeding celery stalks through it. "I told him to get started, but he wanted to wait for you. Said the information in my books is outdated."

The whine of the motor made Taylor's head pound. "It probably is. You bought these encyclopedias when I was a kid." Taylor pushed the books away and rubbed both temples. "Why didn't you take him to the library?"

"He wanted to wait for you."

"Well, by waiting, he's lost at least two hours of time he could have been working."

Charlie peered into the processor's bowl and smiled at the results of his celery experiment. "Just write a note and explain that you didn't know about the report until tonight. Ask his teacher for a few extra days so he can get it done."

Taylor shook her head and the pain ricocheted from side to side. "The fact that I didn't know isn't much of an excuse. I *should* have known."

"His teacher will understand. Life's been kind of different around here lately."

Cody decided to help his grandpa's argument. "You can write a note. That's what Justin's mom did. She wrote a note because she and Justin's dad are getting a divorce."

Taylor pulled her hands away from her temples. "Lisa and Joe Mooney are getting divorced? Are you sure?"

"Yep." Cody climbed onto a chair and pulled a bag of chips from the cupboard. "I went over there today on the way home from school. Justin's dad was carrying boxes out to his truck."

Taylor glanced at Charlie, who'd stopped grating carrots and looked equally shocked. "Well," he said with a deceptively light laugh. "Imagine that. I always figured Lisa and Joe for one of those couples who'd last forever."

"So did I," Taylor said, but the memory of the encounter she'd witnessed at the drugstore left her uneasy. "I know things have been tough since Joe lost his job, but I'm really sorry to see it come to this."

Cody had moved to the refrigerator and emerged with a bottle of some power drink he'd talked Taylor into buying because the bottle was "cool." "They're not getting divorced because of Justin's dad's job. He got another job already."

Taylor nearly asked for details, but caught herself and clamped her mouth shut. If she gossiped about Justin's family troubles, she was no better than the people who talked about her past. "Well, that's great. I hope they'll be able to patch things up. But we're supposed to be worrying about your report, not about other people."

"Yeah, but I know why they're getting a divorce."

"I'm sure you do, but it's none of our business."

"But, Mom—"

"I mean it, Cody." She put a handful of chips on a plate so he wouldn't completely spoil his appetite, then tucked the bag back into the cupboard. "Forget about Justin's family and start figuring out what you're going to do about Spain."

Cody slumped back in his chair and stuffed a handful of chips into his mouth. "I don't know. I don't have time to do a *good* report tonight."

Taylor didn't know whether to help or let him take his lumps for forgetting, but she thought at least half the blame belonged on her shoulders for not paying enough attention over the past two months. "You can get started. If you'll do your best in the time we've got left, I'll talk to Mrs. Wilson tomorrow."

"Then can we go to the library?"

Before Taylor could agree, Sam opened the door and Ruby burst into the kitchen in front of him. "I am *so* glad you're back. I've been trying to find you for hours. You've got to come with me."

Taylor looked at the mess in her kitchen, at the encyclopedias and schoolbooks stacked on the table, at the potato and carrot peelings in the sink, at the mounds of shredded, diced, and sliced vegetables on the counters, and the empty food-processor box blocking the dishwasher.

"Not tonight, Ruby. Whatever it is can wait."

Sam added the picnic basket to the clutter, but at least he set to work emptying it instead of leaving it for her to deal with. "I don't know, Taylor. You might want to hear what Ruby has to tell you before you decide."

"I'm so tired right now, I don't care what happened."

"Oh, you will." Ruby stepped over the empty box and made herself comfortable at the table. "I just heard something that—if it's true—will blow Hutton Stone right out of the campaign water."

"Oh?" Taylor poured herself a small glass of Cody's super-duper power drink. "What did you hear?"

"His wife is going to stay with her sister in Billings."

Taylor took a gulp and wondered how something with so little taste could possibly infuse a body with energy. "How will that blow Hutton out of the campaign?"

Ruby grinned, let a moment lapse for suspense while she looked from one face to the other to make sure everyone was paying attention. "It's not just a visit. It's permanent."

Charlie and Sam shared a confused glance. Taylor took another sip, just in case the stuff actually worked. "She's leaving him?"

"That's what I hear."

"But why? Not that I wouldn't if I were her, just on general principle . . . but *why*?"

Ruby grinned and leaned forward, locking her fingers together and lowering her voice. "What *I* heard is that she's a little fed up. Seems she doesn't like sharing Hutton with his mistress."

Taylor nearly fell off her chair. Charlie dropped the lid to his food processor. Sam tossed the empty sandwich bags into the garbage can.

"Are you sure about this?" Taylor's voice barely came out above a whisper.

"Fairly sure, but I'm not absolutely, one-hundred percent certain. That's why I need you to come with me tonight. I want to verify the rumors."

Taylor still couldn't move. If this were true, Hutton Stone would be exposed for the liar he was. If this were true, it would knock the legs out from under everything negative he'd said about her. If this were true—

"All we'll do is make a few phone calls," Ruby was saying. "I managed to get a number for Mrs. Stone's sister, so one of us can call her. And rumor has it that Hutton's favorite place to meet his lady-love is the Star-Lite Motel out on the Alpine Route. I don't know who she is yet, but if we can find her—"

Cody cut her off. "*I* know."

The instant he spoke, Taylor knew what he was going to say. She remembered Lisa Mooney's car turning into the alley behind Hutton's office the night of the disastrous shoot-out. The mysterious woman leaving Hutton's office. The argument between Joe and Lisa she'd interrupted in the drugstore.

Charlie pieced it together as quickly as she did. He'd picked up the food-processor lid, but now he dropped it again. "Lord." He mopped his face with his palm and let out a breath that seemed to come from the bottoms of his feet. "Are you saying what I *think* you're saying, boy?"

Cody nodded. "Justin's mom. That's why his dad's moving out."

"I can't believe that," Ruby said. "It's bad enough to cheat, but couldn't she have found someone better than *Hutton Stone*? I mean, *really*." She sank back against her chair and looked at each of them in turn. "Now what?"

Taylor held on to her glass to keep her hands from shaking. She had everything she needed to pull the rug out from under Hutton's campaign. She could practically ensure her victory by fighting back using the weapons Hutton had chosen.

And yet . . .

She looked at Cody for a long moment, stood slowly, and turned away. "Now, we keep our mouths shut."

"Shut?" Ruby lunged forward in her chair again. "You're not serious."

"I can't use this, Ruby. Hutton's not the only person involved. Neither is Lisa. Maybe Hutton deserves to walk in mud for a while. Lisa, too, for that matter. But Joe and the kids don't." She tossed back the last of the power drink and carried the glass to the sink. "The news might get out. It usually does one way or another. But it won't come from me. I won't use anyone else's pain for my own gain."

Taylor was half convinced her heart was going to stop beating. The polls would be closing in less than an hour. The election would be decided. She wasn't at all certain she could survive until then.

She stood at the window of campaign headquarters, watching the polls across the street. Behind her, Sam sat with his hat pulled low over his eyes, watching her and pretending not to. Charlie talked softly with Ruby, and Cody had his nose buried in a hand-held computer game.

Taylor was the only one who couldn't seem to sit, couldn't think, couldn't even form a complete sentence. Her fingers were numb and her hands clammy. Every breath she took felt like fire going in and ice coming out again. Her stomach knotted painfully as she watched a couple leaving the polling booths across the street, laughing as if the election meant nothing.

She turned away, kneading her hands together. She'd been right about one thing—news of Hutton and Lisa's affair had quickly become public knowledge, but she'd remained firm in her resolve not to say anything negative.

No matter how often she was asked, she'd maintained a neutral silence.

Tonight, she'd see exactly what the people of Heartbreak Hill valued most. No matter how they'd hurt her in the past, she wanted to believe the best.

"Maybe you ought to sit down," Sam said. "You look like you're about to keel over."

"I'm fine," she lied. "Just anxious for the results."

Ruby looked away from her conversation with Charlie. "He's right, Taylor. Sit down and relax. We won't know for hours, at best."

Taylor shook her head firmly, aware that she was behaving like a stubborn child, but unable to stop herself. "Everything is riding on what happens tonight. How can I just sit here and twiddle my thumbs?"

Sam pushed his hat back half an inch. "Not everything, Taylor. We'll all love you, no matter what happens tonight."

She forced her stiff legs to sit in the chair beside Cody's and slid an arm around his shoulders. "I know," she said with an apologetic smile. "And I'll still love all of you." Her arm grew numb almost immediately, and she shook her hand to get the feeling back into her fingers. "I just keep wondering if I made the right decision. Maybe I should have given Hutton the kind of battle he wanted."

Charlie pulled a chocolate bar from his pocket and bit off a piece. "That's nerves talking, my girl. You made the right decision. We all know it."

"But if I lose?"

"If you lose," Ruby said, "then things go back to normal. I can have my friend back instead of a nervous wreck who looks vaguely familiar."

Taylor kneaded her fingers gently. "And if I win?"

"Then I'll celebrate all night long and deny I ever said that." Ruby grinned and pulled two cans of Diet Pepsi from the miniature refrigerator, handed one to Taylor, and opened hers. "I don't care what happens. I'm just glad it's finally over."

Taylor popped the tab and took a long drink. The cool

liquid felt wonderful against her parched throat. She held the can to her fevered forehead and sighed. "So am I, I guess. It wouldn't be the end of the world if I lose. It would give me plenty of time to go to Cortez with Sam, and more time to spend with Cody. More time to spend on the house and yard. I'll find a job that I can leave behind at the end of the day." She sighed again and wondered why she couldn't get excited over the idea. "But I'm not looking forward to serving as a lame duck for the next few months."

Charlie scowled. "That's pessimism talking."

"It might be realism." Taylor took another drink and set the can on the windowsill behind her. She caught a glimpse of Kip and DeWayne leaving the polling booths—two long, lanky figures surrounded by a cloud of cigarette smoke—and added two more votes to the mental total she'd been carrying in her head all day.

Cody looked up from his computer game. "I won't mind if you don't get reelected."

Taylor slid her arm back down to his shoulders. "Why? Because you miss having me around?"

"No, because then you'll finally marry Sam."

Taylor laughed and ruffled his hair. "I should be hurt by that, you know. You don't miss *me*, you want me to lose so you can have *Sam* around even more than you already do."

Cody grinned sheepishly. "I miss you. Sorta." He shoved the lock of hair out of his eyes and glanced down at the game that was beeping in his hand. He punched a button with his thumb and the beeping stopped. "I'd miss you a lot more if you didn't make me clean my room when you're home."

Some of the tension that had been riding high in her shoulders slipped away. "Sorry, kiddo. I *have* to nag you about your room. It's a law."

Cody rolled his eyes. "Yeah, sure."

"It is. It's in the mother's handbook. Every mother is given one when her first baby is born."

"How come I've never seen it?"

"Because." She barely resisted the urge to kiss the tip of

his nose the way she used to when he was little. "It's invisible."

"Oh, yeah? Well, I have a kid handbook, and *it* says my room's *supposed* to be messy."

He looked so young and happy, Taylor felt a pang. How long had it been since they'd teased each other like this? How long since she'd taken time to laugh with her son, since other concerns hadn't come first?

Maybe it didn't matter whether she won or lost. Maybe fate would have its way, no matter how hard she worked, how fiercely she fought, how much she might want a certain outcome. It had been strong enough to sweep Sam up and bring him here. It could certainly handle a small-town election.

She looked from face to face, from Ruby's dark eyes and the shadows beneath them, to Sam's kicked-back posture, from Charlie's thick eyebrows and laughing eyes to the dusting of freckles on Cody's nose. And she realized that she'd been lying to herself for months.

She'd felt so virtuous, saying that her family came first, yet she'd put them all far below other people in reality. She'd been more worried about people she didn't particularly like than about the people she loved.

All at once, the remaining tension rushed from her as if someone had turned on a faucet. She gave in to the urge to kiss the tip of Cody's nose and laughed at the face he made as he wiped furiously with one curled hand.

"Yuck, Mom. Why'd you do that?"

"Because I just realized it doesn't matter. It really doesn't."

Sam eyed her suspiciously. "What doesn't matter?"

"Whether I win or lose."

Ruby looked skeptical. "Since when?"

"Since about thirty seconds ago." Taylor stood and impulsively brushed a kiss to the top of Charlie's head. "What do you say we quit hanging around here and go to dinner instead? My treat."

Charlie didn't even need a second to make up his mind.

He stood and motioned for Cody to get to his feet. "I vote for Angerbauer's Steak House."

"Sounds great to me," Taylor said, "but why don't you ever suggest Angerbauer's when *you're* buying?"

Charlie looked completely unabashed. "It's too expensive, and I'm a cheapskate."

Taylor reached for the light switch and waited while the others filtered out into the night. "Now that's a lie. Once you have a beer or two, you'll insist on picking up the check. I'm counting on it."

Sam slid an arm around her waist. Cody started walking backward, his computer game forgotten. Ruby laughed at something Charlie said, and Taylor realized that they'd reached a peaceful coexistence while she'd been busy worrying about other things.

She had her family. She had friends. She had the love of a most remarkable man. Even if she had nothing else, she had the world.

Chapter 19

TAYLOR WOKE WITH a start the next morning, dimly aware that a sound had jarred her from sleep. Watery yellow sunlight filtered into her bedroom through the curtains and the low moan of wind came with it.

She sat on the edge of her bed and stretched her arms high over her head, still as filled with contentment as she'd been last night. She'd been so content, in fact, that she'd come straight home after dinner and gone to bed before the results of the election were in.

The only thing that could make this morning better was if she'd woken up with Sam beside her. If she'd come to consciousness slowly, curled in the comfort of his arms. That day wasn't far off, she assured herself.

The election was over.

A flame of excitement licked at her insides. Visions of their wedding day, of setting up house together, danced through her head as she reached for her robe, and the flame grew to an insistent tickle that brought her to her feet just as a knock sounded on her bedroom door.

"Taylor?" Charlie called. "You awake?"

"I'm up, Pop. Come on in." She pulled on her robe as the door creaked and Charlie's face appeared in the opening. "What are you doing here so early?"

"You need to come downstairs, Sweet Pea. Ruby's here with the election results. Hope you don't mind that I let her in."

"Of course I don't mind." She knotted her robe sash and slipped her hand beneath Charlie's arm as she left her bedroom. Even knowing that she was about to learn the results couldn't dull her mood. "If anybody had told me two months ago that I'd be hoping I've lost this morning, I'd have told them they were crazy."

"You don't really hope that, do you?"

Taylor nodded and raked her fingers through her hair in a vain attempt to work through the results of a night's sleep. "All I can think about this morning is marrying Sam and getting on with the rest of our lives."

Charlie stepped aside to let her down the stairs first. "You can do that whether you win or lose. I've always thought home was more a state of mind than anything."

"I told myself last night that I'd be happy with whatever happens with the election, and I will be. But the idea of starting my new life without all the eyes in town on me is kind of appealing."

Charlie chuckled and followed her downstairs. "Sweet Pea, if you think you can do that in a town this size, you're dreaming." He waved a hand toward the back of the house. "Everybody's waiting for you in the kitchen."

She stopped suddenly and looked at her shabby, old robe. "Maybe I should go back and get dressed. I don't want to scare Sam off with the real me."

Charlie swept a glance the length of her. "He's going to have to see it sometime, poor fella. Might as well be now."

Taylor laughed and hugged him quickly. "You old charmer, you."

When she released him, she realized that there was still a tiny knot of nervousness in her stomach—one tiny piece of her that cared whether or not she won the election, one corner that wanted to beat Hutton Stone and prove that truth and honor still had a place in the world.

She took a deep, calming breath and let it out slowly. "Shall we go in?"

"Sure you're ready?"

"Do you know? Did I win or lose?"

"Wish I did, Sweet Pea, but Ruby like to took my head off when I asked her. And it's impossible to read her face. There's something going on in her eyes, but I can't tell if she's happy or upset."

Taylor squared her shoulders and stepped around the corner into the bright kitchen. They were all there, waiting. Cody, still in his pajamas. Ruby, immaculate in a winter white pantsuit and heels. Sam, with his long legs stretched out in front of him and his hands linked lazily across his middle.

The contentment came back immediately, and she knew she'd never truly need anything but the people she loved around her.

Sam stood when she came in and kissed her lightly. She slid her arms around his waist and held on. "So?" she said to Ruby. "What's the verdict?"

Ruby crossed her legs and a slow smile spread across her face. "We won, Taylor. We beat the bastard!"

It took several seconds for the announcement to process. If it hadn't been for Sam's tightened embrace and Charlie's ecstatic whoop, she might have thought she'd heard wrong.

She dragged her stunned glance from Sam's broad smile to Charlie's arm pumping in the air, to Ruby's tear-filled eyes and eager nod. "We won?"

"By a pretty wide margin."

Cody grinned broadly. "My mom *rules!*"

Taylor kept her eyes locked on Ruby's. "Are you sure?"

"One hundred percent." Ruby grabbed her hands and pulled her into a warm hug. "Congratulations, Sheriff." She gave Taylor a little shake and added, "From what I hear, Hutton's as stunned as you are."

Taylor laughed in disbelief. "But—but I was so sure we'd lost. I was *ready* to lose."

"Well, you didn't." Ruby pulled her toward the table and urged her into a chair. "The people have spoken, Taylor. They want someone honest in that office."

Taylor took an unsteady breath and let out a shaky laugh.

"I don't know what to say. I—I was—" She broke off and rubbed her forehead. "Well, shoot. Now I'm going to have to rethink the next few weeks. I was planning to have some time off so Sam and I could go to Cortez and take care of everything."

"I told you already," Sam said, "I'll wait until it's right for you."

"No. You've waited long enough. You've put yourself on hold for months waiting for me. We need to find out if your brother's ledger still exists. We need to find your family. Nothing else is more important than that. Donald can take care of things here for a few days. What can happen?"

Sam sent her a lopsided smile. "Guess I might as well confess that I'm a touch nervous about going back to Colorado. Wondering if I do have family, wondering how they'll react to me showing up, wondering how to explain who I am—or if I even should. Might be that they'll think I'm some crazy man come out of nowhere. I'm not real anxious to go through that again."

"This time will be different," Taylor said firmly. "I'll be with you."

"Guess I could do worse than travel with a sheriff, couldn't I? You'll lend me a touch of respectability."

He was still smiling, but Taylor could see a shadow in his eyes, a sadness she hated to see and didn't know how to help banish.

Would it eventually fade? Or would that shadow always be there?

"I thought you had homework," Taylor said to Cody two nights later. She'd spent the past two days getting things ready for her trip with Sam. It had been a rush job, but she had tickets reserved, mounds of laundry done, arrangements with Donald made. Cody would stay with Charlie. There was nothing left to do now but go.

Cody glanced up from the kitchen table, where he was pretending to study. "I'm doing my homework."

"Really?" Taylor positioned two cloves of garlic on her cutting board and smashed each with the side of her knife.

"That's funny. You haven't turned the page in at least fifteen minutes."

Cody shoved his hand into his hair and leaned his cheek on his palm. "That's because it's boring."

"Maybe so, but you still need to do the assignment."

"I don't know why. All it says is people settled in this place because it was good for farming, and didn't settle in that place because it *wasn't* good for farming. It's stupid."

"Maybe the textbook isn't well-written, but history is important," Taylor said as she minced the garlic. "And it can be really interesting. Besides, you need to know where we've been as a culture to know where we're going."

"I'm eleven, Mom. I don't *care* where we're going."

Taylor laughed and pulled two cans of tomato paste from the cupboard. "You will some day. But look at it this way, then. You'll understand Sam a lot better if you know how things were where he came from. Aren't you even a little interested to know what life was like when he was your age?"

Cody perked up slightly. "Well, yeah. I'm interested in *that*."

"Well, that's history. It's full of all sorts of people just like Sam."

"Then why don't they write about them in schoolbooks instead of just talking about farming?"

Taylor worked the can opener before answering. "With textbooks, you have to read between the lines. When they talk about settlers, just imagine someone like Sam riding into a valley, looking at the land, deciding whether to live there or not. If there were no grocery stores, no cans of food all ready to cook with, what do you think would be the main thing you'd think about when you were deciding where to live?"

Cody sighed, but the blank-eyed boredom had vanished. "Farming, I guess." He stuck a pencil in the center of the book and closed it. "If you *really* wanted me to understand history, you'd let me go with you and Sam to Cortez."

"I explained why I don't think that's a good idea this time. I don't know what Sam's going to find there. I don't

know how it will affect him. I don't know if his family
will be upset when he shows up and claims to be from the
past. . . . There are too many wild cards, Cody. But I promise that if things go well and we go back, you'll go with
us then."

Cody's eyes dulled again. "I don't want to stay here."

"You'll have Grandpa."

"Yeah. But it's not like having you and Sam here."

Taylor pulled eggs and cheese from the refrigerator.
"Look at the bright side. Without me here, you and
Grandpa can get into all sorts of trouble together." She
pointed an egg at him and added, "Just not *too* much trouble."

Cody rolled his eyes. "We probably won't do anything
but watch TV. Grandpa doesn't do anything anymore."

Taylor started to protest, but the truth of Cody's words
kept her mouth shut. Charlie hadn't been himself lately—
not the old troublemaking self that she used to worry about.
There'd been something almost subdued about him for
weeks. She set the eggs on the counter and wiped her hands
on her apron. "I've noticed that, too. Why do you think
that is?"

Cody shrugged. "Beats me."

"He hasn't said anything to you?"

"No. Why would he?"

"Because you're his pal. His little buddy. You and
Grandpa used to always contrive ways to spend time together. I don't think there's anybody he likes being with
more than you."

Cody didn't way a word, but his gaze dropped and a
slight flush tinged his cheeks.

"Cody?"

"Yeah?"

"Is there something I should know about?"

Cody went through a series of gyrations that Taylor
thought were meant to mean no, but looked to a mother's
eye like an evasive technique.

"*Cody?* Did something happen between you and
Grandpa?"

He gyrated a little more, then sighed heavily and flicked the briefest possible glance at her face. "Well, maybe. I mean, sort of, I guess."

She turned down the burner and joined him at the table. "What was it?"

Cody shrugged one shoulder, then the other, readjusted his position on the chair, and toed off one shoe by the heel. "It wasn't really anything. Just . . . well, he sort of heard me asking Sam to go to the father-son thing at school with me."

"How do you know he heard you?"

"I kind of saw him through at the window—but not until after. I mean, if I'd known he was there, I wouldn't have asked right then."

"Did Grandpa say anything to you?"

"Not really."

"He didn't talk to you at all?"

Cody sent her another of those heartbeat quick glances. "No."

Taylor ran her fingertips across her forehead. Charlie wasn't the type to hold anything back unless it hurt him deeply. If it had made him angry, they'd have all known about it. "I know you wouldn't hurt Grandpa intentionally, but I do think you owe him an explanation at least."

"I know. I just don't know what to say."

"I'll help you with that," Taylor promised. "But first, I want to talk to Pop and see how he's feeling. I'll run next door while the lasagna's in the oven, and *you* finish that homework."

Cody looked as if he might argue that point, then wisely thought better of it and nodded. Smart kid. After everything Pop had done for them, after everything Taylor had put him through, all the patience he'd shown, all the sleepless nights when Cody was little, it tore her apart to think of hurting him.

She stood outside on his back porch for several minutes before she could bring herself to knock. She listened to the song of one lonely cricket who apparently hadn't noticed that summer was over and the nights had grown nippy. She tugged the edges of her sweater together and let out a shaky breath, then lifted her hand and knocked softly.

Charlie opened the door and soft yellow light spilled out onto the porch. He looked so dear standing there, Taylor felt her throat close off and tears sting her eyes.

"Sweet Pea? Where's Cody?"

"Finishing his homework. I came alone because I need to talk to you for a minute."

Charlie's expression sobered and he pushed open the screen door with one hand. "Well, get inside out of the cold. You want me to call Sam? He's doing battle with the washing machine, but I can get him."

She stepped into the kitchen and loosened her grip on her sweater. "Actually, I'd rather talk to you alone."

Charlie closed the door and motioned her toward the chipped Formica table where they'd had every major discussion of her life. In all the years Charlie had lived in this house, nothing in this room had changed. Everything in it was worn and old and frayed and endlessly dear. "Is something wrong?"

"Not in the way you think. Cody just told me he asked Sam to go to the father-son activity at school. He says you overheard them."

Charlie dragged out a chair and made a noise with his tongue. "You're worried about that?"

"If it hurt your feelings, yes. You've always gone with him."

"He's just a boy, Taylor. He wouldn't hurt his old grandpa on purpose. I know he loves me."

"Yes, he does."

"And it's natural for him to want to be with someone younger. When you and Sam get married, the boy's finally going to have what he's always wanted. And he's probably going to prefer doing things with Sam. It's only right."

"No, it's not, Pop. It might be how it is, but it's not right. You've done everything for him since the day he was born. You've defended him, helped support him, stayed awake with him when he was sick—"

"And you think he owes me something for all that?"

"I think he owes you respect."

"He does respect me, sweetheart. He just doesn't want to pal around with me as much."

"But, Pop—"

"Now, you listen to me, Sweet Pea. I didn't do any of those things because I expected something from Cody in exchange. And you know I'm pleased that Sam's in the picture, even if it means I lose out on a few things. The truth is, some of Cody's activities are hard on these old bones. I'm happy to let Sam take my place."

"You don't mean that."

"Have you ever known me to lie?"

"Only when you try to keep me from finding about some trouble you've gotten yourself into."

Charlie leaned back in his chair and grinned. "Well, I'm not lying now."

"Your feelings aren't hurt?"

"Maybe a little. But there's no serious damage." Charlie linked his fingers on his stomach. "This is what happens when kids grow up and families change. We've gone on the same way for a long time and things have gotten pretty comfortable for all of us. Change hurts a little, but that doesn't mean it's a bad thing."

"But—"

"Now, Sweet Pea, you know as well as I do that you and Sam are meant to be together. I've never known a man who went through quite so much to get to a woman." Charlie quirked a small smile. "And we both know that Cody needs Sam just as much as he needs you and me."

Taylor nodded, suddenly unable to speak.

"Sam's good for the boy."

"Yes," she managed to get around the lump in her throat. "Yes, he is."

"We're having growing pains, that's all. Just stretching a bit here and there. Now, if Cody changes his attitude or starts smarting off with me, we'll have a problem. But right now, we don't."

Taylor took a deep breath and tried to smile. "It's hard

to see things change, Pop. It's wonderful in one way but so hard in another."

"I've always thought that the hardest thing about love is knowing when it's best to let go."

"And you're letting go of Cody?"

"Not completely. Never that." Charlie grinned impishly. "And you never know what this will mean down the road. Maybe now that you and Sam are settled and I don't have to worry so much about Cody, I might even find me a girlfriend."

That tore a laugh from Taylor's throat. "Are you saying Cody and I have been cramping your style?"

"Not that I've noticed, but it might be." Charlie's grin inched up a bit further. "Maybe I'll start hanging out in front of the feed store with those other old coots and let the ladies get a gander at me. You've got to admit, I'm a sight better looking than Horace Lambert or Arvy Fenton."

"You certainly are." She narrowed her eyes and gave him a slow once-over. "Are you saying that you've been holding the ladies at bay because of Cody and me?"

"Not holding 'em at bay so much as just not offering any encouragement. Truth to tell, I never thought along the lines of romance until Sam came along. But seeing how happy you are together has reminded me of how nice life was with your mother. I think I'd like that again. And it's not as if I'm all *that* old."

Taylor shook her head. "You're not old at all, Pop. You've got years and years ahead of you. There's no sense spending them alone."

"That's how I see it. So if I was to start seeing someone, would you mind so very much?"

She grabbed both of his hands and held them. "I wouldn't mind one little bit. I want you to be happy, whatever that takes."

"Ah, see?" He leaned forward and kissed her cheek. "Now *that's* love."

She started to pull away, but an idea stopped her. "Do you have someone in mind?"

Amazingly, Charlie's cheeks turned a shade of deep pink. "Well, I might."

Taylor sat back, astounded, not only by the admission but by the fact that her father was blushing! She glanced at the counter where his new food processor, blender, and crock full of utensils stood proudly. "It's Betty D'Angelo, isn't it?"

The pink in his cheeks deepened. "She's a fine woman, Taylor."

"I know she is. I'm just amazed that this has been going on under my nose and I never saw it."

"Not much has been going on yet."

"Yeah, but I still should have seen this coming. How many kitchen aids does one man need?"

"Well, now, that depends."

Taylor shook her head slowly. "And I call myself a sheriff. I guess it's a good thing Heartbreak Hill doesn't have any real crime. Apparently, I can't see what's right under my nose."

"I wouldn't say that," Charlie said with a grin. "Maybe it's just that I'm awfully clever."

"Maybe." Taylor leaned back in her chair, suddenly weak as the worry that had kept her going for so many years slipped away. "We're going to be okay, aren't we, Pop?"

"We'll be more than okay, Sweet Pea. Things are as they're meant to be. If you want my opinion, I'd say things are finally looking up for the O'Briens."

Chapter 20

SAM SAT IN the passenger seat of the car they'd rented at the airport and stared in amazement at the changes the years had brought to the land he'd once called home. The city had grown so large, he could scarcely believe it. Huge signs pointed the way to Mesa Verde on one side of the Montezuma Valley and Black Mesa on the other.

He'd grown so used to Montana mountain country, the starkness of the southern Colorado landscape felt familiar and strange at the same time. Even though plateaus rimmed the valley, they seemed short and almost squatty after the jagged peaks around Heartbreak Hill.

He couldn't believe he was actually back.

His heart thudded ominously, a far cry from the rapid pulse it had set when that airplane lifted off into the air. He'd spent the first five minutes of the flight clutching the arms of his seat, but he'd soon relaxed and actually found himself enjoying the bird's-eye view of the land.

But as he looked at Cortez, the years fell away. He might have been looking at modern buildings and roads, cars and flashing lights, but he could see the dirt street, tiny clapboard buildings, buckboards and carriages. There was, just below the surface, a sense of anticipation—as if he thought Jesse might round the corner at any second, or Olivia might rattle into town in that old buckboard of hers.

Taylor drew to a stop at a sign and turned her gaze on him. "Well?"

"It's different, I'll say that."

Her eyes didn't leave his face. "Are you disappointed?"

"A little, maybe. The town doesn't look the same at all, but it feels the same in some ways—probably because the mesas are still there on either side of the valley. I catch a glimpse of them and almost expect to see someone I know."

"Are you nervous?"

He laughed sharply. "Nervous? Of course not."

She dragged her attention back to the road and pulled away from the corner. "Let's get to the motel and then we can start looking for your family."

"Today?"

"You don't want to?"

He shook his head, feeling silly, but not quite ready to take that step yet. "Why don't we just look the town over tonight? Tomorrow will be soon enough to start looking for people."

She let her gaze leave the road for a split second. "You *are* nervous. I *knew* you were."

"I'm not nervous. I'm edgy. God only knows how they'll react to me showing up on their doorstep, or whether they'll let me look for that ledger in Jesse's portrait. I figure we can use tonight to get a feel for what things are like, what *they're* like, before we drive out there tomorrow. It never hurts to know who you're going up against."

"Have you decided what you'll tell them? How you'll explain yourself?"

He nodded. "The truth. Or at least part of it. I'll tell them I'm a distant relative and that I've heard about this ledger and wonder if it's around."

"That's probably best," Taylor agreed. "We don't know if Jesse ever told any of his children about you—or if they believed him if he did. I guess none of his children would still be alive."

"I doubt it. If they are, they'd be over a hundred years old. The most I can hope for is a grandchild."

The conversation broke off as Taylor pulled into the parking lot of the motel. They left their bags in the car and went into the brightly lit lobby to check in. The clerk, a rotund woman with several chins and button-black eyes, looked them over with supreme disinterest. "Can I help you?"

"We have a reservation." Taylor said, and pulled out her wallet without even batting an eye.

Every time she did that, Sam felt a pang of guilt. He had no idea how much this trip was costing her, but he hated every blasted penny she spent on his behalf. The woman quoted a rate for one night that nearly knocked Sam off his feet. Hell, back where he came from, a person could've lived on that much money for a year, maybe more. But he wasn't back where he came from, and used-to-bes didn't matter.

He had no idea what to expect from this trip, but he knew one thing—if he didn't find some way to hold his head up soon, he and Taylor would suffer for it. Already, he could feel himself pulling back a little. Not because he didn't love her. God knew, he loved her with his entire heart and he wanted her more than he could say. But he didn't feel equal to her, and it was damned hard to make love to a woman who deserved more than you could give. His shortcomings just kept getting in the way.

The clerk did something with Taylor's card and handed it back. While Taylor signed the receipt, Sam caught the clerk's attention. "You from around here?"

She nodded her chins into action. "All my life."

"You know the Cinnabar Ranch, then?"

Her button eyes narrowed slightly. "Sure. Why do you ask?"

"I have family there. Thought I might drive out and introduce myself in the morning."

"To the Evanses?" The woman's chins folded themselves in disapproval. "How are you related?"

"Distant cousin."

"Really?" She glanced at the receipt Taylor had signed.

"I didn't realize the family had any relatives named O'Brien."

"*I'm* not related," Taylor said quickly. "But Sam is."

"Oh. I thought . . . that is, I assumed you two were married."

Taylor had assured Sam repeatedly that no one would so much as raise an eyebrow at them sharing a room, but he still worried what it would mean to her reputation, and now, with the look on the clerk's face, he wondered if she would refuse their business.

That would be the ultimate humiliation.

Taylor didn't look even slightly worried. She tucked her credit card back into her wallet. "We're engaged," she said with a brilliant smile. "This is a pre-wedding trip, actually. Sam thought it would be nice to show me where his family comes from."

To Sam's surprise, the clerk's smile warmed and her entire face changed. "Well, that's lovely." She leaned on the counter and made herself comfortable, as if she were settling in for a while. "The Evans family has been one of the most influential and popular families in this area for several generations. They really are lovely, lovely people."

"Who would be the patriarch?" Sam asked.

"I suppose that'd be old Randolph Evans. He's pretty old, though. Celebrated his eighty-sixth birthday just a month ago and he doesn't get out much anymore."

Sam's pulse picked up speed and a strange tingling began in his fingers. "Do you happen to know if he's descended from Jesse Evans?"

"Well, yes. Of course. The whole bunch of Evanses around here come from Jesse and Elizabeth. Randolph is their oldest grandson, and proud of it, I can tell you. He used to brag all the time about how he was the keeper of all the family secrets."

"What secrets?"

The clerk laughed lightly and straightened. "Who knows? I can't imagine the Evans family having any secrets. Every single one of 'em is as honest and up-front as the day is long. But I sure was fascinated when I was a little girl. My mother took me out there to visit Randolph's daughter. She was Mama's best friend, you see, so that left little Jessie and me to sit with Randolph and listen to him talk. That man loved to tell the story about Old Sam Evans."

Sam's heart threatened to jump out of his throat, but he managed to get a few words out. "What story would that be?"

The little button eyes rounded. "You haven't ever heard the story about Old Sam?" She laughed again and found a stool. "It's quite a story, I'll tell you. Not that I believe it, but Randolph does and he claims to have papers that Jesse gave him before he died that he's keeping for the day Old Sam comes back."

Sam met Taylor's excited gaze and tried to remember to breathe while the clerk launched into the story. "It all started over Black Mesa," she said. "You have to make sure you get up to see the ruins while you're here. . . ."

Once they left town the next morning, the landscape began to look even more familiar and a rush of homesickness swamped Sam. He'd expected to feel nostalgic, but he hadn't expected to be knocked flat by it.

Roads and power lines and a few buildings that hadn't been here before broke into the landscape, but the red rock and endless sweep of plains stretching between the two mesas, the stands of juniper and piñon, the scent of dirt and sage brought waves of memories rushing back. He could almost see Jesse riding beside him into town, the spectacles that slid endlessly to the end of his nose, the thin brown hair and wide smile. He could almost hear his voice on the wind. Sam regretted every argument they'd ever had, every sharp word he'd ever uttered.

He closed his eyes and let the memories play. He remembered his father, his mother, pictured Kurt and Olivia, felt again the sun on his face and the wind in his hair. Mixed with the familiar scents, the memories were so real he might actually have been back in the past, but for the slight hum of tires on the road and the soft sound of Taylor on the other side of the car trying not to interfere.

He reached for her and found her hand in his, soft and gentle yet firm and strong.

"Are you okay?" Her voice was barely above a whisper, so soft he could scarcely hear her.

"I'm fine. Just fine. Just reliving a little." He opened his eyes and met her worried gaze. He grinned to set her mind at ease. "Seems like just a couple of months ago I last rode this stretch of land."

She laughed, but it sounded uneasy. "Imagine that."

"Last time I rode here with Jesse, I was angry with him. Or maybe it'd be more accurate to say I was frustrated. Either way, I'm sorry I didn't get the chance to tell him how I really felt about him."

"You don't think he knew?"

He shrugged and let his gaze drift to the window.

Taylor squeezed his hand. "You made the ultimate sacrifice to leave him this ranch, Sam. He *had* to know how much you loved him. He probably remembered every minute of every day. Every time he watched his children play on the incredible gift you gave them or watched the sun rise or smelled the rain. How could he *not* know?"

"You might be right, and I'd sure like to think he did, but that's still no substitute for saying it."

"No," she said softly, "it's not."

Sam dragged his gaze back to her. It didn't seem possible, but he loved her more in that moment than he ever had. There were so many things she could have said, so many ways she could have tried to influence how he was feeling. Instead, she chose to simply acknowledge what he felt, and that somehow made the pain a little less.

Before he was ready, she slowed for the final turn down the lane toward the house where Sam had been born. It was there, incredibly just like it was the last time he saw it. His eyes blurred and his throat stung. His heart slowed and his legs tingled. He couldn't feel anything, yet every breath hurt.

Nothing had changed. In all these years, not a board had been altered—or if it had, Sam couldn't tell. He motioned

for Taylor to slow down and she responded immediately.
The car stopped, and when the dust cleared, Sam opened
the door and got out.

He stood in the road and looked at his home for a long
moment while Taylor waited in the car. This was another
thing he loved about her—that she was sensitive enough to
realize when he needed a few minutes alone. She really
was the most remarkable woman he'd ever met.

Before he could tell her, the front door of the house
opened, and a man stepped out onto the porch. He looked
so much like Jesse, Sam nearly forgot that it couldn't possibly be his brother. Some descendant of Jesse's, surely,
but not Jesse, himself.

The man stepped off the porch and moved closer, and
Sam still had the dreamlike illusion that his brother was
walking toward him. When the man drew close enough,
Sam could make out gray hair against the rising sun and
see that his shoulders were stooped, not the straight posture
of Jesse's in his youth.

He was aware of the sudden silence when the car's engine stilled and the brush of sound as Taylor got out of the
car behind him.

Sam could see the man squinting to see him better, and
then, to Sam's surprise, he held out his arms, tilted back
his head, and laughed. He came forward with surprising
quickness for a man his age. Took Sam's hand and pumped
it. "Welcome. Yes, indeed. Welcome."

Sam tried to remember the speech he had planned, but
he could only manage a garbled, "You know who I am?"

"Do I? I've studied you for so long, I probably know
more about you than you do about yourself. I have to admit,
though, I was about to give up hope that I'd live to see this
day." He motioned Sam forward and held out his arm for
Taylor. "And you must be the young lady who took Sam
away from us. Grandpa always wondered what kind of
woman you'd be."

He studied her intently for a long minute, then patted her
hand. "Well, for what it's worth, I approve. And I know
damn well Grandpa would have. Looks like you have just

enough fire in you to keep Old Sam on his toes, and just
enough satin to keep him happy."

Sam stared at the old man as he led Taylor up the drive,
then chuckled softly and shook his head in wonder. The
old man was Jesse's grandson, all right. No doubt about
that.

He started after them, gazing around him as he walked.
Welcome home, Sam. Welcome home.

Exhausted and exhilarated at the same time, Taylor stood
in back of the ranch house and watched the sun slide toward
the western horizon. The sky was shot with fire—orange
and crimson and gold—and the view was breathtaking.

It had been a long day—one she wouldn't soon forget.
So many people, so much talk, so much she couldn't relate
to or understand. Randolph had given Sam a trunk contain-
ing Jesse's journals, and with Sam locked inside the study,
she'd finally found a chance to slip away and catch her
breath.

Along with all the reunions, the laughing, and the sharing
of stories, with the unbelievable realization that Jesse's entire line of descendants had been told the story and some
had actually believed it, had come a growing sense of fu-
tility. This land was stamped on Sam's soul. This family
was his blood.

This was where he belonged.

She'd been battling the growing awareness all day, trying
to tell herself that she was wrong, that fate had brought him
to her for a reason, but the sense that she was going to lose
him to this place had grown stronger with every passing
hour.

Jesse was here. And so was Olivia. No matter what Sam
said, Taylor could feel the pull Olivia had on him. She was
in the wind and in the sun and in the soil beneath their feet.

She wished she could resent how he felt, but she knew
that if she'd been pulled away from Charlie and Cody,
she'd have gone anywhere, given up anything for a connection to them—no matter how far removed.

Charlie's words from two nights before echoed through

her head over and over. *Sometimes the hardest part of love is knowing when to let go.*

The words found a place in her heart, and she realized that letting go had always been her problem. It's what kept her from allowing Cody to find his father. How could she be so two-faced? How could she encourage Sam to find his family and deny Cody the truth about his? Of all people, she should understand Cody's need. After all, she'd grown up without her mother. She knew how hungry she'd been as a child for that connection.

And her time for letting go of Sam was approaching, as well. She could feel it growing with every breath she took.

A sound behind her intruded on her thoughts. She turned quickly to find Randolph moving across the open ground toward her. He walked more slowly than he had earlier, as if being reunited with Sam had drained something out of him.

He drew even with her and smiled. "It's been quite a day, hasn't it?"

"Yes, it has." She pushed her bangs off her forehead and tried not to let Randolph see anxiety. He'd been waiting for this day longer than she'd been alive. She wouldn't ruin it for him. "Your ranch is lovely. No wonder Sam loves it so."

He gripped the fence rail and looked out over the land that the setting sun was infusing with deep reds and oranges, purples and yellows. "I've lived here all my life, you know. Eighty-six years so far."

She turned to see him better. "And how long have you known about Sam?"

"Since I was a boy. Grandpa used to sit me on his knee and tell me stories about his tall, handsome brother. Some boys had movie heroes—I had my uncle. A real-life cowboy and a story that outdid anything Hollywood ever came up with." He chuckled softly. "It was quite a legend, you know."

"Did you always believe it?"

"Always. Grandpa wasn't the sort to let his imagination run away with him. He was an immensely practical man.

But *he* believed the story, and so did Uncle Kurt and Aunt Olivia. So, of course, so did I."

"You knew Olivia?"

"Of course. They were like family as long as they were alive. The Richards family and the Evanses have always been more like cousins than neighbors. And in some instances, we actually became family. Every so often, the valley sees a Richards-Evans wedding."

"What was she like?"

"Olivia?" Randolph gave her an odd, knowing look. "Sam hasn't told you?"

"A little. But she meant so much to him back then, I can't help but be a little curious."

"Olivia was a lovely woman. Just lovely. And entirely wrong for Sam."

"You're saying that just to make me feel better, aren't you?"

"Not in the least."

"But I'm not competing with the reality of Olivia," Taylor said, shocked by how easy it was to confide in this man. "I'm competing with the memory."

Randolph shook his head slowly. "You're not competing with Sam's memories of Olivia, either. You're at war with your own fears. And they, my dear, are more powerful than any other woman, any memory, anything that might ever threaten to come between you and Sam."

"I am afraid. Terribly afraid that I'll lose Sam to his memories. I don't have the slightest idea what to do. If I try to hang on to him, I'll lose him. But I can't bear the thought of leaving him here, either."

"Are you sure he wants to stay?"

"This is his home."

"He left once."

"Yes, but what if he regrets it? Have you seen his face? He's like a little boy in a candy shop. This place is everything to him."

"I don't agree. I think *you* are everything to him. Coming back here today just gives him—what's that term people toss around these days?—closure. That's all this is for him. He left rather suddenly before."

Taylor's eyes burned with unshed tears, her throat felt parched from the effort of holding them back. "I wish I could believe you."

Randolph turned his back on the sunset. "I'm an old man, Taylor. I've seen a lot of life. Indulge me for a moment?"

"Of course."

"If you remain so afraid of losing Sam, you're going to *make* it happen. When fear controls us, everything we do is colored with it. Every word we speak is shadowed with it. It permeates everything, and soon it gains strength. Before you know it, your fear will drive a wedge between the two of you, and you'll have created what you fear most."

"But maybe it's time to let him go."

Randolph touched her hand. His skin felt dry and almost paper-thin. "If you can get a grip on yourself, you might be surprised at what you find. And now, if you'll excuse me, the day has gotten the best of me. I think I'll find my easy chair and put my feet up."

"Of course." The words came out little more than a whisper, but Randolph was already gone. And Taylor was alone with the gathering dusk, the whispers of a bygone era, and the echo they created in her own time.

It was much later when Sam finally emerged from the study clutching the small leather trunk as if it were a lifeline. Taylor had done her best to believe Randolph's warning, but the look on Sam's face when he came out of those heavy wooden doors wiped away every bit of peace she'd been able to find.

He glanced around for her anxiously and crossed the room to her side. "It's all here," he said with more enthusiasm than she'd ever heard him express over anything. "Everything. From the day I left until Jesse got too old to keep writing." He reached for Taylor's hand and squeezed it, as if he expected her to be thrilled.

And she was—in the part of her heart that didn't love him, in the part of her soul that didn't need him. He needed this. He deserved this. If she truly loved him, how could she ask him to leave?

She maintained her equilibrium as they bid good-bye to Sam's family, through the countless hugs and promises to stay in touch, through the tight hug from Randolph and the deep look he took into her eyes. She listened to Sam recount parts of Jesse's journals as she drove back to the motel and tried to put aside her own selfish interests.

But when they were back in the privacy of their room, Sam flopped onto the bed and linked his hands behind his head. He crossed one foot over the other and started on another tale, so lost in the past, in *his* world, Taylor couldn't take it any longer.

She put a hand on his thigh and waited until he noticed and ground to a reluctant halt. "I'm glad you had a good day, Sam. I'm thrilled that you found your family and that they knew about you."

He grew instantly wary. His hands came out from behind his head and he shifted onto his side. "Why do I sense a *but* coming?"

She pulled away and stood, hurting so much she thought she might die before she could get the words out. "Because there is a *but* coming. I've had all day to think about this Sam, so please don't stop me before I can get it all out."

He nodded, one sharp dip of his head, his gaze watchful.

"Like I said, I'm happy that you've found your family. You're happier than I've ever seen you. And I love you so much, that one part of me is really glad to see you so happy. And that's why I have to do this."

His eyes narrowed, his smile evaporated. "Do *what*?"

"This is where you belong, Sam. I don't want that to be true, but it is. This land is part of you. These people are part of you—"

"Yes, but—"

"*Please*, Sam. Let me finish this before I lose my nerve. I could beg you to come back to Heartbreak Hill with me, and you probably would. But if I keep you from this place, you'll grow to hate me. I know you will. I also know how hard it's been for you to live up there without a job, relying on Charlie and me to support you. I know you'll eventually find a way to support yourself, but I can't bear to see you hurting. At least here, you could work on the ranch with your family. At least here—" Her voice caught and she couldn't take a breath. The tears she'd been battling all day clogged her throat and filled her eyes.

Sam slid to the edge of the bed and stood to face her. "You're telling me you want me to stay here?"

"I'm telling you I want you to be happy, no matter what that means for me."

He reached for her, and she was helpless to resist the urge to be in his arms once more, to feel his heartbeat against her cheek, to breathe the scent that was so uniquely his. She melted against him, weak and sobbing and half-wishing she'd kept her mouth shut so she didn't have to lose this.

"You can't really think I want this more than I want you," he said softly. His voice vibrated from his chest against her ear, his arms tightened around her and his finger found her chin and tilted it so she had to look into those soul-deep gray eyes. "You're right, Taylor. This is my past. A past I walked away from once and am completely ready to walk away from again."

"But—"

He put two fingers on her lips. "I listened to you. It's my turn now. I left the Cinnabar to find myself, and I did. I found my life when I landed in Heartbreak Hill. I found my heart with you and Cody and Charlie. I found my soul in your arms. I know who I am now, and I don't ever want to lose that."

"But—"

"It's no good arguing with me." He bent to brush the lightest of kisses to her lips. "You can go back to Heartbreak Hill without me, but I'll follow you. I know where I want to be, Taylor. I know where I belong. This place was Jesse's, always and forever. I have what I needed. I have my connection with my brother, I have letters and stories of his life. I have letters from Kurt and Olivia, too. If ever

I feel lonely for them—and I'm not saying there'll never be a time—I have them with me now."

She gulped back a sob that rose to her lips. "Are you sure?"

"More sure than I've ever been about anything in my life."

Her heart felt as if it was going to beat out of her chest, the tears pooled in her eyes, but from joy this time. "But what about the other?"

"Work?" Sam laughed and drew her onto the bed. "Well, now, here's the funny thing. I was waiting to tell you until we were alone because I can hardly believe it myself." He reached into the box and pulled out a leather journal. "Why don't I let Jesse tell you in his own words?"

He handed her the journal and she blinked to clear her eyes, then began reading the entry he put in front of her.

Sam, you old coot. I'm still having trouble believing what Kurt and Olivia tell me. And yet I've known Olivia as long as you have, and she seems serious. It must be true because I can easier believe that you somehow went into the future than I can believe you would leave without saying good-bye. Besides, the sheriff has been searching the ruins for days and can't find hide nor hair of you, so it's obvious that you've gone somewhere.

I rode the north pasture today and started thinking about all you've given up. Just as you didn't think it right that Pa left the Cinnabar to you, I don't think it's right that you get nothing from it. The best part of this is, you can't argue with me. I've opened an account at the bank and I'm going to put a percentage of the profits into it from now until the day I die. I'll see that my children do the same. The money will be there for you if you ever come back. And though I know the Cinnabar will never hold you, I must believe that you'll be back some day, long after I'm gone.

Now, just pray to God I make a profit, or your share will be mighty small.

Taylor looked into Sam's eyes. "You have money?"

"According to Randolph, I have a great deal of money. Enough to buy some land and my own string of horses."

Joy, light as champagne bubbles, filled her heart. "In Heartbreak Hill?"

"Just try to keep me away, lady." He dropped to one knee and took her hand in his. "I've been wanting to do this for a long time, and now I finally can. Taylor, you already have my heart and my soul. Will you do me the honor of taking my name, as well?"

She dropped to the floor and threw her arms around his neck. "Oh, Sam. I've never wanted anything more."

"When?"

"The first minute we can."

"I've been waiting a hundred years to find you," Sam said with a grin. "But I can't marry you before we get back to Heartbreak Hill. I've got a ten-year-old best man waiting for me at home, and I don't want to disappoint him. After all, this was his idea."

Home. Taylor didn't think she'd ever heard a sweeter word. "I hope it wasn't entirely his idea," she teased as she drew Sam to the floor beside her. She ran her fingers across his shoulders and kissed his eyes, his mouth, his chin.

"It wasn't *entirely* his idea," Sam said with a grin. "I had a few thoughts about it, myself."

"I would have walked away and left you here, you know. But I'm so awfully glad you didn't let me."

"Never," Sam whispered. His eyes darkened and he pulled her close. "Not if I live a million years."

TIME PASSAGES

FRIENDS ROMANCE

Can a man come between friends?

❏ **A TASTE OF HONEY**

by DeWanna Pace   0-515-12387-0

❏ **WHERE THE HEART IS**

by Sheridon Smythe   0-515-12412-5

❏ **LONG WAY HOME**

by Wendy Corsi Staub   0-515-12440-0

All books $5.99